Dan Jaydid

# TRIPPING THE FIELD

## An Existential Crisis of Ungodly Proportions

GladEye
Press

**GladEye Press**
Springfield, OR
gladeyepress.com





**Published by:** GladEye Press
**Text Design:** J.V. Bolkan
**Production:** Sharleen Nelson
**Cover Art:** Ian Jaydid

**ISBN-13:** 978-0-9911931-9-6



The body text is presented in Garamond.

Ian Jaydid has been writing and creating fine art, illustrations, and cartoons for more than twenty years. Through his creative arts and writing outlet, Iboga Moon Productions, he illustrates the cartoon series Generation Jaded, designs mixed-media fine art, logos, and marketing materials. He regularly partners with news, medicinal plant, and alternative healing organizations to write and edit articles on the topics of meditation, psychoactive research, lucid dreaming, and alternative healing techniques. *Tripping the Field* is his first, fully realized fictional novel. He currently resides on the front range of the Rocky Mountains. Visit his website: www.ianjaydid.com

# DEDICATION

If you have been a part of my life, you have made an impact on me. But I'd like to single a few of you out who left the biggest imprints in my heart as well as this particular story, regardless of distance or our current state of relations. First and foremost, I extend tremendous gratitude to my publishers at GladEye Press, Jeff and Shar who helped make this possible.

Of course, if it wasn't for my parents' unconditional support, the world may have devoured me long before this story saw the light of day. Dad, you taught me how to make logic a most powerful ally. Mom, you taught me to love unconditionally and to see the world in my heart. Both of you encouraged me to be curious, even of that which appears ordinary.

I offer the deepest gratitude to the first love of my life, Eden. Your fearless, irreverent energy inspired our story's hero in so many ways, I simply had to name her after you. I am lucky enough to be able to call the most imaginative, good-hearted man on the planet a beloved friend: Michael Downey. Your unrelenting compassion and trust helped me push through my own hero's journey through hell. I extend great love and appreciation to Brian Ferguson and Jim Pavlik. Each of you in your own way inspired me to be excited about science and to stay objective, even in the face of deeply personal topics. My brother AJ, I thank you for your voice and sense of dignity. Your strength is behind several of the more powerful personalities in this tale.

If it wasn't for modern thinkers and philosophers like Carlos Castaneda, Terence McKenna, Eckhart Tolle, Gangaji, and Adyashanti, my awareness may have never known such brilliance in this lifetime. Highest praise to scientists such as Carl Sagan, Brian Greene, Richard Dawkins, Lawrence Krauss, Sam Harris and Neil DeGrasse Tyson who excel at translating their knowledge into a format even a simple-minded artist like myself can digest. Without your efforts, I may have never seen how wonder and inspiration can be found just as readily in the study of cosmology and physics as it can be through spiritual insight and revelation.

**To the reader,** I guarantee the following tale is absolutely true and a total work of fiction; both particle and wave. In my own defense, I solemnly swear that at no time during the inception or the writing of this story was I sober; in fact, I remember typing very little of it at all. My job was largely about stepping out of the way and letting it happen. If you've found this book, forces larger than "I" intended it so—and I believe they wish to shake you from the limitations of your own story.

*Ian Jaydid*

# PART ONE

## On the Road

*"Only as a warrior can one survive the path of knowledge, because the art of a warrior is to balance the terror of being a man with the wonder of being a man."*

Carlos Castaneda

Everything after the Big Bang could be boiled down to entropy; that gradual—and often not-so-gradual—slide from order into disorder. From time to time the universe employs highly ordered tools to create even further chaos, from black holes to lightning bolts to bacteria. Who am I? Now I see why that is the mother of all questions. At this point I would make one, slight—very relevant—modification: *What* am I? Damn how I wish I had tackled that question earlier on. It takes nerve to ask a question like that. It bears the potential of coaxing the particle into a wave. I finally figured out the joke is on me. I'm Schrödinger's cat; both alive and dead. And I've already endured the unpleasantness of dying once this week. I'd rather not repeat the ordeal.

I pull my eyes from the road to steal a swift, calculated glance behind me. The haphazardly duct-taped slow cooker is still securely strapped to the backseat, rigged to the cigarette lighter. The tiniest smirk rises as I consider how the hallucinogen brewing in that Crock-Pot may be the only hope I have for a future. It's all come down to this: Above all else I must deliver one cup of the Dimethyltryptamine in that cooker to my beloved friend and colleague, Professor Eden Jessup. Once I find her, that is. This has become my sole duty, my unbending intent.

Although I must admit I'm having some bit of trouble deciding what constitutes good decision making lately. Not being brainwashed takes some getting used to. Plus I imagine it takes experience to drive this fast and accurately with a cocktail of psychoactives on the brain, which would explain why I'm doing such a terrible job of it; not enough practice. If my attention freezes to one spot for too long my peripheral is flooded by a dazzling display of poetic, subconscious nonsense. Since I hit the switchbacks to the foothills, the black, leather dash has transformed into a garden of blooming lotuses and a rather lovely pond of glowing, Japanese koi.

Under less intense circumstances I might revel in the novelty. Now I find it distracting. It's important to remind myself from time to time that quantum physics dictates that the simple act of observation can pluck the particle out of a wave of possibilities, which is practical information in my case, considering . . . Shit. I nearly forgot I was behind the wheel again. Keep it straight, Mike. I'm the one driving. I'm Professor Michael Huxley.

And . . . where am I going again? Gold Hill, Eden Jessup. One cup of ayahausca. Unbending intent.

"If worse comes to worse, retell your story," Sadhu advises from some dark corner of the right, temporal lobe. Great, now I'm the one hearing voices. "If you can't bear the lightness of being, tell the tale of you. How did you come to be here, in the

Now? Collapse the Probability Wave into something manageable."

I'm both angered and worried I'm actually considering his words again. To hell with those shaman. If they gave a damn about what happened to this world, they'd be helping me.

"What good is that; talking to myself about myself?" I holler inside the badly damaged, and recently stolen, German sports car. "Didn't we agree I'm narcissistic enough?"

As if in response, the memory of Iboga's voice whispers in my ear: "See your story line through to its illogical conclusion. Then, and only then can you edit your story as you wish; see the full potential. After all, it's the first step to shapeshifting."

Fine. Maybe the shaman were telling the truth about this one. I'll have to pull myself back from the brink of insanity and drive at the same time. Do I really have a choice? If I don't sort my head out before I reach the cult's compound at the top of Gold Hill, what are my chances of preventing an apocalypse this morning? I need a grip and, once again, all my footholds are muddied.

Waves to particles, waves to particles, microsecond to microsecond, all day long, even when we dream.

The Craneo Roto tribe insisted that people maintain their reason, the very order of their world, by talking to themselves incessantly. At the time, I didn't take their words literally. I run my fingers over the roof to inspect the series of savage, parallel cuts torn completely through the ceiling, tracing the holes punched cleanly through the door. It's a miracle that aberration of evolution didn't split me in half. I cringe as I recall what's hunting me.

Stay focused, Mike. Indulge yourself in just a little brainwashing—just enough to take the edge off. You're in total withdrawal from illusion.

It so happens we're all experts at brainwashing. It's so easy we teach children to do it. Brainwashing works by repeating something over and over until it becomes part of the routine, internal dialogue. And it doesn't really matter if the thing being repeated makes any real sense or not. That's the terrible beauty of it. Then again, the truth can be overwhelming in its own right. Because I'm out of my godforsaken mind, I'll tell my story of how I came to be here, in the Now. I'll talk my way back to what "domesticated humans" refer to as sanity. I'll make the chaos linear. I'll coax these waves back into particles.

I'm Professor Michael Huxley: evolutionary biologist, science department head, opium poppy enthusiast, atheist. And I'm going to save the goddamned planet this morning even if it kills me; again. Who can say when it started? However, I can begin on a Friday morning, less than a week ago.

# God is Bullshit

*"Do you, do you really believe —*
*That we were nothing but them monkeys swinging up in the trees?*
*Don't it seem a little likelier that Adam and Eve —*
*Did a lot of humping, and that was the origin of the species?"*

M C Frontalot

**M**y mind was dead-set on slipping off campus early to fill my gut with opiates, but Eden was already 10 minutes late to her own lecture for her Seeds of Religion course, a pre-requisite for majors in Theology and Anthropology. When she didn't show up for our 8:00 a.m. caffeine fix in her office, I took the liberty of greeting her students pouring into the lecture hall of the Science and Humanities building.

A full thirty minutes before class and at least fifty undergrads were already spreading into the stadium seating. I spied a few harsh glances over territorial rights to the highly coveted, front row real estate, mostly from the females. At this point in the semester, the boys had generally given up vying for Eden's attention. Most of them had accepted how pointless their efforts were by now. The back rows were lined with the usual pack of stoners, most of whom weren't students at CU. Over the last few months, it had become a thing for a subculture of the local youth around Boulder to smoke themselves into a stupor and watch the Eden Jessup show. Who could blame them? Recently, her lectures had taken on an inspired vigor, and often a total disregard for boundaries. Almost overnight Eden had blossomed into campus rock star, just another in my growing list of concerns over her.

To my eyes, she was still just Eden; my beloved and entirely platonic friend of nearly twenty years, still every bit as passionate, outspoken, and energetic as she was when we were undergrads ourselves. I knew her secrets; she knew most of mine. I knew the intense doubt she hid beneath the cavalier attitude. She wielded her intelligence and beauty with such careless grace it was easy to mistake it for arrogance. And sometimes it was, but ever since the "episodes" started, she too began questioning her true intentions, perhaps even her sanity.

As usual, a brace of the more conservative students huddled in the center stands. These were the fundamentalists of the crowd who felt it was their god-given duty to challenge Eden's discourses, especially when they contradicted some favorite part of Genesis. She referred to them lovingly as "Team Jesus."

None of the faces before me betrayed any sign of amusement at the prospect of having me as their stand-in. I was third-string in these parts; an egghead from the science department with no imagination, the dry, evolutionary biologist who somehow managed to keep such exceptional company as Eden Jessup. The hell if I cared what they thought. The superstitious, New Age/chic-Buddhist/spiritual-hipster nut jobs who made up the majority of Eden's fan club, who wouldn't hesitate to ridicule the cold rigidity of science and reason would also fail to produce one solid argument against the scientific method. Once it was clearly explained to them. In fact, they would realize that they'd been using this questionable method since the day they were born, or even before, to cope with the world around them. It's the only way to conduct one's life: Hypothesis, test, collect data, analyze results, change beliefs accordingly. Anything short of that is folly.

Eden dashed through the double doors to the left of the stage, tugging at her motorcycle jacket. Her black, chin-length hair was windswept. She hadn't worn her helmet again, with her condition. She darted around me, stole a quick glance off her shoulder to find her bleachers overflowing. She smiled and shook her head with a mild frustration at her tardiness. Her goggles were still around her neck as she not-so-covertly straightened her unprofessionally tight, badly worn "Pixies" T-shirt. I remember Eden once arguing that, since her entire body was plastered with detailed tattoos of deities and religious symbolisms, it was her duty as an educator to expose as much skin as possible during her theology classes. She was also pretty stoned when she arrived at that conclusion.

I was paid with a quick nod and a wink as a thanks for saving my ass again, Mikey. "Rough morning?" I asked quietly. Her gaze fell briefly to the floor. I didn't need to press further. It had been bad, and that made me even more angry. "So you decided to hop on the bike after one of your episodes?" I whisper-shouted.

"At least on a motorcycle, I'll just kill myself," she chirped, studying the sea of faces impatiently awaiting the show—and likely trying to remember what topic she last covered.

"You gunna stick around for autographs, after?" she teased. It would have been funnier if she wasn't occasionally greeted with an eager fan base searching for just that. I disappeared into the wings while Professor Jessup faced her fans and struck center stage. Her two, muscle-bound "assistants," courtesy of the local chapter of Lambda Chi Alpha, took their usual positions on either end of the stage. Acting as emergency backup had become part of the regular hazing process for the frat's bulkier pledges. The addition of security detail had been initiated by Eden herself, and not for her own safety. Of course, she insisted they were only there to assist in the unlikely event of another fit, but we both knew better.

"Well, it's about time! Where you lazy bastards been all morning?" she blared at the crowd after hooking up her mic. Laughter and chuckles echoed through the auditorium.

"So, where were we last?" she prompted. From a quick study, the average onlooker might figure Eden to be somewhere in her mid to late twenties—athletic, petite with a short, punkish haircut. Closer observation would reveal subtle wrinkles, lightly weathered skin, and an air of confidence that generally doesn't reach fruition until the mid to late thirties, if it comes at all. Eden Jessup had just turned 41.

I had always pictured her as the rebellious, popular girl in high school who slipped out between classes to smoke with her cooler-than-Jesus entourage, but she swore that wasn't the case. Her story was of being the weirdo kid who hid under a dark trench coat two sizes too big and a smear of black make-up, scratching out depressing haikus into her forearms.

Now, while our rock-star theology professor claimed to be

just another awkward, misunderstood loner, I could confidently state I was the real deal. I had grown comfortable, or
at least reached a truce with my identity as Science Nerd. Not
that this comfort made it any easier to approach women, mind
you, but I liked to think I had carved out a degree of pride
in my harmless, garish looks: Thick, reddish-brown hair too
course to comb properly, narrow shoulders that rolled forward,
clothing that never seemed to hang right off my fat ass—even
if the pants were tailored. It all became forces of nature I grew
tired of fighting. In fourth grade, Kristin Ruth summarized my
overall appearance nicely, and loudly for everyone: "Mike, you
look like if I threw a ball at you, you'd scream and flinch," she
giggled.

She was the loveliest girl in my class and her frank evaluation
broke my heart. I eventually gave up on cool, and my clumsy,
buttoned sweaters, unruly beard, and small-rimmed glasses
were just my little ways of accepting the ego of an intellec-
tual. At least these days being a geek carried a certain level of
respect. I guess people finally realized that somebody out there
needed to know how to keep their goddamned cell phones
working.

I snapped back to the present when, much to Eden's delight,
an outspoken beauty with flashing eyes waved from the front
row; eager to be noticed, desperate to help. "Professor Jessup,
last week we were discussing how every major religion can
trace its origins back to the ceremonial ingestion of hallucinogens," the student called out, reading her notes from her
laptop. She was a doe-eyed brunette likely not yet old enough
to drink legally. Eden scratched thoughtfully at the back of
her neck, winked at the girl and continued her ruse of being in
perfect command of her domain.

"Excellent!" Eden cheered, turned and darted to the computer tablet on her podium. "There is a very important word
you must remember when considering how the first concept of
'God' came into existence," Eden announced, scribbling thick,
capital letters onto her tablet which projected onto the widescreen behind her. "This is where 'God' really came from."

An array of murmurs and giggles echoed through the auditorium as their professor stepped forward to take in the responses. She had scrawled, "BULLSHIT" onto the projection screen. Team Jesus exchanged a round of sneers but awaited a reaction from the group's alpha, Bethany, an articulate, humorless young woman who shifted angrily in her seat, but remained quiet for the moment.

"As ancient man moved from the trees to the plains, he had to radicalize his survival strategies." Eden continued, pacing the stage. "New sources of food had to be located, proven safe and nutritious. It was most certainly the women of the tribes, the Eves of the garden, who first stumbled upon the curious mushrooms that grew on bovine droppings, just as they do today. At that time, the African plains would have offered the perfect climate and conditions to produce vast amounts of what we today refer to as psilocybin cubensis." While the majority of the audience erupted into note taking, the stoners in back sighed with knowing bliss. Low, mumbling groans from Team Jesus.

"These are edible fungi that require no preparation whatsoever, as opposed to nearly every other naturally occurring mind-altering substance that can produce an experience we might refer to as religious. Cubensis, as well as an array of other hallucinogenic fungi, need no catalyst, they require no boiling, no smoking, no fancy alteration. They can be safely eaten immediately after picking them." Eden paused for a moment to consider her words. "Well, you might want to brush the cow shit off first." More laughter from the crowd.

"So the sacred mushroom was, without doubt, the first consciousness-altering 'drug' humans encountered. The effect they had on us as a species was so radical, we're still just beginning to comprehend how they changed the face of the planet forever. Long ago, the hallucinogenic experience wasn't bound to the limited, societal perspective we find ourselves trapped in today. The conservative-minded generally think of psychoactives as a dead-end distraction that only wayward, unruly kids experiment with. This is one of the largest reasons we're still fighting for the right to even conduct scientific research on their extensive therapeutic values: recovery from drug and alcohol addiction as well as depression and PTSD, to name a few.

"Early humans found that these perception-expanding, boundary-dissolving experiences were often best left to the tribe's elders; only the wisest, most insightful among them. Back then, people had a chance to step into the sacred world of visionary medicine free from prejudice. And, from those stepping stones, some could argue that mind-altering plants put our species on a fast track to global enlightenment—that is, until we discovered alcohol several thousand years later." More laughter and murmurs.

"Those among you with firsthand experience of hallucinogens will certainly not argue when I say that the effect that an eighth of an ounce of cubensis wages on normal perception can alone explain the origins of religion. Now, to the uninitiated, this might be hard to swallow. Why? Because firsthand experience in this case is everything, and the psychedelic "trip" can never be contained in words. Yeah, yeah, I can rattle off a bunch of colorful adjectives and phrases in a futile attempt to capture the emotional, visual, spiritual, even philosophical qualities one experiences under their influence. I could tell you that mescaline is like stepping into a waking dream world where inner and outer stimuli merge in ways beyond normal comprehension. But what does that really tell someone who's knowledge is limited to Bud Light? The primary, most essential question one can ask when the topic is non-ordinary perception is quite simply: Are you experienced?"

"Jimmy!" someone hollered from the rear.

Eden smiled and continued, "If we think of our personal awareness as a sound wave, it's not hard to imagine how every drug on this planet either turns the volume up or down. On the darkest ends of the spectrum we find naturally occurring drugs that seem to shut down all higher functioning, leaving only the base, reptilian brain in charge." Onto her widescreen she projected a photo of a lush, green plant bearing stark white, trumpet-shaped flowers.

"For example, scopolamine, derived from the nightshade plants, is often referred to as a zombie drug. Many have reported that its effects are akin to a black hole that devours the user's awareness and basic free will. We should be wary of anything that acts without conscious intent. Of course, on the complete opposite end of that spectrum, a few peyote buttons can crank your volume so high you'll come face-to-face with your soul's highest potential. Is it any wonder that the powers-that-be have always preferred its citizens drunk and asleep rather than curious and awake? Even the Christian church, an organization supposedly dedicated to bringing us closer to heaven will do everything in its power to frighten us from the thousands of god-given, naturally occurring visionary plants on this earth that we have an inborn right to." Eden's voice was booming, her pulse racing. Her security detail grew uneasy. Thankfully, she calmed herself and reeled it back.

"But, I digress . . . " she smiled calmly, taking a breath. "Let's try to put this all into perspective for a moment: Intelligent, ape-like creatures, who had known nothing except survival until this point climb out of the trees and stumble upon a mind-altering substance which they don't need to know anything about. They don't have to figure out how to roll this stuff into a joint and smoke it; they don't have to catch it and collect a secretion from its skin like the Colorado River Toad. And they don't have to find the right catalysts and boil it down like ayahuasca. They need only pluck it and eat it. The mushroom takes over from there. And it produces an experience beyond anything early humans have known thus far; a world of images and the subconscious, where new perspectives could be visualized that were never dreamed possible; where metacognition was first born.

"Modern magnetic imaging shows that hallucinogens like DMT activate the centers of the brain responsible for symbolism and language. So suddenly we have a planet inhabited by animals with imagination, with the ability to play out scenarios in the mind before they act, to review mistakes and correct them before they're repeated. The potential for an animal to wake up beyond its survival programming is now within reach for the first time. Creativity and insight take a giant leap forward. The advantages this gave us over other species changed everything. Now we could really put our opposable thumbs to work."

"So what does any of this really have to do with God, professor?" Bethany of Team Jesus asked impatiently without raising her hand. "How does any of this connect with the Bible, or any other religion?" Eden smiled knowingly. She couldn't have timed the question better.

"Well, consider the fact that our ancestors knew nothing of microscopic spores," Eden whispered into her mic, taking a few steps forward. "Try to imagine what an early human might assume about these little curiosities. Humanity now has a powerful new tool that puts them in direct contact with an otherworldly realm; one that appeared to have sprouted directly from bovine droppings. What would ancient man have possibly made of all this? To paraphrase Bill Hicks, if the keys to heaven came directly from a cow's asshole, then the beast itself must be the most mystical fucking creature on the face of the Earth." She paused for the laughter to die down.

"We often assume ancient cattle worship was due to the milk, the meat, the hide they provided. Lots of plants and animals gave us the means of survival, we didn't worship them all; no, it was far more than that. God first made herself known to us through none other than bull shit. Irony? I think not." The crowd rumbled into chuckles and note-taking. Eden didn't let up. As her tirade continued, she projected a series of archeological photographs on the screen of ancient artifacts from around the globe.

"And this isn't just speculation or a means to glorify my own preference of drug use," she added. "Archeologists discover signs of hallucinogen worship wherever they dig up ancient civilizations—such as the paintings and carvings of mushrooms here dated around 7,000 B.C. in caves on the Tassili plateau of Northern Algeria. And here we have the Mixtec culture of central Mexico who worshipped many gods and one known as Piltzintecuhtli, or Seven Flower, was specifically the god of hallucinatory plants, especially the mushroom. Some of these sites, like the stone carvings seen on this slide recently found in France date back more than fifty thousand years; centuries upon centuries before anyone had even conceived of a Buddha, a Muhammad, or even a Christ."

This was too much for Team Jesus to bear quietly. Bethany pushed up her designer glasses and straightened herself. "So, you're suggesting that God was simply an invention from some Neanderthal's hallucinations? Is that right?" she called out. "You can't possibly ask us to believe that Fred Flintstone tripping on 'shrooms'—I believe they call them—is whom we have to thank for our relationship with our Lord and Savior? Or for our entire life of devotion and worship? Our church? Our faith?"

"Yeah," Eden replied flatly. "Except that we killed the Neanderthals off, yeah, pretty much."

Bethany gasped with dramatic disdain. "I think that is absolutely the most depraved thing you've suggested yet, professor. Just when I thought you couldn't stoop any lower. I can't begin to explain how offensive that is to me as a Christian." Team Jesus nodded in solidarity, the auditorium went into a vacuum, all eyes fixed to their professor.

Eden cocked her head with a smirk. How she delighted in these little moments, I had no idea. "Ahh, as per the usual, the generation of 'You hurt my feelings, and even though I have no rebuttal to your information, I won't let that detail stand in the way of me complaining about it.'" Eden replied, stepping closer to the crowd. If the woman ever cared about who she pissed off, she never betrayed the slightest indication.

"That's the inconvenient bit about evidence and facts, isn't it?" she continued. "They don't always agree with your beliefs." Eden moved in with a rapidly deteriorating tone. "And since you've changed the topic to what offends you, allow me to share the same." This was also why I adored her. She often scared the hell out of me, and maybe that was part of her charm. Eden inched her way closer to the edge of the stage while the fraternity guards prepared for action. "I'm offended at how religious zealots judge other world views as superstitious nonsense while your own magic book would have us believe that man's role on this planet began in a magical garden with forbidden trees and talking snakes. And all the while you completely miss the obvious message behind Genesis: That long ago, early people, who lived in a greater harmony with their environment, stumbled upon mind-altering substances that stimulate unique, neural connections for communication—with ourselves and with others. I'll say this, if there has ever been a literal Tree of Knowledge on this earth, it's been the very thing fundamentalists like yourselves have gone through great effort to keep out of everyone's hands."

At that, Eden strolled back to her podium. The frat-guards eased up and backed away. ". . . but, you'll never be able to consider that because you're too busy voicing your opinions," she added gravely.

"Eating the forbidden fruit was the original sin," Bethany called out, "so if your version of Genesis is correct, are you suggesting we were kicked out of Paradise for doing drugs? Maybe there's a lesson to be learned there."

"There's no lesson!" Eden shouted. "We weren't kicked out of a garden by an old, white man floating in the clouds, who people just like you used to refer to as Zeus, by the way. We woke up and walked ourselves out of the jungle, we left the wild quite willingly to chase after agriculture. We wanted more control over chaos! THAT was our sin, if there is such a thing. Your Bible would have us fear the Tree of Knowledge that woke us to begin with. Fundamentalists in every part of the globe always want the same thing: They want everyone to stay subservient to the 'mystical' teachings of their church, that we all smile, walk a straight line and forget we're still animals. The Church doesn't want us to be personally enlightened, it wants our obedience! You know what really scares the shit out of you? You're afraid of people who seek their own connection to God. That's why these discussions bother you. Christians prefer slaves, not thinkers."

Her temperature was out of control again. This wasn't good. Applause and a few whistles rang out while I sighed quietly. Her general attitude about the church mirrored my own, but for rather different reasons. She can complain about Christianity all she wants, I thought. Her own beliefs are considerably more bizarre. She'll scoff at virgin births, raising the dead, and walking on water, but astral projection and mystical energy chakras were all somehow within the bounds of reason.

"So, if it were up to you, we'd all just say to hell with the rules, go back to beating on drums and dancing naked in the mud, acting like wild animals?" Bethany shot back. Eden glared at the girl with a fire in her gut.

"What makes you think we're not still wild animals?" Eden asked with surprise.

"Well, for starters," Bethany replied slowly, stalling to mull an adequate response. ". . . we're sitting in a university lecture hall, not running around clawing at each other's throats, fighting for survival. Or are you too stoned to see that, professor?"

"Ah. I get it." Eden sighed. And something shifted. What it was exactly, I couldn't say, but it was like watching some invisible leash fall away. It all happened very fast. Limber as a mountain lion, Eden darted around her podium and sprinted full speed to the edge of the stage. With claws outstretched, she lunged headfirst and sailed into the air, over the seating and directly toward Bethany who shrieked with stupefied terror. A moment before impact, Eden Jessup's body snapped to a sudden, midair halt; caught by her security detail, her fingernails inches from the student's throat. The guards carried the professor's horizontal body backward and returned her upright, back onto the stage. While Eden regained her composure, Bethany remained a frozen, shriveled heap in the crook of her chair. I wondered if she peed herself. The entire lecture hall went silent as everyone held their breath.

"Religion would prefer we forget our connection with the wild," Eden said thoughtfully, straightening her T-shirt, which had nearly come off during the commotion. "It would like us to keep our clothes on and talk pretty—all so we can forget our roots. And that's more than just shortsighted and it's worse than arrogant: It's downright dangerous. Especially at a time when our social constructs are about to implode. So, gotta ask yourself: Are you experienced?"

With that, Eden smiled and took a bow before an auditorium that exploded into cheering and applause. I quietly slipped through the rear exit. I alone knew that wasn't part of the show.

# How to Make Liquid Heroin: A Practical Life Hack

*"Junk turns the user into a plant. Plants do not feel pain since pain has no function in a stationary organism. Junk is a pain killer. A plant has no libido in the human or animal sense. Junk replaces the sex drive. Seeding is the sex of the plant and the function of opium is to delay seeding. Perhaps the intense discomfort of withdrawal is the transition from plant back to animal, from a painless, sexless, timeless state back to sex and pain and time, from death back to life."*

William S. Burroughs

I crept up to the third floor and into Eden's office; a place she was rarely found. To her, it was just a storage locker, "a place to keep her stuff," as one of her late heroes, George Carlin, might have said. Here I would be left to my own devices. I had just started sensing the first tingles of withdrawal an hour ago as my last shot of opium was last night. The plan was to knock off early, go home, and refuel. But after what I had just witnessed, I felt obligated to check in with her after the lecture. I needed to know if her situation had worsened, and if it was beginning to affect her decision making.

It bordered on superstition, but some days it seemed the universe intentionally threw obstacles between me and my love. That was what opium tea was for me: Love transformed, shapeshifted, into a tangible thing that could be ingested. The lingering, warm ecstasy that massages the body after a life-draining, intense orgasm is the only comparison I could draw for the "inexperienced"; however, an opium tea high wasn't nearly as fleeting, or as unreliable as sexual gratification. Tea dulled the edges of my loneliness in ways I wasn't even sure a woman could for me any longer. I could blame it all on what happened with my parents, but what good would come of it? After dozens of attempts to hold miserable relationships together, I suspected that in some way I simply traded my need for a girlfriend with a need for junk. The votes were still out as to which posed the greater threat to my health. Yet, lately, I had begun to sense some agitation even when I was high; some part that still wasn't satisfied beneath the ecstasy.

I closed Eden's door behind me quietly, flipped the deadbolt and twisted the blinds shut on the window that faced the hall. Her office would best be described as something from the basement of an ancient world history museum that had been the target of multiple break-ins. Stone and wooden relics from India, Japan, and South America were strewn haphazardly over shelving, filing cabinets, and the floor. Maps of Mexican pyramids, old scrolls illustrating sacred waterfalls in Tibet, and Chinese diagrams of spiritual energy centers in the body all fought for wall space with prayer flags, Australian didgeridoos, and Native American flutes. A common observer might think this was the work of some Indiana Jones character who relentlessly scoured the globe for some ancient, religious artifact. But, alas, no, this was just typical Eden. Her apartment was far, far worse. The only thing she was searching for at times through this mess was her cell phone.

Woven throughout the many piles of treasures were hundreds of photos of her perched atop snowy mountain passes, clinging to the side of a sheer cliff or squatting near a raging river in God only knows what jungle. The pictures that vexed me the most were the ones of her in a beaming embrace with some indigenous tribesperson she couldn't have known for more than a month, two at the most, while conducting research on ancient religions in some forgotten part of the globe. I didn't have photos of me hugging my own grandparents where I looked that content.

If it were left to her, there wouldn't even be a path cleared between the door and the desk, but as luck would have it, the old custodian was shamelessly, cartoonishly in love with her. I could only guess that his poor English skills were the reason he hadn't picked up on the fact that Eden had no interest in men. That, or he just didn't care.

I plopped into her chair and removed my "baggage" from my shoulder pack. I generally kept a ziplock of ground up, dried poppy pods stuffed into a corner somewhere for emergencies, but in the case of my addiction, an "emergency" was any time I was out of pods. I dumped the powder into a French press and flicked on the kettle. This all started with a six-week prescription for Percocet several years ago, courtesy of my own family physician after removing a "benign but concerning" patch of discolored skin from the center of my chest. Not that I blame the man directly, but one would've hoped for a system in place when they hand an amateur like me a month and a half's supply of powerful narcotics, maybe a goddamned phone call from a nurse after a week or so to check on me.

I soon found myself lying to physicians about lingering pain long after the surgery to score refills and later rooting through my grandmother's medicine cabinet. After finding it too difficult and unreliable to secure pharmaceuticals, I had to weigh my options on maintaining my newfound habit. Due to my position at the university and the sheepish intellectuals I was generally surrounded by, finding a hard drug dealer wasn't likely. Sure, maybe Eden would've known how to make a connection like that, but frankly I was too ashamed to share my secret with her.

My only option was to do what I do best: Research. I studied precisely what it was I was addicted to. I scrutinized it. I examined it. I broke it down logically. After a few short hours of research, I was a minor expert in the field of opiates. My CliffsNotes went as such: Morphine is derived from the poppy flower and, while harvesting opium is illegal, owning and purchasing the dried flower pods in the United States is, technically, not. In fact, one could find them rather easily at floral, craft and hobby outlets to be used strictly for "decorative purposes only". These dried poppies aren't "slit" by drug seekers to extract the milky latex containing the morphine and codeine, so instead these compounds are absorbed into the walls of the flower pod—and, to some extent, the seeds—during the drying process. Furthermore, all these desired alkaloids are water-soluble, which means one can extract the morphine and codeine by making a tea from the grounds.

I had found a loophole to have all the ingredients I needed to create my own supply of morphine shipped directly to my house. All I needed to do was run the pods in a coffee grinder and toss the resulting powder through a coffee press and voilà! A dark brown "tea" that tasted like dirt mixed with vomit, yet stronger and longer-lasting than OxyContin. Over the course of the eight years I'd been an addict, I'd only had to tolerate withdrawal about four times. Generally, I was able to extinguish the burn within a couple days with a fresh supply of pods.

In my case, detox takes place in very specific stages. It starts with a sort of hollow buzzing that slowly intensifies in my joints and chest. It's tolerable at this point, but the sensation is disturbing and stressful, much like the onset of the flu. After that, the next 12 hours are consumed by my body not knowing if it's freezing or burning up. This is followed by relentless nausea until finally a crescendo is reached where I am engulfed with the physical and emotional terror of which, I would imagine, could only be compared to the initial stages of drowning. The process can be so torturous and nerve-racking that people have been known to have strokes, seizures and heart attacks during withdrawal.

I was about to push the filter down on the French press when I heard the jingling of keys outside the door. My heart jumped and I shoved the press off to the side, out of sight, and stared into my phone as casually as possible—as if I had fully expected company. The door opened and the light flipped on. It was Eden. This never happened. Her lecture wasn't over for another forty minutes.

"Hiding from your students in the dark, again?" she joked, tossing her belongings to the floor before collapsing into her rolling guest chair across from me.

"I already taught my BIO 410 this morning. What's your excuse? Why so early?"

"Someone pulled the fire alarm on the first floor. How the hell didn't you hear that? After all the drama, I just let 'em go early. The attention span of today's youth is … alarming."

"Maybe you should try leaping into the stands at them now

and again."

She barked out a strained laugh she probably imagined sounded easy and carefree, but then peeled her eyes at me. "Mikey, don't pretend a wild part of you isn't constantly pissed off with the domestication you've agreed to."

Classic misdirection: A bizarre observation that, although may indeed be accurate, only served to shut down any discussion on her ever-mounting frustration with the total lack of control in her life. I let it go for now and remembered I had indeed heard a blaring alarm far off in the periphery while I was brewing my tea. Funny how attention works. Eden flung her feet onto the desktop and pulled a small, blue jar along with a pack of rolling papers from her briefcase. With precision and skill she tapped out a green/purplish row of fuzzy nuggets into the crease of her paper. Somehow, this was something she genuinely was easy and carefree about and I couldn't fathom her total lack of concern. Even though Colorado had fully legalized marijuana and she held a legitimate script for it, lighting up on campus was obviously forbidden.

"Today's kids are leading their lives staring at screens where they get to pretend they're safe," she mumbled as she rolled her joint. "We have an obligation to remind them that the world wants to devour them."

The topic of how she's been coping with the chaos was clearly off limits, so I went for the jugular instead, to the source of the chaos itself.

"So you had another 'episode' this morning?"

"If by that, you're asking if I had another seizure, then yes," she replied flatly, firing up her lighter.

# Lucidity in the Dream World

*"Things have been tough lately for dreamers. They say dreaming is dead, no one does it anymore. It's not dead it's just that it's been forgotten, removed from our language. Nobody teaches it so nobody knows it exists. And the dreamer is banished to obscurity. Well, I'm trying to change all that, and I hope you are too. By dreaming, every day. Dreaming with our hands and dreaming with our minds. Our planet is facing the greatest problems it's ever faced, ever. So whatever you do, don't be bored. This is absolutely the most exciting time we could have possibly hoped to be alive. And things are just starting."*

*Waking Life*

I glanced briefly at the French press. It was better not to draw attention to it. "How bad was your seizure this morning?" I pushed a little further. She slouched into her chair and rubbed her eyes. She hadn't processed it yet, that much was clear.

"I didn't even make it out of bed when the first wave hit. I felt it coming on as soon as I opened my eyes, but my meds were just out of reach—might as well have been a mile away. You know, they gave me this giant syringe that I could theoretically inject into my rear end when I feel these coming on. It's supposed to put a stop to it before it starts. I've never used it, though; it's always been just out of reach. So strange for your last, rational thought to be, 'Man if I could just reach that thing on my nightstand and shove it straight up my ass, everything would be fine.'

"Anyway, an hour later, I found myself face down on the carpet a few feet from my bed," she lamented, staring at the floor. "When I come to, it's like my brain's operating system is rebooting after being wiped. It's fuckin' spooky. After these 'fits' I don't know what happened for a while. I don't even know who I am. Panic sets in because I have no idea where the hell I am, how I got there. I mean none. I could wake up on the fuckin' moon and I wouldn't know it was unusual. So, as always, I lose my shit for a few minutes inside my head. I tell ya, when you don't know who you are, that's hell." She clenched her fists. "There's just nothing to hold onto. And I can't move; not even the energy to lift a finger. I can almost see the little spinning computer icon in my mind sayin', 'Loading … Please wait'. Then slowly, slowly everything starts coming back, a little chunk at a time."

"Did you have another vision?" I asked casually, trying not to sound too nosy. I wanted to convey my genuine concern but the outlandish visions that accompanied her seizures were fascinating, and often worrisome. It's not uncommon for people to experience intense hallucinations during seizures, but it's generally considered a side effect. In her case, the vision-ary states themselves had begun devouring a troubling amount of her attention. Plus, these experiences increasingly took on a quasi-religious quality that worried me further about her emotional stability. Eden continued staring into space as she nodded quietly in response to my question, the smoke from her joint slowly filling the room.

"I was ten years old again," she began. "I was walking to school in the morning just like I really used to. And, just like every other vision, everything was an exact replica of real life. I could feel the sun on my face, the grass was lush and damp; I could smell it. It was a perfect playback of the path I must have walked a thousand times back in elementary school, yet it was totally happening in the Now. My old metal Star Wars lunchbox was in my hand and I was happy. I was innocent. And, then, as per the usual, something struck me as wrong about the whole scene. It's like a part of my adult-self wakes up and realizes none of this is right, I'm not supposed to be here. Then it dawns on me that maybe I'm dreaming, so I do the thing."

The "thing" she was referring to was literally raising her hands in front of her face so she could stare at them. It was a simple tool to determine if she was awake or not; an admitted-ly clever trick that a self-described "shaman" had once taught her. Boulder is teaming with them. When these seizures first started, seemingly out of nowhere, I insisted she consult a half dozen physicians and neurologists. Each of them had a slightly different diagnosis and opinion on just what was going on and why, but none of their scans could find one, solid anomaly. Every blood and urine sample, every x-ray, every magnetic imaging scan from every angle, head to toe, all confirmed she was in excellent, physical health. But that didn't keep every specialist from prescribing a slightly different medication for her condition.

With no solid answers from the medical community, Eden fell back to her initial instincts and began asking advice from local spiritual healers in the community. That too revealed another series of varying diagnosis: Her chakras were out of alignment, her "Qi" was either blocked or there was too much of it, or she had unresolved past-life trauma. Her yoga teacher swore she just needed to start eating raw kale. Some charged just as much, if not more than the doctors. One man who claimed to be of ancient, Mexican Toltec heritage took a greater interest in the fact she was becoming aware that she was dreaming during these fits. He insisted that the relevance of this alone far outweighed the details of the dreams themselves, or even the fact that she was having seizures.

The ability to consciously "wake up" during a dream-state is commonly known as lucid dreaming. It's an unusual skill many people have claimed to possess; one that has only recently begun to attract some degree of respected, scientific attention. In Eden's case, the Toltec man recommended that whenever she felt the slightest suspicion that she was in a dream-state she should immediately stare into the palms of her hands. Stare and hold the gaze. He claimed it was a universal truth that whenever one closely observes an object in a dream long enough, the object of focus will eventually shapeshift; changing texture or color or whatever. Because our hands are our primary tools to manipulate the world, they are always present in a dream—no matter how bizarre the dream may be—therefore, the fastest way to prove to our ego whether we are awake or asleep is to stare at our hands. If they shapeshift, then witnessing the change triggers a deep-seated point of self-awareness within the experience, and we know beyond a shadow of a doubt that the world we're experiencing isn't our normal, waking state. This knowing endowed the dreamer to consciously steer the content of their vision. What the dreamer did from that point on was limited only by imagination. Or belief.

Of course, only now do I know the truth: In the daily world, our attention pulls waves into particles. In our dreams, our attention pulls particles into waves. So are you awake or dreaming? Stare at your hands. Bizarre advice for sure, but it seemed to help her cope with the intense hallucinations. It was no longer just something happening to her, she was now an active participant. After discovering the technique to be surprisingly practical, she remarked how it was the first and only thread of control over the random fits thus far.

"There's no way to explain how bizarre it is, Mike," she continued. "I mean, I become totally awake, as completely aware as I am right now. In fact, more so. Like a hundred times more. But, the dream doesn't stop. It continues playing around me and I'm just left staring in total awe. Where else do you get to literally watch your subconscious play out in living color, and texture and sound, even taste! It's so odd: I know I'm having a seizure, I know what time it is for Christ's sake, I'm conscious of everything that's going on, and yet I can't feel my body. But, still, here I am: Fully submersed in this world that appears to be operating on a will of its own."

"So, did you wake up after that?"

"No," she considered, "that's when it always takes a turn for the worse. Every time I 'wake up' in a dream, I always come to the same conclusion. I always figure that, since this is my dream, I can go anywhere, I can create anything, right? I should be as good as God in this place, right? And that alone scares the shit out of me. It freezes me up with all the choices."

"Why?"

Wide eyed with excitement, she bit her lip and took another drag. "Because it's all too big, I guess. It forces me to ask what I would actually do if absolutely anything was possible. That's gotta be our base truth, right? I mean, if the world is completely lain at your feet, what do you really want from it?"

"So, what do you do when you're in that state?" I asked. She failed miserably to contain her enthusiasm at the mere thought of it. A sly smile crept over her lips.

"None of your damn business," she replied giddily, giving into the adrenaline. She began bouncing in her chair from excitement. "Oh Mike, you don't understand! This is so more real and intense than your virtual reality! This is pure power that you can touch! You can do anything!"

"Anything?"

"Let's just say I've done some awesome and, yeah, sometimes terrible things in my lucid dreams." Her mood suddenly took a nosedive. "But, so what? They're my dreams. It's not like I'm actually hurting somebody." Her troubled expression told me she somehow didn't believe her justification. I couldn't see why. What we do in our dreams is our business; that's an arena where you can forget your moral compass, right? "Anyway, after I've worked out all my insane fantasies about power and desire, I always finally remember that all I really want is to swim in my lake at sunrise."

"You mean *the* lake?" I asked. "Little Big Crooked? The one near the cottage your family used to own?" As far as I could remember, every vision she ever described featured this lake in some respect. As a child, Eden had spent her summers with her family at a small cottage in southern Michigan which her father and grandfather built by hand sometime in the 40s. The property was surrounded by a quiet chain of forest-lined lakes all interconnected by small canals. The original, native inhabitants of the area had named them Sister Lakes.

"Same lake," she confirmed. "So, there I am thinking about how I can transport myself to Little Big Crooked and suddenly, out of my peripheral, a giant hole appears like the very fabric of my dream was torn open. At first it's just a black hole, but then a scene appears on the other side and I can see the shore of my lake. The water is perfectly still; it's pure bliss. It's every bit as beautiful as I remember it, way before they allowed motor boats and jet skis to fuck it all up.

"I turn and start walking toward this portal when something else catches my attention. I can see something growing on the horizon—a violent storm; black and terrifying. Clouds are twisting and growing like some giant sea creature writhing up from the ocean floor. My demons won't let me rest. All of a sudden, the wind swept up with enough force to knock me off my feet. And it was real in every sense; completely vivid, yet I'm still totally aware it's all just a dream."

Frustration twisted her face the more she considered it all. Her words gained momentum.

"And I always wonder: Where is all this coming from; the clouds, the wind, the storm? Was it invented in some deep-seated corner of my subconscious? Is this just some part of my brain that my ego isn't connected with? Mike, when these visions take hold I have no idea what's going to happen next, so how is that possible? Who the hell wrote this scene? Who's the director here? And how am I not aware of it? Next thing I know, a deep, rolling thunder starts shaking the ground beneath me. And off in the distance, blinding daggers of lightning are crashing into the field, scorching the earth. You know how I've always been scared to death of lightning, just the raw, unbridled power of it all, so I lost myself and I ran. I ran as fast as I could in the other direction."

"If you know it's a dream, why do you run?" I asked. She let out a knowing laugh. She had tortured herself with the same question.

"I know. It doesn't make any fuckin' sense, right?" she considered with a pained expression, "It's like every, evolutionary, creature-like, preservation instinct still manages to kick in and take over. It's all so damn real. There's some part of me that flips out and starts doubting. Some corner of my brain screams, 'What if this isn't a vision? Safe trumps sorry, right?' So, I run. I run like a crazed lunatic. The lightning's crashing down all around me, burning hot, shaking the earth. I'm out of my mind with panic. Then my whole body is suddenly held in a field of static electricity; my skin tingles and my hair stands on end. Static charges start buzzing around my hands and for a split second, I know, I know I'm going to be struck by light-ning and there isn't a damn thing I can do about it. So I threw myself to the ground and curled into a little ball."

"Did that help?"

"Not. At. All." She smirked. "Next thing I know an angry freight train of pure, chaotic energy slams into me. Every cell in my body burns and all I can see is white, scorching light. I'm being struck dead-on by a bolt of lightning and I'm going to die, I know it. I didn't think it was possible to feel that much power coursing through my body. So, I figured this is it, so I just let it happen; no point in fighting the finger of God."

"So, you died in your dream?"

"No, it passed right through me, down into the earth. But at that point, I've totally forgotten it's all just a dream. I'm in total shock, I mean fuckin' traumatized."

"Do you ever make it to the lake?" I asked. With that ques-tion, she lowered her head with watering eyes, and I felt stupid for prodding.

"No," she said quietly. "I never get to the lake. There's always something that stops me. Sometimes I find myself a few feet from the shore and someone or something's in the way. Always. Once I forget it's all a dream, everything starts going black and that's all I remember. Sometime later I wake up sprawled out naked on a floor somewhere. At least I was home this time."

Her office now wreaked of smoke and I feared an admin-istrator barging in. She noticed the discomfort on my face. "Come on, Mikey. You know I need this for my glaucoma," she chirped, blowing a giant cloud across the desk.

"You don't have glaucoma."

"Ah, must be working then," she smiled. She leaned over and offered me the joint. To both her surprise and my mine, I accepted. I guess I thought it might ease the nausea and aches starting to come on; a discomfort I was trying to hide behind a façade of irreverence. If I brought attention to the French press in any way, she would ask what I was brewing and then I would have to pull something out of my ass. And then, of course, she might want some of whatever I made.

Feigning confidence, I pulled hard on the joint and immediately regretted doing so. I erupted into a coughing fit when my lungs collapsed under the smoke. My throat exploded with searing pain and my eyes turned to fire. I ripped my glasses off and rubbed my face, trying to hold back more embarrassing choking.

Yes, I had tried smoking pot when I was younger, but it never really seemed to have much of an impact. The subtle dizzy spells I encountered weren't powerful enough to convince me the effects weren't merely psychosomatic. I concluded it just didn't work for me, and perhaps feared the idea of becoming the stereotypical slow-witted, slack-jawed stoner. After I befriended Eden, I was shocked at how razor-sharp she was in spite of her heavy consumption. Marijuana rather seemed to energize her mind and instill her with inspiration, but still I couldn't help but think of it as a dirty haze that fogged rational thought. I had to stay in control.

But, now . . . now, a heavy wave engulfed my body and the sensation of weightlessness arose. This was not my imagination. Eden was delighted with the look on my face. For a moment it appeared I was witnessing the scene, Eden and her office, unfold at a slower pace, allowing me to watch the play manifest out of the ether, from microsecond to microsecond, yet still chained by the neck to Plato's Cave. That's great: One hit from a joint and I'm having "stoner" thoughts.

"Good stuff?" she joked.

I briefly played with the notion that I couldn't remember how to form words. The very idea of transferring "meaning" into auditory symbols seemed suddenly alien. Gradually, all linear thought sprouted wings and took flight, and that, in and of itself began to consume my attention. I sank into a stupefied awe that soon turned to anxiety. I had never really considered the possibility that perception was even a thing that could be altered, not simply clouded. This experience was far stranger than a fogged mind; this was a transformation. As wondrous as this all was, I felt a dark, gaping hole opening beneath me; a mysterious unknown that I had remained blissfully unaware of. It began to make me uneasy. If perception can be flipped on its head with one drag from a joint, is it really trustworthy? What else have I placed my trust in that might not deserve it?

"I've never . . . " I muttered, but I didn't know what I intended to say. More stoner thoughts. A heavy knock on the door jolted me from my trance.

"I'll bet that's the DEA, buddy," she giggled quietly. "Comin' to take your dirty, hippie ass to jail." With both feet, she pushed off from her desk and propelled her rolling chair into the window blinds with a small crash. She peered through the blinds for so long, I feared time had shut down altogether. In my altered state, the possibilities of what may lay on the far side of that door seemed endless. I finally gave up trying to be cool.

"Who is it?!" I nearly shouted. Eden shot a devilish grin at me and continued to study the hallway.

"Relax. It's not the DEA," she said, trying to understand the view herself. "It's the FBI."

# Tribal Myths

*"It'd be like a bunch of rivers, the Amazon and the Mississippi and the Congo asking how the Atlantic Ocean might affect them… and the answer is, of course, that they won't be rivers anymore, just currents in the ocean."*

Douglas Adams

I had had enough of Eden's jokes, but I tossed the joint over her desk and into her lap nonetheless. She snatched it up into the corner of her mouth and threw open the door without leaving the comfort of her rolling chair. Standing firm in the entrance were four terribly serious people: A heavyset, gray haired man in a navy blue suit and matching tie stood front and center. Just to his left was a raven-haired, athletic woman with dark, almond eyes. Native American, perhaps? She wore a sleek, black skirt and a pressed, white buttoned shirt with the sleeves rolled up. Positioned in brick-wall formation behind the mysterious man and woman were two male soldiers clad in green, Special Forces attire with machine guns strapped over their shoulders at the ready. My attention finally fell to the white badge hanging from the older man's lanyard, specifically to the bold, capital letters printed on it: FBI.

"Wow," Eden exclaimed, pushing her chair backward, joint still burning in the crook of her mouth. "You guys have really taken the drug war to brand new levels." She peered between the man and woman to the armed soldiers. "You don't think you went a little 'overkill' with the machine guns, though?" she added before stealing a drag. The young woman broke into a restrained smile.

I couldn't unclench my jaw. They weren't here for her; I was their target. They traced my poppy pod connection to my house, then back to campus and . . .

"We're not here for . . . that, Professor Jessup," The young woman said with a lovely accent I couldn't immediately place. "May we come in? It's rather urgent." Eden was already charming the poor woman before she stepped a foot into the damn room. I swear, competing for a female's attention with her was a losing battle. Luckily, she was generally only flirting for sport as she was strangely picky when it came to her actual choice in partners.

"I only go for the batshit crazy chicks with crop circles shaved into their pubic hair." I recall her explaining once. Again, she might have been high when she said that.

My nerves stiffened as Eden giddily welcomed the odd foursome into the room, delighted with the novelty of it all. I, however, was petrified. This couldn't be real. One of the soldiers struck a strategic position near the rear of the office while the other blocked the doorway after mechanically locking the deadbolt behind them.

The federal agent and the dark-haired, olive skinned woman seated themselves next to Eden on the far side of the desk. The man unloaded a briefcase full of file folders and thumbed through them until he found one with Eden's university staff photo clipped to it. I caught Eden's eye for any signs of comprehension. She only smiled with raised eyebrows. She didn't know what this was all about, but was thrilled to find out.

"Professor Jessup," the agent sighed with exhaustion, or possibly irritation. "I'm Agent Tom Downey of the FBI and this is Special Agent Tina Flores of the Peruvian National Police. Professor Jessup, your name came up as a local expert on South American tribes, their customs, beliefs, and such. Before I explain the reason for our intrusion, may I assume you are familiar with the Craneo Roto tribe?"

I eased back in my chair slightly. Maybe this really had nothing to do with me after all. With eyes peeled, Eden leaned forward and shook her head slightly, trying to wrap her own head around this sudden, strange turn of events.

"Well," Eden said hesitantly, "I can tell you about the myths surrounding the Craneo Roto, but short of a few superstitious villagers, no respected academics believe the tribe actually exists. The Roto tribe isn't even supposed to be a proper tribe at all. They're said to be a clan comprised exclusively of shaman; the most powerful medicine men from around the world." She paused to see if our guests wanted to hear more, or if she was even heading in the right direction. The two agents continued to listen patiently.

"But, they're Bigfoot, ya know?" Eden continued, "There's a version of this story on every continent. In Australia, some of the Aborigines call them the Bina Tribe and they appear in dream states. In Tibet they're known as the Dug Gtong and they live deep in the Tsangpo Gorge; farther in than anyone else has managed to step foot. And the name of the tribe changes depending on what part of South America the story pops up. I found tribes in the Amazon basin who call them the Kothoga. But the details that most seem to agree on is that these sorcerers banded together to form a sort of heaven-on-earth, a Shangri-La, if you will, where they could meditate and hone their spiritual powers without the distractions of modern society, which they're said to despise. They're generally thought to be mischievous, if not extremely dangerous. And for those who actively search them out, deadly.

"Some believe that anyone who manages to find their camp is thrown into a 'bottomless pit that passes directly through the bowels of the earth.' It's a fantastic story, one of my favorites, but there's never been any evidence to prove their existence."

"But there isn't anything to prove they don't exist, either." Agent Flores added. She was dangerously ravishing, but I zeroed in on her fallacious logic—and, in my current state, I couldn't catch my mouth before it ran away from me.

"Ye-ah," I snorted arrogantly, "and, maybe there's a, oh, I don't know, a little teacup and saucer floating outside Earth's atmosphere. You can't prove it's not there somewhere. So let's have NASA search for it. Does that sound about right?"

I immediately regretted speaking. Agent Flores peered in my direction before rummaging through her own briefcase full of documents with a knowing smile. Fuck, I'm so miswired. My first indication of how attracted I am to a woman can be reliably measured by the lengths I'll go to turn her off. Better to burn that bridge to the ground intentionally before she has a chance to size me up, I always say. How my male ancestors managed to breed at all remains a mystery.

"Either way," Eden continued, trying her best to smooth over my outburst, "the Craneo Roto story carries a good deal of weight with a few villages in the Chambira Basin in Peru. The Roto have been attributed to every sort of strange event you can imagine: Butchering cattle, murdering competing shaman with incantations or deadly potions, shapeshifting into vicious creatures to attack other tribes. They're the bogeymen of South America."

"Shapeshifting?" Downey asked, his weary eyes showing the first signs of life. He peered at his notes before searching Agent Flores for a cue. She nodded her head in agreement, clearly satisfied with Eden's knowledge on the subject. Apparently, she had now passed some sort of test to get into "the club," whatever that meant. I wondered if there would be a password or a secret handshake. At that, a childish giggle escaped my mouth to a round of confused glances.

Jesus, I thought. The entire room wreaks of weed. Pull it together, Mike.

Flores reached over to shake Eden's hand for the first time. "Professor Jessup, my unit investigates cartel and terrorist cells," she explained. "We monitor drug trafficking mostly, but I've requested access to a particularly troubling case in my homeland that I believe you can help us with." I found myself increasingly enamored by this woman's cool demeanor. She was stunning and confident. It didn't hurt that her shimmering black hair was parted down the middle and pulled into a tight ponytail. I couldn't take my eyes off her.

"Your government has been kind enough to cooperate with us in an ongoing investigation into a terrible massacre," Agent Flores continued.

"A massacre?" Eden gasped. "Jesus, that's awful. Where exactly?"

As much as I wanted to stay and see the conclusion of this odd turn of events, and, perhaps, gaze upon "Special Agent Tina Flores" a while longer, I had to somehow make a break for it, with coffee press in hand.

"I hate to interrupt," I announced, rising to my feet, "but, this clearly doesn't concern me, so I'll just . . . "

"But, you are Professor Michael Huxley, yes?" Agent Flores asked, "science department head?" She removed a file folder with my own staff photo clipped to the front. My head buzzed anew to unravel this next twist.

"Your dean, Doctor Tyson, said that you two are thick as thieves," Agent Downey wearily explained. "Professor Huxley, we're requesting your cooperation on this matter as well. The situation is complex."

Flores shook her head at the understatement. I slowly returned to my seat. At this point, my curiosity was surprisingly more powerful than my urge to dowse the growing flames of withdrawal. The government was requesting my help? The tea could wait just a bit longer.

"We've brought with us a piece of video footage of the massacre in question." Flores explained. "Footage that we'd like you to analyze. It'll help explain why we've tracked you two down in ways that are difficult to summarize in words alone." She motioned to one of the Special Forces soldiers stationed at the rear of the office. The young man stiffly marched to the desk, unzipped a vinyl bag strapped to his chest, and removed an ultrathin, state of the art, widescreen computer tablet and a flash drive, both of which he positioned strategically on the desk before Agent Flores.

"Thank you, Corporal Pavlik," she said as she booted up the system, inserted the drive, and moved a video file over to the tablet.

With a skilled hand, she removed the tiny storage device from the computer and returned it to the soldier. As serious as a heart attack, Corporal Pavlik placed the drive within a vinyl case with foam padding containing an indentation shaped specifically for it. After zipping up the bag, the soldier returned the case to an inner pocket behind his armored vest and resumed his post at the rear of the office. The whole thing was completely absurd. Why would a video file be kept under armed guard? I began to wonder whether this was some elaborate practical joke of Eden's. It certainly wouldn't be the first.

Or perhaps this was payback.

For more than five years now, Eden and I had been engaged in an ongoing, cutthroat game of "Bullshittery." What had begun as a moronic way of wasting a bit of free time back in the dorms as undergrads had steadily developed into a moronic way of wasting massive amounts of valuable time. Out of the blue, one of us would suddenly offer up the most outlandish factoid, a random piece of trivia that sounded insane. The trick was to keep the best poker face during the explanation and for the opponent to quickly decide whether the information was, in fact, correct (without looking it up, of course). As of this morning, with a score of 71–77, I was ahead.

I had celebrated my last victory just a few weeks before. Eden and I were heading to one of the better cafeteria lounges across campus for lunch on an unseasonably hot, dry afternoon. We were both sweating bullets when Eden lamented how her lack of faith made her uncertain as to whom she should direct her wrath for the ungodly, sweltering conditions. "Stupid ball of hydrogen and helium!" she finally barked, shaking her fist at the sun.

"Don't blame the gas," I said. "It's not their fault. We could replace all that hydrogen with the equivalent mass in avocados and it would still be just as hot."

"Right," she sighed dismissively.

"Is that challenge accepted?" I smirked. She looked at me with suspicion, realizing we were back in play.

"You're saying that if we instantaneously replaced the hydrogen and helium in the sun with avocados it would give off as much heat?"

The player is allowed up to three clarifying questions. "That is correct." I said carelessly, disinterested.

She bit her lip and searched for any "microexpressions" I might let escape as we crossed the courtyard. "Tick-tock, ticktock" I reminded.

"Fuck you, no way" she concluded and pulled out her phone. It took only a minute of searching for her to realize her loss.

"It's about the pressure," she said, nodding in comprehension. Admittedly there was some debate later concerning a lack of nuclear fusion eventually leading to temperature loss, it was agreed the point still went to me.

Now, as Agent Flores dragged this mysterious video file into a secure folder on the laptop, Eden once again was studying my face for microexpressions, perhaps wondering just what dramatic, new levels to which I had brought the game. Then again, I pondered, her show of suspicion could just be another ruse in her elaborate plot of mounting bullshittery.

"So, the video's on this?" Eden asked offhandedly, reaching for the computer while studying my face.

"No!" Downey and Flores shouted in unison. Eden jolted back. "I apologize, professor. Please don't touch the computer," Flores said quietly, calming herself.

"Professor Huxley, I understand your physics department has developed some sort of revolutionary particle analyzer," Downey said mechanically as if he memorized it from a document. Upon processing the question, my mind seized. I was in no state to assess whether I should now feel this confused or not. It took some time to extract the relevant information in my altered awareness.

Feynman . . . Damian, Kyle. Oh . . . that particle analyzer . . . Wait, what?

The federal agent was referring to what the techs who created the device dubbed the Feynman Squid. Damian and Kyle, the quantum physics undergrads behind the project, must have blabbed about it online. Memories slowly emerged in my altered awareness how the two of them had rambled excitedly about what the proposed instrument would do when they originally talked me into signing off for the funding to build it. That was more than a year ago. Looking back, I wish I had been paying closer attention to what the two of them had said. My primary field was biology. When it came to living organisms, the laws Newton devised hundreds of years ago worked just fine. Particle physics didn't factor into what made the human body tick. Or so I imagined at the time.

"So, you're saying this device of yours will construct an

image of a . . . probability field?" I recalled asking Kyle and Damian at the time. "Do I have that right?"

The two undergrads had burst into my office early on a Monday morning with a stockpile of notes, textbooks, and laptops in tow. Apparently, they had shared an "epiphany" for a never-before-dreamed-of method to analyze "spooky behavior" of particles over the weekend. Neither of them had slept in days. Kyle, fueled by caffeine and adrenaline alone, was a giddy mess bouncing from the walls.

"Professor Huxley, you know how quantum physicists proved that particles, photons, and electrons and such, don't appear as solid, physical objects until someone is looking at them, or observing them somehow, right?" he rattled, pacing back and forth before my desk. He fired that insane sentence off so fast, I assumed I heard him wrong. Damian and Kyle were both caught off guard with my ignorance on the subject.

"The Double Slit experiment?" Damian asked suspiciously. "You know, Schrödinger's Cat? Probability waves? Wave collapse?! None of this rings a bell?"

I could remember reading an article once where someone asked Einstein for his opinion on some theory in quantum mechanics that stated something akin to, "Reality didn't take physical shape until it was actually observed". Einstein scoffed at the notion, responding that he couldn't imagine a world where the moon was only there when he looked at it. It sounded like pure nonsense to me, too.

"Yeah, didn't Einstein say that the moon . . . "Einstein was proven dead wrong."

"Dead wrong," Kyle agreed.

"Yeahh, wow . . . and quite long ago, too," Kyle added, feeling sorry for my stupidity. He dramatically paused for a moment to decide how best to communicate with the ape of a department head sitting before him. I knew he was only half-joking, but he wouldn't patronize me; I was comfortable with my handle on current, scientific research. He didn't know the mysteries of cellular energy conversion like I did. His mind would be blown away by my insights into enzymatic reactions alone.

Kyle was a heavyset junior with a blast of prematurely graying hair and a scratchy voice. His remarkable intelligence first caught my attention three years ago in my Evolution of the Brain course. Even back then he was bursting at the seams with enthusiastic questions, primarily on how everything we studied could hypothetically be related to some aspect of quantum physics. To him, theoretical physics was the real forefront of, according to him, everything. I couldn't help but take an immediate liking to someone with such unabashed passion for a subject. He was excitable and awkward, and he prided himself on his brilliance.

"So, are you suggesting that the file folders I have locked in the cabinet behind me aren't really there now, because I'm not looking at them?" I asked sarcastically.

"Yes," the two replied.

"The particles that make up our universe, everything from black holes down to your ugly sweater, are in every position possible until we observe them; we refer to that as superposition. Only when we look at them do they fall into a single position. We call that wave collapse, by the way." Damian mumbled as if he'd said it a thousand times. Maybe he had. But not to me. He had no patience for explaining physics to a dung beetle.

Damian was quite a bit older than Kyle, somewhere in his early fifties and working on his sixth degree in a science-related field. This time around he chose quantum physics "for the challenge, because astrophysics was too freakin' easy". I could confidently say, without hyperbole, that Damian was the most intelligent person I'd ever met. His oddly shaped, completely bald head gave one the impression that the high acidity of his brain power made for poor soil to grow hair. Damian's interest was only on the solid, experimental science, not the theoretical. Yet, that never stopped him from debating it for hours on end with Kyle.

"This is ridiculous." I snorted. "The files are there because I remember putting them there a week ago."

"Some physicists would argue that's just a convenient story

we tell ourselves to make the world seem linear," Kyle added. "Some would go as far as to say that when you open the drawer, the files appear out of hyperspace or the Zero Point Field and your mind feeds you some memory about how you put them there earlier. The universe is just gonna do whatever the hell it wants to do. And then our narrow, linear brains are left scrambling to try to make it all fit into a tidy box."

My head dropped into my hands and I found myself rubbing my temples. Damian sighed heavily. "Waves to particles, waves to particles, all day long. This was all proven with the Double Slit experiment years ago."

They both gawked at the stupid look on my face. "When a single particle, like a photon, is fired at a wall with two openings, it goes through both at the same time," Kyle added.

"Wait, what?" I mumbled. "How can a particle be in two places at once? That makes absolutely no sense."

"You heard him right," Kyle sighed, reaching over my desk to tap at my forehead. "Your brain just can't and, I mean, it can not, understand it. Quantum physics has shown us that the universe is stranger than we can imagine it. The Double-Slit experiment proved that as long as we can't see it happening, a single photon will pass through both openings at the same time. As long as it's taking place behind closed doors, particles dwell in a vast field of possibilities, or a probability wave. And that's where your file folders are at the moment; in a vast field of possible locations."

"Okay, so you're suggesting that if I open the cabinet drawer behind me, only then do the particles arrange themselves back into the documents I left in there, is that about right?" I huffed in disbelief.

"Yup," Damian said.

"Well, the particles in your file cabinet will probably arrange themselves back into those documents once you open the drawer," Kyle added. "There's always the one in a trillion billion chance they'll arrange themselves into something completely different. Of course, you'd probably make up a bizarre story in your mind that fits that scenario as well." My confusion grew deeper.

"Oh, it gets stranger," Damian promised with a wide grin, basking in the confounded look on my face.

"So, as you might imagine, for years physicists were confused as hell over this," Kyle continued. "How the hell can one, single particle go through both slits? It must only travel through one or the other, right?! That's just common sense. But it seemed the rest of the universe wasn't restricted to those rules.

"So, physicists tried to solve this once and for all. They put tiny indicators near each of the two slits in the panel, so they could see exactly which hole the particle went through. And if it really went through both, they wanted to actually see that in action! And that's when the strangest thing anyone thought possible happened. What they discovered with that experiment changed our view of the universe forever. We still don't know what to make of it." Kyle trailed off, staring above my head, lost in fantasy.

"Kyle?" I said quietly. He snapped from his trance.

"Sorry. God! How do you not know all of this already?" he said, coming back to the present. "Okay, so this time, when they fired their particle gun with the indicators placed at the holes, it resulted in a specific, individual blast pattern. The photon only went through one of the holes this time!" He beamed with excitement, searching for my shock. His heart sank when he only found more confusion.

"So, this time the photon chose only one hole to go through?" I stammered. "Okay. Why? What changed?" Kyle exhaled dramatically with defeat. Damian just smiled at the floor shaking his head.

"What changed? What changed?!" Kyle whined. "What changed is that they were recording which hole it went through! That's it! Don't you get it? They proved that reality only takes the form of a single, individual particle when someone is fucking looking at it! Otherwise, it acts like a wave, a field of energy."

He immediately apologized for cursing. I looked at Damian

for help. "It's true," Damian agreed. "Look it up. Brian Greene does a nice little video on it. Particles are in superposition until we bring attention to them or measure them in one way or another." I eased back in my chair, trying to determine if they were both serious or not. Damian broke in before the implications began to take root.

"Some physicists compare this to living inside a video game," Kyle said with childish delight. "Like in the *Return to Dragon's Lair*, the coding for a dungeon chamber only springs to life when the player moves to that part of the game. Until then, all that information lies dormant; in potential, if you will."

"Okay, so where is the moon when I'm not looking at it?" I demanded. This was becoming frustrating for some reason.

"In a wave of possibility," Damian replied, holding back frustration. "The particles that make up our universe are in every position possible at the same time until we observe them. Only then do they choose a single position. We call that Wave Collapse. Why do I feel that's still not the last time I'm going to have to say that?"

"Okay," I finally surrendered. "So, what do you need fifteen thousand dollars for?"

Damian stepped forward and leaned over my desk. "Professor Huxley, the guys at MIT developed a camera that records at over a trillion frames per second. They're using it to photograph photons in motion. Idiots. We believe we can use this technology to analyze particles moving in and out of a probability wave. Kyle and I can build a device that will generate an image based on a particle's range of possible locations before it's literally photographed."

"Pics or it didn't happen, right?" Kyle said with poorly contained excitement. I understood why this project was so important to them, but I didn't comprehend it for a second. At least they had done their job at piquing my curiosity. It was clear to both of them I was still completely lost.

"Let me put it this way," Kyle started anew. "If we're right, we can use this device to take a mathematically generated picture of those file folders in your drawer before you open the drawer. We'll peel back the illusionary world of solid matter for a fraction of a second and see what's behind the veil while getting a ton of data on waves becoming particles. Help us do that, professor. It would be revolutionary technology for a relatively small price tag."

I slouched back in my chair, exhausted with the conversation. "You found a way to take a photo of something . . . " I began, "before you photograph it?"

Damian leaned over my desk with a grin. I anticipated another lengthy explanation, but instead he simply said, "Yup." As peculiar as the two of them were, they were great salesmen.

"When we observe something, we say that all of those possible locations a particle could appear in are collapsed down to one, single possibility," Kyle explained slowly. "This is happening nanosecond by nanosecond, right now, in this office. By observing the space around us, our attention is pulling order from chaos. At every moment, we are literally forcing the world of nearly infinite possibility to choose one, single path. We believe we can create photos and generate data of that process taking place more precisely."

"I mean, it all really makes sense when you realize the entire universe is only made up of one electron," he added with a wry grin.

"He's not ready for that," Damian grunted. "Don't confuse him again."

Don't confuse me. That's a laugh. This realm of physics they were suggesting was pure blasphemy to my tidy world of reason on a number of levels, several of which I didn't want to consider. But now something very specific wasn't settling with me. I thought I had somewhat understood the basic insanity my undergrads were suggesting here about the universe's underlying mechanics: At the particle level, the world as we know it, and everything in it, lived in some kind of bizarro state of "all possibilities" until we looked at it. Then, and only then, did the world "collapse" all the possible options into one, coherent form, a form that we could sense and analyze. And hence the problem. "I still don't get it," I admitted. "How the hell does matter know it's being . . . well, looked at?"

At that, both of them went completely silent. I could not believe what I was not hearing. It seemed like the most relevant question of all, and they had no insight whatsoever. "Well, about that," Kyle stuttered, "we both have theories."

"Yes," Damian agreed sheepishly, "We both have theories."

In retrospect, maybe I should have been paying closer attention to the rather lengthy debate that followed between the two of them, but as events unfolded that day, I had run out of pods the night before and was itching to get home to a fresh shipment. All I heard was Kyle shout something about, "Conscious attention must be another wave in the Zero Point Field" or something similar. All the relevant details of their theories on the actual connection between observation and wave collapse were pushed into my periphery in lieu of an escape plan to my house between classes.

While the two of them jabbered on from the far end of my desk that day, I discreetly glanced again and again at the tracking updates for my new shipment of opium on my phone. Whenever I tried to recall this conversation, I only saw the words, OUT FOR DELIVERY.

But now, my attention was abruptly snapped to the present moment, back to Eden's office and to our unusual guests. Agent Downey of the FBI dropped a photo of Kyle and Damian's revolutionary device, the Feynman Squid, onto Eden's desk before me. "You're going to want this nifty little toy of yours pointed at this computer tablet when we play the video we have here," Downey explained gravely.

"What?" I stammered. I was slowly moving out of my trance and logic was beginning to move back into normal focus. "Why? The Feynman Squid was designed to analyze spooky behavior of particles. I don't need to bring a bunch of fancy lasers and sensors into the mix to tell you about the computer you have there. You've got a rather pricey, Apple workstation tablet with a high def . . . "

"Yes, we're aware of that," Flores interrupted. "But that's only what it is now."

# Schrödinger's Computer

*"No one intuitively understands quantum mechanics because all of our experience involves a world of classical phenomena where, for example, a baseball thrown from pitcher to catcher seems to take just one path, the one described by Newton's laws of motion. Yet at a microscopic level, the universe behaves quite differently."*

Lawrence M. Krauss

Within a couple of short hours, I and a small team huddled around a dusty table in a darkened physics lab in the bowels of the Math and Sciences building; shades drawn, doors locked. The room was primarily used for storage so it was likely we wouldn't be noticed, and, if so, certainly not disturbed. I imagined our two rifle-toting companions posted outside either door wouldn't allow it. It didn't take long to track down Kyle and Damian in their dorm rooms to join our bizarre entourage. Kyle was now balanced on a rickety folding chair atop the lab table rigging the Feynman Squid to a nylon line through an eyehook in the ceiling while Damian failed miserably to hold his friend's makeshift ladder steady.

Their invention was appropriately named. Had I asked my brain-duo to build me their interpretation of a squid with six tentacles using only outdated computer parts, I imagined the results would have been identical. Six opposable plastic arms, each between two and four feet in length, fanned out from an oval, central hub that resembled a small, fat Frisbee. A series of tiny camera lenses lined the interior of each arm as if to mimic the suction cups of an actual cephalopod.

"It can't be any closer than five feet above the table, boys," Downey instructed them with a groan. "If it's any closer to the computer, it'll be damaged by the ensuing phenomena."

I considered it wasn't fatigue I was sensing from the federal agent as much as frustration. Perhaps he was angry he had no better play for answers than a couple of stoned teachers and their eccentric students. "Believe me, Agent Downey," Damian snorted. "If this nylon line fails, your computer will be fine. Doctor Feynman here only weighs 26.8 ounces."

"That ain't the point, son. I'm saying your device there will be buggered if it's any closer than five feet," Downey replied. Both students shook their heads in disbelief.

"Destroyed by what?" Kyle whispered. Damian shrugged. The only light the agents allowed in the room came from a single desk lamp at the center of the table aimed at the computer directly beneath it. Flores propped the large screen into standing position and loaded the media player.

"That goes for the rest of us," Flores added. "We'll all have to move beyond a specified radius when the video starts." We each took a moment to process her warning.

"If this computer of yours kicks out some kind of electronic virus that makes me impotent for some black ops experiment, I'm suing the Feds," Damian snapped. It was impossible to tell if he was joking or not. Damian's mouth was always pulled into an odd sort of grin someone might make who was acting intentionally bizarre for laughs. Yet, he nearly always had this expression smeared across his face; perhaps a quirk developed from a lifetime of being thought of as "weird."

"The phenomena that ensues at the end of the playback here is being studied by . . . a number of other resources," Downey explained gruffly. The man had unloaded his considerable girth into the only padded chair in the room. Eden couldn't contain her curiosity.

"The phenomena that ensues? Care to elaborate?" she chirped.

"Short of a bunch of fancy guesses, no one really knows what the hell to make of this yet," Downey said. "Brighter minds at the Bureau have, regrettably, started searching 'outside the box' for answers. Hence our intrusion."

"Only a handful of people have been allowed to view the full recording you are about to witness," Flores added. "It has become a highly classified piece of evidence in the mass homicide I mentioned earlier. Our technicians analyzed the original recording and have assured us that no digital alterations were made to this video." Kyle choked back a laugh and shook his head.

"The point is, this video hasn't been shopped in any way," Flores explained. "What you're about to see is real, this isn't CGI. It was originally captured on a state-of-the-art, shoulder-mounted camera by a soldier under the direction of one General Roberto Hernandez who, subsequently, asked for my input on this situation. Several months ago, Hernandez ordered all military operations to be recorded on high-def video/wide-range audio cameras. The investment paid off; it proved to be a powerful tool in improving field tactics. This footage is what they captured when three units were dispatched to the Chambi-ra Basin of Northern Peru in response to a series of desperate cries for help from the Chambira tribes. They claimed that . . ."

"Wait," Eden interrupted, "The Chambira people asked the government for assistance?"

"Unlikely, right?" Flores agreed. "They pride themselves on their resourcefulness. Their requests for military intervention on their behalf were unprecedented. It's what piqued General Hernandez's curiosity into this matter to begin with. The Chambira compared what was taking place in their homeland to a plague."

"Those people have survived in that basin for twenty thousand years," Eden said in disbelief. "What the hell would drive them to ask the government for help?"

"Okay, we're ready," Kyle hollered, inserting a flash drive into a port on the Squid's central hub. Agent Flores centered the laptop on the table below the students' device while Damian powered it up. A surge of tiny electrical flickers pulsed through each of its six, mechanical arms that seemed to reach like an outstretched hand for the comparatively small computer beneath it. Immediately after pressing "play" on the video, Flores quickly backed away from the table, trailing a thin measuring tape behind her.

"No one steps beyond this line," she warned firmly, placing a piece of tape on a seemingly arbitrary spot on the tile floor. Except for Downey, who appeared fed up with the entire ordeal, we all gathered around Flores to get a prime view. Following a few bursts of audio feedback, the video sprang to crisp, clear life,  along with an impressive audio system for its diminutive size.

The video opened with a single, rounded light source jiggling back and forth across a black screen. Above the muffled rumble of tires over rough terrain rose a number of male voices, all in Spanish. As the jittering slowed and the light crept into focus, it was clear the video was shot from the rear of a covered flatbed of a military truck. Our cameraman was facing toward the back, open-air stern beyond two rows of soldiers seated on benches. Soon, a second truck came into focus through the canvas flaps trailing just behind, tearing through the green overgrowth of a muddy road carved loosely through the jungle.

"This is the Seventh Commando Infantry Battalion," Flores interjected. "Our cameraman here is Sergeant Torres. Colonel Edward Panza sent in 24, fully armed soldiers and a medical team to assess the threat, if any, that the situation posed."

Suddenly, the video snapped to an outdoor scene shot from a high vantage point. As the camera swept the landscape, three military trucks came into view below, parked single-file at the edge of a sandy clearing, their engines rumbling beneath a thick canopy of foliage and bird cries. Our cameraman, Torres, had struck a strategic position on the roof of the truck closest to the action. As he panned back and forth, the scene below became increasingly bizarre.

The soldiers had spread around the military jeeps with weapons readied. Less than a few meters from the muzzles of their guns stood a quiet mass of people, maybe a hundred or more. All but a handful appeared to be native inhabitants of the region. The camera zoomed to the far edge of the crowd where four Caucasian adults stood shoulder-to-shoulder atop a fallen tree trunk. They were the only ones who appeared out of place: three males and one female. All four of them were caught up in a kind of trance as they towered over the natives.

Their eyes were closed and their lips murmured in unison while their torsos undulated to an unheard rhythm. I could only guess they had been captured by this mob of angry tribesmen, possibly drugged, and were now praying for mercy.

Most of the Indians, if they bore any clothing at all, were clad only in leather loincloths, handwoven tops, large ornate jewelry of hammered metal and colored beads. Only a few wore sandals. The straight bangs of jet-black hair framed faces that I assumed carried an expression of deep, ceremonial worship. But the longer the camera panned over the grounds, the more it became evident: These people were terrified.

"Que demonios?" our cameraman, Torres, mumbled to himself.

From the far dark edge of the jungle strode a thin, pale man wearing a powerful grin. He stepped into the open, anxiously carving his way toward the line of military personnel. Everything about his appearance was also completely wrong, not only because of where he was, but when. The man's dark slacks, black jacket, and white, buttoned shirt were fresh and unsoiled. The bolo tie that adorned his collar held a dark, reddish stone at its center. Only his pointed, black boots betrayed any sign that he had been walking through the jungles at all. The longer I studied the man, the more I imagined a hole had been punched into Salem, Massachusetts, 1692, one just large enough to allow an ancient, Puritan minister to pass through.

He removed a flat, wide-brimmed hat to reveal frizzled, white hair and a patchy beard. Infected bald spots pockmarked his ashy skull. As the frail, sickly man stepped closer, something even more unsettling became apparent. Overall, his muscle structure revealed a man in his mid to late fifties, yet he seemed unnaturally aged. Transparent, hazel eyes sank into withered, dark caverns, his long nose was a beak curved ungracefully downward, hints of blue veins and stringy muscle shown clearly through tissue-paper skin. We were witnessing a skeleton suffer the agony of remaining alive. A pained labor hid behind each joyous step the man made toward the militia. "Reverend Edward Kane," Downey announced. "He is the leader of a small parish called the Church of First Life ministry here in the states." Eden and I shared a brief, confused glance. We'd heard that name before: Edward Kane. But where?

"What's wrong with him?" Damian asked.

"Records indicate he was diagnosed with stomach cancer," Flores replied.

"Twelve years ago." Downey added. "It's a miracle the man's still walkin'."

"Or a curse," Flores said. As if stepping from a showroom floor, Reverend Kane confidently approached one of the commanders. Each lead-footed step was marked with a tall walking staff topped with a tarnished, silver crucifix. The camera struggled to tighten in on the reverend's features, yet never seemed to maintain total focus on him. Many of his facial features always remained slightly blurred. His wide grin stretched the corners of his mouth into daggers, showcasing an unusually white set of teeth separated by black slits.

"Good Afternoon to you," Reverend Kane bellowed with the distinguished accent and charm of a Southern gentleman. He stooped down to read the commander's name badge. " . . . Captain . . . R-R-Ramirez. Good afternoon to you!" Kane snatched up the captain's hand and shook it with enthusiasm. Ramirez pulled back while Kane leaned his weight into his walking stick.

"Hablas Englis, captain?" Kane continued, nodding his head, anticipating a response. His smile crept higher. He did not appear to take notice of the cameraman a few meters above him, yet I was certain he was aware of his presence.

"Yes, I speak pretty good English," Ramirez replied with a heavy accent.

"Excellent!" the reverend cheered. "I am Reverend Edward Kane from the Church of First Life back in the United States of America. My companions and I have traversed earth, air, and sea to be in this wonderful land of yours," he beamed, intertwining his fingers, leaning closer into Ramirez with a lowered voice. "You know, sir, we are here to bring salvation to these desolate people you have here; folks who have never had the opportunity to hear the good word." Graying gums appeared behind cracked lips as Kane enunciated each and every syllable with a molasses-slow, forceful determination. He lowered his tone further, only slightly relaxing his concrete smile as he continued.

"So many of these good people do not even know how to read. The Good Book, sir, remains inaccessible to them. Here amongst the filth of the unforgiving wild, these unfortunate savages do not know the word of Christ, and that, Captain R-R-Ramirez, is why we have come here to them; to lend a guiding hand away from their animalistic tendencies, into the promised land that God's son did give his life for." Ramirez looked around at his troops, removed his black beret to wipe his brow with a handkerchief, relieved the situation posed no real threat.

"We will need to see your passports and permits to be visiting with these people in their territory, please," the captain replied sternly.

"Absolutely, sir, we are more than happy to oblige. I shall return directly," Kane announced. He returned the wide, dark hat to his head and steadily wove through the obstacle of natives, passed his team of trance-induced missionaries, back into the dark foliage. The camera panned again, surveying the scene, briefly focusing on the natives prostrated beneath the four, white missionaries. We pulled in on the face of an elderly man amongst the crowd who, hazarding a quick glance at the soldiers, carefully mouthed a single word. Yanapay.

"Save us," Flores translated. Captain Ramirez could be heard just offscreen speaking to one of his soldiers. "Por que estan todod en sus rodillas?" he rumbled.

"He's asking his lieutenant why the natives are on their knees," Flores explained. A moment later, Kane resurfaced from the jungle carrying a leather satchel from which he produced a stack of yellow forms and laminated cards. Ramirez studied each of the permits before dismissively returning them.

"These passports have expired many months ago," he announced, "I need you to gather your companions and your belongings and come with us. We will arrange for your departure back to the States through your embassy." For the first time, Kane's smile wilted from his lips. His eyes flared and his head shook vigorously.

"No, no, no," Kane muttered, staring into Ramirez, drawing ever closer. "This just will not do, sir, this just will not do! We have yet to finish our work here with these people." His voice cracked, his breathing quickened.

Ramirez jammed his fists into his hips. "And what exactly is your business here with the Chambira?" he demanded loudly. "These people look frightened. Can you explain all of the requests for help we have received over the weeks from the tribes in this basin?"

The reverend did not move. His body grew still. "I am astonished with your audacity, sir," Kane said firmly. "How am I under question here? We have come to you on a mission of mercy to save these uncivilized animals from their own ignorance. Will you stand in the way of . . . "

"These 'animals,'" Ramirez aggressively interrupted, "have been doing very well without your help, Mister Kane, for a very, very long time. Please, gather your belongings."

Kane stared intensely at the Captain before turning to his four companions at the edge of the jungle, just beyond the prostrated tribesmen. He whistled a signal that resembled a high-pitched bird cry that briefly pierced the computer's tiny speakers. Our camera pulled back to focus on the four missionaries who suddenly stopped chanting.

I took note that Kane's companions were at least dressed a little more appropriately for the terrain. Their camouflage pants, earth-colored T-shirts, tank tops, boots and gear appeared military. Or maybe they all shopped at the Army Navy Surplus.

One of the missionaries, a tall angular man with a crewcut and unusually broad shoulders, emerged from his meditation and opened his eyes wide. Slowly, he knelt to one knee and removed a canteen from a backpack at his feet, poured a dark liquid into the cap, and swallowed it with a pained wince. He then handed the bottle to the next missionary in line who did the same, until the woman at the end of the row emptied the canister.

"What are they drinking?" Eden asked in a whisper to Flores.

"The residue recovered from the canteen we found at the scene was determined to be a unique concoction of Dimethyl-tryptamine and other psychoactive agents," Agent Tina Flores replied.

"Ayahuasca," Eden muttered.

"Similar, but a bizarre mixture we've never heard of," Flores said.

With his back to Ramirez, Reverend Kane bowed his head in prayer. There was a long, awkward silence before he spoke again. "Are you a man of faith, Senor Ramirez?" Kane asked quietly.

"Catholic, yes," the captain sighed, his impatience growing.

"Catholic, ah. That's good, that's very good. Of course, the final decision will rest in the good Lord's hands on what's to be done with you. Now, if I were to hazard a guess, sir, I would say that after God has witnessed how you have attempted to block the way of His will being done, He will find no heavenly use for you. Oh, I suppose your faith in His son may stay His hand, but when He takes account of your idol worship, your misplaced worship of the mother, your support of pedophiles, and oh-so many blasphemies of the church: Sir, I believe that moments after your death your insides will be boiling in a never-ending lake of fire."

Ramirez turned to the soldiers at his back in disbelief. Did he hear that right? "Excuse me Mr. Kane?" Ramirez demanded, raising his voice.

Kane turned to the captain, fire welling in his eyes. His thin, cracked lips stretched around dark gums as he enunciated each consonant and vowel with determined precision: "I say your agony will be eternal as you piss blood and choke on maggots in the bowels of hell! I've tried being reasonable with you, but now you're in my way." At that, Kane turned and quickly made his way directly into the band of huddled natives. When he reached the center of the crowd, he stopped abruptly to lower his head in prayer once again.

Eden nudged me and whispered, "Spoiler alert: I bet he turns out to be the bad guy."

I couldn't help but break a smile. I didn't know what to make of what we were watching. The whole scene was insane.

The camera zoomed in to catch Ramirez lowering his shaking head in disbelief before barking at his troops with a finger leveled squarely at Kane. "Take that man and his four missionaries and throw them into the truck, now! I'll waste no more time with this bullshit. Go! Move!" The lieutenant behind Ramirez shouted a few orders to his troops immediately drawing two dozen men into a flurry of action. With weapons trained on the Americans, the battalion divided into two teams to flank Kane's four missionaries from either side.

Suddenly, a number of screams and cries rang out. The camera swept the clearing and focused on the source of the horror: Kane's missionaries had broken from their trance and appeared to be struggling for their very lives, as if simultaneously poisoned. Their bodies convulsed in violent waves, sweat poured from their skin leaving dark spots on their clothing. Throughout the commotion their feet remained cemented to the ground, somehow holding their bodies upright while they shuddered in agony. The color drained from their skin and, one by one, their necks snapped backwards and to the side in a series of powerful cracks and pops. "What . . . in the hell am I watching?" Eden murmured, frozen to the screen. "They almost appear to be seizing."

"Are they, are they . . . dying?" I blurted. My mind spun for a diagnosis. It seemed as if Kane's missionaries were being electrocuted. Yet that made no sense at all. Our camera rolled back to the encroaching soldiers on the ground who now stopped dead in their tracks. Some of them looked back to their Captain for new instruction or perhaps answers. A few of them lowered their weapons, overwhelmed by the sight while others tightened their grip around the trigger. Captain Ramirez paused, gawking at the terrible scene playing out before him.

He managed a few cautious steps forward to make sense of it all while the good reverend continued to stand his ground amongst the Indians, his head still lowered in prayer.

Gradually, the intensity of the missionaries' spasms slowed. As their erratic convulsions came to a halt their limbs stiffened until their bodies hung motionless in contorted, unnatural positions. And impossibly enough, they all continued to stand upright. Our camera pulled in and panned over their frozen faces. Horrifically, their eyelids, along with the surrounding skin, began to shrivel and collapse into the eye sockets while their lips dried away to expose graying gums and yellowing teeth. All soft tissues on the missionaries' bodies began decomposing at an ever-increasing rate. Eden gasped in terror while Kyle and Damian exhaled in disbelief. I simply shouted, "Oh, to hell with this!"

Okay, this is the punch line. Electricity doesn't do this to people. No earthly force does this to the human body. Now it was obvious. The agents, the armed guards, the video—all one, elaborate joke. And for what? Why? Revenge for being ahead six lousy points? I had no idea, but this was clearly directed at me personally, the head of the science department. For some reason, I was the target of the most expensive, outlandish prank in campus history. Nevertheless, I continued watching the footage play out while shaking my head with a quiet, knowing smile.

And the horrors only multiplied on the video. In pulsating waves, the missionaries' faces withered and pulled into the spaces between jaw and cheek bone, eye sockets, and nose cavities. This "'rapid-aging" process quickly spread to the neck, arms, and legs. Everywhere, their bodies collapsed as if some impossible vacuum had opened inside their chests to devour fat and muscle tissue from within. Soon each of Kane's people violently deflated down to erect skeletons; bones and ligaments shrink-wrapped by actively decaying skin.

Even though I knew this was all a dazzling work of special effects, the sight was no less stomach-turning. The graphic design for this must have cost a fortune. Somehow, watching the ordeal play out was making me intensely aware of my withdrawal sickness. I found myself ever more nauseous and clammy. On the video, unhinged terror had now spread over the natives like an airborne plague. People were shrieking uncontrollably, some going insane right where they stood from witnessing the impossible events taking place, several of the soldiers vomited. A handful of natives closest to the missionaries appeared to lose consciousness altogether. And that's the first time I was subjected to the frequency; the most agonizing sound I ever imagined possible for the ear to process.

This deep, resonating hum poured—oozed—from the computer's speakers before plummeting to a sickening, low rumble that shook me to the core. While the suffocating hum intensified in the space around us, the trucks' engines could be heard sputtering out one at a time on the video. Soon the footage began fluttering with electrical static and the screen jumped to a blur of frantic movement, flashes of light and chaotic sound, during which, the terrible frequency dropped into ever-deeper canyons of decibel range.

A few moments of video static interlaced with random images and sound rippled from the computer: bursts of screams and gunfire from several positions around the jungle's clearing. It seemed that all manner of violent commotion was raging on in every direction on the ground. The jungle floor had erupted into a full-blown battle. Or more precisely, a massacre. The camera darted from one shaky point of action to another so quickly, it only managed to focus for a fraction of a second before the screen was swept into more chaos. As the tiny fragments added up, it became evident that the soldiers were under siege by wild animals. But the blurry predators tore through bush and over rock with such speed and agility, a proper identification was impossible.

Most of the natives fled aimlessly into the underbrush while others huddled low to the ground, hands covering their heads and faces. Women draped their bodies over their children while men swung helplessly at their attackers with flailing arms and sticks. A few managed to arm themselves with spears and arrows, but their efforts appeared equally futile.

And the terrible rumbling noise dropped even lower, filling the lab with heavy vibration that imbued me with panic. This is a joke, right? On the video, the skeletal forms of Kane's missionaries were now nowhere to be found among the bloody action. Only a small pile of natives now filled the area where they had stood just moments prior.

The only creature not in motion was Kane himself. The man held his ground in the center of the clearing; a statue in a burning building, his head still lowered in prayer, never flinching a muscle, not even as body after body fell mangled and lifeless at his feet. Every few moments the hazy shape of one of the mysterious animals flashed across the screen, and each time repulsive shrieks followed directly behind. This happened again, and again. The more fractions of images I pieced together, the more it appeared that the animals were generally ignoring the Chambira natives. Their primary target was the soldiers.

Through the commotion, it occurred that more than one type of predator was behind the carnage; I noted a variety of body shapes and color, but none of it made any goddamned sense. It was as if different species had joined forces to wage a highly coordinated assault—something that obviously doesn't happen in the animal kingdom. I glanced at Eden to gauge her reaction. Her wide-eyed, open-mouth expression told me she was utterly taken by this nonsense. And completely horrified by it. "Come on," I whispered. "You aren't buying this?"

She ignored me. Our cameraman's strategic position on the jeep's rooftop had now become his refuge. He paced back and forth whimpering, praying to himself in Spanish while searching for better cover. Finally, he managed to pull into a wider shot of the jungle floor. Only a few spots of naturally colored sand remained in the blood-soaked clearing. The Chambira vanished into the distant foliage in every direction. At this point I could barely stand upright, nauseous from the sound waves that smothered the air we breathed. Electrical discharges of white pops and fizzes began to overwhelm the video's playback, threatening to crash the system at any moment.

The final seconds of clear footage revealed shattered bodies and stray limbs scattered over brush, trees, and demolished military jeeps. Eventually, the shrieks and random gunfire were drowned far beneath the rumbling frequency that now cancelled out all other sound, even within the lab itself. I looked down and snapped by fingers without hearing a sound. The deeper the vibration sank, the more my heart threatened to explode inside my chest. How in the hell are those tiny speakers kicking out this kind of decibel range? It didn't seem feasible. It wasn't feasible. This wasn't a joke.

And there it was. The first moment the notion crossed my mind that I was witnessing an event that, for all rational means, would be classified as impossible. Riding the tails of that notion, there was an abrupt crack in the atmosphere; not the crack of breaking glass or plastic, this was all-consuming, massive. This was akin to a load-bearing wall crumbling. I had to lean toward the buzzing computer to discover the source of it. There, before my eyes, extending into midair from the center of the right speaker was a split, a crack in space itself, darker than the night sky. This frozen, black lightning bolt surged with an electrical hum I could feel in my nerves.

I couldn't help myself. I leaned in closer, desperate to make sense of what I was witnessing. Flores' hand landed firmly on my shoulder as a warning to not move any further. I pulled off my glasses and examined the hairline fracture suspended in midair approximately a meter long. On closer inspection, I could hear the air in the room quietly whistling into this three-dimensional "crack." Of course, I began to suspect I had gone mad. Whatever space lay behind this fracture was somehow emptier than the atmosphere in the physics lab.

And then another crack formed, this one extending from the other speaker. And then another, and another. I stepped back in terror while the very fabric of the space around the computer shattered. As each new crack appeared, more air whistled into the gaps. Fear pulsed through my spine and pulled at my chest. I had no way to categorize what was happening. This growing network of fractures suddenly collapsed inward leaving behind a three-dimensional shape around the computer screen: a pitch-black sphere suspended just above the floor. While the air in the lab rushed into this featureless orb from all directions, it devoured the table, the desk lamp, and finally the computer itself. But this wasn't a proper orb or even an object of any kind. It was a goddamned hole, emptier than space itself.

I felt Eden slip around me, mesmerized, moving on auto-pilot. Absentmindedly, she wandered toward this black hole, beyond the tape on the floor. "Professor Jessup!" Tina Flores cried. "Do not take another step forward!"

With all my strength I wrapped my arms around her waist and yanked her backwards, onto the floor. As I did, a blinding shock wave of rippling, white energy burst from the impossible depths of the black hole. Eden and I fell to the floor as a pulsing wave of electricity ran through our bodies, leaving behind a painless, tingling sensation on the surface of the skin.

In the wake of the shock wave, the hole vanished and the room went silent. All that remained was a quiet, barely audible buzz off in the distance; a vibration trailing beyond the walls of the physics lab and off, into the distance. In the darkness, Kyle stumbled his way toward the door and flipped on the overhead lights.

My mind couldn't process the sight that now lay before us. In the wake of the . . . event, there now lay an impossible structure in the center of the lab. The entire table, along with the computer had vanished and was replaced by a twisted, abstract structure; an absolute flurry of material. Damian stepped closer and doubled over with realization. "Oh God," he wheezed. "That is the table and computer." And promptly ran to the trash can to throw up.

I, too, felt ill upon the terrible realization that he was right. Every object that had been within a given radius of the computer was now a twisted jumble of random shapes. The very fabric of the table had been blended, fused, splattered together with those of the computer and the desk lamp. Or, rather, what used to be the computer and lamp. Plastics and metals stretched and jutted out in chaotic angles and curves to mix randomly with wood and glass as if everything in the center of the room had briefly turned to liquid and then blended for a moment before returning to solid form. If I hadn't witnessed it myself, I would have assumed the desk, the computer, and the lamp had been instantly replaced with pop art, an artist's rendition of a desk, computer, and table lamp.

Other than rapid heartbeats, the only sound in the room came from the random pieces of metal and plastics which had suddenly found themselves unattached to the new structure that lay before us. Fragments of all sizes trickled through a beehive of holes.

Well after the clinking of matter onto the tiles died down, I couldn't unglue myself from the sight. No one spoke a word. Only a chorus of heavy breathing reassured me that everyone else was still alive. Unfazed by the event, the Feynman Squid quietly hummed, safe in its perch in the ceiling above the "war zone." Downey leaned forward and rubbed his temples.

"That always gives me a goddamned headache," he growled quietly.

"Well," Eden said quietly, "that's a hell of a thing." She slowly turned to me, still in shock. "I have to go to there," she said firmly. "We . . . have to go there."

# PART TWO

## Chasing Dragons

*"They say it started with a big bang*
*But they say it came out of a small thing*
*Lately I'm feeling like a big bang, 'cause I've been making something out*
*of nothing.*
*Like my soul."*
*Mother Mother*

*Infinitesimal*

Ishoved the filter on the French press into the murky solution of ground poppy pods, lemon juice, and hot water with such force that the water squirted up the sides and scorched my hand. Normally, I would let the tea brew for a few minutes, but at this point I chose speed over quality. I didn't even let it cool; I slurped the foul liquid straight from the spout, burning my mouth in the process.

It was hard to determine what disturbed me the most, but Eden's ability to remain aloof in the face of current events was topping my list. She didn't bother to hesitate when Agent Flores asked us to trot off to Peru with her, along with a "small military detail" to pursue the homicide investigation anew from a "completely unorthodox perspective". I could only assume this translated to chasing after a fucking frequency through unforgiving rainforest.

The tea couldn't kick in fast enough. The phenomena in the physics lab had left me damaged worse than a flesh wound. Any trouble I had experienced in life—my parents walking out and leaving me in the care of my grandparents, the half-dozen failed relationships, a general sense of isolation from my fellow man—I could always fill those gaps with reason and logic. Some linear, rational explanation would always mend the agony of the unexplainable. Even a strong hypothesis would suffice to keep my world together. And now? Now, I couldn't even muster a farfetched guess, even if I did know which part of the series of impossible events we had witnessed I should attack first. An impossible massacre of armed soldiers, reality breaking down at the particle level, solid materials twisting and misshaping instantly.

Christ, I would've preferred Downey and the beautiful, Peruvian agent had simply dragged us all into a room and had the shit beat out of us for no reason whatsoever. A literal ass-kicking would've been far easier to deal with. And to just lay that in our laps like that! Where did they get off? Was this how the government operated when they're lost on a case?

My only hope was that Kyle and Damian would make some sense of it all after they analyzed the data from The Squid. But who knew what kind of shape those two were in after this afternoon?

And, finally, there it was. The first wave of relief washed up my spine and into my chest. I dropped onto the couch and let the tea seep in. Soon my shoulders unhinged and my knees un-buckled. I released the loudest sigh imaginable; one held back under far too much pressure for far too long.

"Are you okay, Mikey?" my grandma called worriedly from the kitchen. It was after 8:30 so my grandpa was already asleep in bed; "reading," as he called it. Grandma was a night owl like me.

"I'm okay, ma," I replied blissfully, "just a very long day." I only managed a smirk at the understatement, but it was enough to make me feel I still had my wits about me.

"I could heat up some of that sausage and sauerkraut if you like," she said, poking her head into the living room. She broke into her favorite, heavy Polish accent: "Sauzage und kraut guud for you. Make strong! Put hair on chest!"

"I'm good, ma. I'm hairy enough," I said, smiling. "Really, thank you. I'm not hungry."

"Okay, I love you, sweetie."

"Love you too, ma."

She disappeared back into the kitchen and the tea pulled me

deeper into the cushions. How does anyone break an addiction like this? Every muscle loosened as the warm ecstasy flowed into my chest. Well, you have your opiates. This is what you've been waiting for all day, so are you happy now? I must be. Comfort equals peace, right? But, of course, the tea couldn't mend those holes.

Moments after the "event" in the physics lab, I begged Agent Downey and Flores for more information. I could not accept that our government would drop something that volatile onto goddamned civilians. And to have the audacity to offer almost zero explanation in the aftermath!

After I helped Eden to her feet in the lab, I paced the room working madly to formulate my first question while everyone else dealt with the shock of it all in their own, unique way. Except for Downey and Flores, of course. They'd seen this all before and were just about sick of it. Downey was downright frustrated with our reactions. He was well beyond the point of shock with the phenomenon; now he wanted answers. Eden stood motionless in the center of the room, staring intently at her hands. "No. No," she repeated quietly. "I can't be awake."

Wide-eyed with disbelief, Damian moved toward the new-found "structure" in the room in slow motion, gently running his hands over the curves and edges of the twisted jumble of plastic, wood, and metal of what used to be a table, a desk lamp, and a computer tablet. It was almost grotesque. There was something sickeningly organic about the entire structure, as if every molecule within and around that computer had suddenly found itself alive and ran screaming in every direction.

"It's not even hot," Damian muttered. "Not that heat would really make any more sense." He carefully ran a finger along a thin, curling wisp on the edge of the mess. "Look, this part here is clearly the black plastic from the tablet but here it transitions into the metal from the lamp. Yet, this entire section has a wood grain from the table top." Kyle, on the other hand, appeared unfazed by the whole ordeal; his concern was the Feynman Squid. He leapt onto the chair and began frantically detaching it from the ceiling. Flores spoke slowly to calm our nerves. Her gentle tone was the only thing keeping me from bursting into total hysterics.

"I know you're all confused right now," she said quietly, slightly mechanically. She had given this speech before. "I apologize for how traumatizing this all may be, but please know we've tried every approach to introduce this phenomenon to newcomers. We've tried offering detailed descriptions to those about to witness the event, we've tried . . . "

"In the end, it doesn't make a bit of difference." Downey sighed. "Nothing can prepare you for what you don't think is possible."

Flores nodded in agreement before continuing, "Although we do not understand the exact nature of the phenomena that the video recording produces, I guarantee that it generates no physical damage to anything outside of the event boundary."

"You have no idea what that frequency did to us," Damian growled through clenched teeth. "If you don't understand how this can happen to physical matter, then you have zero clue what side effects it wreaked." Oddly, I was relieved to hear someone else held the same hypothesis: That the terrible, droning sound at the end of the video was the ultimate culprit behind turning everything around the computer into chaos.

"She's just sayin' that it doesn't kick out any radiation, microwaves or whatever, outside of that radius," Downey barked from his chair while massaging his temples. "Some of the smartest guys on the planet have run a thousand and one tests on the recording and . . . "

"Yeah, and those guys sent you to us 'cuz they don't have a freakin' clue what's going on here, so don't tell me . . . " Damian began before agent Flores interrupted.

"Wait, how did you know that the sound wave at the end is responsible for the event?" Flores asked, derailing Damian's tirade. He paused to consider.

"I'm assuming this recording does the exact same thing to everything it's played through," he began. "In fact, I'm guessing you can just play back the sound wave alone and get the same results." Downey and Flores both agreed.

"As long as it's played through a speaker system capable of at least six hundred hertz," Downey wearily replied as if it were the thousandth time he'd repeated it to someone. "Except for the patterns the materials take on within the boundary, the results are always the same: All physical matter within about a five foot radius of the speakers is randomly . . . flung together . . . twisted up, whatever. And as you can see, the phenomenon buggers solid materials like wood and metal in ways that, so far, no one will hazard a guess as to how they'd reproduce the effect—even with all the time and resources in the world."

"But the pattern is always different?" Damian asked, waving his hand over the jumble of matter.

"Always," Downey agreed. "Why's that important?". Damian and Kyle looked at each other with shared suspicion.

"Luckily, the first tech who handled Torres' camera equipment recovered from the scene followed protocol and made a backup of the memory card before he analyzed the footage." Flores added. "He was even luckier that he had backed away in fear from the computer speakers moments before the event took place. I can't imagine what the frequency would do to organic matter."

"Are there witnesses?" Eden broke in. "In the basin that day in Peru: did anyone survive?"

"We don't believe anyone in Captain Ramirez's battalion survived, no," Flores said. "It's difficult to say, though. Forensics are still sorting through little more than chunks of torn body parts and bone. It could be some time before we can make solid identifications from any of it. At this point, we believe only four of the Chambira natives were killed that afternoon, but there isn't a consensus yet as to how they died, exactly."

"Four missionaries," Eden said quietly to herself. "Four dead natives."

"You're saying the natives killed weren't ripped apart like the soldiers?" I asked aimlessly. I didn't know what I was looking for. I wasn't even convinced that whatever the hell was taking place in the footage had anything to do with the frequency. These could have been isolated incidents.

"Not at all," Flores replied. "There weren't any noticeable wounds on any of them. Toxicology all came back negative. Maybe they dropped dead from fear, we just don't know, but it's been known to happen."

This whole ordeal was beginning to piss me off. "What about DNA at the site?" I demanded. "There must be something that identifies what those soldiers were being attacked by?"

"Inconclusive," Flores replied. "The DNA they recovered so far makes no sense. Some of the tissue samples they believe came from the attackers contained highly unusual, or more specifically, impossible configurations of stem cells. They say it's as if two dozen different predatory animals, many of which aren't even found on the continent, charged through the basin that day."

"Stem cells," I repeated. Flores smiled.

"One of the guys in the lab joked that maybe the animals weren't finished being built yet," she added. I nearly laughed out loud I was so frustrated. This was asinine.

"Kane and his four missionaries," Eden said anxiously. "Where are they now? Were they killed in the attack?"

"Two members of the Church of First Life survived," Downey replied. "The reverend himself and one Christopher Aldon, the muscle-bound missionary with the military cut, were picked up five days later attempting to board a plane back to the States with expired visas. Aldon is a former marine, discharged for disorderly conduct in Afghanistan several years back. Some reports suggested he liked to gun down Muslim civilians while reciting his favorite Bible passages. Of course, none of it could be proven.

"Except for a bit of dehydration and jungle rash, there wasn't a solid mark on either of them. Both men have been questioned repeatedly by the National Police and the FBI. We had nothing to hold them on. We were forced to allow them to return to their compound where Kane and a parish of some two dozen members reside, under regular surveillance, of course."

"They live on the church grounds?" Eden asked.

Downey jumped in. "The Church of First Life claims to be a Christian-based religion, but its worldview isn't consistent with any sect of Christianity anyone's ever heard of. We classify them as a cult."

"Well then, I'd love to have a talk with them," Eden said, exasperated. "I can't believe you just let them go."

"Both men's stories were fairly consistent with what we've discovered at the scene." Flores replied. "Edward Kane and Christopher Aldon claim that as they were preparing to co-operate and return to base with Ramirez's troops, a pack of unidentified animals attacked the entire camp; possibly rabid dogs, wolves, or mountain lions. They say that their other three missionaries were killed in the carnage; Giddeon, Braun, and Bowen."

"That was their explanation?" I shouted. "Dogs?!"

"A bad case of mange can severely alter an animal's appearance and mental functioning," Damian offered.

"It doesn't make them imperious to machine gun fire!" Kyle scoffed.

"I'm just sayin' . . . " Damian surrendered, but the two continued arguing amongst themselves. Flores nodded in agreement with eyes closed; she'd obviously trekked these roads long ago. But our anger and confusion was fresh. I couldn't keep my thoughts straight. I began blurting out question after question.

"And what was Aldon's explanation for what was happening to him and the other three missionaries in the video? Why did they look like they were dying? And mountain lions?! Why would they spare Kane or . . . "

"Ha!" Flores snorted. "Can you guess his response to that very question?"

"That his faith in God shielded him from evil," Eden said knowingly.

"Pretty much word for word," Flores said, "but we also don't have a better story. Aldon claims that he and his companions were wrestling with a bad case of Malaria: his only explanation why they appeared so ill in the video."

"Appeared 'ill'?" Eden scoffed. "Being drawn and pale can

make you appear ill. Those people were decomposing."

"Try holding suspects for breaking the laws of nature, professor," Downey sighed.

"Believe me, I understand your frustration," Flores said. "Kane and Aldon claim to be victims just like the rest. Besides having expired visas, they've done nothing wrong that we can prove. They maintain complete ignorance on all other details; they say they know nothing about bizarre sound waves or what killed the four natives, or how a team of armed soldiers allowed themselves to be torn apart by sick dogs."

Flores handed Eden and I a sheet of paper with an illustration of a molecular chain with a chemical breakdown. "And neither Kane or Aldon can tell us why this was found in their canteen," she added.

"That's a tryptamine with two methyl groups," I said.

"Which doesn't make any sense either," Eden added. "That concoction was either given to them or they stole it. I guarantee Kane and his people didn't brew it themselves. Except for these other alkaloids I don't recognize, maybe a form of nightshade, this is essentially liquid DMT. It goes by a lotta names; Yage, Vine of the Soul, but it's generally known as ayahuasca. Aya means dead body, waska means rope, or vine. It's arguably the strongest psychoactive on the face of the earth. Natives of South America have been brewing it for thousands of years."

While staring at the diagram of the molecule, I realized how closely it resembled the neurotransmitter serotonin. When it came to the human body's ability to regulate mood and social behavior, serotonin was the end-all, be-all of molecules.

"Any thoughts on how a powerful hallucinogen may play into any of this?" Downey asked.

This was a waste of time. Who cared what the hell those missionaries were drinking? But I tried to remain calm and share what little I knew for certain.

"Well, we know that dimethyltryptamine is found in a surprisingly wide range of plant life, but it's also found naturally in the human bloodstream. Some evidence supports that it's manufactured in the pineal gland near the center of the brain.

No one can say for sure just why the body makes its own psychoactive, but, some believe . . . now, this is all speculation, but . . . "

Eden picked up on my line of thought and ran with it. "Some believe the body secretes DMT in order to increase awareness during times of intense crisis. Psychoactives have been shown to substantially improve acuity, problem solving, and reaction time. Some researchers claim it can be generated during REM sleep on occasion, producing intense dream states. It also may be released at the time of death, possibly to make the transition smoother. Why that would be an evolutionary advantage, I can't say, but there's a strong argument that near-death experiences are aided by DMT."

"Whatever," I interrupted. "None of this begins to explain what we see happening with those missionaries."

Eden couldn't help but agree on that point. "So, the only eye witnesses we can possibly trust are the Chambira. What's their take on this?" she asked. The corners of Flores' lips drew back as she lowered her head.

"The natives in that region are very suspicious of the government," she said quietly. "Our investigators could hardly get any of them to talk. What little information they did gather was disregarded as gibberish."

"And why is that?" I prodded. "What did they say happened out there, exactly?"

Flores smiled gently and hesitated before taking a deep breath. "The only information they pulled from the Chambira was this," Flores began, unsure of whether she should share this piece of information. "They claimed that Kane and his four missionaries showed up in their village a few weeks earlier asking about the Craneo Roto tribe. The Chambira claim that he hired a member of their clan as a field guide to make contact with the Craneo Roto. They believe that the Roto shamans taught the white men how to conjure up the devil from their Bible at will. When Kane returned to their village, they were "not natural," their souls had changed. They claim that what attacked them that day was not . . . human nor animal."

"Meaning what?" I demanded.

"Specifically, they say the devil rose from hell that afternoon, entered the bodies of Kane's missionaries, stole the 'soul-energy' from four members of their tribe as 'fuel' and then massacred Ramirez's soldiers in an altered, more powerful physical form," she explained and stepped closer. "I'd say this adds up to a bit more than tales of orbital teacups."

"Demonic possession," I sighed. It was right about this point I wished these guys were from the DEA.

And now, in the aftermath of it all, in the comfort and safety of my living room, the tea's effects were just beginning to peak. I curled into a ball on the couch and pulled my grandmother's afghan over me. I can't go playing detective in South America. What am I going to do, carry around a supply of ground poppy pods, a grinder, and a French press? Or, a gallon jug of highly concentrated, premade tea? Both options were about as reasonable as going through withdrawal while drudging through a humid jungle. One of the major drawbacks to my particular addiction was that it certainly wasn't a very 'portable' one. This generally wasn't a problem given my homebody lifestyle.

Despite the rest of the day's unanswered questions and loose ends, I could at least put this one dilemma to bed: There was no way I was going to Peru in my condition. With that minor achievement under my belt, my eyes grew heavy and I plummeted to a dreamless sleep. For nearly three blissful hours, I slept deeper than I would for the next week.

I was ripped from my cozy, opiated womb by my phone screaming from my back pocket. Eden was already chattering on the other end before I fumbled it to my ear. "Don't you see?! That's why the FBI was in Boulder, Mike! That's why they said the connection was local!" she squealed. "Get your jacket! I'm coming down Arapahoe now. I'll be there in ten!"

"Wait. Wait." I muttered absently. "What's goin' on, now?"

"The Church of First Life!"she hollered. "It's up in Gold Hill! We can be up there in an hour. You and I are going to talk to Reverend Kane ourselves."

My heart thumped. "I really don't think that's a good idea—" I began, but she had already hung up.

# Pilgrimage

*"We all have a Monster within; the difference is in degree, not in kind."*

Douglas Preston

The 1950 Hudson Commodore skidded around yet another of Mapleton Drive's neck-breaking curves, turning my muscles to lead. The car was a massive beast that swallowed the entire lane; dark blue and badly rusted with a frame designed to smash through brick walls. Eden nicknamed it the "Furious Cock." I preferred to call it the "Sub." She had inherited the ancient, rolling tank from her grandfather who was evidently 'quite the character' and had little respect for the law.

Eden hardly noticed the dark, treacherous road ahead as she blurted out everything stream-of-consciousness style; her unique way of dealing with stress and anxiety. Mine was to go fetal and wrestle with my internal dialogue quietly.

"So, I'm thinking why CU Boulder, why us?!" she barked, "It's not like we have the most renowned science or theology departments in the states . . . no offense. We were just convenient when they started looking outside the box on this!"

While I was snuggled in a pocket of bliss on my couch, she had been digging. It seemed that Edward Kane and his family bought up twenty acres of forest on the western peak just above Gold Hill more than thirty years ago, but no one paid much attention to it. According to the maps, there was only one unpaved road in and out of that peak, and for years no one built anything on it. It was nearly forgotten altogether by the locals, until four years ago. Seemingly out of nowhere, a ten-foot, wrought iron fence appeared one morning around the entire property.

Soon after, a small blurb ran in the *Daily Camera* stating the owner of the estate, a Reverend Edward Kane, was constructing a church in the center of the property at the peak's apex. Officially, they were listed as a religious service, but there was no mention of any public events offered. Ever.

Now that she and I had time to think about it, we both

recalled a few, off-handed comments floating around a couple years ago about an out-of-state, private construction company doing work up in Gold Hill, but there was never any solid information or real concern over it. Once a mining village, Gold Hill was a quaint mountain town about an hour's drive into the foothills, just west of Boulder. The inhabitants generally preferred their privacy and had no interest in gossip. As long as Kane didn't disturb the peace, what he did with his property would have been his business.

While listening to Eden's diatribe, I hoped her enthusiasm had moved beyond trying to convince me to come with her tomorrow. I already felt ashamed turning down my beloved friend and the government at once. The goddamned FBI had come knocking for my input as a scientist, and I had to make lame excuses like a child. As terrified as I was over the whole situation, I also needed answers for my own well-being. Furthermore, I wanted to look after Eden. She was too skilled at convincing newcomers she was in fearless command of her faculties. I accepted some responsibility, probably too much, for being the only one who really understood how fragile and unstable she was becoming.

"Okay, so why keep this from us?" I asked. "Why wouldn't Downey and Flores tell us their little cult compound was situated right above our heads?"

"I'm guessing they didn't want us to do something stupid," she considered, reaching across my lap to dig in the glovebox. "You know, like, drive up there and try to talk to him ourselves, or some crazy shit. Maybe they think I'm reckless." She pulled an enormous revolver from the tiny compartment—seemingly larger than the glovebox—and tossed it into my lap. "See if that's loaded."

I jerked back with enough force to throw the handgun to the floorboards. "Are you fucking kidding me?" I shouted. "Where the hell did you get that?"

"What?" she said. "It was my grandfather's! It came with the car. Hey, these religious nutjobs might be dangerous."

"Dangerous how exactly?" I barked. "As in dark magic and

sorcery dangerous? Is that what Agent Flores thinks? Look, I have no idea what insane fantasies you two are planning on chasing after in one of the deadliest jungles in the world . . . ”

“. . . insane fantasies *we're* chasing after in one of the deadliest jungles of the world,” she added.

I shook my head; she was trying to change the subject. “I say this as your friend.” I began slowly, trying to keep my cool. This was the last thing she needed in her life right now and I grew angrier the longer I spoke. “Eden, I know you've got your ideas about how the universe works, but you're still a woman of science and reason. You can't believe there's something supernatural going on with any of this. You know how ignorant that kind of approach can be! You're imagining this Reverend Kane is some kind of monster. Has it occurred to you that he really might be a victim of . . . whatever as yet unexplained, completely natural phenomena is at work here?”

“You're scared,” she replied, laying a hand on my lap. “I get it. This is a frightening situation.”

“Goddamn it, don't reduce my logic to an emotional outburst!” I shouted. “You can't go into this thinking you're hunting monsters! You study religion, Eden! You of all people know where that kind of thinking leads: You end up finding them! Don't be so quick to think you're immune to the same errors in judgment Team Jesus makes.”

“Aww,” she whimpered. “You're worried about me.”

This was her way of changing the subject. My last comment had cut her deeper than she let on. I fell back in my seat. “Of course I'm worried about you,” I said, exhausted.

“That's why I need you to come with me,” she said, veering into yet another sharp turn. The wheels screamed beneath the friction. “I admit it: I'm a total mess. I need that big, sexy brain of yours to keep me on track. I need you to fill in the gaps for me on this.”

Her sudden humility and honesty made me feel terrible all over again. I remained quiet for the rest of the drive. Our tires rumbled onto Gold Hill's dark, gravel roads around 11:00 p.m. I rolled down my window as we slowed our pace, watching for the break in the trees that led to Kane's church. Except for a few raccoons and deer scampering from our headlights, the town was asleep. The air was cooler and thinner at this elevation and everything seemed quieter. The whispering rush of wind over pine needles was the only movement beyond our rumbling engine. Only the occasional glow from a porch lantern reminded us the place wasn't deserted altogether.

"There!" I whispered, pointing to a dirt road hidden by pines, wondering why I was whispering. Somehow, the situation seemed to call for it. Eden directed the Sub into the tight, black slope and flipped on the high beams. Branches scraped at our doors as we slowed to a crawl along an impossibly sharp incline. Just after passing a wide-open iron gate, the forest grew sparse and soon we found ourselves spiraling up a barren driveway toward a low, darkened structure positioned at the top of the peak. I could only assume we were climbing above tree line, but our elevation didn't seem high enough. We drove just beyond what appeared to be the building's main entrance where three figures stood silhouetted beneath a single, yellow bulb. Eden parked at the far end of the drive and killed the engine.

"I'll do the talking," she said.

"Damn right you are."

When we stepped from the car, the church proved far more massive than it appeared from the road, much of it hidden by the curvature of the peak. As we drew closer, we were treated to the sight of intricate, stained-glass windows wrapping the entire periphery. Each section of colored glass was illuminated by candlelight from within. Eden deciphered the pictures and symbolism depicted in the windows as hailing primarily from Genesis and Revelations. "Odd choices," she muttered.

The three figures we spotted from the drive turned to us as we approached: Two men and one woman. We immediately recognized one of them: the bulkier, barrel-chested man was Christopher Aldon, the missionary from the video. He appeared very much alive and in fine health; a far cry from what we witnessed in the footage. Both men were clad in well-worn, black motorcycle jackets and camouflage, military pants. A stout woman with a smart, blue suit and an intensely red beehive hairdo pushed the men aside to greet us.

"Why good evening to you!" the woman called with a cheery, southern hospitality. "I'm Miss Cartwright. And who might you two be at this late hour?"

After a curt introduction, Eden closed with, "We're working with the FBI on a matter of grave importance concerning your church and we need to speak with the reverend." So much for subtlety.

The man positioned behind Christopher Aldon scoffed. "When's our own government gunna stop harassin' us?" he hissed. Aldon shot an intense stare at his partner.

"Brother McGhee," he reminded firmly.

Brother McGhee lowered his head submissively and stepped aside while Aldon moved his wide frame before Eden, towering above her with arms crossed. "Whatch' you need to know, little lady?" he grunted. "We already told you folks everythin', just as it happened."

"You nor your reverend here have explained what happened in that jungle," Eden replied sharply. "We need to know what really killed those soldiers."

"Hell Hounds, I s'pose," Aldon smirked with a low, raspy voice. "Dragged them poor souls straight back to where they belong."

"Oh?" Eden replied. "Why did they spare you?"

"Come on, now," I whispered.

Aldon stared into her for a long moment. A smile crept up his lips. "What you teach down there at the university?" he demanded, sizing us up and finding nothing to be concerned with. Deep shrapnel scars stretched the left side of his shaven head, thick muscles pulsed in his neck, and blackened dog tags hung over his bulking chest.

"Theology," Eden answered without breaking eye contact with him.

"You mean religion?" Brother McGhee asked. "You two Christians?"

"No, you a Zen Buddhist?" Eden fired back with a southern drawl of her own. Miss Cartwright squeaked out an awkward laugh and brushed the two men from the porch.

"Now, Mr. Aldon, Mr. McGhee, let's let our guests know they are welcomed," she cooed nervously. Aldon took another intense, emotionless stare at us before he and his companion moved on.

"The devil got no reason to cut down real Christians," Aldon called out as he walked away. "He know they just gunna end up in heaven, far from his reach."

"So the other three missionaries who came with you: Giddeon, Braun, Bowen; they weren't real Christians?" Eden shot back.

"My friends is jus' where they supposed to be," Aldon replied before disappearing around the corner into the dark.

"You'll have to excuse Mr. Aldon," Cartwright said brightly as a pair of Harley engines roared to life around the building. "We welcome all shapes and sizes here who want to make themselves right with the Lord."

The thick, tiny woman led us through a set of tall, wooden doors, into a dimly lit interior. We followed her along a tight corridor that rose on either side into a beautiful arch high above our heads. The highly polished walls of knotted wood were dotted by tea lights nestled within dozens upon dozens of intricately carved crevices. Upon inspection, tiny slivers of quartz lined each crevice to refract the candlelight, creating a rather dazzling sight that left me with the feeling I was moving through some celestial gateway.

The narrow passage abruptly gave way to a large, empty hall with a wide oak counter at the far end that seemed to stand guard before a set of ornate, double doors. Miss Cartwright took her station behind the desk, placed a pair of old-fashioned reading glasses on the tip of her nose and opened a heavy, leather-bound scheduling book.

"Now, do you two have an appointment with the reverend at this late hour?" she asked politely, firmly.

"No, we do not," Eden replied kindly, leaning into the desk.

"But if he is here, you need to collect him. Wake him if necessary." My anxiety rose steadily. I wondered how far she could push her inflated authority before we were called to task on it.

"Oh, the reverend does not sleep," Miss Cartwright replied with a subtle hint of disgust, as if sleep was some form of sin. "After everyone retires to their dormitories, the reverend is often in his private sanctuary at this time. Do kindly wait here and I will try to retrieve him." Without another word, the woman disappeared down another, candlelit corridor heading the opposite direction.

"She's a well-manicured Hobbit," Eden sighed. For several, long moments we waited in silence. The array of corridors leading away from the large hall betrayed no signs of life, except for a gentle breeze that lazily flowed in one direction, and then reversed itself as if the place was breathing.

"Apparently, that is not the reverend's private sanctuary," I finally mentioned, nodding to the double doors behind the desk. With the grace of a gymnast, Eden leapt over the counter on one hand and landed without a sound. She gently pulled at the handles to find them locked. From one of the many, inner pockets of her motorcycle jacket, she produced a spool of lock picks and, despite my strong protests, began to jimmy the door.

"Why don't you just shoot the damn thing open?" I whispered angrily. She considered my suggestion with an arched eyebrow just as the door gave way. Begrudgingly, I followed her into the depths of an even more spacious, darkened service room. The only light and sound came from a half-dozen, sparkling waterfall features gracing each of the six corners of the great hall. On each, the water appeared to flow directly out of the walls before draining into a series of glistening white, marble pools carved seemlessly into the wood flooring. I nearly gasped at the beauty and craftsmanship. The degree of artistry behind each detail was astounding.

Most churches I'd been in were gaudily decorated; cheap looking yellow-gold pillars, obnoxious, tacky artwork—an idiot's vision of the splendors found in heaven. But this space was refined, inspired, and elegant. A place where I'd actually enjoy worshipping, if I ever did such a thing.

A large stone crucifix weighing perhaps a thousand pounds or more hung behind a wooden lectern. At the center of the cross was a tiny chain of interlocking circles carved into the surface surrounding a large infinity sign. Eden and I both found the symbolism confusing, but something far stranger grabbed our attention in the room. All the pews had been pushed haphazardly against the walls to face not the pulpit, but the very center of the room.

"What do you make of this?" she asked, brushing her fingers along the floorboards. It was hard to determine in the dim lighting, but the wood appeared to be scuffed, perhaps burned. Dark brown stains that survived several bleachings intermingled with severe, random cuts and scratches.

"Maybe they use this space for illegal cock fights on the weekends," I halfheartedly joked, studying the door behind us, wondering how long it would take our host to find us lurking around her church in the dark.

"They would have to be some really big cocks," Eden replied flatly, but I wouldn't encourage her. Beyond the podium at the far end of an unlit hallway a red light flickered behind a small, smoked window on a narrow door. Eden immediately disappeared into the dark recesses of the hallway to investigate. Miss Cartwright's high heels clip-clopped through the corridors behind us while Eden quietly turned the handle on the recessed doorway. Upon finding it unlocked, she shot me a wide grin. "I won't have to shoot this one open," she whispered.

"Eden!" I barked, but it was too late. A pressure differential between the chapel and the entryway forced the door violently open, slamming into the opposite wall with a shuddering thud. A cloud of dark, red steam poured from the open doorway that brought with it the pungent stench of sulfur.

"A door to hell," Eden mused, "how apropos."

"Hurry!" called a familiar voice from behind the red mist. "Come in! You'll let the heat out!". We both stepped inside and wrestled the door closed. Swirls of hot vapor enveloped us to make vision impossible. We could only hear water bubbling from somewhere near our feet.

"Please, set your clothes just outside the door and have a seat," the disembodied voice offered. Though we couldn't see the source, I recognized Reverend Kane's unique manner of slow, careful enunciation.

"What is this?" I asked, "A steam room?"

"A steam room!" Kane replied. "Ha! This, my son, is a natural hot spring. That is why I chose this spot to build my church."

Eden had nearly finished introducing us, punctuating again that we were "working with the FBI" when the door behind us burst open. Miss Cartwright's voice was shrill at our backs.

"I do apologize, reverend! These visitors strayed beyond the lobby!" she squealed. Kane quickly thanked and dismissed Miss Cartwright, assuring her we posed no threat. Enough steam escaped during the intrusion that I could begin to make out a few details of our strange surroundings. Damp wood paneling fell tightly around us to merge with a bed of smoothed, sculpted lava rock edging the periphery. The center of the rock-bed held a rounded pool of rolling water that nearly swallowed the entire floor. A series of red candles were melted into various spots throughout the obsidian which illuminated the silhouette of a frail figure; an elderly man draped in a robe, seated atop a plush, white meditation cushion. His thin legs dangled into the rumbling water below.

"I am afraid you'll both have to leave your clothing just outside the door if you're stayin'." the reverend explained with his polished, Southern accent; one far more dignified and measured than the brutes' we encountered outside. He breathed heavily as he spoke, yet didn't seem bothered by the labor each syllable required.

We faced an awkward decision: If we wanted to meet with Kane, we would have to undress. As I considered my options, the intense humidity steadily soaked my clothing and fogged my glasses. When I turned to gauge Eden's feelings on the matter I found she had kicked off her shoes, pulled off her shirt and pants and was tossing them onto the floor outside as if she just arrived at a beach. Before I could protest, she was already gingerly lowering herself into the hot spring.

I fidgeted with my sweater and wondered which pair of boxers I had put on this morning. After a short wrestling match with shame, I joined the two of them at the edge of the bubbling pool. Perhaps it helped that we were all reduced to blurry shadows in the dim glow of red candlelight.

I attempted to charge straight in behind Eden, but the water was far hotter than I anticipated. Even with all the opiates flooding my system, I could barely go further than ankle-deep.

"I apologize, but you two did not call ahead, so you'll have to adapt to my nightly routine if you'd like to meet with me." Kane explained matter-of-factly. "An herbalist I met in the Congo informed me that the natural minerals such as the sulfur you're smelling bubbling up from below would help ease the many side effects of the tumor in my gut. Good advice, for sure. Twelve years ago my own doctors told me I had better put my affairs in order. Said I wouldn't survive the year. Never did I imagine the bowels of the earth would keep me alive."

"And they can't operate?" Eden asked with enough gravity to fool most into thinking she was genuinely concerned, maybe even herself. I was certain her kindness was tactical. Kane's skeletal shadow shook its head in the mist across from us.

"No, ma'am," he replied firmly. "They say it's got its claws in all the right places as to not make that possible, almost as if it knew what it was doing. Maybe it does."

"What about chemo?" I asked with a warm tone of my own. "Is that an option for you?" At least my compassion was sincere. I had no logical reason to doubt we had just barged in on a suffering, perhaps slightly confused, elderly man who recently witnessed a terrible slaughter including members of his own church.

"Oh, I tried that for a time, son. I'd rather die of the cancer," he chuckled softly, enunciating every last bit that passed his lips. "So, you two are working with the government?"

He painfully straightened himself to shake our hands. His grasp was so fragile and cold, I felt I should check for a pulse.

He leveled a knobby finger in my direction. "Now let me get this straight . . . you're the scientist," he said before moving his aim to Eden, "and you're the theologian."

"Well, then, tell me son," he mused, "no one's ever been able to explain this to me: If we used to be monkeys, why are there still monkeys?"

I cringed ever so slightly. I abhorred this asinine question. Not only did it demonstrate a complete ignorance of evolution, the dim-witted religious masses always used it in debate as some kind of "gotcha question" under the bizarre assumption that a real scientist would flounder for a response. In fact, the question would only make sense if evolutionists suggested that species actually morphed into different animals along the way, as if chimpanzees at some point all simultaneously shapeshifted into humans. Now, that would indeed be unnatural. I was about to explain evolutionary advantages of mutated offspring when Kane laughed quietly to himself, waving his hand to let me off the hook.

"I'm just havin' a go at you, son," he said. "I don't tolerate that kind of arrogance myself. I generally find it insulting when Christians challenge scientists. They always end up demonstrating their own ignorance on the subject." I could hardly believe what I was hearing. For a reverend of a Bible-based religion, this seemed a rather enlightened viewpoint.

"I'm impressed," I nodded. "Since I've been teaching, no one who's challenged me on evolution bothered to educate themselves on the theory."

"Or bothered to know what the word 'theory' even refers to in such a discussion," he added. He chuckled again as I shook my head in pleasant disbelief. "I believe you'll see we all actually have quite a bit in common," he continued. "I assume that's why you made the trip up at this hour: To figure me out, to pick my brain."

"Well, we—" I began, but Eden held back a laugh.

"You think we have a lot in common, do you?" she asked.

"Oh, absolutely, young miss," he replied. It began to bother me that I couldn't see the expressions on his face. The details of his emaciated outline would occasionally flicker in the candlelight and illuminate the stark features of his skull and jawbone, but his face remained perpetually cast in shadow. Kane slowly pulled his feet from the pool to sit cross-legged atop his overstuffed, white prayer cushion.

"You see, I'm a Christian, but I'm also a man who appreciates the scientific method that God allowed us to discover. In fact, I have devoted a good deal of time and resources to studying the last thing that, in my humble opinion, is the only subject worth studying in this world. Do you know what that is?"

"Faith?" Eden answered automatically.

"No, there's no need to study faith, miss, you either have it or you do not. If you do, then you know your life is in God's capable hands. If you do not, then you lead a life filled with worry and doubt," he said. "God's love is never-ending and eternal; His grace alone. Studying that which is infinite seems pointless; no, I'm interested in those lesser manifestations, those which are finite, that which appears to stand in the way of God's light. If we can only remove those deceptions, we would all be right with the Lord." Eden and I were both caught off guard now. She nor I had ever heard a Christian speak quite like this.

"You're talking about evil," Eden replied.

"Call it what you will—darkness, malevolence, wickedness— the underlying force that convinces men to commit atrocities to themselves and to each other. 'Evil' is as good a term as any for conversation's sake. I study the work of Satan the Deceiver. I aim to know my enemy as was instructed. And I have spent a lifetime doing so."

"I think personifying the whole scope of evil into one ultimate source is as dangerous as imagining the totality of goodness originated from one, all-knowing man in the sky," Eden replied.

"Yes, but you're still young and closed-minded," he laughed quietly. "Did you know that the largest organism on the planet is found right here in Colorado?"

"That's still up for debate," I replied. I knew where he was going with this, but had no idea why. Eden was silently reeling from a Christian daring to call her close-minded.

"Yes, yes, but my point is still relevant," Kane interrupted. "We now know that our Aspen groves are actually one, interconnected biomass beneath the earth. I've found that the nature of evil is like that as well. I think it's dangerous to not realize that all of these seemingly various forces in the world, those which cloud the eternal grace of the Lord, are all various manifestations of one entity. Even the two of you must admit that evil exists in this world, yes?"

"I suppose, yes," Eden reluctantly answered. "But it's all about those troublesome definitions, isn't it? What you call a sin I might call a typical Friday night."

"So, what benefits have you found in studying evil?" I added to keep the conversation constructive.

"The way I see it, there are only two forces in this universe of any consequence," Kane continued, "the work of the Lord, and the work of the Deceiver. Divine truth and wicked lies. Now, we humans have no tools to understand God. Even your modern science has proven that God created this world in ways that are beyond human understanding, and yet the atheists still claim dominion over the truth. How arrogant indeed. But the work of Satan is lower than God; it is beneath Him. And so it remains a force that can be researched. In fact, our science can only truly study the finite illusions created by the Father of Lies. And, again, you may call this source whatever pleases you. I'll call that force 'Maya' if you prefer, Professor Jessup." Eden crossed her arms. This discussion wasn't going the way she had anticipated.

"But whatever you call it, its intention is always the same," Kane continued, "to confuse humanity; to make us forget that we are presently in God's eternal embrace. So I have put a good deal of time and effort into dissecting darkness. If we can see the deception through and through and we can understand its nature, its habits, all its itty-bitty cracks and crevices, and we truly "love our enemy" as Christ directed, then it holds no power over us. And what is left but the grace of God?"

"That's an interesting take on it, for sure," Eden remarked. "Most Christians devote their life to stamping evil out and running in the other direction. Or, so they'll claim."

"Well, that's the problem, isn't it?" Kane mused. "Most people who call themselves Christians wouldn't know what true faith was if it was burned into their foreheads. How many people will swear that, after they die, they are certain the gates of heaven await them? And yet they fear death! Many won't even utter the word 'death'. It's always been the convenient Christian's folly to hide behind words, has it not? Oh, she's passed on, she's in a better place. And, mind you, that's what this country is filled with: Convenient Christians. I have no use for them, hence my church here is so very, very small. True faith is so rare. So few hear the word of their own creator any longer. I say that a genuine servant of the Lord carries no doubt on his shoulders. The limited power of Satan is his plaything; a tool to herd the masses."

"You believe evil can be used for righteous purposes?" Eden asked.

"Absolutely," Kane replied, "everything possible can hold a greater purpose. We just have to discover it."

"So where do you find this evil that you study?" I asked. "Evil has so many faces, so many forms. How do you research something like that? What are your methods, exactly?"

"Yes, indeed, Professor Huxley!" Kane beamed. "So, many, many forms, indeed! You should join our church, sir, we'd love to have your insight!" He coughed hard on his words. With a shaky hand, Kane took a sip from a teacup next to his cushion. "That was the very problem I myself was faced with as a young minister. I had no idea where to begin! It took quite some time to find the core of evil. I have spent my adulthood hunting for its roots in all the darkest, filthiest corners of this earth and by using the processes of logical, scientific deduction, I can confidently say that my church now knows the true face of hell. We have stared the Deceiver in the face and we have unmasked the truth. Darkness is now a tool for us to be waged in the war against ignorance of the Divine."

"And what is that truth you have found?" Eden asked with growing curiosity.

"Just as I have said, that Satan and all his works are finite." Kane happily replied. "We don't simply preach salvation; my church is free. Because of that, our determination to bring others into the light of God is unmatched, that I guarantee you. Now I aim to provide proof to the world that there is a real choice to be made in this life; one that must be addressed before the flesh rots from our bones. Our small voice here at the First Life will roar triumphantly from the mountaintops."

"Just what do you mean by proof?" I asked.

"Let me ask you this, professors: If you knew that hell was absolutely real; that it was an actual place devoid of love, filled with fire and agony, and that you were headed there immediately following your last breath on this planet, would you then turn your life over to the Lord?"

"If I had flesh and blood proof," I considered, trying to be fair. "If there was convincing evidence, then, I don't think I'd have much of a choice."

"Yeah, if it was clear those were my only two options, that doesn't leave a lot of room for creativity," Eden agreed. "You show me Satan, and I suppose I'd do whatever was necessary to stay out of hell. That certainly wouldn't make me a good person, though. I'd be no more pious than the other shmucks chasing the carrot. That's just me saving my ass. But to get me to behave like that, yeah, you better have some pretty damn amazing proof that's the way the cards have been stacked."

Kane gently chuckled to himself. "And I disagree," Kane replied thoughtfully. "I realize that academics like yourselves would like to think your beliefs are all based on reason and personal experience, that you're open-minded enough to see the truth when it's in front of your nose. But I disagree." He leaned forward. "I may be wrong, but it is my hypothesis that you'd turn from God even if he was sitting right in front of you. I think you've already made your choice, just like much of humanity. But we'll see soon enough. I'm a man who lets experimentation come before belief."

The man made my skin crawl for sure, but in a weird way I had to admit I found him compelling, even strangely charming. If nothing else, he genuinely believed what he was saying. Eden, on the other hand, had never heard a Christian talk like this. She didn't know what to make of it. That alone seemed to anger her. She decided to go for the jugular. "And what happened in Peru?" she said flatly. "Was that also the work of Satan?"

Kane returned fire without hesitation. "What happened in Peru was a miracle," he stated triumphantly. "The first of many. God himself has told me that he is calling all those without faith, like yourselves, professors, back to where they choose to be: Trapped in the illusion of suffering. He has allowed me the opportunity to offer this Earth back to His children and it starts here with my church, with the next evolution, the true First Life of a new world. Those who chose to accept it, that is. And when it comes to surrender to the Almighty, acceptance is key."

"God said that to you personally, eh?" I asked. It was at that moment a distant word echoed through my mind. Bicameral. Yet at the time I couldn't recall what it meant or what it referred to.

"Yes, that's right," Kane replied cheerfully. "I know you've been brainwashed to believe that sounds insane. Such a shame to have your own culture teach you that communication with your own Creator is some form of mental impairment. I do realize it's not possible for an educated man as yourself to wrap your brain around this notion, but every single member of my parish hears the word of our Lord directly. There has never been a separation between God and his creations."

"Well, that's all very cryptic," Eden retorted. "And it doesn't answer my question."

Kane took a long sip from his tea and released a weary sigh. "I regret that, although I have truly enjoyed our conversation, it is quite late, professors. I do miss elevated conversation like this. Unfortunately, the faithful I am often surrounded by are not always the strongest of thinkers. Sometimes I want to put my hands around their throats," he said, pantomiming strangulation, "and shake them awake."

"You'd resort to violence to get your point across?" Eden asked, "even with your own parish?"

Kane paused and lowered his hands. "Well, of course," he said sternly. "When you know the Truth, it burns uncontrollably in you. Sometimes people need to be rattled from their complacency, wouldn't you agree?"

Eden leaned in slightly. "No, I would not," she said sternly. In the dim light, no one saw me roll my eyes.

"Perhaps you lack conviction," he said. "Regardless, professors, I don't believe there is any more I can tell you that you're going to hear. Maybe someday soon, when you see where your atheism and New Age nonsense has led you. Until then, you'll believe what you've been trained to believe about this world. And that is a shame, indeed. I would hope we could continue conversations like this after we shed this mortal shell, but I don't imagine either of you will be . . . accessible to me."

Eden smiled, shook her head, and quietly lifted herself from the spring. While she gathered her clothing I held back, thanked the man for his time, and shook his icy cold hand once more. For some reason, I didn't want Eden to overhear my words of gratitude for his time. Perhaps it was the cloud of warm water and opiates I was sailing on, but I felt completely at ease in Kane's presence.

The frigid air through the open door startled me back to my senses. The moment I slipped from the room, I heard Kane utter to himself, "Now, what use does the FBI have for you?" Just before I shut the door, he seemed to arrive at his own answer. "It makes no difference," he sighed.

# The Bicameral Mind

*"The mind is still haunted with its old unconscious ways; it broods on lost authorities; and the yearning, the deep and hollowing yearning for divine volition and service is with us still."*

Julian Jaynes

Eden remained quiet on the slow, winding drive back down into town. Both our minds were in a tailspin, but I suspected for very different reasons. Kane's unique version of Christianity was unusual to say the least, but he held a sincere sense of curiosity. He questioned how the universe worked, and he was going to push to his last breath to find his answers. How could I not respect that? Most religious fanatics seemed to read their dialogue from a cue card. Rarely did I find evidence of any genuine consideration behind their words.

I thought back to my own parents' gradual slide into total abandonment of rational thought. The more time they spent at their "Guru's Home," as they referred to the cult they had become entangled in, the less curious they became. After years of trying on new religions and philosophies, they were at least asking the tough questions along the way. As a child, I would often lie in bed hearing my mother and father in the living room talk through the night, questioning and philosophizing over the meaning of life, death, and everything in between. At first, it was quite jarring to my young mind to realize that even my own parents didn't have all the answers to the big questions, but eventually I enjoyed listening to them. Often some part of their discussion inspired me to start asking my own questions about the nature of reality.

And then they found "Rajneesh." And he had all the answers. My parents were overjoyed. I wasn't much older than thirteen when they shared the "good news" with me: They had found a man who filled in all the gaps; a man who promised to make them whole. And, naturally, I was happy for them. My mother and father who I had watched search high and low for life's answers for years had finally won the battle. There was no space for troubling doubts and questions; there was no need for them. And little by little, I watched the curiosity trickle from their eyes. The late night philosophizing stopped, and eventually they hardly spoke at all; to each other or to me. With no siblings or other family around (my parents had gradually cut them all from the picture; they weren't "elevated" enough to grasp the finer truths they had attained) I soon found myself isolated and alone in my house. Even my own questions for them were often met with prescribed responses.

"Mom, can I watch TV after dinner?"

"Son, television is a distraction from the Ever Present truth." When they left, I swore I would punch the next person who preached to me. I suppose one of the reasons I was drawn to Eden was because she actually had the balls to do just that. She seemed to hold no reverence for any belief system. Nothing was above evaluation.

Bicameral. There was that word again. Shortly before my folks moved into their guru's compound in Oregon, before they sold our home, before they relocated me and all of my belongings to my grandparent's house, they told me their guru's words were always with them. When I asked what they meant by that, my father explained that he could hear "Rajneesh" speaking to him all the time. He said he just had to be quiet enough to listen. What's more, he said he realized that he had always heard his guru's words, even long before he met the man. His reasoning for this was that Rajneesh's truth operated outside of normal time and space. Like a raindrop in a puddle, his voice sent an expanding wave forward and backward through time.

Perhaps Kane was running in circles within the maze of his religion, but he had maintained a curiosity, a thirst for knowledge. And what's more, he seemed willing to bend the traditional boundaries of his belief system to get the answers he sought. But, his assertion that everyone in the church spoke directly to God, that's what bothered me more than anything else he said that evening. Whenever I heard such things from the devout, I always assumed they were speaking metaphorically. Or, I hoped they were.

Bicameral. I remember the word. I once met a professor from Princeton, Julian Jaynes, who suggested that up to somewhere around three to five thousand years ago, the average human brain functioned as, what he dubbed, a "bicameral mind" where ordinary cognitive processes were divided between the two hemispheres. Either side of the brain performed very different tasks—tasks that the conscious self wasn't always privy to.

In one part of the brain, basic functions such as planning and organizing took place unconsciously to be later "downloaded" to the other, conscious hemisphere in a series of visual and auditory "hallucinations". Jaynes imagined that, up until quite recently on humanity's timeline, all the planning humans did all day took place in a section of the mind they weren't conscious of. Once the plans were made, for the day, for the year, for oneself, and for the tribe, the end-product was then "passed over" to the conscious self in the form of a grand "realization."

If he was right, there would have been no experience of: "We really need to keep that village on the other side of the ridge from infringing further into our hunting territory. The best strategy would be to attack them at night and run them far from our land." All formulating and planning would take place behind closed doors, resulting in an alien message appearing seemingly out of nowhere; a final conclusion not recognized as one's own. Something like a disembodied voice that whispered: "Attack the invading tribe at night."

The hypothesis was that the introduction of spoken language did this to us. He believed that language changed the very structure of brain matter in ways we still can't imagine. Early versions of humans were nonverbal, they didn't suffer from this dilemma; their minds weren't tainted with an "internal dialogue" that we all suffer from today. If we hadn't been raised with a language of any kind, what exactly would go on in our heads all day? Spoken language, Jaynes explained, was an absolute shock to our gray matter. It was akin to introducing completely new software to the same hard-drive that had been around for millennia.

If that were indeed the case, what option did ancient humans have but to believe that unseen, supernatural forces were regularly intervening into their life; a mystical force that presented preformulated thoughts, ideas, and insights to the conscious observer? What would any of us assume to be true about our world if our brain's executive functions all took place behind closed doors only to be exposed to us at intervals throughout our day? Perhaps we would believe that magical entities spoke to us regularly; guiding us from one experience to the next. Perhaps we would believe our own dreams to be divinely inspired, as we would never realize we were its authors.

According to Jaynes, that's just what everyone on this planet believed up until quite recently on the larger scale of humans upon Earth. Every single piece of literature we have found before a few thousand years ago has one thing in common: No one ever "thinks" about anything. All great schemes, knowledge and insight are handed down from some divine source. Odysseus never once thought to himself, "Hey, I should sail around in this boat full of gladiators and get into a bunch of wild adventures." No. Zeus and the powers that be were always blazing a path for him.

It was further suggested that mankind's modern experience of being conscious of the "little voice in our heads" and identifying it as our own represented an actual, physical alteration in the hardwiring between the left and right hemisphere; a quiet, yet powerful evolutionary change in our very biology, within the last few thousand years! I couldn't help but marvel at the possibility. It was a farfetched idea for sure, one hard to prove or disprove. Soft brain tissue doesn't survive long after death; we don't have access to our ancestor's gray matter. Doctor Richard Dawkins, the famous evolutionary biologist, once said something to the effect that Jaynes' theory was either a work of pure genius, or that of a raving lunatic. No middle ground was possible.

I was briefly snapped from my trance when Eden squealed the tires of the Hudson around another tight bend in the road. I couldn't help but wonder if some vestige of this ancient cognitive functioning was still alive and well in humans today. If Jaynes was right, there would almost have to be. The problem with evolution is that it's not neat and tidy. Most changes like this happen gradually over time; incomprehensible amounts of time. So incomprehensible, in fact, that I suspected that the majority of evolution deniers couldn't grasp just how much time some of these transitions took from generation to generation. What if the nutjob, extreme religious fanatics out there were actually walking around with outdated hardware in their heads? Brains hardwired to hear the word of a god?

As the Sub barely cleared the next turn, a rundown biker bar appeared around the bend nestled into the hillside, denoted by a sole, neon TEQUILA sign in the window. Eden yanked the wheel and skidded into the parking area, screeching to a frightening stop just short of the ledge. In the last ten years, I couldn't recall seeing an alcoholic beverage in the woman's hand more than a few times. After a long gaze out the window, she finally spoke. "I need a drink."

# A Cliché Bar Fight

*"The brain itself does not produce consciousness. That it is, instead, a kind of reducing valve or filter, shifting the larger, nonphysical consciousness that we possess in the nonphysical worlds down into a more limited capacity for the duration of our mortal lives."*

Eben Alexander, Neurosurgeon

Eden stood firm on the platform of tequila for the evening's drug of choice and I was too exhausted for a debate. Whether it was the late hour or isolated location, we enjoyed the small, dingy bar we had pulled into nearly all to ourselves. Besides the bartender, the only soul in sight was a heavyset woman stamped with faded, green tattoos. She busied herself with stomping in and out of the kitchen as she swept, cleaning up glasses, and ignoring us. Nirvana's *Nevermind* rumbled quietly in the background from a pair of speakers suspended above a deeply scarred pool table. I grunted under my drink when it occurred that today's kids would consider this album an "oldie."

Eden didn't speak again until she had downed her second shot. "I need a drink," she repeated to herself. "That's what we've been taught to say when the world is fucked: 'I need a drink.' I can't think of a worse way to deal with your problems. Hell, the body recovers from heroin better than it does alcohol."

She held the amber liquid up to one of the greasy, yellow bulbs looming over the bar. "Before alcohol, psychoactives were the only drug humans knew," she mused. "What a world that was; a world where no one got drunk. Can you imagine it? Ancient cultures found that psilocybin mushrooms could be stored in honey as a preservative. Down the road, they realized that the honey itself would eventually become psychoactive from contact, so they would seal it away to preserve it long after the cultivation season had passed. Eventually the honey would ferment and bam! the world's first liquor was invented: Mead. Just like that we moved from a hallucinogen-based to an alcohol-based culture and we wonder why our world is fucked.

We shoulda stuck with the 'shrooms.'"

I didn't know if I agreed with her or not, but I was happy she was talking again. "We probably shouldn't have left the trees," I added. She smiled and nodded, staring at her reflection in the darkened window behind the bar.

"That man is dangerous," she decided. "We've got to get to the bottom of this. We have to find out what happened out there, retrace Kane's steps. Love thy enemy, my sweet ass. I prefer my Christians scared to death of evil; only thing keeping most of them safe."

"I still don't understand what you think you're going to find back in Peru."

"What *we're* going to find," she reminded again, tipping her glass with a wink. "Kane was telling the truth when he said he's been searching the globe for something for a long time. Whatever the hell he was looking for he found in the Chambira Basin. We need to know what that is exactly, for all of our sakes. And, his relationship with darkness . . . "

"What about it?" I asked after a lengthy pause.

"What if they're allowing themselves to be possessed? Surrendering to it?"

"You mean if possession were possible," I grunted and downed the rest of my shot. She smiled as if it were a joke and shifted gears.

"Mike, let Damian and Kyle do the lab work, study the recording, analyze that frequency, but I need you with me out there where this all started."

When I shriveled back, she leaned closer to force eye contact. "They're bringing three, combat-seasoned marines with us and a fully loaded Humvee," she said, trying to console me as if I were a coward, "and your hot-ass, police woman guaranteed we wouldn't be gone longer than ten days, two weeks tops. They even found the field guide Kane hired when . . . " She stopped, realizing my attention was elsewhere. My eyes were on the door leading to the kitchen and my concern finally dawned on her as well. The place had gone dead quiet, even more so than before. Our bartender hadn't emerged from the back for quite some time. No trace of movement anywhere.

"Now that I think about it, I heard Harley engines a couple minutes ago," she added, looking around the empty room with growing concern. She got up, jogged around the bar top and poked her head through the swinging doors leading to the kitchen.

"Lots of people drive Harleys out here," I reminded her.

"The kitchen's empty," she said.

I moved to the window to see if the two employees decided to take a smoke break. Except for a couple cars, the dark, gravel lot next to the bar was empty. I could barely make out the lines of our Submarine across the lot, but just enough moonlight highlighted the chrome on two motorcycles parked further off the road.

"Bathrooms are empty, too," she whispered, jogging cautiously back to me. "This place is deserted." Her panic began scaring me more than the situation itself.

"What?" I asked. "What are you thinking? There's probably a smoking area in back." The moment I said it, I knew that probably wasn't true. The shack we were in was heaped right up against the slope; there wouldn't be more than steep, unforgiving land at the back of the building.

"I know we didn't make any friends tonight, that's for sure," she said, peering through the window with me. Hesitantly, I followed her lead and moved near the exit, but not before I threw a twenty on the bar top. The Sub was maybe forty meters away. I felt her press the car keys into my palm and I glared at her. She glanced up briefly, knowing damn well I had never been behind the wheel of a beast like her Hudson.

"Sorry," she said sheepishly. "You know I'm a lightweight with liquor. You'll do fine. It's an old three-shifter by the way."

"A what?" After scanning the parking area through the windows and finding no signs of life, we decided to head directly for the car. Without looking back, we pushed straight through the doors and walked quickly, stiffly toward the road. The moment the screen door clattered shut behind us, all the lights inside went black, followed by the neon sign and finally, the lamp above the parking lot. We froze in our steps. From behind the building, the compressors could be heard powering down. It was several, long moments before my eyes began to adjust to total darkness. The only sound was the wind moaning through the canyon.

"Okaaay," Eden whispered. "Maybe they're closing down for the night?" Before we managed another step, a terrible roar blared out from the rear of the bar. We searched each other, hoping the other could identify the terrible noise.

"A bear?" I whispered. She didn't answer, but didn't look convinced. The roar was deeper than any animal I had ever heard. Then a second, more savage bellow echoed from the same direction; this one carried a wet, gurgling finish as if the creature was coughing on phlegm. Or blood? We remained glued to the gravel lot, waiting, needing more information on what we were hearing. After another bout of silence, the sounds of crashing metal pierced the air, a violent rumble akin to garbage cans launched into brick walls.

We knew one thing for certain, whatever the source of the commotion, it was moving around the back of the bar and right toward us. This was all the motivation we required. We hurled into furious action and bolted for the car. I broke into a sprint I didn't know I was capable of while a frantic, earthshaking gallop closed in from behind. We erupted into full-blown panic at the undeniable reality that we were indeed being chased by something massive. Enormous, hollow breaths followed each thunderous stomp at our backs. A bear attack this aggressive was nearly unheard of. I skidded through the gravel around the front of the car and fumbled with the giant, chrome handle. It was locked. Eden pounded on the roof from the passenger side.

"You need to unlock it!" she squealed.

As I jammed the heavy key into the lock, I couldn't help but gawk at the dark mass growing behind her as it closed in. From but a stolen glance under a sliver of moonlight, all I could determine was it was the size of a Volkswagen and nearly on top of us. I unlocked the wide, heavy door, dove in and pulled the passenger lock. Eden swept into the seat just as the black silhouette reached the car. Using both hands and all her weight she pulled the handle and slammed the door shut a moment before impact. The beast crashed its massive head into the side of the car with unbearable force, crumpling metal and cracking glass. Gravel rumbled beneath our tires as the entire car skidded several inches sideways. I was thrown into Eden's lap, dropping the keys in the process. Judging by the jingling clatter, I guessed they landed somewhere just below the steering column. Eden quickly shoved me back onto the driver's side.

"Get us out of here!" she screamed.

I curled to the floorboards with furious hands, searching every square inch of the mat for the ignition key. Eden did the same on her side, but she pawed for the handgun. Outside, the animal moved around to the front of the car, possibly stunned by the impact. While we crouched beneath the dash, our mystery attacker sprinted up, over the hood and slammed a massive forehead into the windshield. The metal frame crunched beneath the blow, spraying shards of glass over our heads. Try as it might, it seemed the opening was too narrow for its skull. It twisted its head to the side and forced its snout as far into the cabin the frame would allow. Eden and I shrunk into the floorboards as pungent, acrid breath poured from the vicious, snapping jaws overhead.

Finally, the creature stumbled back from the hood, deciding on its next attack when I heard a metallic click-click to my right. Eden had found the pistol. I felt a metal ring beneath my fingers and snatched the keys into my hand as she shook my shoulder.

"I'll shoot, you run this fucker down!" she shouted. We both crawled out and slid low into the seats, just enough to peek over the hood. I fumbled the key into the ignition as Eden braced her legs against the dash, barrel pointed at the recently shattered windshield. The small cannon in her hand looked bigger than she did. Her elbows were locked, the pistol was rattling, and I realized the obvious: she had never held a gun in her life. Upon seeing movement in the car, the creature reared onto hind legs, lifted an impossibly bulky arm into the air and swiped down with terrible force. Our ears rung from metal tearing when the hood on the Hudson broke free of its hinges and flew into the night air off the ledge like a Frisbee.

"Jesus Christ!" Eden yelled and fired blast after deafening blast out the window, filling the car with blinding light. I turned the key and the blessed sound of our engine roaring to life filled my ringing ears. The beast shook its head, dug its front paws into the exposed motor, lunged back and prepared to pounce.

"Run it off the cliff!" she shouted.

I threw the shifter into Drive and stomped the gas pedal just as the crazed animal leapt up and swung its paw down once again. Metal hosing and rubber belts exploded in every direction, sending the car sputtering to an abrupt halt. After a brief moment of horrifying silence, the giant, decapitated engine crashed into the parking lot next to us. Eden stared blankly through the window in horror.

"That's an eight cylinder," she whispered to herself. "That's gotta weigh what? . . . Five, six hundred pounds?"

Dreadful reality set in that the Sub was now forever dead in the water. Bracing itself against our front bumper, the giant, enraged animal lowered into a crouch-and-pounce stance once again. "Back seat!" Eden shouted, smacking my arm. "Back seat!" We scrambled up and over the seat back as another blow to the windshield exploded behind us. The creature had blasted open the frame wide enough to reach an angry arm into the cabin. Inches away, the leather and metal springs of the front seat shredded beneath furious, swiping claws, forcing us as low as possible.

"Now what?" I shouted. She threw open the gun's chamber and locked it back into place.

"I have one left!"

"Don't miss this time!"

"I didn't fucking miss!" Suddenly Eden remembered something and began studying the seat back between us. "Grampa ran moonshine in this! He converted the seat!"

She reached inside a split in the leather backing and yanked on a hidden handle to expose a small opening connecting the backseat to the trunk. "Crawl in!" she shouted.

I hesitated, weighing the terror of being stuffed, trapped in the trunk, with being mauled to death. As I considered, she slipped easily through the narrow opening. Metal crunched and squealed as the beast began ripping the roof from the Hudson like a tin can.

"Come on!" Reluctantly, I wedged my fat ass head first through the hole, scraping my hips in the process. Eden pulled at my shoulders from inside the trunk, but before I could slip my feet through the opening I felt something grab my ankle.

"It's got me!" Eden yanked hard and I jerked my knee upward, tearing my foot from the vice-like grip, pulling the shoe clean off in the process. There was barely enough room in the massive, dark trunk for us to lie side by side in fetal position. That felt like a hand around my ankle. A human hand.

"Find the crowbar!" she yelled. I didn't ask; I trusted she had a plan. With stifled movements, I pawed for any sign of metal on the floor. The beast had now burrowed itself into the cabin, tearing angrily at the final, thin layer of cushioning and metal that stood between us. It would be mere moments before it dug its way into the trunk.

"It's near my feet!" she yelled. I shrunk back as far as I could to allow her enough room to curl into a ball and snatch up the crowbar. In the dark, she grabbed my foot that still wore a shoe and positioned my heel at the back of the steel handle.

"You need to kick this in as hard as you can!" she screamed. I couldn't understand her plan. She wasn't trying to open the truck and break us free; she was holding the crowbar near the sidewall.

"But . . ."

"Stop thinking and do it!"

I stomped with all my strength, pounding the crowbar into the wall. Inches away from my head, the beast ripped into the seat back. I kicked again and again until the tool punched through the metal. With a terrible screech, Eden pulled it from the hole and liquid rushed down between the panels onto the gravel below. Soon the smell of gasoline filled the air. The seats shredded apart under the bear's unrelenting claws while Eden jammed the crowbar into another crevice at the rear, and the trunk unlocked! I instinctively pushed up on the lid to free us when she grabbed me by the collar.

"Wait! Let the gas drain to the ledge!"

For what seemed like an eternity we held fast, crouched blindly in the trunk as the hole between us and the creature grew ever wider. "Okay. Together, on three! . . . One . . . Two . . ."

A savage, powerful arm punched through the seats and clawed at my leg. I screamed in pain as Eden yelled, "Three!"

We threw open the trunk and tumbled out, over the bumper tearing my shin free in the process. My flesh ripped under massive claws as I stumbled down onto the gravel in searing pain. Eden pulled me to my feet and nearly dragged me to the edge of the slope. Behind us, the furious rumbling in the cabin suddenly stopped. We turned to see the animal lift its head through the demolished roof to find its prey escaping. With renewed anger, it began to wedge and wriggle itself backward to free itself. In a few moments, it would be on top of us again. Our efforts had merely provided us a few more breaths of life. I began to scramble down the rocky incline as Eden seized me by the arm.

"No! Take cover!" She aimed the pistol at the ground beneath us. In the moonlight, I found the trail of gasoline shimmering and snaking its way from beneath the Hudson, down the slope, toward our feet. The animal roared in some bizarre comprehension at its predicament as Eden fired her final shot into the road, igniting the stream. I knew I needed to duck, but I couldn't pull my eyes from the orange flame racing to the car. Eden lunged up, wrapped her arms around my neck and forced me to the ground, just as metal, rubber, and glass exploded in every direction over our heads. Smoking shrapnel rained into the road and the rocky slope around us.

"Well, I'm fresh out of bright ideas," Eden muttered next to me, exhausted. "If that didn't kill it, it's all up to you now, buddy." The final growl that bellowed from the burning car was somehow human.

# No More Excuses

*"Lifting me up like a garage door*
*I need to feel it when the drug starts coming on*
*I know you Lord are a jealous Lord*
*I know the tablet is your competition…*
*But I need for you to be reasonable"*

*Soul Coughing*

After a lovely series of antibiotic shots and a zig-zag of stitches, the ER nurse carefully wrapped my leg. The puncture was deep, but luckily the claws had passed between the heads of the gastrocnemius; i.e. high pain, minimal damage. Somehow, Eden had walked away with little more than a few scrapes and bruises. She was now just outside my hospital room talking on her phone with Agent Downey. I would have loved to hear her version of tonight's events, but she hung just out of earshot.

"I've been working in the ER on the front range for over twelve years," the nurse mentioned. "I've never seen a bear flat-out attack someone like this. You don't realize how lucky you are to be alive."

"Oh, I realize," I sighed. The nurse exited the room to get my discharge papers just as Eden ended her call. Apparently, the only action we took that Agent Downey was pleased with was that we contacted him before the police. He wouldn't say any more about the mess we walked away from up there except that he would "take care of it" and that we were to stay put in the ER. Furthermore, we were instructed to await Agent Flores who, for some reason, was already on site speaking to the hospital administration.

"A bear, huh?" Eden said with raised eyebrows.

"Huh?"

"That's what you told the nurse. You know that wasn't a god-damned bear," she said leaning into me, "Right?"

"Okay, what the hell do you think that was?" I whisper-shouted.

She moved in closer. "It wasn't a fucking bear."

I shook my head and turned away. "Well, then it must have been something supernatural," I grumbled.

"This is a 50 caliber," she said a little too loudly, brandishing the giant revolver she had stuffed inside her jacket. I shoved her arm back to hide the weapon. "I shot that son of a bitch right in the face five times! You saw what it did. It shook it off like I slapped its nose with a flyswatter. And do you have any idea how much that engine weighed? . . . in one swipe, Mike!"

"It was pitch black!" I hollered. "You missed! And bears rip apart garbage cans all the time! They're five times stronger than humans. When Downey and his men-in-black team checks out the burning mess we left for them, that's what they'll find: The carcass of a bear."

Agent Tina Flores burst into the room just before Eden could launch her next talking point.

"Your timing is perfect." Flores smiled. "Can you walk?"

I could walk. Indeed, my lower shin was ripe with stinging pain, but it didn't impair walking. Flores ushered us to an adjacent wing in the emergency department, down a darkened corridor where the power had been shut down. Oddly enough, it began to bother me how easily she shrugged off us sticking our noses into her case. "I was kind of expecting to be reprimanded for going up there," I mentioned, limping behind Flores' elegant form. She turned and smiled wryly.

"Did you expect a spanking?"

While my jaw froze, Eden raised her hand quietly next to me and whispered, "Yes, please".

We arrived at the last room at the end of a sterile hall to find it decorated with yellow police tape. Tina held the plastic strips open and motioned for us to climb through. As I fumbled through the hole, she added, "It shows me you're curious about this case. That's what I need."

Lying in a sad heap before us was the shredded remains of a restraining gurney with torn Velcro straps for hands and feet. The entire room had been demolished, sliced apart. Streaks of dried blood stained the walls, metal tables, trays, the floor and ceiling. Even the windows were blown out. The concrete walls were splashed with hundreds of slash marks running every direction. I endured the pain to kneel and inspect a section of the metal railings on the bed that had been cut in two. A hand grenade was the only reasonable culprit that came to mind. Eden knelt beside me, examining a section of the shredded gurney and whispered in my ear, "Those damn bears are really getting out of hand." I shook my head for her to shut up.

"This happened two days ago,." Flores began. "We've been tracking any bizarre activity in or around Gold Hill, specifically incidents connected to the First Life cult. Originally, we ignored this report. It didn't seem to have anything to do with our situation, but I just got out of a meeting with two administrators and, clearly, the hospital severely minimized the stranger details in their report. They made it sound like some homeless meth addict flipped out in their ER. Earlier today we cross-referenced anyone we know to be connected to Kane's church with police reports."

"One of Kane's people was involved in this . . . " I asked, gesturing to all the damage. " . . . this . . . whatever this is?"

"This is another homicide scene," Flores replied and began reading aloud from a file folder in her hands: "At approximately 10:30 p.m. Wednesday, an unidentified woman was nearly run over by two teenage girls on Mapleton Drive in Boulder County just below Gold Hill town limits. The girls reported that, as they rounded a sharp turn, a woman appeared to be convulsing in the middle of the road. They just barely missed her. Their cell phones were out of range, so they transferred her to the backseat of their Subaru and proceeded back to Boulder to get her to an ER. They both stated that, as they were transporting this woman, who they both guessed to be somewhere in her mid- to late-twenties, her body began to "shrivel up and age". When they arrived at Foothills Medical, the staff reported that the woman they removed from the car appeared to be in her late nineties, probably older, yet highly aggressive and impossibly strong. It took three security guards to restrain and transfer her to the room we're standing in now.

Moments later, a nurse entered with a syringe of medication to subdue the patient. What happened after that is conjecture."

"Jesus Christ," Eden whispered.

"Only the nurse survived; a Jessica Vonfeldt," agent Flores explained. "How she survived, we don't know. The original statement from the hospital read that the three security personnel who were restraining the patient had been stabbed to death. But I've seen the autopsy reports: those men were gutted. And Vonfeldt hasn't spoken since the incident. She's been remanded to a psychiatric facility in Fort Collins. Whatever she saw take place in here shattered her mind. She won't eat or sleep."

"Won't speak either?" Eden asked.

"It's like she's gone brain-dead they say," Flores replied. "Apparently she's just been sitting in her room staring at Fox News all day." The sound of two drum beats and a cymbal crash filled the room: Buh-Dum-Tishh. "Sorry, that's my cell," Tina explained and stepped aside briefly to study an incoming message.

"So how did this all end?" I asked, mesmerized by the damage.

After reading her text message, Tina said, "After hearing a terrible commotion and bizarre sound waves blasting from the room, more staff rushed in and found the remains of the security guards and a very traumatized Nurse Vonfeldt huddled in the corner, covered in blood, wielding her syringe like a knife."

"And the patient?" Eden asked. Flores gestured to the window.

"The only sign she left behind was her shredded clothing. She must have gone through the window, but, as you can see, these metal frames look like they were blown out with some kind of explosive."

"Okay, so what the hell does any of this have to do with Kane?" I asked.

"You mean except for a woman aging seventy years in a manner of minutes?" Eden added sarcastically. "People being ripped limb from limb? Bizarre sound waves? You mean apart from those details? Are you being willfully ignorant?". I closed my eyes to shut her out. Once again she was making wild assumptions to force connections.

"Early this morning, police in Lyons, Colorado picked up a woman limping down the side of Highway 36," Flores continued. "One Brea Felluci, a former legal assistant from Broomfield, age 24, and a member of Kane's church for six years. She was wrapped in a hospital bed sheet and couldn't explain what had happened to her. They gave her a Breathalyzer, she was negative for alcohol. She refused medical attention, so the officers returned her to the First Life church upon her request. Short of being disoriented and poorly dressed, she was apparently quite polite and well spoken. Brea Felluci has to be the woman they brought in here that night."

"Could the hospital staff identify her?" Eden asked.

"No," Flores replied quietly. "All anyone here saw was an old woman shaking violently, but I sent a recent picture of Felluci to the families of the teens who picked her up. That was the reply I just received: Both girls are almost certain it's the same woman they picked up on Mapleton Drive two nights ago. The FBI will still have to gather more evidence, but I'm telling you, One of Kane's people did this."

"They're almost certain?" I said, shaking my head.

"Those girls aren't sure of what they saw," Flores admitted. "They're both still in shock. I've seen it in the field dozens of times. People have a way of doubting their own memories when something happens that they can't handle. Some people alter or block out details altogether."

"Or some people will make wild connections and toss all logic right out the window, no matter how idiotic," I added, growing more frustrated. "So, okay, what if one the cultists did this? How so? What tool do you even use to slice metal bars and concrete walls like this?"

"The same tool you use to rip a Hudson Commodore apart," Eden replied. I scoffed at both of them.

"You know, I've dated eight women in my life," I snapped. "Each and every one of them thought they were psychic."

"You think I'm crazy, fine." Flores snapped. "Then go with us to Peru and give us your brilliant idea about what's going on!

Prove there isn't a connection here!"

"You can't prove nonexistence," I mumbled. She ignored me, regained her composure and laid out her grand, "far outside the box" plan as to how to proceed with the investigation:

She, Eden, and her "support team" of marine bodyguards would depart Denver International tomorrow afternoon in a military cargo plane from a private hangar. They would take a direct, fifteen-hour flight to a small military base just outside of Lima, Peru where the same field guide Kane hired to navigate the rainforest would be awaiting their arrival. From there, the guide would lead them mostly by Hummer deep into the Chambira basin where he claims he knew how to make contact with the same tribe of shaman that he led Kane and his missionaries to, the Craneo Roto.

The words, "mostly by Hummer" hung heavy in the air.

"Give me ten days out there," Flores pleaded. "If we can't find the Roto, you go home. If we find them and there is no connection between these incidents, you go home. Either way, you'll be paid your government stipend for your time and efforts."

I didn't give a damn about federal bribes. I was about to reiterate my bullshit excuses for my refusal to travel when my nurse walked in and handed me my discharge paperwork, along with a prescription for thirty tablets of 20mg OxyContin; enough to survive without pods for two weeks or more. I was fresh out of excuses.

"Fine," I said with defeat, as if Flores had finally convinced me. "The idea of the two of you roaming the jungle, fueling each other's psychotic fantasies scares the hell out of me more than whatever the hell the rainforest has to offer." After a moment of consideration, I added, "But we're not going anywhere until Kyle and Damian brief me on what their Squid picked up from the event."

Flores and Eden shared a surprised look with my sudden change of heart.

"I'd expect nothing less," Flores agreed, with a shrug. "See you tomorrow. Bring your shit-kickers cause it's gunna be one hell of a trek through the jungle."

# The Universe with Its Pants Down

*"The particles that are the very building blocks of all things, are in all possible locations until observation/measurement causes them to choose a specific position."*

Kevin Michel

The doorbell jolted me wide awake at 6:00 a.m. I managed to stumble into the living room before the racket woke my grandparents. As soon as I unbolted the latch, Kyle and Damian burst through the door arguing wildly.

"Well, we know it trips the observer effect!" Kyle hollered. "Obviously it's all connected to the Zero Point Field! That frequency harmonizes with it and temporarily . . . destabilizes it or something."

"That would change everything we know about wave collapse!" Damian returned fire. "The observer effect is like a built-in failsafe."

"Built-in by who?" Kyle sneered.

"It's a manner of speaking," Damian shot back. "You know damn well I'm not turning this into an argument for intelligent design. I'm saying if we found a loophole to the observer effect, maybe someone else did too."

I hushed them up and ushered them down the hall into the kitchen where their voices wouldn't reach my grandparents bedroom. The two of them babbled and talked over each other as I rubbed the sleep from my eyes at the breakfast nook. I could barely focus on what they were saying. Clearly they had been caught in heated debate long before they arrived, and now they hardly noticed where they were.

Kyle finally made the first attempt to pull me into the discussion. He reminded me about my original question a year ago: Just how does the universe know when it's being looked at?

"Look, let's assume the observer effect you asked about once, Professor Huxley, is fundamentally just another transfer of information," he began, turning back to Damian, "so why wouldn't that transfer rely on the Zero Point Field? The frequency on the FBI's recording matches the frequency of the ground state, then it shuts it down; it trips it somehow. You're just scared of change, admit it, Damian!"

"Yeah, that's why I'm hesitant to throw out everything we know about quantum measurement!" Damian laughed angrily. "You're just trying to fill gaps in knowledge with any lame idea when . . . "

"I take it the two of you had a chance to analyze the data from yesterday's event?" I hollered to pull them back around. Both of them took a moment to breathe and to stare blankly at me.

"Yeah," Damian answered flatly. "Jesus, man, keep up. The frequency on the recording temporarily flipped the observer effect somehow. Every particle around that computer moved into a probability wave while we watched it happen. But, once the computer, well . . . stopped being a computer, it was like a game of musical chairs when the music shuts off! It left all the matter around those speakers in a complete, random mess. And we were all in the room observing it happen! That shouldn't be possible because probability waves only collapse when we're observing them. Or, at least they're supposed to."

"It was as if the moon continued to not be there even though we were looking right at it," Kyle added.

"Okay." I began slowly as my brain eased into second gear. "Do either of you have a hypothesis on this that would make sense to my gorilla brain? I need to catch a plane in a few hours. I'm talkin' the basics, here, guys. What do I need to know before I go chasing after this signal?"

Damian sighed and pinched the bridge of his nose as if my question gave him a headache. After silent deliberation he finally gestured to Kyle. "You take a shot at it. I don't know where to start."

"Then don't interrupt me!" Kyle snapped, enthused to have the spotlight. He jumped to the center of the kitchen floor and swung his hands back and forth. "Okay, so we live in a sea of virtual particles . . . that's energy to you," he began. "Every-thing, even the empty space between you, me, that chair, the sun, and Neptune is bubbling with an underlayer of massive amounts of force created by particles that are constantly popping in and out of existence everywhere, all the time."

"Popping in from where?" I asked, knowing my question wouldn't be answered to my satisfaction.

"Bizarro-world, Universe X," Damian grunted. "We don't know. Maybe from another dimension or from dark matter. It's just the nature of empty space. Deal with it. Emptiness, it turns out, is full of energy."

"Even in a total vacuum with zero degrees of heat, physicists are able to detect a steady, underlying field of energy," Kyle continued. "We refer to that field of spontaneous energy as the Zero Point Field; it's the ground state of all fields of energy in the universe: Magnetic, electric, Higgs. Look, if we're fish in the ocean, the Zero Point Field would be the water, got it?"

"I guess," I said cautiously. "Except that you're saying that energy exists even in a total vacuum. I mean, the very definition of a vacuum is a space that is devoid of energy, so . . . "

"Yeah, well, quantum mechanics doesn't give a shit about our definitions," Damian added as he booted up his laptop in front of me on the kitchen counter.

"That's true," Kyle agreed. "It really doesn't. I know it seems illogical to think of there being energy even in cold, empty space, but it turns out that particles are zipping in and out of nothingness all the time." He held his palms a few inches away from each other. "With the energy that exists in this amount of space, we could literally, not figuratively, boil all the oceans on the planet five times over."

"If we knew how to harness it," Damian said.

"Can you put those hands to work to make some coffee while you're up?" I grumbled. Kyle snapped his fingers and began scrambling through my cupboards.

"Okay," I said. "What does any of this have to do with our event on the recording of theirs?"

"Well, remember how matter exists in a field of probabilities when no one is looking at it?" Damian asked.

"I suppose."

"It's possible that when matter isn't being observed, that energy falls back into this sea of background noise, this Zero Point Field, only to be pulled into solid position once it's being observed again," Kyle explained. "If we think of the very act of observation as some measurable, physical occurrence, another type of energy that affects waves to particles, then it's not hard to imagine that connection can be altered, or cut off in some way. Just like you can cut a power cord and stop electricity flowing into your computer. Maybe the same thing can happen to the fundamental act of observation itself."

"You're saying that consciousness is just another field of energy that shapes matter?" I asked, trying to follow their logic.

"I'm not prepared to say that," Damian replied.

"Our data on that event would seem to suggest that, yes," Kyle said cautiously.

"That's nuts," I argued. "How can just looking at the world be an active process? It's the most passive thing we can do!"

"We know for a fact that observation itself actually alters the world around us," Kyle replied. "Our data from that frequency suggests that consciousness is another quantifiable field just like a radio or magnetic wave; waves that can be focused, or altered."

"Or neutralized altogether," Damian broke in. "It reminds me of that Zen Koan: If a tree falls in the forest and no one is around to hear it, does it make a sound? The scientific answer, by the way, is a definite, resounding, 'No'. Sound waves need to be interpreted by a brain or a recording device in order to actually become an audible experience that we refer to as 'sound'. Otherwise, they're just vibrations moving through the air." He suddenly appeared troubled by his final thought. "God, that's like a metaphor for my entire life."

Kyle distributed coffees while Damian rapped on his computer keyboard. I was only barely following their logic. "Okay, you guys said this before; that the act of observation pulls matter into physical existence. So, how do you think that dynamic can be altered exactly?" I asked, not even sure if I was asking the right question.

"By harmonizing with the Zero Point Field and then tripping it, so to speak," Damian replied as if it were obvious. He turned his computer screen toward me to reveal a sound frequency grid with a vibrating ess curve in the middle. A number flickered at the bottom reading 528.

"Just like everything else in this world; the table here, the windows, this coffee cup, your brain, everything vibrates at a certain frequency," Damian continued. "The Zero Point Field vibrates at 528 Hertz. Remember Agent Downey said that the recording can only produce its magic trick if the speakers are capable of around 600 hertz. I think there's a reason for that. Now watch what the Feynman Squid picked up just before the computer, and everything around it, flipped its shit back in the lab. This is the last few seconds of the event."

He pulled up a second frequency grid and pressed "play". I watched the straight line gradually bend into an arch and then slowly bend further into a snaking curve while the numbers at the bottom rose to 528. Upon reaching 528, the ess curve collapsed back into a straight line again on the scale.

"Do you see that?" Damian asked. "The frequency that video recording emitted harmonized with the Zero Point Field long enough to alter its pattern dramatically, which changed the connection between the observers and the observed. It's almost like it reached out and jammed the ZPF; it threw a giant, temporary roadblock between us and the computer! So everything around the source of the sound, in this case, the computer speakers, moved into superposition, a probability wave, even though we were standing right fucking there looking at it! For a few moments, everything within that radius around that computer behaved as if it was not being observed."

"Essentially," Kyle stepped in. "It temporarily punched a hole into our reality. Whatever technology is at work behind all of this has the capacity to match the frequency of the Zero Point Field and then temporarily trip it."

"So what does that really mean?" I asked.

"It means that pile of twisted, jumbled metal and plastics we have sitting in the middle of that physics lab is just one of an infinite number of possible combinations that those atoms could have been arranged in," Kyle said, exasperated. "It's a little disturbing that our government has a recording of a frequency that allows us to catch the universe with its pants down; a pattern that breaks the structure of our reality at the most fundamental level. I mean, we've invented ways of blowing things up, but this . . . this is total chaos in a bottle! A chaos no human consciousness could have dreamt."

Kyle rolled his eyes when he found no "ah ha!" expression on my face. His gaze fell onto my grandmother's bulky, old microwave sitting in the corner of the kitchen counter. "My God, is that an old Raytheon?" he asked.

"I have no idea," I replied. "My grandma's had that thing for, like, two hundred years."

"And might there also be a house cat on the premises?" he asked innocently. "I think I can create a visual representation of this process for you. For science, that is."

"Yes," Damian agreed excitedly at the idea, "for science!"

I wearily followed the two of them as they tiptoed into the living room where my grandmother's cat, Agnes, was fast asleep on the far edge of the sofa; currently the only section of the cushions bathed in sunlight. As they approached, the old gray and white Tabby opened her eyes, suspicious with the sudden attention on her. She let out a disgruntled moan as Damian gently lifted her from her warm nest. With only minor complaint, they carried her into the kitchen and lifted her up to the microwave oven door.

Upon realizing their dastardly plan, Agnes burst into hysterics. Fur and claws exploded in every direction as the two students pushed and struggled to shove the ball of fury into the belly of the appliance. After managing the bulk of the angry feline inside the compartment, Damian poked at her swiping, angry paws around the edges while Kyle carefully shut the door behind her. By the time the locking mechanism clicked shut, their forearms and hands were covered in bloody scratches. The old windowless, heavy construction of the device made it impossible to detect any sign of the pissed-off feline trapped within.

"I doubt Schrödinger had to deal with this shit," Damian said, sucking on a particularly deep wound on his knuckle.

"That's nothing compared to what my grandmother will do to you if she wakes up to find her cat in the microwave," I explained, sipping my coffee. "She will literally, not figuratively, beat the shit out of both of you."

"The cat's fine, this'll just take a second," Kyle explained, catching his breath. "Besides, it's really important you catch onto this new way of thinking about the world. Okay, professor . . . what's in the oven?"

I stared at both of them blankly. "You kiddin'?" I asked. "Open it up and you'll see exactly what's in there. Just make sure you lean your faces in real close when you do."

"No, you don't get it," Damian said. "Right now, we have no sensory connection whatsoever with that cat. We can't hear it or see it. Her existence isn't being measured by the outside world. Let's say that our field of consciousness isn't interacting with whatever is inside. The line of awareness is temporarily severed between us and her."

"Okaay."

"So, because we don't have that connection with your cat right now, we might say that her particles have fallen back into a field of probabilities," Kyle added. "We have no observation of her, so we literally can't say what's in the microwave at this point. Not until we open it up and our observation collapses the field of all the many possibilities into one, solid reality. Until then, we could say that the particles of that cat are in every possible combination at once."

"So is she alive or dead?" I asked. They were both enthused with my question.

"Exactly!" they replied. I sighed angrily.

"Fine." I consented. "Then why will the particles arrange themselves back into a cat when we observe it again?"

"Yes!" they both shouted simultaneously. "Now you're getting it!" Kyle cheered. "Now you're asking the right questions!" Somehow, hearing I was catching on to this absurdity was making me feel even more stupid on the subject.

"In quantum physics, we can only speak of the way particles will appear as a probability," Damian explained. "It's only probable that there will be a cat sitting there when we open the door. Highly probable, but still not entirely certain. It's simply easier for the particles to go back into the position from where they started. It requires no additional information or energy. Now consider the frequency in that recording on that video: it throws the microwave door open without the particles collapsing back into their probable position!"

"But!" Kyle interrupted. "If we were to add energy to the equation, like, for instance if we were to turn this thing on . . . " He pantomimed pressing the "power" button. "We increase the probability that what would come out of there would be something very different. But again, you need to get available, free energy from somewhere."

For some unknown reason, I now pictured the four dead natives back in Peru Agent Flores had mentioned; the ones closest to Kane's missionaries. The ones who displayed no signs of bodily damage.

As interesting as this all was, I had no more time for hypothesis. Plus, I had no idea how any of this information was practical to our investigation. Damian and Kyle agreed to keep working on the data they had, and to keep me updated with what they found. Both of them were thrilled I was going to Peru to track down the source of the frequency, but they also agreed that nothing could convince them to go out there themselves.

"I mean, look at me," Kyle said, panning his entire body. "The jungle would eat me alive."

"Any ideas as to what I'm really looking for out there?" I asked.

"It would be something like a radio," Kyle said. "Short of that, instead of receiving radio waves, it picks up the Zero Point Field."

"And then jams the station," Damian added.

"You're looking for a revolutionary, incredibly high-tech piece of equipment out there," Damian concluded. "I couldn't even tell you how big it might be. It could be the size of a phone or the size of a truck; I just don't know."

"What the hell would cutting-edge technology like that be doing in the jungles of South America?" I asked rhetorically. They only shrugged, wished me the best of luck in the rainforest, and immediately continued arguing the moment they reached the front porch.

Even though I was still having a hard time picturing just what this frequency did to matter, I was feeling slightly more content knowing there may be some sort of scientific explanation at work behind the phenomenon. Just hearing Damian's contention that an electronic device lay at the source of the mystery made me feel better. Why, exactly, I did not know. I didn't care that none of this explained what killed those soldiers; there was a reasonable explanation behind that, too. I just needed to find it. I would fill those gaps and I'd have my tidy world back in no time.

Eden called the moment I shut the door behind the two of them. It appeared that sleep was impossible for her as well. Agent Downey had updated her on the scene we left up at the biker bar.

"Besides the burned wreckage of the Sub, they found three bodies on site," she explained.

"Was one of them found inside the car?" I asked hopefully.

"Nope. They didn't find anything in or around the burned out car," she explained. "Two of the bodies belonged to the bar employees we saw. Their remains were found out back behind the building, shredded just like the soldiers. But, get this: The third body they found was Trevor McGhee, the man with Christopher Aldon outside Kane's church."

"Okay," I sighed, resigning myself to the fact that I couldn't ignore another connection like this. Regrettably, I was forced to admit: this was too much to be coincidence any longer. "How was he killed?"

"No one can say yet," she said. "His body doesn't have a scratch. They're still waiting on toxicology reports, but so far it appears he dropped dead like the four natives in the basin. Like the life was sucked right out of him."

Now I had to face the reality that we were on the trail of a real sort of danger. I didn't know what to do with the tension twisting my stomach, so I decided to prepare one last press of tea for the plane ride before I would have to survive on Oxy-Contin in the rainforest. I popped open the microwave oven to heat the water, and was greeted rather suddenly by a furious ball of claws to the face and neck before Agnes returned to her warm spot on the couch. Evidently her particles had managed to arrange themselves right back into the same, pissed-off feline.

# PART THREE

## Stacked Cards

*"We were once so close to heaven Peter came out and gave us medals, declaring us the nicest of the damned."*

*They Might Be Giants*

After spending far too long packing for the trip, I collected Eden outside her apartment to find her dressed like she was heading to Burning Man: weathered cargo shorts, a tight fitting, handmade tie-dye shirt and her scuffed up motorcycle jacket. I wondered if she still had her grandfather's gun on her, but I didn't ask. She carried a single backpack slung over her shoulder; half the size of mine. Earlier, I had spent an hour at REI choosing the right socks that matched the new hiking boots I just purchased.

"I'm bringing two ounces," she shouted through the passenger window and tossed a baggie stuffed with marijuana onto the seat. "Do you think that'll be enough? Tina said we were bypassing security, so I figured . . ."

"Get in the car," I hollered, hitting the gas before she shut the door. We met Agent Flores in a private hangar at DIA where we were ushered into a military cargo plane they had flown in from Peterson Air Force base in the Springs. At the top of the loading platform we were joined by the same machine gun wielding soldiers who escorted Downey and Tina Flores yesterday; Corporal Sabol and Pavlik. They had both traded the military fatigues for casual hiking gear, which put me a little more at ease. It made this all seem like a camping trip; something I could relate to, even though I hadn't actually been camping in years. Then again, it was a little disturbing to see a large, automatic rifle strapped around a bright red Hawaiian shirt, but Sabol wore them both as easily as one might hold their morning cup of coffee. He greeted us with a smile and a polite handshake when we entered. His lean, muscular form was that of an avid runner or biker more so than the stereotypical marine.

Pavlik, on the other hand, carried more of the typical build one might expect: round, broad-shouldered, weighing at least 240. At first glance he could nearly be mistaken for chubby, but it was clear he was packing a heavy load of muscle beneath all the baby fat. Pavlik and the military lead for our expedition, a Sergeant Ronald Gomez, poured over a table of tactical gear, knives, and weaponry while we loaded ourselves into the massive cargo plane.

"Do I get a gun, too?" I asked, but was ignored.

After briefing our pilots, Tina mentioned that Sergeant Gomez had fled to the States twenty years ago with his sister and her son from Colombia where he had worked for the police force. Apparently, he wouldn't play ball with a nasty drug cartel and the US military was happy to have him. The man had "seen some shit," as Flores eloquently put it, quoting Agent Downey. Downey believed that Gomez's intimate knowledge of the dangers South America could pose made him the perfect point man for the expedition. Apparently, the man rarely spoke, but he pulled himself from securing the dark green Hummer into the wheel locks long enough to introduce himself before takeoff. He was soft spoken and at least twice the age of Sabol and Pavlik. The first thing that caught his attention were my boots.

"Those brand new?" he growled softly.

"Yeah, just this morning," I replied confidently.

He shook his head with a knowing smile. "Sabol, find that man a size ten and a half before takeoff," he hollered across the hangar. I didn't see his problem, but I really didn't care. With the bottle of Oxy stuffed into its own private pouch in my backpack, my fears about detox were behind me. Now I had the luxury of worrying about the real bodily harm that lay ahead. With a deafening whine of hydraulic pressure, the loading platform at the rear rose up and sealed into place with a terrible thud! of finality. There would be no backing out now.

The flight was unpleasant to say the least. There were no indications that our airborne, metal coffin was still in regular military use, and the random corners of the cargo hold we were crammed into was clearly not designed for civilians. There were no windows where we sat, which was fine with me. I didn't need to be reminded of our elevation.

A string of dull, yellow bulbs overhead provided just enough light to see what a heap we were in. Seating arrangements consisted of two narrow metal benches running the length of the fuselage. Short of the newer-looking military Hummer parked behind us in the bay, the plane looked more like a storage facility for forgotten equipment. Dusty machine guns lay in a wooden box bungee-corded to the sidewall. Who knew if they would ever fire again. Behind them lay a mesh bag filled with old grenades. Well, that's just fuckin' great. The few nylon straps that weren't securing some discarded military junk to the hull swung hypnotically back and forth throughout the flight. Clearly, they spared no expense on this leg of the investigation. This all endowed me with a new level of anxiety as to just how "off the books" this mission was.

I had downed my last shot of tea moments prior to takeoff in hopes of easing my fear of flying. Where I first picked up this irrational anxiety of heights in general, I did not know. I have vivid memories from childhood where I didn't hesitate to scale up trees that soared above the rooftops. I loved spying down at my neighborhood miniaturized beneath my feet. It wasn't until I flew to Colorado with Eden after college that I first realized I couldn't stomach the view from the window. I now found the enormous, yawning spaces nauseating. Great, I thought, I'm moving to the front range of the Rockies and now a fear of heights kicks in?

For the first several hours of the flight, the three marines kept to themselves, using the opened trunk of the Hummer for rounds of Texas Hold-em. Tina sat across from Eden and me staring into her laptop. Her shimmering, black hair was now pulled into a tight bun atop her head with a red bandana. Strapped to her upper thigh was an enormous handgun that hung just below her khaki shorts. She was Tomb Raider come to life. Not the manicured Angelina Jolie Tomb Raider, no. She was the real deal.

"Are there a lot of women in your line of work out there, Agent Flores?" Eden asked.

"I think it's safe for you to call me Tina, professor," she replied peering over her screen with a smirk. "We might as well get comfortable with each other."

"So, do I get a gun too, or . . . " I tried to interject.

"Well, as long as you drop this 'professor' shit," Eden replied with feigned awkwardness, "I guess I'm asking, 'What's a nice girl like you doing on a dirty cargo plane full of grunts?'"

Eden's style of flirtation was to pretend she was bad at flirting. And it never failed, even if her target was straight as an arrow. Quite to the contrary, Eden observed how even the straightest-laced bent the fastest for her. Her confidence was generally enough to catch her prey flattered, curious, and off guard. Personally, I just hoped this banter wouldn't be joining us for the duration of the trip.

"I don't generally do field work," Flores explained. "I usually work safely behind a desk. Occasionally I have to venture out to analyze evidence at the scene or in another lab, but nothing like this. My superiors in the National Police would rather keep their names as far from this escapade of ours as possible, so where's the harm in sending the crazy woman who dreamed up the plan to begin with? I alone was forced to convince your government that they had a responsibility to support this operation. So now I have two countries who think I'm insane for chasing after a lost tribe, but the responsibility is mine and mine alone. That's why you're stuck with me. I hope you aren't disappointed."

"Now you're talking crazy," Eden said. "I'm fucking jazz-hands to be here. It takes real courage to ask the insane questions."

"Despite some minor progress, my culture continues to be very male-oriented," Flores added. "In the upper echelons of the government, my ideas are not taken with the same consideration as a man's. It was the same in America not so long ago, yes?"

A boisterous "Ha!" burst from Eden's mouth. "It seems every minority group in America has made more progress than women," she said. "Trust me, the fight to be taken seriously outside the kitchen is still raging on. And wealthy, white men cringe with every inch we gain." She punched me lightly in the arm.

"Yeah, okay, everything's our fault," I added. "And I'm not rich. You know damn well there's also a lot of unspoken confusion with what equal rights should look like. I'd say we have too many women nowadays who've confused real empowerment with getting whatever they want. Sometimes you think all men are pulling the strings and have a road paved with gold ahead of them. So we get blamed for everything that goes wrong. That's not power."

"Ah, poor baby." Flores cooed at me playfully. "Must be rough being an educated, middle class, white man in America."

"You know, it's funny," I shot back, "but that's pretty much the exact response I get from American women when I make that observation. If they want real equality, they need to be able to take real criticism. You need to recognize when you actually are being treated as an equal. It may not look quite the way you fantasized it would. Believe it or not, women aren't infallible."

"You think men are any better?" Eden laughed and winked at Tina. "The male ego today is frighteningly delusional."

"Men?" I laughed. "Oh, hell no. I'll freely admit that most men are absolute children. And you know damn well I hardly identify with the male ego in this country. It's a superhero fantasy most of the time. But I didn't hear any women complaining that they should be added to the draft list along with us. None of you moan when a woman commits the same crimes as a man and gets less than half the sentence because society has a hard time thinking of you as dangerous. All the while, real minorities out there are being executed in the streets by their own police force."

"Can you believe he's still single?" Eden said to Tina. I decided to end my little tirade on a high note and salvage whatever respect Flores may still have for me. My ugly reaction to her was beginning to worry me. I never pushed women off this hard, and there was no reason for it. I tried to salvage any shred of respect she might still hold for me.

"For what it's worth," I said quietly, trying to unbury myself. "It's refreshing to meet a woman who genuinely isn't afraid to think outside the lines, to take the risk on following a case in a nontraditional sense, as Eden said. I respect that, I do. I wish there were more women pursuing areas that are typically male dominated; science, law enforcement, politics. Men need the balance in the field. We need female insight. Now more than ever."

Eden glanced at me a with a condescending grin that said, "Well, look at you, trying to cock-block me! Good for you!"

"Well, thank you," Flores replied, still somewhat suspicious of my attitude. "I have to admit, even I have a hard time relating to many women with the type of work I do. My mother and both of my sisters couldn't believe it when I told them I wanted to study criminal investigation. I remember my father just laughed and shook his head. Law enforcement was no place for a woman." She stared at the floor for a moment. "Anyway, it wasn't easy to get my superiors to listen to my ideas about this case. They were desperate for suggestions, but we're not going to see a lot of support from my government on this excursion of ours."

Though I was afraid to ask, I felt it was finally time to take the blow and hear her grand theory on the case. "Okay, Agent Flores," I sighed playfully, "let's hear it. My boys in the physics department tell me we should be looking for a revolutionary piece of technology out there, something like a receiver and tuner for what they call the Zero Point Field; the ground state of every field in existence from magnetic to quantum. Personally, I'm still not convinced that these attacks and the frequency are even connected. So, what's your idea behind all this?"

At that, Flores shut off her laptop and straightened herself.

I buckled in tight for the response. "First and foremost I'll say that I don't know," she admitted. "All I know is that I have a lot of unexplained deaths on my hands, in my country and now in yours, that follow the same pattern. I have a recording of a sound wave that can alter matter in ways no one really understands. I know this all started in Peru, and I know Kane's little cult is connected to all of it somehow."

"I respect that," I assured her, "but, you didn't answer my question."

She smiled shyly. "True," she said, taking a measured breath. "I believe that the Craneo Roto shaman do indeed exist, in some form at least. I grew up hearing those stories, too, and I think, if nothing else, there's a source at the heart of those stories somewhere. The guide we're rendezvousing with is the same guide Kane found in Peru. I believe this man took Kane and his missionaries to meet with the Roto tribe; why, I cannot say," she answered flatly before taking another deep inhalation. "And I believe those shamans shared some kind of ancient knowledge with them; knowledge concerning hidden powers of some sort. How or why, I do not know. But I think it's clear that the members of Kane's church are now incredibly dangerous in ways that defy logic."

"Hidden powers, huh?" I asked incredulously.

"Like shapeshifting?" Eden asked. She took no issue with Tina's hypothesis whatsoever.

"I don't know," Flores replied quickly. "I can't say that I know what that even means."

Luckily, the tea was just kicking in, so I managed to swallow this complete load of bullshit with a fair temper. Opiates always helped me accept the unacceptable. Hell, if it wasn't for the morphine I was doped up on at the hospital the night before, I didn't think I would've mustered the courage to agree to this trip on my own. My blood felt warmer, my muscles loosened, and my mood lightened. Soon, the metal bench beneath me didn't seem so unforgiving and cold. I rerouted my urge to get angry into more questions.

"Shapeshifting . . . okay," I said calmly, trying to find a shred of common ground. "I've heard of the idea of shapeshifting in tribal cultures, but from what Eden's mentioned, I always thought it was just a metaphor. The old stories of the medicine men transforming into eagles and wolves during their ceremonies; I thought it was just another way of expressing their 'oneness' with nature, or whatever. I didn't realize anyone took those stories literally."

"In many ways, you are right," Tina explained. "From my experience, shamans have a number of ways to describe their journey into other realms; realms which they generally agree cannot be described with our limited language. But yes, when their experience involves a dissolving of boundaries—emotional, spiritual or physical—they often describe how their soul merges with the life around them. Most shaman don't recognize a separation between what animates their body and every other organism. So, in that regard, you're right. When they speak of their spirit or awareness expanding out to touch other life-forms on this planet, they generally aren't suggesting that their physical body literally shapeshifts into a different animal."

"However," Eden interjected, "in nearly every branch of shamanism and religion practiced throughout the world, you find tales of shapeshifting which were clearly not meant to be metaphorical. Carlos Castaneda's teacher claimed that the Mexican shamans of the old world would literally become other animals, even other people. Gods, saints, and holy men from around the globe from the Aztecs, the Egyptians, to the Greeks are attributed with the power to transform their physical bodies. The Greeks believed Athena could turn into whatever she wished. Odin and Loki could alter their age and sex at will. Gurus throughout India were believed to be able to take the form of animals or other people after a lifetime of meditative practice. We have hieroglyphs and carvings from every walk of life depicting chimeras; half-human, half-animal creatures."

"Half animal," I replied, "if you're saying Kane's people shapeshifted, then just what the hell are you suggesting they shapeshift into? Whatever killed those soldiers wasn't somebody's wayward spirit animal, Eden. It sounds like this power you two are describing should only be accessible to holy men or saints; people who've dedicated their life to a spiritual practice. Your hypothesis on shapeshifting, if it did exist, which it absolutely does not, sounds like some reflection of a deeper oneness with the universe. So, how does that apply here? We met Chris Aldon outside their cult compound last night. Did that man strike you as a shaman or a holy person of any kind?"

"No," Eden admitted thoughtfully. It was clear she hadn't thought this through completely.

"Professor Huxley, if I've given you the impression that I have all of this figured out, then I apologize," Tina offered. "I was simply the only one who didn't outright disregard the unanimous, eyewitness testimony of every other adult on the scene that day simply because they were tribespeople."

"What witnesses are you referring to again?" I asked.

"The Chambira," Tina snapped, shocked that I didn't know who she was referring to. "They claim Kane's missionaries transformed into monsters right in front of them. They said the devil from the 'white man's' Bible crawled out of hell and possessed Kane's people that day. I don't know what that means, but I find it irresponsible to call the whole ordeal a mystery when we have an entire tribe of men and women telling us what happened out there."

The words took a running start from my mouth before I could tackle them. "Yeah, a tribe of illiterate, superstitious Indians!"

Eden bit her lower lip, feeling the sting of my embarrassment. Tina stared into me with fury. To make matters worse, Corporal Pavlik, aroused from his card game, concurred with a bellowing, "No, fuckin' shit, man. Dumbass natives."

"And, there it is, right there," Tina said emphatically, slapping her palms together. "That's the sentiment in a nutshell: 'Dumbass natives'."

"Do you have any idea how racist that is?" Gomez mumbled disinterestedly to Pavlik.

"How the fuck am I racist?" Pavlik said with shock, slapping

Sabol across the back of the head. "Sabol's my friend and he's black."

Everyone's eyes, except for Tina's, turned to Sabol. "It's true, I am." He smiled and promptly smacked Pavlik so hard his ball cap flew out of the Hummer onto the floor. "And we've never hung out outside of work."

Tina's eyes were still digging into me. "Let me explain," I stammered. Shit, the bridge is already burned. You don't need to kick the ashes. "I'm only saying that due to their lack of formal education we can't know what they consider to be logical or reasonable, or if they were even speaking literally. Who knows how their culture . . . "

"You should probably stop explaining yourself," Eden whispered, trying to save me.

"Fine!" I hollered. Fuck the bridge. "You're gunna let goddamned political correctness get in the way of looking at this case rationally? Then why the hell did you need me to come with you? I'm saying we need to approach this with a little more skepticism."

"Let me tell you what illiterate villagers are capable of, Professor Huxley," Tina began gravely. My throat clenched and my stomach sank. I could feel her momentum building as she paused before her attack. She had been waiting for this opportunity to fire into me since yesterday in Eden's office, but now I was on her turf. Her eyes burned as the words shot from her lips. "I grew up in the village of Camalau in Bolivia. Do you know where that is?" she seethed. "It's nowhere, because it's not a tourist destination. You'd see it as just another village full of stupid, poor natives. As far as the rest of the world was concerned, we weren't hated, we weren't loved; we were invisible.

"My grandfather was a medicine man in Camalau. He cured everything in that village, and I don't mean lifting curses or exorcising demons; he set broken bones, sewed, disinfected and healed wounds, treated infections of all types. He used his immense knowledge of plant medicine to pull family and loved ones back from the edge of suffering and death countless times. He cured cancer, Parkinson's, Alzheimer's; diseases that you in the West are still scratching your heads over.

"And he did this all without reading a single page from a biology book. He knew more about how the human body worked than you, professor, with all your education and research; more than any of your doctors or pharmacists in America ever will. He wielded a knowledge of plants that's been handed down for thousands of years; knowledge that you've been taught to ignore because it wasn't conducted by men in lab coats. His lineage has known for generations that White Willow eases pain and prevents heart attacks, but today you call it aspirin. In fact, 80 percent of the medicine on your drugstore shelves—the ones that actually work—originated from plants found by people like my grandfather. He was illiterate and the most intelligent man I've ever met. When he died, a thousand years of medicinal knowledge died with him. Your attitude about the worth of indigenous people is precisely what allows our homes and our lands to be bulldozed for your rubber, your coffee tables, your cheeseburgers, all without anyone raising an eyebrow."

"That's just survival of the fittest," Pavlik barked from his poker match without looking up. "Just science and nature. Ain't that right, professor? And, lady, if your grampa knew how to write, he woulda wrote all that voodoo shit down somewhere."

"Please stop helping me," I cried before turning back to Flores. Pavlik glared angrily in my direction. The elaborately detailed, black tattoo on his bare shoulder of the crucifixion wasn't quite intimidating enough to counteract the boyish freckles sprinkled over his chubby cheeks. But I suspected he compensated with overt aggressiveness. "I wasn't trying to attack you," I pleaded with Flores. "Honestly, I'm more on your side than you realize."

"I know you don't think you're attacking me," she said. "You're just quietly allowing the notion of hierarchy to spread; that mental disease that would have us all believe that only the white, educated males are capable of understanding the world and making valid observations. While on the other end of the spectrum are people with only half of what you possess; those half-naked, half-humans who dare live directly off the earth. Surely, those people must be incapable of rational thought. Otherwise they would have realized that what they really need in their lives are designer clothes, high-tech phones, maybe a sports car or a mortgage payment on a condo with a view of the park. That attitude is literally suffocating the life out of this planet. My guess is that we'll be all out of air and water before you face the truth that you've buried the people and the natural resources that could have saved you."

"Marry me," Eden smiled at her. Pavlik mumbled something inaudible at Flores' reference to global warming, something about it all being a hoax, but she didn't take notice. I was her sole target.

"Didn't you come to me for help?" I asked quietly, trying to bring her back around.

"In his defense," Eden began, "this man knows nothing of fashion or sports cars."

"And I don't have a mortgage," I added. "I still live with my grandparents."

Flores let out a sigh followed by a restrained smirk at our attempts to lighten her mood.

"I think you've jumped to a few assumptions about me," I said. "I'm not The Man. But I am a man of science. I would doubt anyone spewing tales of the supernatural. I don't care if they lived in the jungle . . . "

" . . . or in Boulder," Eden added.

"Especially Boulder," I replied. "I don't disregard the Chambira's story because of where they live or the color of their skin. I disregard their story because monsters aren't real, and demonic possession is nothing but a mental disorder, pure and simple. It's dangerous to think otherwise. Superstition like that is what led to young women to be burned as witches. And, while we're at it, organic flesh doesn't shapeshift. The amount of free energy alone required to alter the chemical composition of . . . "

"Well, actually, octopuses can change shape and color in an

instant," Eden mused. I growled and clenched my hands.

"They don't have BONES, Eden!" I yelled. "They can manipulate chromatophores in their skin through muscle contraction. Do you honestly want me to go into the insane biological differences between cephalopods and mammals?"

"You said 'organic flesh'!" she surrendered with raised hands.

"Are we really doing this?" I barked.

Eden smiled. She had already lost interest in debating me and instead changed the subject altogether. "Frankly, I can't imagine Evangelical Christians being able to communicate with shaman from such a dramatically different worldview. It seems like there would be absolutely no points of reference. I don't see how Kane and his people could comprehend a holistic philosophy with so few boundaries."

"You're assuming the Craneo Roto's beliefs would be similar to any other documented philosophy," Flores noted. "If they're an isolated, uncontacted tribe, their beliefs, their customs, everything about them may have no connection to anything we've ever seen. I can only hope we can find some way to communicate with them if we do find them."

"And you assume Christians can't understand other religions," Pavlik called to Eden. "If anything, it would be those witch doctors in the jungle who didn't understand them." The young soldier threw his cards down on the trunk bed and leapt down to stretch. "I fold, boys."

Eden sank her head into her hands and sighed. "Oh, God. What is so hard to understand about Christian theology?" she asked, her voice muffled through her fingers. "Your god calls the shots and you either buy into the obnoxious idea of Original Sin and obey him or you get punished for eternity. You could boil Christianity down to a master/servant relationship. Dogs understand that relationship."

"Oh, it's that easy?" Pavlik snapped. Gomez and Sabol grumbled in vain to pull their opponent back to the game. "God gave us free will to do whatever we choose. You have no idea how much courage it takes to follow the path He laid out for us."

Gomez let out a sigh of resignation and tossed his cards to

the Hummer's floor. "Must we do this?" he mumbled. "Do any of you idiots think this is going to go somewhere? Or change anyone's mind?"

"What choice do you think you have as a Christian?" Eden fired back. "If you don't follow the word of God, he sentences you to an afterlife of eternal suffering. What courage does it take to do exactly what you're told to avoid hell? Where's the bravery in that?"

"God doesn't want us to go to hell; he loves us," Sabol added quietly. "He wants us to follow him, but it's our choice. It's all up to us."

"Et tu, Sabol?" Gomez sighed, lighting a cigar. Tina and I exchanged glances and lowered our eyes. Neither of us had any interest in joining this particular detour.

"Right. We've got free will," Pavlik agreed.

"You're not free," Eden replied. "The cards were stacked from the beginning and somehow it's always our fault. I love that logic: God, in his infinite wisdom and compassion de-signed the entire universe from absolute nothingness yet he's not ever responsible for any of the awful shit that goes down afterward. How can anyone less than a god be free in a system like that?"

"Hey, choosing evil was man's decision," Pavlik declared. "And we've been paying for it ever since."

"Do you have children, corporal?" Eden asked.

"I got a three-year-old boy, yeah?"

"Then tell me," she snapped. Her intensity grew, and my pulse quickened. This wasn't the time or place for her to lose her mind. "Does it seem reasonable to put your gun to your child's head and demand that he tells you that he loves you, because otherwise you have no choice but to pull the trigger?"

"Fuck that," Pavlik spat. His breathing quickened. "What's that got to do with anything?"

"Of course you wouldn't," Eden replied calmly. "Anyone who behaved like that would be a lunatic. Yet, you have no trouble believing that the god you kneel down and pray to has dealt you the same hand but far, far worse."

Pavlik pushed out a laugh and slapped Sabol's shoulder. "Do you have any fuckin' clue what this chick is talkin' about?"

"I'm not sure," Sabol replied thoughtfully, growing troubled by the conversation.

"You justify the most abusive relationship by rationalizing that it must be your own damn fault for choosing evil," Eden barked. "And, even if we did everything in our power to be good, we somehow still inherited Adam and Eve's punishment for their mistakes? Why God believes we're responsible for our ancestors' choices we'll never know, but it seems to me if the machine you built from scratch with your own hands ain't workin' up to specs, you have only yourself to blame. Every mistake humans make only proves your Christian god is a terrible engineer."

"Hey, you can choose to be saved or not, it's up to you!" Pavlik hollered. "Clearly, you made your choice. Let's see where your books and your science get you guys." Losing momentum, he plopped onto the Hummer's rear bumper.

"Yeah," Eden said, easing against the wall. "Christians always say that all the evil in the world is because of the choices we've made. I mean, it's got to be, right? Otherwise, your Almighty is either a real prick or he just isn't powerful enough to stop all the evil shit from going down, so you go out of your way to make every awful thing that takes place on this planet someone else's fault: the gays, the Jews, the atheists, the liberals, or whatever group you've decided the Devil is working through now."

"Are you hearing yourself?" I quietly asked Eden. She didn't hear me.

"Everyone has to make their own decision," Pavlik grumbled. "You either put your faith in Christ or you don't. God can't make that choice for you."

"Oh, but he did; he already has!" Eden hollered, rising to her feet. "If I'm choosing what to eat at Denny's, I didn't create the choices that are listed, did I? I wasn't the one who put 'evil' on the menu to begin with. And, furthermore, I didn't create the brain that had to decide if any of the options sounded reasonable in the first place."

"Yeah, so you go eat somewhere just as bad?" I mumbled. She continued to ignore me.

"Okay, what are you saying, Professor Jessup?" Sabol asked with genuine curiosity, "that we don't have free will?"

"I'm saying you can't make a choice that belongs to you within your system," she said. "I'm saying that Adam and Eve, just like the rest of us, were choosing from a list of possibilities; preexisting possibilities, mind you. So, who the hell is responsible for creating a universe where these evils are even possible? Who designed the menu?"

"God did, obviously," Pavlik replied.

"Exactly, so why did God put 'evil' on the menu as an option?" she asked. "Can't you see what a fucked up game that is?"

Looking ever more troubled, Sabol considered for a moment while Pavlik stormed off to the rear of the cargo hold. "He does it to test us," Sabol responded slowly, uneasily. "I mean, he wants us to choose a life with him, but it's our choice to turn our backs."

"Says the delusional boy with a gun to his head who thinks daddy loves him," Eden replied with a finger to her temple. "If he made us, he's the one who endowed us with the capacity for decision making, for better or for worse, so who's really being tested, us or him?"

"Fine!" Pavlik yelled from the rear. "If there's a gun to your head, why not just accept Him into your life! Why do you agnostic liberals have to make this all so damn complicated?"

"Cause it would be a lie!" she hollered. "I'd just be saving my ass! And a real deity would be smart enough to know that! So, I say 'Pull the trigger, asshole! I won't play that game'." Pavlik returned to the Hummer shaking his head, trying to erase Eden's words from his head like an Etch A Sketch.

"You know what?" he grunted. "I can't explain it to you guys. You ain't ever gonna get it 'less you got faith. For me, my reward is in heaven."

"I heard that, Jimmy," Sabol concluded upon hearing something he could agree with.

After the two of them bumped fists in solidarity, Eden turned at me. "And to think we've put our lives in their hands. Ironic, isn't it?" This brought much delight to the soldiers. They laughed and resumed their card game.

"Damn right, lady," Pavlik laughed. "If the shit hits the fan out there, you'll be lucky to have a man of faith covering your ass."

Gomez, who appeared to have fallen asleep in the corner of the flatbed, lifted his head in hopes the storm had passed. Exhausted, Eden eased back in her seat and exhaled loudly. "Why do I bother?" she lamented.

"Because you're afraid of other people's beliefs," I replied. She twisted her face.

"You're damn right I am," she grunted. "I'm never worried about the hard facts swirling around someone's head. I'm worried about what they think is true."

"I heard that, Eden," I joked quietly and offered up my own fist-bump of solidarity. She declined with a smile.

"God, you're lame" she groaned. At that, I retreated from the crowd. The opium was pulling at my eyelids and I figured we all had enough of the "getting to know you" phase.

My bed that night was pieced together from musty sleeping bags and rolled-up sections of tarp. I constructed my sorry excuse for a nest in the front corner of the cargo hold past the Hummer, as far from the rest of the crew as I could manage. The cold of the metal flooring quickly crept its way through the thin padding and into my spine. Normally, the chill would have twisted my back into knots, but with the tea moving my body into an ecstasy coma, I could've slept upside down in a refrigerator.

Traditionally referred to as the "nods" amongst heroin users, this special state of consciousness lies somewhere between sleep and the waking state. I found the sensation rather pleasant. It was the supreme state of dozing where I was aware just enough to remain conscious of my body in full surrender. The womb didn't feel this safe. The deep, steady rumble of the plane engines induced a low vibration throughout my body that I found sedating; nothing like the nightmarish frequency we were chasing down. Even the wound on the back of my leg was emanating little more than a soft buzzing I couldn't rightly refer to as "pain".

As I drifted deeper into the nods, a dark vision took hold of me. I envisioned I was back home, walking into my kitchen toward my grandmother's old microwave. Something scratched and pounded at the walls from within. As I reached out for the handle, the latch exploded and the door burst from its hinges. A terrible, indiscernible mass leapt at me with a furious rage, snapping me from my trance. It took a long while for my nerves to settle enough to slip back into my coma.

For some reason; now more than ever, I realized the tea wasn't putting me at ease like it was supposed to. I still yearned for something, a deeper sense of safety perhaps. My dope had given me the confidence to step into a danger it could never protect me from.

# Warm Greetings

*"You can not simultaneously believe in spontaneous healing and not in shapeshifting. Meditate on this and you will know the two are inextricably linked."*

Iboga, Shaman of the Craneo Roto clan

**M**y senses snapped back when the rear, hydraulic platform screeched to the tarmac, flooding the cabin with blinding, morning sun. Behind it, a dense wall of humidity permeated the fuselage with the heavy smell of damp earth and pollen. I knew this area of Peru would be hot this time of year, but I was shocked by the suffocating heat. Overcome by claustrophobia, I found myself grabbing my backpack and running down the platform in search of relief.

We had landed at a small military base some fifty kilometers east of the Chambira Basin with a single airstrip cut into dense, green foliage; the same outpost from which Ramirez and his soldiers had dispatched to confront Kane and his missionaries. The base itself was little more than a featureless, concrete building of muted, earthen colors hidden by snaking vines. Had it not been for the massive antennae and satellite dish protruding from the roof and a short row of military jeeps parked along the side, the structure would have been indistinguishable from an abandoned park ranger's station. Around the corner of the base I spied a rusting stash of discarded military equipment, vehicles, even a single-prop airplane. I began to wonder if we landed in a junkyard.

As the propellers wound down, the thrumming of our engines was soon replaced by an orchestra of bird and animal cries from every direction. The moss-drenched palms towering overhead left the impression that we had stepped into a prehistoric landscape. When the rest of the team made their way down the tarmac, we were greeted by the head of operations, a Colonel Panza, a rotund man with a swath of black hair and a thick, Salvador Dali moustache.

"This place is hidden pretty well," Sabol exclaimed, shaking

Panza's hand. "Almost looks like a secret base. Our pilots had a hell of a time making the landing."

"That was the intention," Panza grumbled in a thick, Spanish accent as he escorted us through the gates, "but not our intention. This landing strip was carved by the Quiza drug cartel. It was made for something the size of that old Aeronca Champ there." He indicated one of the small, camouflaged planes covered in rust off to the side. "The cartels grow more bold and ruthless each year. They will stop at nothing to get narcotics into the States, but because our two governments can't seem to agree on how best to deal with criminals and murderers, I suppose this is just our fate here in the 'lower' Americas." He paused, staring into the jungle behind the base.

"The Quiza kidnapped all the young men from one of the Water Basin tribes to clear out the trees and do their shit work. When we finally shut down their operation, we realized we needed an intermediate base deeper in the jungle as the cartels push further into uncontacted territory."

"Uncontacted?" Sabol asked. Tina began to explain the word, but Panza quickly shut her down.

"Tribes that have never had contact with the outside world," he explained sternly. "As far as they're concerned, it's still year one. And there aren't many of them left. It's very dangerous to get close to them. They should be left alone. Especially by outsiders."

"Why they so dangerous?" Pavlik called from the rear of the group. "They cannibals? They gunna shrink our skulls or somethin?" Panza hesitated. Was this idiot serious? He searched Tina for a cue. She shook her head with an eye roll that begged, please ignore him.

"Shut your mouth, colonel," Gomez demanded quietly. Pavlik immediately shrunk back and fell into line.

"Ehh, no, son," Panza replied dismissively as if to a child. "It's for their safety, not ours. We carry viruses they have never had to contend with."

Of course, he was absolutely right. When the Spaniards landed on these shores hundreds of years ago, the Indians' fate was sealed long before the first sword was drawn. When we think of invasions throughout history, the subject of focus is the differences and superiority of the weaponry, the size and organization of battalions. The real fight, the one that consumes the most lives, is the battle that takes place in the immune system in the form of influenza and typhus when people from faraway shores engage each other. Cortez and his meager army of 500 men didn't wrestle the Aztec empire of a million souls to its knees with fancy armament as some versions of history would like us to believe. Smallpox did the work for them.

Because I myself hailed from one of those faraway shores, I decided it best to keep my mouth shut on the subject. Nevertheless, recalling how Flores explained that the Chambira referred to the mysterious forces terrorizing their villages as a "plague" made me feel ill. Throughout ancient Mexico, Central and South America, a few diseases instilled enough fear to send entire cultures running for their lives, abandoning entire cities in a matter of days. Anyone who saw the effects of these plagues firsthand would rather die by sword, and who could blame them? Within a few short weeks of catching smallpox, the blackened, puss-filled skin would begin detaching and sliding off the body in sheets, leaving the victim to bleed out in a slow, agonizing death.

Our team followed Colonel Panza through a quiet control room holding a meager handful of old computers, and into a warm, empty hall. The base didn't appear to be manned by more than a half dozen soldiers. We came to a stop just outside a closed door which Panza unlocked, but not before he paused to address us in a grave tone. Much of his frustration appeared to be directed at Agent Flores.

"If the Craneo Roto do exist, and I believe they do, as does the person behind this door, they're just another uncontacted tribe; uncontacted for good reason," he began slowly, pointedly. "I hope to God you people don't find them. It will only bring more death. And although I have been ordered to cooperate with your government, I will tell you all this: We don't need more Americans here. You've done quite enough." His tone quickly grew darker. "I knew Ramirez for twenty years and whatever happened to him and his men out there was because white people don't know how to mind their own goddamned business. It's an historical problem. Never in my career have I seen men murdered in the manner Ramirez and his troops were."

He slapped his chest. "And I know this land; this is my home. Whatever tore those men apart didn't come from my country, not my jungle. You come here to a people with a culture and history you cannot possibly understand. Every time something terrible has happened here, it's because outsiders are looking for resources of one kind or another; rubber, lumber, a place to hold their cattle. And it never ends. Whatever your missionaries brought to Peru is still here. We're still receiving cries for help from tribes, peaceful villages, all over my territories." Panza leaned in to stare Tina directly in the eye.

"And you should have known better, Agent Flores," he seethed before pulling himself into a professional posture and gesturing to the door. "With that said, the Water Basin tribe say that this is who guided your missionaries through our land. Senora Flores, I understand you speak Quechua, so my duty to your investigation is finished. In case there was any question, it was I who insisted you bring your own transportation and resources into my jurisdiction. All I did was allow you to land here, so I'll let you all see your way out. I assume you have maps of the region. I have work to do. I have more dead tribespeople to deal with." At that, he turned, glared at both Flores and Gomez in disgust and thundered down the hallway.

"Wait!" Tina called after him. "Are you saying natives are still being massacred out there?" Panza didn't answer. He vanished into the operations room and slammed the door.

"Again," I said quietly, "you guys came to us, right?"

"As I suggested, not everyone is pleased with the direction I'm taking this," she admitted.

"Including members of your own team," Eden said with a grin, looking back and forth between me and Pavlik.

"Hey, keep me outta this," Pavlik said sheepishly. "I'm just here to keep you assholes alive."

Tina and I opened the door to find ourselves in an emptied storage room lit solely by candlelight. Sitting cross-legged in the middle of the floor, surrounded by neatly arranged piles of dried leaves and roots, was a young native Indian girl no older than nine, maybe ten. She shot us a glance sizzling with raw, untamed energy, but immediately returned to her work grinding various plants and roots in a wooden bowl with a smooth stone. Clad in leather and highly polished ornaments of bone and hammered silver, her attire appeared to match the Indians' from the video, except for a necklace of red and yellow beads wrapped tightly around the full length of her neck; jewelry that looked African to my untrained eye.

Peeking through the door, Pavlik slapped the back of his hand against Sabol's chest. "What is she? Is she black or what?"

"I'm the race expert, huh?" Sabol said shaking his head. He knelt to take a closer look at her features. "If I had to make a wild guess," he said, mildly irritated. "I would say that beyond her Chambira roots a large percentage of her DNA is central African, Namibia perhaps. But that seems unlikely."

Although her skin and hair looked clean, a faded residue of red and white dyes remained streaked across her face and a rust colored clay coated several strands of her hair. "Hey, sweetie," I said, bending down to greet her. "Is your mom around?" As soon as the words left my mouth, I felt stupid for speaking. She had no idea what I was saying, and I already knew where this was heading. "Shit, this is our guide, isn't it?" I asked rhetorically, rubbing my forehead.

"Is this a problem because she's a native?" Tina replied wryly. Before I could fire back, she slapped me on the shoulder. "I'm kidding," she smiled, patting my cheek. "It's because she's brown, right?"

"It's because she's a child, goddamn it," I whispered.

"Well, we're fucked," Eden sighed, stepping in the room, "Girls are terrible with directions."

# The Thick Abyss

*"Perception colors reality. How many times have we mistaken someone's identity or drawn a conclusion after observing a situation? Our narrow perspectives deceive all too often. When we clear the field, truths develop. However, even then fluidity twists even concrete. Subatomic physics claims that there is no actual, solid matter . . . so what is there? . . . maybe just our consciousness playing out. Let's enjoy the trip."*

Andrew J. Wichlinski

Our pilots fired up the engines minutes after we unloaded the Hummer. Panza refused to allow a plane carrying two American pilots to await our return on his base, so they would have to fly to La Paz until we radioed for an extraction. Evidently, Bolivia was more willing to cooperate with Agent Downey for some reason. With the stress of being in foreign, unwelcome territory weighing on our shoulders, we piled into the military vehicle and left the premises as quickly as possible, with our newest, youngest team member in tow. Shortly after Panza's base disappeared into the foliage at our backs, the gravel roads morphed into dirt trails, which eventually became little more than tire tracks cleaving rugged terrain and tall grass.

The world beyond our military vehicle was intensely alive. Lush moss dripped from every branch, vibrant algae and bacteria carpeted rocks and tree trunks. Somehow, being immersed in the rainforest made it easier to breathe; that, or I was adapting to being near sea level once again. I occasionally let my mind slip from the suffocating heat as my awe with the vast biology around me intensified.

Road conditions limited our speed to 25 miles per hour, which didn't provide enough air current through any window for relief. I considered asking if the AC worked, but I didn't want to be the high maintenance tourist. I felt out of place enough. Everyone, even the child, appeared better equipped than I for this environment. My profuse sweating was an obvious indication of my sad, physical shape, and my body always took full advantage of any humidity to flush out toxins.

"Akaylahshantisumvhardi," the child replied when Tina asked for her name. Luckily, we were allowed to refer to her as simply "Kay-lah." Kaylah situated herself on the floorboards behind the front seats and continued her work grinding her dried plants into a powder. She had now accumulated several cups worth of this mixture in a leather shoulder satchel. Although Tina seemed to grasp the girl's particular dialect of Quechua, Kaylah would only reply with brief, vague answers.

Frustrated with her inability to identify the herbs, Eden finally asked Tina to question our guide about the concoction she was working on.

"She says she's making an offering so that we may pass into the land of the Craneo Roto," Tina replied. "She says she still needs to find one more ingredient so that the Dreaming Tree will accept us into her roots. Besides that, she'll only say that we need to hurry. The waters are rising and we're running out of time."

"Any idea what that means?" I asked.

"Besides the fact that we're moving into the rainy season? None. She instructed us to head north of the basin for now."

Kaylah spoke quietly in her native tongue near Tina's ear before briefly glancing up at Eden.

"She said the Roto clan is expecting us. Her mother needs to bring balance to the horrors that Kane has unleashed," Tina explained with a blank expression, as baffled by the response as we were.

"Ask her about her knowledge of the Roto," Eden suggested. Tina leaned down and questioned the girl. Kaylah answered without looking up from her work.

"Or where her parents are?" I added to no reply.

"She said her grandmother taught her how to 'rest in the blossoms of the Dreaming Tree' before she passed on. Now, she is the last soul on this continent who knows how to reach the Craneo Roto," Tina explained. "She says she has contact with a number of hidden realms including the one where the Roto reside."

Realms? I began wondering if the girl was delusional or

just being a typical, imaginative kid, but I kept my thoughts to myself. For all I knew, she had no idea where we were going and had never met Kane or his people. Regardless, the girl was making me uneasy. There was nothing childlike about any of her mannerisms.

"Why did she take Kane to the Roto clan in the first place?" I asked. The girl's response to my question appeared to confuse Tina more so than the others.

"Because Kane and his people were dying," Tina translated. "The Rotos were the only ones who could heal them."

Even if I doubted the veracity of Kaylah's information, I found some comfort in the idea that the people we were seeking were healers of some sort. If they did, in fact, exist. "Do we have anything to fear from the Roto clan?" I asked. Before Tina had even finished translating my question, Kaylah exploded into laughter. It was the first expression of emotion we had seen from her, and I desperately wanted to know what it meant. Upon composing herself, Kaylah offered a final word on the topic.

"She says the Craneo Roto shaman are perfectly safe," Tina explained. "They will only tear your world apart."

"You do know what 'Craneo Roto' means?" Eden asked with a devilish smirk, nudging my shoulder. She knew damn well I didn't.

"Broken Skull," she whispered in my ear with delight. I tried to ignore this novel information and focus on what brought me here. If Damian and Kyle were right, there was an electronic device at the heart of this nightmare; a device that could level this quantum field of theirs, and all particle organization along with it. I hung my head out the window and gaped at the green landscape beyond. How a bunch of shaman were connected with technology like this, I couldn't begin to fathom.

Five hours of unforgiving terrain later, I awoke from a hazy nap when Sergeant Gomez slowed the vehicle to a crawl in a sandy clearing. Half a kilometer ahead, the flat terrain abruptly exploded into another wall of dense vegetation where the road forked into three directions. The gravel-covered path on our far left led to a wooden bridge over a ravine where a pale green pickup emerged on the far end of the overpass, at the very least proving the bridge was in some degree of working condition. Short of a couple of mopeds, it was the only sign of human life in this region. The other two roadways ahead appeared similar to what we had been rolling over: Little more than tire tracks snaking their way into dark brush below a thick, green canopy.

We came to a complete stop several meters before the fork. When Gomez killed the engine, the high-pitched hum of a billion insects arose from the wall of jungle ahead. After a brief pause we all turned to face Tina, who finally realized our predicament.

"Should I go cut us a dowsing rod?" Eden asked, surveying the landscape. She suddenly grew very excited about the view from her window. In the middle of the clearing just off the road stood a sole cactus with yellow flowers at least three meters high.

"Oh, shit! That's a San Pedro!" Eden hollered.

Kaylah leapt up to the window next to her and exclaimed, "Pani!"

Before Tina could ask our young guide for directions, the first in a series of violent crashes thundered through the Hummer, catapulting everyone to the left side of the vehicle. We all tried to catch our bearings when a heavy, metallic grinding screamed through the cabin with deafening roars as the driver's side of the truck thrust several feet into the air before slamming back to the ground. The final collision threw me face-first onto the floorboards next to Kaylah who had curled herself into a tight ball. I could hear Tina shouting above me and the rumbling of another large engine just beyond the door.

"Nine o'clock!" Sabol shouted to Pavlik in the rear cab. "Nine o'clock! Everyone stay down!" I lifted myself onto hands and knees, trying to understand what was happening when I realized Eden had slammed her head into the window. She was dazed but didn't appear injured. I scanned the cabin to find Gomez with a trickle of blood running down his temple while Tina fumbled for her sidearm in my peripheral. Eden absentmindedly began pulling herself up before I dragged her down to the floor next to Kaylah.

I peeked out the window to find the front bumper of a pale green pickup buried into our sidewall. A small team of men were leaping from the flatbed. Soldiers?, I thought: My brain ambushed by disjointed information. Through the commotion, I struggled to register the men's features: jet-black hair, high cheekbones. They wore T-shirts, ball caps, jeans and each brandished an automatic rifle. Jesus, these are armed civilians. The driver of the pickup outside our door struggled to throw his vehicle into reverse, but the front end was tangled with our side panel. He cursed loudly in Spanish as his rear tires spun angrily in the sand.

"He's trying to break free to ram us again!" Gomez shouted. "Front axle's blown! Pavlik, get them out of here!"

Outside, a half-dozen men had now scattered around the perimeter of our truck. Suddenly, Pavlik and Sabol rolled from the passenger's side into a storm of gunfire. The noise was unbearable, rapid explosions followed what sounded like hammers beating against the metal exterior. Gomez tried to restart the engine while firing his pistol through the window at our assailants, transforming the air into a spinning fury of blasts and metallic ricochets.

My body froze, I dared not move. In the next moment, I found Pavlik dragging me by my collar through the passenger door, flat onto my back onto the sand. When I looked up to find Sabol and Pavlik take cover near the front tire, Kaylah led Tina far from the truck behind the wide base of the lone cactus Eden had spied. As soon as they made cover, Tina shielded the child with her body.

Before I could catch my bearings, Sabol and Pavlik signaled each other and simultaneously launched to their feet to unleash a hellfire of bullets over the Hummer's hood. My body automatically contracted and I rolled into a low, kneeling position, while poorly avoiding the searing hot casings showering around me. From under the vehicle, I glimpsed several of our attackers dash behind their truck and dive over a large, downed tree trunk for cover. Gomez gave up recovering the engine and focused on firing his pistol through the driver's window, sending two Indians to a sudden, bloody death.

I had never witnessed someone killed in real life. I couldn't even recall seeing a gun fired in my presence. It was surreal and far more mechanical than I imagined, like watching a plug pulled from a socket. My heart rate skyrocketed as bullets slammed into the truck's side panels and blasted our windows and mirrors into a powder. A high-pitched duet of explosions shook the Hummer when the tires on the far side blew out. In a crazed panic, I scanned our desolate surroundings: Nothing but sand and low rising brush; nowhere to hide. And Eden was nowhere in sight.

When Sabol stopped to reload he screamed, "I couldn't pull Jessup from the backseat! You need to pull her out!"

Without thinking, I crawled between the two soldiers, ducked my head through the back door and searched the shredded cabin. Laid out on the seats on the far end of the truck, huddled in a fetal position was Eden, panicked and shaking with terror. I shouted her name over the metallic ping of bullets. She didn't respond. Her body just kept trembling. Oh, God, no. Not now.

Staying low, I stretched out my hand to grab hold of the scruff of her T-shirt. With all my strength I managed to slide her closer to me over the vinyl seats. Nuggets of glass zipped everywhere as the windows gave way and indentations in the side panels spread like wildfire around us. As I tugged again, Eden's neck arched backward and her eyes fluttered chaotically. Only then was I sure she wasn't shaking from fear; she had entered a full blown seizure.

My adrenaline exploded and I yanked at her collar, pulled her from the truck, into my lap and down into the dirt. With shaking hands I searched for any suitable object to shove between her teeth. Short of preventing her from tearing out her own tongue, there was nothing I could do for her. The piercing gunfire began drowning beneath an echo of high-pitched ringing as my eardrums reached their limit. I spotted the military-issue knife dangling from Sabol's utility belt and snatched it from its sheath. The soldier was too focused on the gunfight to notice. I shoved the leather-wrapped handle sideways into her jaw and stuffed my jacket under her head. Pavlik leapt to the ground beside me to reload. "Keep her behind the tire!" he shouted. "Even if it blows out, keep her here!"

As soon as he leapt back into action, a deep thud rang through the air like a baseball bat into a leather couch. Pavlik's feet launched upwards and his body went airborne. I spun around to see him land flat onto his back behind me. He let out a low, agonized wail and clutched the center of his chest. That's a really bad area of the body to be shot in, was my first thought as I dragged him by his ankle from the line of fire.

"Jimmy!" Sabol shouted, trying not to pull his attention from the numerous targets closing in. "Talk to me, brother!" Gomez crawled out from the passenger door and tumbled onto the ground next to me. He reloaded his pistol and slammed a plastic med kit into my stomach.

"You gotta help him!" he hollered before leaping up to join Sabol. Without thinking, I crawled on my belly to inspect Pavlik as he gasped for air, gripping his chest. I knelt over him and grabbed his wrists while he struggled.

"Let me see!" I shouted. He strained in agony to tear his fists from his bloodied chest. I ripped off the Velcro holding his body armor, grabbed his knife, and sliced through his shirt. A red, dime-sized spot in the center of his breastplate quickly grew into a purple, blotched mass. It took but a moment to comprehend what I was seeing. His vest had only partially stopped the bullet from passing through, but the tip of the slug had broken the skin and snapped the soft cartilage along the center of his rib cage.

"You're going to be okay!" I yelled at him. But, goddamned is this going to hurt. I tore open the med kit and fumbled through gauze, arm slings, aspirin, and creams to find butterfly bandages, blood-clotting powder, and field-grade Lidocain patches. I doused the wound with powder, pulled it closed, and dressed it. "Keep pressure on this!" I shouted.

Locked into the lid of the kit I found a syringe and three glass vials, one of which was labeled "Morphine". I fought to ignore the brief excitement that we were packing liquid opiates. After a quick calculation of Pavlik's weight and blood pressure, I jammed the needle into the bottle and loaded 30ccs. As I worked, I realized the gunfire hadn't slowed overhead. Closer to the truck, Eden continued to convulse, but was still hidden behind the tire.

I turned back to see Tina struggling to keep Kaylah low to the ground. Oddly enough, the girl was using one of Tina's blades to hack away at one of the lower arms of the cactus they were using as cover. With the speed and precision of a hummingbird, Kaylah removed a small chuck of the flesh, skinned it, chopped it into tiny bits, and then crammed as much as she could manage into her mouth. Tina flew into hysterics as the girl escaped her grip and darted across the clearing—chewing vigorously as she ran—past me, past Pavlik's body, and over to Eden. This forced Gomez and Sabol to suddenly reposition to cover the child's movements.

"What the fuck is she doing?" Gomez hollered. Kaylah came to a skidding halt at Eden's side, pulled the knife from her mouth, tilted her chin backward, pried open her jaw and, to my utter shock, regurgitated a juicy slosh of cactus mush directly into Eden's open mouth. She then returned the blade handle back between Eden's teeth and deftly sprinted to her hiding place under Tina's protection. Bullets pelted the sand around her every step.

From my unique angle further back from the Hummer, I spied two of the natives make their way to the far end of the downed tree trunk. It occurred that if they went unnoticed by Gomez and Sabol for a few moments longer they could easily make their way to our side of the truck. Without a plan, I picked up Pavlik's machine gun.

"Sabol!" I shouted with all my force. It was no use; my voice was a whisper beneath a sea of explosions. I clumsily pawed at the rifle, trying to find the proper grip and positioning. It was lighter than I imagined, but its flat-black, serious-looking construction was intimidating.

Pavlik reached out and wheezed next me, "I just reloaded. There's no safety. Flip the dial on the right side to 'semi', look through the scope, put the red dot on your target, and pull the fucking trigger. Aim for anything in the upper torso."

I looked up and found the two assailants readying themselves for an ambush on Sabol and Gomez. Panicked, I flipped the weapon onto its side and did as instructed: I turned the knob from "auto" to "semi," only half-aware I was still shouting Sabol's name at the top of my lungs. I shoved the butt of the rifle into my shoulder and peered through the scope. It only took a moment to center the glowing red dot on one of the native's heads. Can it be that easy? Could I just pull this trigger and end this person? On who's authority do I take a man's life?

"Do it, goddamn it!" Pavlik coughed at my feet. "They're not gonna hesitate to murder us!" As I doubted my next move, the most peculiar realization washed over me, followed by an intense burst of consciousness. I became aware of the trajectory of every single body in motion within my vicinity. I could clearly see the impacts and debris from the many bullets, but my train of thought had become foreign. Indeed, thoughts continued to stream through my mind, but it was all noise; a chaotic jumble of synaptic firings. Somehow, none of it had anything to do with me.

With that, an odd, quiet bliss emerged from a hidden place. Drugs don't make men this high. With a clear head, I lifted the barrel of Pavlik's gun to take aim and I watched helplessly as the two men slipped around our Hummer, leapt over Eden, and tackled Sabol from the side.

And this is what bliss gets you, you fucking idiot.

I immediately resumed my previous state of unhinged panic. The three men wrestled briefly before one of the natives slammed his rifle across Sabol's temple, instantly rendering him unconscious. I ran forward for a closer aim as Gomez spun to discover the commotion at his feet. With a thundering crack, Gomez swiftly fired his pistol into the forehead of one of the men. The sight was terrifying and grotesque. The native's head snapped backward, instantly collapsing his body. I tried to process all the stimuli and stiffened to a mere witness to all the horrors.

Before Gomez could take down the second attacker, the driver of the pickup leapt over the Hummer's hood and slammed his rifle into the back of his head, sending Gomez to a heap on the ground.

A third man with blood seeping from his brow bolted around our truck and jammed his barrel into Gomez' chest. All three of them shouted furious orders in Spanish before Gomez raised his hands in the air and surrendered his pistol with a small thud. And everything went quiet.

Somehow, my presence had not yet been noticed. I was the only one on our team still brandishing a weapon. This is it. If I don't act now—right now—we're all going to die.

"Stop thinking!" Pavlik hissed near my feet. "Just shoot those motherfuckers." I've always relied on my intellect to navigate danger. I always had the benefit of time to form a strategy. I didn't know how to simply act. From my far right, one of the men began dragging Tina and Kaylah from behind the cactus as the other forced Gomez to his knees. The driver of the pickup suddenly made burning eye contact with me: a short, barrel-chested man plastered with grizzly, tribal brands and faded tattoos. My chest turned to ice. "Shoot him you pussy," Pavlik whispered angrily.

Ever so steadily, the driver approached me while removing a pistol from behind his back. My weapon was still raised, but he continued moving forward until the tip of my barrel pushed into his throat. The man was at least a foot shorter than me and positively chilling. He seemed charged head to toe with anger; every muscle in his face, neck and arms rippled with a ferocious intensity. He searched my eyes and found nothing to be intimidated by. With a dismissive swipe of his hand, he snatched the rifle from my grip and, on the return swing, smacked the butt of it across my cheek. My knees buckled and I sank into the ground, not so much from the impact but from humiliation and defeat. Pavlik growled a list of insults from the dirt next to me. "Goddamned, tree-huggin, liberal, atheist, faggot, motherfu . . . "

After aggressively smacking Sabol back into consciousness, the three surviving natives forced us to kneel in the sand with hands locked behind our heads, including Pavlik, who agonized to remain upright. Eden still lay unconscious just a few yards in front of us. The most violent spasms seemed to have passed, leaving her body intermittently twitching and contracting. Our captors didn't know what to make of her condition, so for the time being, they ignored her.

The driver, who his two cohorts referred to as "Alto," tore through our equipment and supplies in the Hummer, throwing every electronic device to the ground while the other men loomed over us. They bashed in our radios and crushed our satellite phones under their boots and against rocks. All the while, we could hear the groans and wheezes of at least two other natives on the far side of the truck who were suffering nonfatal wounds.

Upon exiting the shredded Hummer, "Alto" kicked Eden hard in the side. When she didn't respond, he kicked her again with more force. I cringed with anger and Kaylah whimpered next to me as if she felt the blow herself. When Eden continued not to respond, he paced back and forth before his hostages.

"Who is in charge of this operation?" he demanded in rough English. Tina cleared her trembling throat.

"I'm agent Tina Flores from the National Police. You've attacked a peaceful operation from your own government. You've . . . "

"My government?" he interrupted, laughing angrily. He spat while he growled at her. "I have no government. Where are you going?"

"We're investigating the murder of innocent civilians and soldiers in the Chambira basin," she replied. The driver resumed his pacing.

"Those people were not innocent," he said quietly, barely

containing his rage. "And you did not answer me." He leaned into Kaylah's face. When the girl lowered her watering eyes, Alto angrily grabbed her by the hair and yanked her head backward.

"Kastillanuta rimankichu?!" he shouted at her. She shook her head. "I know who you are," he sneered. "You're taking them to the shaman? You're a little troublemaker, much like your grandmother, aren't you? Where is it!?" He shook her head violently with his fist. "I know your ancestors trained you to keep your mouth shut, but I will make you speak! Where is the Beyul now? We know it changes locations. Tell me or you'll never speak again."

Beyul? Eden had used that word before.

"Ripuykuy!" Kaylah shouted.

"Leave her alone, you coward," Tina demanded. "What do you want from us? We're no threat to you!".

Alto knelt before Tina to stare fire into her eyes. He caressed her cheek before reaching down to squeeze her throat. "Not a threat?" he asked, releasing Kaylah from his grip to jam his revolver under Tina's chin. "You killed four of my men, and that little shit is taking you to the Craneo Roto because you seek knowledge. Knowledge, not faith. You would stop the return of Yahweh upon this earth."

"Yahweh?" Tina muttered. "That's not your religion."

"Reverend Kane warned us someone would come," he replied. "He knew the godless would come here seeking his power next." Realization drew heavily that these men were Kane's faithful converts from his months of preaching in the region. A silence hung in the air until Alto stepped away, knelt to one knee and unclipped an old, military walkie-talkie from his belt.

"Señora Giddeon," he called into the receiver. Several moments later a muffled, female voice hissed from the speaker.

"You have them?"

"Si,"

"And the child?" the woman asked.

"Si, señora."

More static over the receiver followed by dead quiet. "Will

she speak?"

"No, señora. The Beyul's location would not have been passed down if she would speak so easily. We could torture her. But, even so, I would not trust anything she said." Further silence.

"Dispose of them," the voice concluded.

"Si, señora." At that, Alto rose to his feet and addressed his men. "We'll pile the bodies back in the truck. They'll say it was the Quiza."

My mind raced for a solution. I looked into the eyes of the brainwashed man hovering above our little team huddled in the dirt and found nothing but hatred. I would not talk my way out of this, not this time. My intelligence was useless here. Alto walked around to our backs, directly behind Sabol positioned at the far end of the line. His intent was clear. He would murder us one by one, execution style. Alto pushed the muzzle of his pistol into the back of Sabol's head.

"You have no honor," Gomez said firmly, kneeling next to Sabol. "At least let the women go. Don't kill us like animals."

"This is nothing compared to what comes next for you," Alto growled, holding his gaze on Gomez as he pulled the hammer back.

Sabol muttered, "How about you put down that gun and face me as a man." Alto chuckled. And then squeezed the trigger. The gunshot exploded with a deafening crack and a spray of sand launched into the air near Sabol's right knee. The shot missed the soldier's head by an inch. Slowly, Alto lowered himself to Sabol's left ear.

"Face you like a man?" he said quietly. "What makes you think I'm a man? Ending your lives with a bullet was mercy, soldier. I don't need a gun. If you want to face me, it'll be with my true face." Alto muscled Sabol to his feet and led him forcefully behind the truck. Before they disappeared, he barked a final order to his men: "Execute them." The two remaining Indians moved behind us with their rifles.

With Kaylah's arms wrapped around her waist, Tina quietly wept and apologized under her breath. The men readied their weapons as she turned to me with swollen eyes. "I'm so sorry," she whispered. "I had no idea." The men raised their barrels to the back of our heads and, just before I closed my eyes, I noticed Eden regain consciousness, and my heart sank even lower. She came around just in time to see us murdered right in front of her.

"En tres," one of the men ordered. On three. Still laying flat on her back, Eden lifted her hands to her face and studied them.

"Uno," the man counted behind me. Eden appeared confused, then mesmerized as she wiggled her fingers in fascination. "Dos."

Eden smiled and threw her hands to her sides. "Ahhh," she mumbled with the knife still between her teeth, "I'm dreaming!" (although, with a mouth full of blade handle, it sounded more like, "Eye Threaming"). Still on her back, she looked to her side to see me on the verge of execution. Eden raised her eyes and winced at the men taking aim behind us. "Oh, you fuckheads are toast," she mumbled. And that's the second time it happened: Another event that would unhinge my mind.

In a glorious contradiction of physics, or rather, in a vile insult to the forces of gravity and propulsion, an equally invisible and impossible explosive appeared to detonate directly beneath Eden, blasting her body straight into the air. She spun into a lopsided axis before landing in a savage, crouching stance: A mountain lion prepared to pounce.

"Lo que la cogida?" one of the men behind me mumbled.

Like a weightless rocket, Eden launched herself directly toward us, four, maybe five meters through the air, and sailed just above our heads. As she passed, she pulled the blade from her teeth and sliced the man's throat standing just behind me. We all spun around to see the wounded Indian begin to collapse while his partner fumbled his aim toward her. Eden alighted to the earth amongst an explosion of rapid gunfire as the gunman haphazardly unleashed his weapon. With the speed of a humming bird, she spun and shielded herself behind the falling Indian she had just dispatched. Just before both of their bodies met the ground, Eden whipped the knife out from behind her human shield in a powerful, spinning beeline. The knife whizzed through the air as if it were on a rail. With a splatter, the blade burrowed directly into the other man's eye socket. He clutched wildly at his face, swinging the barrel aimlessly.

With yet another explosion of energy, Eden leapt into a dizzyingly wide arc directly onto his chest while simultaneously pulling the weapon from his skull and slamming him to his back. With both hands gripping the handle, she reached high into the air and pounded the blade into his heart. She kept twisting until every muscle in the man's body stopped twitching. Blood dripped in long threads from her hands, forearms, chin, and hair.

"The driver!" Gomez whispered loudly, pointing beyond the Hummer. "He took Sabol!".

Perched like a starved animal atop her prey, Eden placed a finger to her pursed lips. "Shhhhh," she whispered, leaving a bloody slash across her mouth. With careless ease, she slipped off her shoes, snatched up the dead man's rifle, and leapt over the Hummer's hood without a sound.

And that was the second time I heard it.

The moment Eden vanished from sight, the horrible frequency penetrated our ears with its gut-wrenching orchestra. Even though the sound filled every cubic centimeter of space, it seemed to emanate from just behind the truck. The thunderous vibration was even more agonizing in real life. Everyone doubled onto their sides from the engulfing sound waves. Before I could comprehend what was taking place, Gomez forced himself to his feet, grabbed the dead man's rifle and chased after Eden.

Just as the rest of us struggled to stand, another round of automatic gunfire rang out, bringing the frequency to a sudden halt. For a few moments, everything went still. Nothing stirred; not the birds, not the insects.

In a confused panic, I sprinted around the wreckage of the Hummer to an insane sight: A half dozen bodies of bloody locals were draped over tree trunks, strewn over rocks, and laid out on the sand. Most of them appeared to have fallen under our soldier's bullets. Jesus, maybe Panza was right.

Trapped in a thick haze, I was still hearing gunfire when I found Sabol near my feet. He lay on the ground curled into a ball, screaming in horror into his chest, out of his mind from shock. I shuddered trying to imagine what would drive the soldier to this level of hysterics. Just beyond him, Eden and Gomez were madly firing at something escaping over rock and sand toward the wall of jungle in the distance. I turned my attention to Eden and gawked, wondering how her stance and command of her rifle appeared to rival that of the trained soldier standing beside her. Gomez was firing wildly on full-automatic while Eden fired in controlled, three-round bursts.

Several moments passed before I decided their target was indeed human, and not animal. Although their target wore the same attire as the pickup driver, Alto, this person was enormous, even at a distance; almost twice his size. His movements were unnatural, like watching some four-legged creature forced to run for its life as a biped. In my current state of shock, however, I couldn't trust what I was seeing. Several streams of blood poured from bullet wounds down the back of Alto's shirt and, just before he disappeared beneath the canopy of trees Eden made a direct hit to the man's upper leg, but it didn't slow his progress. When he vanished from sight, Gomez stopped firing. Eden did not, or perhaps could not.

After several more rounds, a sliding mechanism on the top of her rifle snapped backward and her trigger clicked without report. Realizing she was out of ammo, she threw the weapon into the sand, swiped the knife from Gomez's belt and darted toward the jungle. Gomez snagged her by the waist just before she dashed out of reach, sending them both crashing to the ground. He threw his weapon aside to free both arms to hold her back, a struggle that required all of his strength. She had become total, unbridled power. I stared at the furious energy kicking and fighting to break free of the soldier's powerful grip and didn't recognize it. This wasn't the woman I had known half my life; this was some unrestrained force wearing Eden's skin. Her tattoos weren't even recognizable; somehow, they seemed to have come alive.

"Professor Jessup, calm yourself!" Gomez hollered as he tried and failed again and again to pin her arms to her sides. "That man won't live through the day. We put too many bullets into him."

"No!" Eden roared. "We need to kill it while we still can! We have to send it back!"

"Professor Jessup!" Gomez shouted.

"Professor Jessup is asleep!" she hollered in a voice that wasn't quite her own. Impossibly enough, she began lifting her arms away from her sides, overpowering the soldier's hold. "Don't make me hurt you!" she growled.

"Eden!" I shouted. I leapt down, forcing her to make direct eye contact with me. "Your name is Eden Jessup!" She glanced at me and recognition flooded back to her eyes. Her body went limp and she slipped between Gomez's arms. I caught her head before it hit the ground.

Her eyelids slowly closed, but not before she quietly asked, "Mike, are we safe?"

"Um, well," I stuttered. "We are now, yes." Satisfied by my response, she fell out of consciousness. In turn, Gomez collapsed backward with a heavy sigh of relief.

# Reconfiguration

*"From the perspective of the thinking mind, Enlightenment is the essence of boredom. It isn't attractive, sexy, exciting, or even interesting. Rather, it is far more dangerous. It is supreme knowing and contentment. And that frightens the absolute hell out of the limited world of thought. It will run from it in a thousand and one ways and will waste lifetimes of your energy trying to convince you to remain forever preoccupied with trivialities."*

Sadhu of the Craneo Roto clan

After pulling ourselves together the best we could, we attempted to hold a rational discussion as to our next move. All of our radios and phones were bashed to pieces, and the truck was totaled. It seemed our only viable option at this point was to admit defeat, endure the day-and-a-half walk-of-shame back to Panza's base, and head back to the States.

While Kaylah busied herself with hacking at one of the larger arms of the cactus, she explained to Tina offhandedly that our truck would have soon been useless to us anyway. She said from here we needed to head into the lowlands just north of the basin to an area with no roads or encampments.

I couldn't believe what I was hearing. We had almost been executed, in over our heads and laughably ill-equipped for this mission; whatever the hell it was about. Eden still hadn't awoken and from my estimation, the only reason Pavlik was able to stand was due to the morphine I had filled him with. Sabol was now in a catatonic state and Gomez discovered, at the very least, he could get him to follow basic commands by shouting an order at him. Whatever Sabol had seen had shaken him beyond the ability to communicate. He sat on the bumper of the Hummer staring at the ground, shaking his head. Neither Tina nor Gomez could make sense of it, either. Before I could voice my many burning concerns about moving further into the jungle in our collective condition, Kaylah spoke up.

"She says we have to move forward; our lives depend on it." Tina translated. "She says Eden will be okay, that she's 'reconfiguring' to account for a massive imbalance of energy."

"Whatever that means," I replied angrily.

"We could carry Professor Jessup until she comes around," Gomez considered.

"She needs a hospital," I grunted. "This is insane. Even your own men are in no condition for this." From the look on Tina's face, she agreed. Her concern deepened the more she studied Sabol in his frozen, seated posture.

"What did that man, Alto, do to him?" Tina asked. Gomez shook his head.

"I've only worked with Sabol a few times," Gomez explained. "But, he served four years in Iraq. I know he's seen action up close. I don't know what this is. By the time I came around the truck, Wonder Woman here (gesturing to Eden) was already firing at Alto, and Sabol was already huddled in a ball."

"Yeah, well, superheroes aren't real, so what the fuck was that?" Pavlik demanded under slightly drugged speech. "She landed that blade into that fucker's eye from a dozen feet away, while falling."

"While hiding behind the other man," Gomez added. "I've known maybe one other person who could have made that shot. What kind of training does she have?"

"Training!" I laughed. "She's a fucking college professor!" I tried not to run calculations in my head while studying the distance between where Eden had been seizing and where we had been held captive in the dirt: A five-meter jump from a stationary position. I found myself wondering what the world record for that was. My thoughts churned back and forth, uncertain which discordant piece of information should take priority.

And there was something else that didn't make any sense, which I decided to keep to myself: I was looking at six dead natives, four of whom had clearly died from gunshot blasts to the head or chest. But two of the men had only tertiary wounds. One had a superficial hole in his upper thigh and another had taken a shot to the inside shoulder. Damage like that doesn't kill a man in a manner of minutes. While I conducted a brief examination on one of the bodies in question, I heard Sabol whimper to himself, "That man Alto took their souls." I approached him, desperate for information.

"What does that mean?" I demanded. "Why did you say that?" The young man lifted his head and stared at me in quiet horror.

"They gave their souls to him," he whispered. "That's how those two men died. I watched it happen. They willingly surrendered to him." It would be the last he would say on the matter.

"The driver was taking orders from a woman he referred to as Señora Giddeon over his radio, Tina reminded us. "That can't be coincidence. Kane brought four missionaries with him to Peru: Christopher Aldon, who you had the pleasure of meeting (nodding to me), Corey Bowen, Tim Braun, and Charlene Giddeon. We were told the only members of the church who survived the attack here were Kane and Aldon. I think it's clear that's bullshit."

"Wait," I interrupted. I had been theorizing how the pickup driver must have escaped with the mysterious "frequency device" in hand when I realized I was worried about the wrong piece of electronics. "Did that man Alto still have his walkie-talkie on his belt when he escaped?" I asked.

"I believe so, yes," Gomez admitted, shaking his head. "Fuck." It wasn't long before everyone realized my point. Whichever direction we were heading in, we needed to move fast.

We collected what water, food and gear we could carry from the truck as Gomez ordered Sabol to his feet and threw a pack around his shoulders bearing the few pieces of electronics that may still be of some use. Although the casing of the satellite phone was badly damaged, Gomez thought Sabol may be able to repair it once he was operating normally again, assuming the soldier ever came back to his senses. The only other devices that survived were a small GPS unit, a few flashlights, and a laptop Sabol had been carrying in his backpack loaded with a copy of the original video footage containing the frequency. At this point, I didn't care to ask why Tina decided to bring it along.

As we attempted to head out, we had some difficulty pulling Kaylah from her work on the cactus branch. The girl had carefully removed and skinned one of the arms to chop it into small chunks, just as she had before.

"She says it's the last ingredient we need to travel to the Roto clan," Tina said and hesitated before speaking again. "Eden was right. That is a San Pedro cactus. It's used in religious ceremonies by many of the tribes here. Highly hallucinogenic. Kaylah says the cactus is the one who is responsible for saving our lives. She says it saw we needed help and it chose to intervene."

"Oh, it chose that, did it?" I grunted.

With Tina at the helm under Kaylah's navigation, we continued into the jungle with a pile of bodies and wreckage in our wake. Gomez managed to order Sabol to assist him in carrying Eden in a makeshift stretcher. I had done what I could to wash the blood from her hands and face, but the stains were persistent.

Without road or trail underfoot, we moved into muddy terrain that gradually sloped downward. Progress was slow as Tina slashed away at low hanging vines and twisting branches. There were times when we were pelted by a continuous shower of flowers and twigs from her machete. Although it was the middle of the afternoon, there was barely enough light to navigate. The thick, green ceiling of enormous leaves allowed for only the occasional sunbeam to sneak through.

"Those weren't just brainwashed villagers," Tina explained as I followed her lead. "Their leader, Alto, I recognized the brandings on his chest and shoulders. He was a Brujo, a shaman trained in black magic. They can be hired as hit men, but this wasn't just another job for them. They believed killing us was the moral thing to do."

"Shamanic hit men?" I asked incredulously, "I thought they were healers."

"Usually," she replied. "They say that sometimes when a man of knowledge sees the root of the powers he is working with, he doesn't choose to use it for healing. Those men back there were choking on their own anger. It's a miracle we're still alive. Kane has gone through considerable effort to erase his steps out here. That's a good sign." She surmised my confusion from the shock on my face. "It means they think we could be a threat to them; we're onto something. Clearly, they don't want us to find the Roto."

I wasn't sure if Kane was directly behind all of this or if he just had a way of leaving a lot of confused and dedicated followers in his wake. It certainly wouldn't have been the first time such a thing happened in the history of religion.

After hours of trudging through heavy brush on a slow decent, out of nowhere Eden reached out and weakly grabbed at my wrist from her stretcher. "Mike" she whispered and we all came to an immediate halt. Her irises were drowning behind dilated pupils. Gomez and Sabol carefully lowered her to the ground as I knelt beside her.

"Am I still dreaming?" she asked. I searched the group for suggestions for an adequate response and found nothing but blank faces. Eden's face gently twisted with anxiety. "I think . . . I feel like I killed someone. It's like . . . I can smell death on me."

Her eyes drooped and her head fell to the side as she began to fade once more. Before she lost consciousness, she mumbled one, final phrase; an arrangement of words that frightened me nearly as much as her killing spree. "The Christians are right," she whispered, "I've been so blind."

When I gave up trying to revive her, we continued along our path through unrelenting rainforest. I worried we had made a terrible choice and feared the worst. Maybe Eden was suffering brain damage and I was actively killing her by not seeking medical attention. For some reason, I had allowed a child to assure me that Eden was "okay," a child who thought it best to feed a seizing woman a powerful hallucinogen. But it was all fine because Eden was just "reconfiguring". Maybe I was suffering brain damage.

The farther we moved, the less dense the jungle became and more patches of blue sky opened overhead. My back and knees ached terribly. I wasn't habituated to extended physical discomfort. I was raised in a world where temperature and humidity was altered with the flip of a switch. In the uncontrolled wild it was painfully obvious: my compulsive need to control my environment over to my physical body via chemicals was simply a matter of time.

At some point I gave up trying to wipe the sweat from my forehead. It was impossible to tell how much of my misery was from the transition I was making from the tea down to the pharmaceuticals, or simply from excessive strain and heat. Each time I stared at the pocket on Pavlik's backpack where I saw him stash the morphine, I cursed myself. I knew that morphine would pack a punch far stronger than my pills, but I fought to push those troublesome thoughts aside, chewed up another OxyContin and forced my attention onto just how much I knew about the strange woman swinging on the stretcher before me.

Eden and I had known each other for years, but short of her cherished memories of the cottage in Michigan, she rarely spoke of her childhood, or her family for that matter. All I did know was that her mother and father were both college professors who strongly encouraged her curiosity. Her mother was a zoologist who researched social structures of predatory animals, but it must have been her father who inspired her academically. The man had been intently fascinated with aboriginal cultures and their religious beliefs. In the 1970s, he conducted a number of highly controversial experiments at Harvard where he placed students in isolation tanks after feeding them massive amounts of LSD.

Later in his life, he had become devoutly Christian, a turn no one anticipated. He started reading the Bible and attending church services twice a week. It was Eden's opinion that he simply saw too much, that he'd traveled the farthest reaches of reality and found it cold and empty. The Bible provided him a direction, it put his mind at ease. Perhaps it filtered down all that troublesome curiosity that got him into trouble in the first place. He even began preaching to Eden about her "lifestyle choices." I remember more than one occasion in college where

Eden slammed her phone into a wall after a heated debate with her father concerning her "moral scope." Yet, none of that explained what we had just witnessed.

The team stopped to rest at the edge of a steep, muddy cliff that disappeared into a low-lying blanket of white mist below. I had no idea there were still even lower valleys ahead. A steady rush of water could be heard emanating from somewhere beneath the fog, but it remained out of sight. Kaylah said we needed to climb down the side of the cliff and then follow the river hidden below the clouds upstream "until the sun sets."

A roll of thunder boomed through the valley to the west as we studied the near 90-degree ledge hanging before us. I shivered at the cool breeze rising from far beneath our feet; a welcomed relief from the heat, yet there was no telling just how far it had traveled to reach us. We tried throwing rocks into the ravine with the hopes of judging the distance from the sound of impact, but any report was swallowed by the roar of the river. Kaylah either wasn't familiar with this particular area, or wasn't willing to share it with us; Tina couldn't tell which. But she suspected the girl was reluctant to share any information about the landscape ahead.

"What's the GPS say?" I asked Pavlik.

"It says we're in Peru," he barked, angrily tapping on the device. "It won't bring up a topographic, though."

Gomez finally decided we had no choice but to repel down. Within moments, the soldiers were securing the only nylon rope in our possession to the closest tree trunk. The longer I watched them work, the less restraint I had for hiding away from all of this. While Pavlik's attention was on tying down the line, I nonchalantly slipped my hand into his backpack and snatched the bottle of morphine, along with a clean syringe. I carelessly approached him while he knotted the rope.

"It's been over four hours." I said with professional concern. "You're going to need this, especially for the climb down."

"No thanks," he replied with unsubtle machismo. "The lidocaine is enough, bro. The pain keeps me focused."

"Okay," I said with a strained reluctance. "But, let me know if you need another dose."

No one noticed that I didn't return the syringe to his back-pack. I knew he would turn me down. You tend to pick up a lot of underhanded scheming when you're a drug addict. We anxiously followed the coiled line through the air as Gomez tossed it over the edge. When it vanished below the cloud cover I felt ill, hollow somehow. I'd never be able to do this.

"That looks treacherous," a voice exclaimed next to me. I turned and found Eden staring over the ledge along with us.

"Can I go first?" she chirped.

# Slippery Slopes

*"Indigenous groups living in isolation are isolated because they choose to be. It's not for complete lack of contact, but precisely because previous experiences of contact with the outside world proved so negative."*

Scott Wallace, *The Unconquered: In Search of the Amazon's Last Uncontacted Tribes*

While the soldiers attempted to reconnoiter the "rope situation," I pulled Eden back to the edge of the jungle, out of earshot of the group. Pavlik insisted I take his M-4 along. "You can hand it to your girlfriend there if you run into trouble," he added with a sneer.

Eden, I soon found, had no recollection of anything that had taken place in the "real world" after seeing the San Pedro cactus. She was eerily calm and focused; detached. It wasn't like her. I tried to shake her up by explaining exactly what took place, blow by graphic blow. I didn't omit a single, horrid detail.

"Well, that would explain all the blood," she said smoothly, studying her hands. I asked her about her remark about Christianity. Her eyes lit up at the mention of it. "Yes!" she exclaimed, grabbing my shoulders. "Michael, I was with Christ! He's real, my GOD, he's real! He must be who stepped in when I saved you!" She never called me Michael.

"You mean you had a lucid dream while you were seizing?" I asked hopefully. "You do remember the part where Kaylah spat a wad of that cactus juice into your mouth, right?"

"No!" she demanded. "They aren't dreams! I only called them dreams so your thick brain would listen to me. They're revelations! Michael, the Testaments are real. It all makes perfect sense now!". She took a moment to collect herself before relaying her experience during the attack.

"In my revelation, I was at the old cabin in Michigan, just like always. But, I noticed something about the scene wasn't right; the world looked different. Everything had an aura around it: the trees, the grass, even the cabin itself. Every object vibrated with these intense, translucent waves of blues and violets. I looked at my hands and, after a few moments, they turned invisible; I could see right through them. And I knew: I knew I was in God's Eye. And I was awake.

"So, I started walking along the little dirt path that led to my lake, Little Big Crooked, passed the weeping willows. I could see the water peeking through the branches, the sun had just begun to rise and oh, the water, Michael. It was the most beautiful sight. The morning breeze and the light touched the surface to make diamonds in the water. I walked to the shore and I could see straight to the bottom the water was so clear. I was standing in the essence of bliss.

"I took off my clothes, about to step in and I remembered: Every time, in every vision I've ever had, something keeps me from my little lake. I can never get to it. Some horrible thing always stops me." She was on the verge of tears; overwhelmed by emotion. My pulse was rising. Her fists drew tighter around my shirt the longer she spoke.

"I'm about to step in and my foot slams into a wall: some invisible force field. I panicked! I try punching my fists into it. I pounded, I kicked! No amount of force would break this invisible barrier. I fell to my knees and cried. And, I mean, wept. I've never wailed so hard in my life. I could see my lake right in front of me! It was inches away and I wasn't allowed in!

"But then this music fills the air, this beautiful symphony coming directly from the lake. The water was literally singing to me; a song I've never heard and yet, the most familiar, intimate melody. For a moment I thought this music might somehow make the force field vanish, but what happened was even more surprising. I realized that I was the one vanishing. I looked at my body and my skin became clear. Only the slightest, bluish outlines of my muscles, bones, and nerves remained.

"So, ever so carefully, I stepped out again. This time, my toes passed right through the force field! I could feel this thin, electric layer pass through my body as I moved into the water, the same we felt from that shock wave in the lab. The deeper I moved into the lake, the more I became engulfed by serenity. When the water reached my chest, I let myself fall back in utter surrender until I sunk low, beneath the surface. I've never felt so content in my life; I could have drowned right then and there and my incarnation would have been complete. My soul would have been at rest. Michael, I was baptized.

"But, then something pulled at me; some agitating force. It wasn't my time to die! There was something left undone! I swam back to the surface and wiped the water from my eyes. And I saw Him. He was standing atop the water right before me. There is no way I can describe Him to you, Michael. All I can say is: When you meet God face to face, you KNOW it. You know it from the most ancient part of your soul."

My concern about her emotional state at this point could not have been more severe. "Okay, who do you think it was . . . Jesus?" I asked apprehensively, trying to pull her back to some objectivity. "Did he say anything to you in the dream?"

"Yes," she said before searching my eyes, "but I already told you it wasn't a . . . "

Suddenly, she pulled away. "You don't believe me," she said severely. I was at a loss. There was no doubt something unusual had happened to her, but I had no idea what it may have been. The electrical activity in her nervous system was a mystery, that much was certain.

"I cannot believe you," she said. "Are you hearing anything I'm telling you? Michael, you need to drop this nonsense about biology and physics being the answer to everything, and I mean now! We don't have time for this. I know what's hunting us! It's all clear! Kane found a way to make evil a flesh and blood reality. And I'm sorry if that doesn't jive with your atheist mindset, but your doubts on all of this are going to be a liability to this mission!"

My mind spun to catch up. "What do you mean?" I asked. "What are you saying?"

Her jaw dropped and her eyes widened. "Seriously?" she hollered. "You can't be this thick! I appreciate your logic and reasoning, I do, but you need to get with the program here! You're a scientist, remember? Your beliefs need to change when you're presented with new information, no matter how detrimental it is to your old framework, remember? That's the beauty of science, that's what you said! You just said you saw it with your own eyes! You witnessed a supernatural force use my body to save all of you! How else can you explain that?"

"Well, I didn't say I saw a supernatu . . . "

"You said my body flew five meters through the air. Do the math! Or have you convinced yourself I'm physically capable of doing all those things? You can't believe I killed those people by myself! You're not even following your own rules now."

At that, she stomped off to rejoin the group on the cliff's edge. I was frozen in place. My mind refused to process a single thought, like a box of tiny wrenches had been dumped between every synapse. My eyes went blurry after several minutes of not blinking. Some corner of my brain barely registered the sound of branches and brush crunching underfoot far off in the jungle behind me, something large and heavy moving our way, tearing the forest as it approached. But it was nothing more than a tiny "blip" on a screen far off in my peripheral. Slowly, from beneath a cloudy haze, a few random thoughts floated upward and took hold. What if she's right? Was I refusing to change my mind in the face of new information? Who would I be if everything she said was true? How would I continue? I am the head of the science department at a respected university. Could I even go back and continue my job? Instinctively, I lifted my hands in front of my face and stared. What if this isn't real?

In some distant part of my mind, some part that had been running on autopilot with perfect, mechanical efficiency began to bleed into the present. The past twirled with the now and the two snapped together as one, complete whole. I've trapped myself in memory as some defense mechanism. I'm not really here right now. I forgot all over again. I'm the one driving! I'M BEHIND THE WHEEL OF A SPORTS CAR, HALLUCINATING MADLY, SPEEDING STRAIGHT TOWARD . . .

With a sudden, violent crash, the doors of perception slammed shut like a curtain falling to the stage at the show's end. Once again, the jungle took form around me with vibrant colors and sounds. My gaze slowly fell to my lower, left side to find I was actively injecting the morphine I had stolen from Pavlik's bag into my forearm. A concentrated rush of numbing ecstasy mixed with acceptance and all that is welcoming flowed through my spine and branched into my extremities. Ahhhhh. The flood of opiates left me with the oddest sensation that I had just been daydreaming about the future.

I'm letting myself get distracted by a bunch of utter bullshit. I need to focus on the task at hand. Don't get ahead of yourself.

I looked back to the cliff's edge where Eden was reuniting with the group. She made her way over to Sabol, who was huddled on a boulder near the ledge, staring blankly into the oblivion below. I watched as she sat by his side and began speaking to him.

For reasons unknown, my mind drifted to a debate Eden and I had a couple years back. We were in a movie theater waiting for the show to start and, before the previews, we were treated to a short documentary that had the look and feel of an independent production. The film opened with a series of black-and-white clips about an African American Olympian's back story of adversity and struggle growing up in the inner city. The little narrative concluded with the man's glorious victory of breaking two world records and winning several gold medals. The entire progression was dubbed over by the now-aged athlete's message of hope and his triumph over racism and self doubt. By the close of the short film, I felt genuinely moved. When I mentioned this to Eden she turned to me with a mix of shock and horror.

"Mike, that was a fucking commercial for a sports drink," she said. "How could you not see the product placement? Or who sponsored that tripe? They made it seem like that man's troubles with adversity are suddenly in the past! I guarantee that dude still has trouble getting fair treatment from police."

"Yeah, I get it," I replied. "I saw all that, too. But, still . . . "

"Still what?" she snapped. "It's worse than shrouding an advertisement around a cloak of social justice! It's propaganda. Fuck all that noise."

"Okay, but the message he had, it still has merit. It doesn't have to be all one way or the other. Besides, I'm pretty sure the movie we just paid for was sponsored by a whole lot worse."

"Shhh," she whispered as the lights dimmed. "The previews are starting."

Beneath the soothing blanket of morphine, surprise pinched at me when I saw Sabol speaking with Eden. She was actually pulling him from his catatonic state. I hoped that was a good sign. Maybe I do have new information that challenges my worldview. I don't care. God didn't come down and intervene. I won't believe that.

The sky had grown darker by the time I rejoined the group. Each successive lightning strike came faster than the last as the storm closed in. A nearly invisible mist began to fog my lenses to the point of uselessness. Sabol appeared to be functioning fairly normally again and he now volunteered to explore the rope situation first. His plan was to make his way below the cloud cover in hopes of finding, if not the bottom, at least a suitable ledge that would support us. He explained that we could theoretically reconnect the rope to something farther down the wall and continue down to safety.

As the other two soldiers gradually lowered their comrade into the muddy ravine step-by-step, Gomez questioned Eden as to how she brought Sabol back to life. A grave suspicion of her was evident in his tone.

"He just needed to hear he wasn't crazy," Eden explained unemotionally. "He needed to know that I saw the same thing he did."

"Yes, and what was that?" Gomez demanded.

"We saw demonic forces crawl out of hell," she replied. "I see how they do it, now. The individual soul is a sort of energy that can be handed, surrendered over to another ego. That ego can accumulate this power and then hand it over to pure evil, a 'demonic entity' if you prefer."

"I absolutely do not prefer," I grumbled. She ignored me and continued.

"Evil is a choice. Demons can only take a soul that is freely given. The more souls they devour, the stronger they are. I think that's why Kane preaches. His missionaries need willing participants around them who will surrender their soul energy at a moment's notice. Kane's converts are just food to them; free energy. I'm guessing that's why Christopher Aldon kept a brainwashed, faithful servant like Trevor McGhee around: Free energy to shift into monsters. It's the reason our crime scenes are littered with bodies with no visible cause of death."

Eden paused, staring into the ground with troubled consideration. "But, it's never enough," she concluded. "Kane wants more. He has a plan to win even more power. We're following an evolution of horror."

Somehow, this jumble of utter bullshit seemed to make some kind of sense to Pavlik. He nodded at the newfound severity of our situation. Tina and Gomez seemed uncertain. I took it all mostly in stride. With the help of the morphine, Eden's words slid off along with the rain droplets that fell with ever-increasing frequency. It was only then that I noticed just how much discomfort I had been dealing with before I shot up. Funny how life-threatening danger has a way of pushing the lesser bodily concerns aside.

I laughed out loud when I imagined a detox clinic that kept its patients running for their lives for two weeks straight to distract them from withdrawal. Everyone glared at me in confusion at my outburst, especially Eden who assumed I was laughing at her. I couldn't protest strongly enough that her explanation was anything but funny. After several minutes, Sabol breathlessly returned to the ledge with his findings.

"The only landing in sight is a solid twenty feet below the end of the line," he explained. "We could salvage belts or nylon straps to cut that down a bit. It's a narrow ledge, but I think it'll hold us all. We'll have to climb down to the last thread of rope and leap down to the ledge from there. Oh, and the fog is still thick as hell; we'll be doing this blind. I'm guessing the river isn't too much farther below the ledge, but I can't be sure."

"There has to be another way," Gomez said. Tina questioned Kaylah on our options which only resulted in more dire news.

"She says it would take a half a day to reach an easier incline and we're running out of time," Tina explained.

"Okay, so it's near death or time delay," I growled, surveying our options. "How would we even untie the rope up here at the top so we can use it again down there?" Everyone stared at me quizzically. I was dismayed to find I was the only one to consider this error in logic.

"Fuck," Gomez mumbled.

"I have rock-climbing experience," Tina offered reluctantly before breaking into a pep talk for herself. "I've had a couple years of training and I've done some free-climbing just recently in Colorado. That cliff face is mostly loose dirt, but I think there's enough rocks jutting out. It's doable. I'll go last. I'll untie the rope and scale down. It's not quite a 90-degree angle. It'll be fine. I can do this."

Lacking a better plan, we connected our belts and extra nylon straps from our backpacks onto the end of the rope to give it more length. With options in short supply and the storm growing ever stronger, Pavlik headed down first to help "catch" us as we free-fell from the line to the ledge.

Imbibed with a renewed sense of confidence (or a diminished sense of danger), I volunteered to go next. It seemed like a fine idea until I actually positioned myself over the brink of the cliff. Nervous and jittery, I swung my ass over the open chasm while gripping the thin, nylon line under white knuckles. Sabol talked me through each and every movement; how to position my shoulders and legs, how to leverage my weight into the face of the cliff and, the hardest of them all, how to "trust" the rope. In comparison to the yawning abyss stretched beneath me, the flimsy line in my hands felt absurdly fragile.

My blinding, white-hot fear of heights exploded behind a force field of chemically induced numbness, which allowed maybe half of the total fear to reach me. Noticing my body seize up, Tina began pacifying me with gentle words of encouragement. I was embarrassed by her mothering, but it did help calm my nerves. "Just do me a favor," I said, struggling to make light of the situation, "don't tell me shit like 'Don't look down', cuz I'm gunna look down." Tina smiled, and a booming roar of thunder stiffened my shoulders back into place.

"That's on top of us," Gomez said, searching the darkening skies overhead. We were losing ambient light by the minute. "We need to move, professor."

I took a breath and eased my weight backward; shaking and sweating, inching down hand-under-hand. Regardless of my vice-grip hold, the rope occasionally slipped through my soaked, burning palms. After a few minutes of clamoring down on wobbly legs against the earthen wall, I was swallowed by white, swirling mists. Visibility was shut down to just over a meter just as I heard Sabol's voice echo softly above, "Shit, I should've given him gloves."

Upon literally reaching the end of my rope, I cranked my head around to find the hazy form of Pavlik with his back against the wall, standing on little more than a narrow outcropping of stone, dirt, and roots. Sabol thought that would hold all of us?

Panic sizzled my blood when the soldier instructed me to simply, "Swing my ass over to the right and drop straight down," an impossible feat of gymnastics for me. To make matters worse, when I let go I had to be sure my body didn't fall too close to the cliff's edge, where I would certainly bounce off the side and drop to my death; nor too far, which would send me diving past the ledge completely, also to my death.

Another burst of lightning transformed the space around me into an ocean of light in the diffuse mist. No more than two seconds passed before thunder vibrated the earthen wall through the souls of my shoes.

"Don't think about it!" I heard Eden's voice echo in the distance. She couldn't even see me, and I despised that suggestion. As if thinking was something we could just turn off. With all the many ways my leap could go dreadfully wrong swimming through my imagination, images of my bones cracking against rock, my skull breaking wide open, I swung my body over Pavlik's shadow, exhaled, and somehow managed to let go of the line. Fear reached a blinding, white apex as I raced down with a deafening rush of wind in my ears. My stomach sailed into my throat, and I was tackled to a violent, sudden stop into the cliff wall.

"You're okay!" Pavlik hollered, gripping my shirt by both hands. "I've got you! You can let go now." It took me a moment to realize my frozen, white knuckles were locked around his wrists. "You . . . you can let go now," he repeated.

I meekly freed him from my creaking fingers with a heartfelt, "Thank you."

He quietly responded with what would normally be insipid pain to my ears, but now his reply, "No problem, bro," filled me with awe and gratitude. Only then, propped against the narrow ledge, did I appreciate just how much of his own leverage he'd jeopardized to "catch" my fat ass.

While the rest of the team made their way down single file, I wrestled with a ball of pain in my gut from the height, which was cutting ever deeper below my opiate blanket. Strangely enough, I couldn't even see how far we were from the bottom through the haze, but that fact didn't ease my fears. The not knowing was worse.

Standing room on our sliver of earth quickly diminished as everyone made their way to the ledge. Kaylah gleefully slipped down the line as if she were above a padded playground. I dug my fingertips into the soft, muddy wall at my back in a fruitless effort to "stick" better. It was all I could do to resist the urge to cling to Pavlik like a frightened child.

That's when the storm burst wide open. What had begun as a gentle sprinkle exploded into a torrential downpour. I didn't know rain could be so brutal, so ear-piercingly loud, especially after living in high desert where rain storms last ten minutes. Each drop bore enough weight to be heard and felt through clothing.

As planned, Tina was the last to come down. She had to shout her intention to untie the line over the noise which now swallowed all other sound. My boots began to slide from our ledge as it grew more slippery by the second. Time and again, I found myself stepping back to dig my heels further into the wall for more traction. This is taking too long. We need to move.

Another crash of thunder echoed overhead, but this strike was unusual. There was more friction behind the rumbling.

We all stared into the clouds, anxiously awaiting Tina's descent when something came swirling down, spiraling in wide, lazy circles through the air as it passed before it vanished into the mists below. It was our rope. Our only rope. From the momentary glimpse of its frayed end, it appeared to have been chewed off the tree.

Tina's scream pierced the rains above, followed by a trio of gunshots and finally a series of animalistic, savage howls; sounds that transported me back to Eden's car outside the bar. That's not thunder. Judging from the depth and intensity, I surmised whatever lay at the source had an enormous lung capacity.

"Christ, it's back!" Eden shouted.

"Who?" Gomez cried, "the truck driver, Alto?"

"Not anymore it isn't."

The sounds of skidding and scraping along the cliff wall above managed to trickle through the rain and thunder. It was Tina, clamoring down the muddy slope in a panic. Rock and debris tumbled around us as her shouts grew louder. The further she made her way toward us, the clearer her voice grew. She was screaming for us to run. The moment her body emerged from the swirling mists, I watched in helpless terror as her foot slipped from a smooth, wet rock. She struggled for footing, but it was too late. In the blink of an eye she lost her grip and fell. All we could do was shout as she plummeted down the cliff.

For a brief instant, the force of her falling body parted the mists and allowed me a direct line of sight to the top of the cliff. The dark figure that hovered over the edge was pure, organic impossibility. It had the torso and horns of a bull and was well over twice the size of any mammal walking the earth today. Its hairy, thorn-laden arms held its considerable mass over the ledge in a manner that was almost human. The vision was fleeting, but I knew it looked directly at me. Its facial features reminded me of some dark, forgotten image from childhood.

As Tina's body sped passed us, my arm shot out a moment too late. Did I hesitate on purpose? Did I instinctively know her combined speed and weight would rip me off the ledge right along with her? A splattering THUD rang out below and we all cringed. I had not the stomach nor the heart to look at the carnage. I knew her body had broken against the rocks below. I couldn't deal with this. I wouldn't deal with this. I flat out refused. No! We can't lose her now. This can't be how this plays out.

"A little help!" came a shout from below. Leaning over, we spotted Tina laying face-down atop an elongated, rounded mound of earth jutting from the wall a few meters below. I held back tears of joy knowing she was still with us. Her fingers were spread wide, hooked into the soupy mud: a cat on a screen door. Slowly, her hands disappeared below the brown, mushy surface as the rains transformed all solid dirt on the cliff into liquid. We watched breathlessly as she began sliding backward down along the hump, toward the chasm. My body shivered from utter desperation to reach her in some way.

Each time she reached for another grip farther up, the mud squished through her fingers and seeped from under her flailing legs as she fought to stay atop the bulging earth. Every move lessened her traction further. In a few moments, she would slide off to certain death. Tina cried out as everyone's mind raced. We had already used every scrap of suitable material on the rope; we had nothing to throw to her, not that our own predicament was any better. The team gave in to chaotic outbursts of cursing and nervous, half-baked solutions. As we searched our gear for anything of use, the entire wall at our own backs began shifting into chutes of muddy water.

More rock and debris tumbled around us when the terrible, unseen animal slashed and pounded hysterically at the ledge above once more. We could only hope that whatever lay at the top of the cliff couldn't manage its way down to us. Eden and Kaylah were the only ones not shouting; they simply stared as Tina lost her grip. With final desperation, Tina yanked a knife from her belt sheath and slammed it down high above her head into the mud. Ever so briefly, her makeshift anchor slowed her descent, but soon the blade began slicing through the earth.

"What if she had more points of contact?" Eden shouted.

"Using what?" I cried. Panicked dialogue shot from our mouths in rapid fire.

"Us!" she said. "You're the scientist! More points of contact against a surface creates more friction. What if we all slid down together in one big mass? There's enough room on that slope for us to all line up alongside her. In one big chain we'd create enough surface friction for a controlled skid. It's less than a 90-degree slope; it would work!"

Wait, I thought. DID that make any bit of sense? It kinda sounded like it did. Then again, it also sounded like utter bullshit.

"You're suggesting we fucking join her?!" Pavlik shouted.

"That's insane!" Sabol added, inching further away from the wall rapidly melting at our backs. "But, whatever we're gunna do, we need to do it fast."

Eden gently placed her hands on Pavlik and Sabol's shoulders. "I need you to have faith," she said with a smile. "I need you trust me and know that I'm right."

The two soldiers struggled internally for a brief moment. Then Sabol's eyes widened vacantly while Pavlik nodded in agreement.

"Yes!" Pavlik hollered. "I have faith! We can do this!"

Gomez shrugged. "Sure, okay," he grumbled, clinging to a branch beneath the mudslide. "I got no better play here."

The entire group then turned to stare at the sole atheist among them. Even Kaylah looked up at me, though I imagined she was unsure of what we had been discussing. As I tried to unlock my brain, the mud flow rose to enough force to wash us off.

"Fine!" I shouted. "How do we get down to her?"

"Well, what's wrong with the way she did it?" Gomez replied. "We'll jump."

Eden explained how the heaviest in the human chain needed to go first, and how the rest should follow in procession down to the lightest of the group. I nodded. Somehow, this all had something to do with physics, or so she assured us. It took a moment for it to dawn on me that I had just agreed to be the first to make the death leap down to Tina.

This required me to place the tip of the toes on the rim of the ledge, facing the cliff wall. I would then have to take a giant step backwards. Pavlik and Sabol held my hands and helped me aim so that I would hit the rounded bulge at the correct distance from Tina; not too far to be out of arm's reach, nor directly on top of her. Sabol handed me his dagger as mud begin to fill my boots.

"Slam this into the earth when you land and angle the handle away from you!" he ordered, slapping me on the shoulder with confidence. "It's a K-Bar! Marine's finest blade! It's going to save your life."

Even while blinded by muddy water, I could feel sweat streaming from my forehead. I looked down and was sickened with the sight of the cliff wall retreating into obscurity.

"You just have to step backwards," Eden explained, moving in between Pavlik and Sabol. "Just let go; allow yourself to fall straight down and you'll land right next her on the bulge. Lock your arms together as soon as you land."

"It's not going to work!" I yelled. "This is impossible. I'm going to slide off!"

"No you're NOT!" she demanded, staring into me. "You're going to stick just like she did, even more so with your fat ass! Jam your blade into the mud and grab her!"

"Eden," I stammered. I searched her eyes in desperation. I was about to die. I was about to die and all I wanted to do was confess. "I'm addicted to opium," I said. We shared a moment's pause as we silently stared into each other. She smiled, leaned in and wrapped me in the warmest embrace I had ever received from her.

"So, you've been self-domesticating," she whispered with a nod.

As she pulled back, she placed her hand over my heart. "Do you want to save her?" she asked. I didn't hesitate. "Yes," I said firmly. She smiled while her hand on my chest turned into a push that sent me clear off the ledge. The muddy wall raced before my eyes as I fell. For a fleeting stretch there was no sound. No past. No present. No thinking whatsoever. I was perfectly still. Rather, it was the world that rushed around me.

I slammed into a mound of wet soil face down while planting the blade into the earth above my head with all my strength. Tina immediately snaked her arm tightly around mine and we dug ourselves in. We locked our fingers together and sank them as deep into the mud as our combined strength would permit. To my utter amazement, it seemed to work. Our combined surface friction had temporarily stopped our slide over the edge. I fought the awkwardness of being desperately wrapped up with her in the most intimate, combined plight for survival. When we seemed to be relatively stabilized, her eyes met mine for the briefest moment; more than enough time to instantaneously heal the bridge I'd been carefully dismantling. Not that I had the breath or the energy to spare, I kept my stupid mouth closed this time, nonetheless.

The rest of the team soon followed. One by one, everyone dropped onto the melting bulge and immediately interlocked themselves into one long row. Gomez and Pavlik leapt down to either end of the line to balance out the weight; each burying their daggers into the earth as they landed. Eden, positioned in the middle, became the "driver" of our slippery train.

"Ok," Eden hollered. "At the same time, we need to slowly release our footholds. You all need to let go and control our descent!"

Everyone held their breath under pounding hearts as our train began sliding down in a series of controlled jerks along the wall. The current rushing into our faces forced us to travel completely blind. All I could do was listen and feel everyone's momentum and muscle contractions on either side of me. I was soon overwhelmed by the sensation that the team had transformed into physical extensions of my arms.

While shouting commands like: "More brake, Sabol!" "Less footing!" and "Ease up, Gomez!" Eden expertly navigated our team down along the cliff. With every meter gained, we fought against the growing loss of friction beneath our bodies. My mind struggled to understand how this was actually working, but the combined weight did indeed feel as if it were helping to control our slide.

An angry shriek from the creature looming above sent my mind spinning into doubt. Fear filled my spine and I could no longer feel the team; my perception was limited to my own reach. No, our combined weight should be ripping us off this wall. As if in response, Eden suddenly shouted, "Stop thinking about it, Michael!"

Instead of arguing, I forced myself to focus and blindly follow her commands. The farther we slid, the more the angle of our decent eased as the wall gradually merged with the canyon floor. When level ground came into view below, everyone broke from the chain one by one to scramble on hands and knees over a small field of glistening, sharp boulders that lined the foot of the ledge.

With solid earth beneath our feet once again, we stopped and listened intently, scanning the ledge overhead that vanished into the mist. When Gomez appeared content that we were no longer being hunted for the moment, the team moved downstream of the mudslide and collapsed atop a pile of giant boulders on the shores of a fierce, blue-gray river. Our appearance was comical. Every inch of our skin, hair, and clothing was coated with a spongy layer of reddish mud. It was hard to tell who was who.

"What we just did was physically impossible," I gasped in fatigue. The intensity of the downpour soon withered, allowing an occasional hole of crisp, blue sky in the dark blanket of clouds.

"And yet, here we are," Eden replied breathlessly. "Your lack of faith nearly pulled us from that wall."

# The Dreaming Tree

*"Hundreds upon hundreds of other scientific studies over the last fifty years have consistently revealed that "invisible forces" of the electromagnetic spectrum profoundly impact every facet of biological regulation. These energies include microwaves, radio frequencies, the visible light spectrum, extremely low frequencies, known as scalar energy. Specific frequencies and patterns of electromagnetic radiation regulate DNA, RNA and protein syntheses; alter protein shape and function; and control gene regulation, cell division, cell differentiation, morphogenesis, hormone secretion, and nerve growth and function."*

Bruce Lipton, PhD

According to Kaylah, our final destination wasn't much further ahead; we should reach the 'contact point' by sunset. We followed the banks of the river Southeast, trudging over wet marsh and tall grass. Marching single file in near silence we soon reached drier terrain between the raging waters and the piles of boulders carpeting the base of the cliff. Pavlik and Sabol stuck to either end of the line with weapons readied.

After finding an iota of equilibrium again, I noticed odd sound patterns throughout the jungle. Every twenty to thirty minutes some massive area far behind us would suddenly go quiet. All the bird and animal calls would abruptly stop simultaneously. Each time this happened Gomez would throw his hand high into the air, motioning for us to stop. He would then spend a full, nerve-wracking minute studying the forest at our backs in troubled silence before he allowed us to continue. I finally decided to question him on it.

"We're being hunted," he said flatly without an offer to elaborate. Judging by how little the man spoke, I guessed he rarely explained anything he wasn't forced to. After a couple hours of silence, Eden motioned me to join her in a short lag behind the others.

"How long you been on opium?" she asked quietly.

"A few years," I replied, contemplating how much I wanted to share at the moment.

"Why did you hide it from me?" she asked. "You know I'm not the type to judge, especially when it comes to drug use." I'm no longer certain what I know about you.

"I know," I replied. "It had nothing to do with you. I guess it's more about my own shame than your acceptance. It's embarrassing." I heard the words coming from my mouth, but didn't recognize them. Was that the truth?

"There's no shame in getting addicted to opiates," she assured me. "Our bodies are wired to seek pleasure and eliminate pain as much as possible. It seems opium is just more efficient at that than anything else nature's invented. Maybe your only fault was that you ever came into contact with it in the first place. The rest is nature. Who doesn't want to feel like they're in heaven all day long?"

"You don't see this as a problem?" I asked, growing somewhat irritated. I suppose I half expected a scolding, or at least a lecture on the pitfalls of addiction, but her open-armed acceptance put me at a loss. This was either a whole new Eden; one I was growing more suspicious of by the hour, or I never really knew her.

"It's a problem to the degree that your mind has convinced you that it's a problem," she replied. I rolled my eyes. "Everyone's addicted to something and everyone knows the right way to deal with addiction: Other people's addiction. Pavlik's bright idea was to just take away your pain meds, and that's every bit as idiotic. I can't have you going through withdrawal now."

"No shit."

"But you believe you're wrestling with an unstoppable force," she continued. "Soon you'll look at this relationship you have with narcotics in a completely different light. God is returning to lift the veil of perception. At that point, you'll be free from your bondage instantly."

My chest tightened and I tried to pull her back to Earth. "There is no such thing as 'instant' when it comes to addiction," I argued.

"If that's what you believe, then that's your bondage," she replied. This was starting to piss me off. I'd prefer to be hollered at. "But, if you open your mind, Michael, and let go, then you will hear what God is saying to you."

"You're talking about prayer," I said flatly. "You realize how hard it is to hear these things coming out of your mouth? I don't know what you're going through, but it sounds like you've exchanged your New Age psychobabble with Christian mysticism."

"Revelation isn't always a gradual thing," she said, ignoring my concern. "And prayer is talking to God. Meditation is listening to the answers." She searched me for a reaction. I sensed wisdom behind her words, but that didn't make my own problems any less troubling. None of it offered a direction, or actual steps to follow.

"You know I'm telling you the truth, but, you also think I'm being lofty for the sake of sounding poetic?" she asked rhetorically. "Why do you think you chose that moment on the cliff to admit your addiction to me?"

"I have no idea," I honestly replied. "I was so goddamned frightened that my mind went blank and the truth just sort of dribbled out. I guess I had to get rid of the garbage in my head."

"There you have it," she said. "Pray from that place." That was the last we spoke on the matter. Eden trotted ahead next to Sabol to talk about the power of Christ, or some other nonsense.

Over the years I had tried to really see, really understand where Eden was coming from, but I never could grasp her perspective completely. I knew she always meant what she said and she despised sounding insincere. Knowing that made me think either she was now delusional, or I really was too dim to see her point of view. And, now her wisdom had been instantly blended with some mysterious belief in Christ. I didn't know what to make of her. She was still the Eden I knew and loved, but a version of her possessed.

We fell to a steady pace as the river's edge evened out and I began to relax for the first time since we had landed at Panza's base. It was hardly a peace born of mental or emotional balance, rather a sort of defense mechanism that was forcing me to "give up." After everything that happened thus far, I realized that I no longer recognized myself either. The impact of what I had endured had yet to settle and I felt like a stranger in my own body. I repeatedly had to remind myself that this journey had just begun.

Of the vast array of possible reactions I might have to staring death and impossible circumstances in the face, I wondered where I would end up. Would I spend my remaining days in psychiatric care? Perhaps this sort of thing would turn a guy like me into an antisocial, homicidal maniac. Or worse yet, would this experience just make me even more awkward and alone?

My only comfort came from knowing our final camp was, reportedly, only a few miles ahead. Maybe we could build a fire. The thought of warm food and rest was the only motivation I had left to keep moving forward. I was confused how I managed to drop the rest of the details at this point. This must have been how ancient humans experienced their reality: constantly pushing toward sustenance and sleep, no time to rationalize or philosophize. As I considered this, I lumbered over rocks and crushed grasses underfoot, noticing my torso had been arching slightly downward from strain and fatigue. I imagined I was some protohuman, barely managing a bipedal stride. As a biologist, I knew our spines weren't designed to be walking around on two legs. There was a strange calm in this vision. My face must have betrayed some rare, inner peace because at that very moment Tina fell back and interlocked her fingers with mine, just as we had back on the cliff. Without making eye contact, she smiled and continued walking. My nervous instinct was to rip my hand away, run behind some foliage and shake, giggle, cringe, then possibly throw up. Why is she doing this? Is she just mothering me? Is this pity?

"You were brave back there," she said shyly. "I was a second away from losing my grip before you jumped down. I would've tumbled into those boulders for sure. There's no way I would have survived. Thank you. You're a good man." I nearly laughed out loud.

"You should thank Eden; it was her idea," I admitted. "They had to shove me off of that rock. I'm deathly afraid of heights."

"Then I'm even more impressed," she said. "That's the bravery that counts."

This was just a pep talk to keep the weakest link moving forward. It was a kind gesture, but her praise made me uncomfortable. I changed the subject and questioned her on just what happened to her back at the cliff. It also allowed me to break the handholding naturally when I turned toward her. Her eyes froze at the question. After a pained hesitation, she slowly shook her head.

"It's like it was meant for me," she whispered. "Catholicism runs strong here in South America. I guess the Christian missionaries who invaded our shores over the years got their wish, but it probably wasn't what they had in mind. In my culture, we took the vision of the Bible in a slightly different direction; our brand of Catholicism has a stronger flavor than what I've seen in your country. We often revel in the visceral qualities of our religious figures more so than you; the pleasure, the pain, the blood, the sacrifice. I find we carry a more tactile connection to our saints. We tend to imagine emissaries of God and Satan as flesh and blood creatures that live among us, in our world; not your pristine, white polished statues of angels, the ones that seem too ephemeral to touch. When we depict the nature of evil in my culture, we really indulge in the visual and physical terror of it all." She paused and stared into the depths of the jungle ahead before grabbing and clenching my hand even tighter.

"What attacked me up there was some perfect, awful blend of every image I've ever been exposed to of what dwells in the pits of hell. It was as if this thing was designed directly from the old religious paintings of horned creatures, an impossible mix of hoofed animals, with spikes and tails. Its features, even its movements, were unreal, imaginary. And that's what made it all so terrifying: This thing wasn't just an image; it was alive, it was flesh and blood. Mike, it charged at me, it sliced that rope as if it understood exactly what it was doing . . . "

She gasped as the incident flooded back to her. Her breathing quickened and the words stumbled from her mouth. "Jesus Christ, it was intelligent and savage at the same time. I fired my entire clip right into its horrible face and it just kept moving! And, my God, its face. It was freakish, otherworldly. Yet it was still human beneath it all. And even though it had three eyes, they were the eyes of a man; eyes I recognized. They belonged to that driver, Alto. But, his body . . . it's like . . . it was designed to scare the life out of me. I know you don't believe me, but that's what happened."

"I believe you." I said, as shocked to hear the words come from my mouth as she was.

"You don't have to say that to make me feel better," she said with a nervous smile.

Disturbingly enough, I did believe her. How I could believe something that didn't fit with any of my schemas made me feel that much closer to the edge of sanity. Eden, who had been eavesdropping on our conversation, glared back at me.

"Her story makes sense, huh?" she smiled with piercing eyes. Yes. I don't know how much sense it makes, but I do believe her story.

Tina and I walked hand in hand in silence into the early evening. That is, we didn't speak aloud, but my internal dialogue Ping-Ponged between the endless possible reasons this woman wanted physical contact with me. I finally decided that holding hands, just as in many Indian and Asian traditions, was simply a sign of friendship in her culture and it meant nothing.

By dusk, our weary crew reached our destination, or so Kaylah informed us. There was nothing out of the ordinary in this part of the jungle, and certainly no sign of humans, much less an entire tribe. We had stopped at a point where the river branched into two canals; the smaller of which fed into a narrow waterfall, a thin veil of water bubbling into a stream a couple meters below.

We came to rest on a sandy clearing just beyond the mouth of the tiny falls. Gomez objected to the location as the rushing water would help drown out anyone, or anything, that might approach. Kaylah explained that we would be hidden out of sight during the night where we wouldn't be discovered. Before we could question her further, the child leapt onto the muddy banks and slipped behind the sheet of water, completely out of sight. We all stared in confusion waiting for her to emerge.

After a moment, a tiny forearm poked through the falls from behind with a curling index finger, motioning for us to follow. We collected our gear and clamored down the bank along slippery stones coated in bright green and yellow algae to the base of the crashing water. Moving in near darkness, we slid behind the arch of the waterfall where we found Kaylah perched inside the entrance of a small cave. Oddly enough, she was illuminated from behind; by what light source, I could not guess.

With an impatient wave of her hand she disappeared further back into the crevice. As we began pulling ourselves into the opening, I realized that the morphine I stole had run its course and the early stages of tingling and cramps had begun to set in. As I didn't dare take any more morphine, I opted to follow up the rear so I could chew up a couple OxyContins. By crushing them down, more of the Hydrocodone would hit my system at once, but the effects wouldn't last more than a few hours. I wasn't sure why I still wanted to hide my addiction, but I did. Habits die hard.

After an ungraceful clamor up, into the opening, the tunnel narrowed into a tight cylinder of rock and mud that shot deep below ground, far below the river. We crawled along the steep shoot as rainbows of dazzling lights shimmered from an unknown source further ahead.

When our eyes adjusted to the dimly lit surroundings, we found the tunnel had emptied us into an enormous, roughly circular chamber. Brilliant white stalactites hung from the ceiling, dripping with milky water. The air was stagnant and musty at this depth, but far cooler. I guessed we were some fifty meters below the surface; only a muffled rumble of the river overhead could be heard through the layers of earth. But, it was the sight which lay before us that froze our feet to the floor of the giant cave.

A weak offshoot from the river high above poured down though a crevice near the ceiling of rock on the far side of the chamber. I could only guess that the water picked up a phosphorescent algae along its descent: it remained the only reasonable explanation for the gentle, bluish light it emitted. The glow from the stream reflected from the stalactites overhead to bathe the entire chamber with a soft, blue light, which in turn illuminated the largest, most incredible geological feature I had ever laid eyes on.

The blue stream flowed into a spiderweb of crevices in the rocky floor which branched into a complex network around, what at first appeared to be a line of seven, enormous bowls carved of stone. I soon realized I was staring at natural, geological oddities: a series of crystal laden geodes split directly in half, lain in a perfect row on their backs like turtles flipped onto their shells. For several moments, I couldn't make sense of the hemispherical structures.

The largest geode I had ever seen had been in the Science and Industry museum in Chicago during a rare rock and gem exhibit when I was a child. I recall musing over a spherical, gray stone the size of a coffee table that had been sliced down the middle to expose the dazzling, hollow core embedded with hundreds of violet crystal points. The seven hemispheres that lay before us now were the size of automobiles.

Upon further inspection, we discovered each of the crystal-line centers were comprised of a completely different color. The geode closest to the mouth of the luminescent river held a bowl of crystal points cast in deep reds, some so dark they appeared almost black. The next geode in the row held tints of fiery oranges and the one after was comprised of bright yellows and golds, followed by the fourth geode filled with rich jades and electric greens. The fifth stone held crystals of ultramarine blues, deep purples and finally, the concave surface of the geode closest to us was a hypnotizing blend of whites and brilliant, intense violets. Each of these massive stones had a hollow center encompassed by hundreds, thousands, of tiny crystals pointing inward. Their interiors were the size of small, upside down igloos; enough to cradle a full-sized adult.

The hollow, translucent cores glistened with their individual color spectrums as we stumbled around the massive boulders in silent awe. I studied the weight and texture of each as I passed. If these aren't real, the workmanship is uncanny. Upon making my way to the far end of the line, I reached up and slid my palm over its damp surface of swirling crimsons and pinks. Disturbingly enough, it was as smooth as glass. I couldn't fathom what instrument was brought down here that would cut through something this size, with such precision. I studied the empty space above it and tried to imagine how impossibly massive these stone spheres must have been before they were split in half. Even with the hollow cores, I estimated that each weighed a half a ton.

"This is more incredible than Puma Punku," Eden gasped.

"Puma what?" Pavlik asked.

"Megalithic ruins in Bolivia," Tina replied, "a series of precision cut stones that weigh ten tons apiece built hundreds, maybe thousands of years ago. No one knows how."

"So, these rocks are really big," Pavlik said. "So what?"

Sometimes I envied those not burdened with imagination and insight. My mind raced in a futile attempt to unravel how humans had managed such a feat of engineering. There was clearly no feasible way anyone rolled boulders this size down here even if there had been an opening large enough for them to pass through, which there absolutely was not. Hell, there was barely enough space for me to crawl down here. And, furthermore, what did they do with the other halves of these massive stones? Those points alone left me with two possibilities: Either the entire section of earth around us, from the dirt flooring up to the river had been constructed with cranes, bulldozers, and an untold amount of man hours, or this was a natural phenomenon.

The first option left me with: Why? The second left me with: How? The solution to both seemed equally mysterious, so my mind was left cleaved, split down the middle. Kaylah seemed uninterested in the chain of boulders lined before us; she went right to work carefully removing her ground-up plant mixture from her satchel and dispensing it into small piles atop a flat-tened rock. After she created seven, equal mounds she began speaking at length with Tina. Tina's eyes widened as she pro-cessed the girl's information. During the explanation, Kaylah made a series of gestures between each of us and the geodes. It was some time after the child finished her tirade before Tina could translate for us.

"She says that this arrangement of rocks is known in her lineage as the Dreaming Tree and it's the only way to reach the Craneo Roto tribe," she began. "In order to make contact with them, she says, the 'vibration of our consciousness' has to align with the roots of the tree."

"Its roots?" Sabol asked.

"I already don't like the sound of this," Pavlik said. Gomez hushed him into submission.

"So, how does she suggest we do that?" Eden asked with a knowing smile.

"First we have to consume the offering she made," Tina continued.

"That would be the 'offering' made with the hallucinogenic cactus and God only knows what else," I interrupted. The same mind-altering chemical that possibly had a hand in turn-ing my best friend over to Team Jesus.

"The same, yes," Tina confirmed. "After we ingest the medicine, we will have some time to ourselves to 'adapt' to the change in vibration. As long as we don't travel beyond the waterfall above, we can do as we please. But tonight, we must all sleep inside the hollow cores of these geodes."

My head fell to my chest, I couldn't hold back a smile any longer. At this point, everything had become so ridiculously absurd, my rationale was about ready to call it quits. "And what if I can't stuff my considerable girth into the center of those rocks?" I asked, laughing quietly.

"That's not all," Tina continued, ignoring my anxiety. "She says each of us must reside within a specific 'flower' on the tree. Pavlik, you have to sleep in the red geode at the far end. Sabol, you're in the orange one next to him. Eden, you're in the yellow, and I'm in the green. Gomez is in the blue geode after mine. Mike, you're in the purple, and Kaylah will be in the last one."

After a round of blank stares, Gomez spoke up with authority. "I'm sorry, but there was nothing in our contracts about consuming psychedelics out here," he said firmly, unemotionally. "Do what you need to do, but our job is to protect you. We've got a sat-radio to fix if we ever plan to make contact with Agent Downey, or our lift out of here. We'll sleep in your rocks if we must, but we're no good to you if we're not sober."

"She says we all have to participate; it's all or nothing," Tina replied. "Each of us must become a key to unlock the full potential of the Dreaming Tree. Every link in the chain must harmonize at the proper vibration. And it must be done in unison. She says that our individual energies have already been primed to bond with one another's, now we're prepared to make the next journey."

"Oh yeah?" Pavlik snorted. "When were we 'primed' to 'bond' with each other?"

"Back at the cliff," Eden replied with authority. "It's all part of the plan. The universe is using us as a catalyst. There's seven of us and seven geodes. That isn't coincidence."

"Yes, it is," I said, clenching my fists. The soldiers began arguing loudly until Tina held up her hands in surrender. "I'm just translating, guys," she barked. "I don't know what to make of this either."

"There's plenty of time to fix the radio," Eden explained quietly. "Trust me. Whatever the girl has there won't last much longer than five or six hours. I guarantee you energy drinks are more toxic. You'll be fine."

"Toxicity wasn't really the issue," Sabol mumbled. Gomez sighed and shook his head.

"Well, then, we're not responsible for your safety tonight," Gomez announced. "Consider us off duty."

"Fair enough, we're on our own tonight," Eden agreed with a sarcastic smirk. "What could possibly go wrong?"

# Altered States

*"Why don't all objects we see do all these weird and wonderful things that quantum particles can do? The answer is that, down in the microscopic quantum world, particles can behave in these strange ways, like doing two things at once, being able to pass through walls, or possessing spooky connections, only when no one is looking. Once they are observed, or measured in some way, they lose their weirdness and behave like the classical objects that we see around us. But then, of course, this only throws up another question: What is so special about measurement that allows it to convert quantum behavior to classical behavior?"*

Johnjoe McFadden and Jim Al-Khalili—*Life on the Edge*

It was disturbing how quickly Eden managed to change the soldiers' minds on the subject of consuming mind-altering chemicals. It seemed she had been officially elevated to the position of religious leader. I was quite familiar with some types of drugs, but I had never done anything hallucinogenic. Apart from Eden's reverent praise of magic mushrooms, all I knew about "tripping" was what I had been taught in school.

The first time I had ever heard of psychoactives was in a short film in elementary school about the dangers of LSD. The movie summed up the psychedelic experience in three basic stages: First, the 'victim' is exposed to ecstatic images of rainbows, unicorns, and flying dolphins. Soon after, the visions turn dark and sinister, filled with fire and terror until finally, now completely psychotic and suicidal, the victim plunges himself through a window or down a flight of stairs to his death. "Tripping," in my shallow understanding, was essentially unicorns, terror, then suicide. Eden laughed out loud when I related my story to her.

After a light meal of dried meat and slices of a papaya Tina had snagged from a tree along the way, we sat in a circle on the cave floor in the shadows of the towering geodes. Kaylah had placed a small pile of plants and herbs on a flat rock before each of us. Following her lead, we shoved the entire 'offering' into our mouths at once and washed it down with water. The taste and sensation was akin to stuffing a handful of moldy, bitter dirt down my throat. After several swigs from the canteen to rinse away the bits stuck to the roof of my mouth and between teeth, Eden turned to me with a strained look of reconsideration. "Well, okay, there was this one guy back in college we had to pin to the floor so he wouldn't jump off a roof after he ate three tabs of blotter, but I mean . . . that almost never happens."

Sensing my grave apprehension, she cut the sarcasm and put an arm around my shoulder. "Thank you for being here with me," she said, squeezing tighter. Remembering just how much I cared about her, I returned the embrace. At least she wasn't preaching at the moment.

"I couldn't let you have all the fun to yourself," I mumbled in an awkward attempt at levity.

Everyone's heart jumped when delighted laughter echoed through the chamber. It was Kaylah. She leapt to her feet, danced her way to the spiderweb of blue streams and pounced playfully in the water, splashing with carefree wonder. It was the first time she had acted like a child. In fact, I nearly forgot we had been traveling with a ten-year-old. She was more confident and adapted to this environment in so many ways, I hadn't felt the slightest concern that we all had just shared a pile of mind-altering drugs as equals. Now here she was, singing and playing like an actual kid. It seemed her job was done; she had performed her task. She got us to this place and fed us her medicine. Like the soldiers, she was now off duty. I only hoped her intentions were pure, given the fact we were at her mercy.

No more than twenty minutes passed before the first effects settled in. It washed over me as if a steady stream of foreign consciousness had slowly penetrated my brain, bathing it with its own alien rhythm. Gradually, my senses responded to my altered awareness and I realized that I was having some difficulty determining if I was awake or dreaming. The cool, luminescent stream weaving through the floor created a gentle flutter on the stalactites overhead and a jittery dance through the geodes' crystals, endowing everything with a false sense of movement.

The patterns created the illusion that the spirals of calcium deposits were actually reaching for the floor right before my eyes. The earthen surfaces became a semiliquid; indeed, every solid undulated with an organic intensity, a sort of "breathing" that inspired even the rocks to become silently alive.

I stood and stared, mesmerized by the sight of the pulsating gems within the massive geodes. The longer I gazed, the stronger the illusion set in that I was no longer seeing solid stone and crystal, rather, I was witnessing living blobs of light sheathed behind a thin, translucent membrane. The energy contained within these pods were quietly, passionately waiting for me, and I became steadily aware of a rising intensity in the chamber. I searched the space around me and found the boulder that pulsated with rich purples and dark blues pulled at my attention with an unbending, gravitational force. Something deep within me stirred at the sight of the otherworldly colors contained within this particular geode's core. Yes, that's where I want to be, wrapped up and drenched in those electric blues.

I realized that I was now doing far more than simply "seeing" or "hearing" my surroundings. Perception became a unified combination of incoming data, an illogical blending of sight, sound, thought, and emotion. I sensed that a hidden, preset dial within my brain, one that had always allowed only a specific amount of information to enter had now been dangerously tampered with, and switched to full blast. I stared at the center of the geodes and actually felt the nonorganic quality of their beautifully symmetrical, crystalline structures. Yet, I was continuously drawn to the one cast in purplish hues. Was this some placebo-style reaction to being told earlier that this was my stone, the one I was to sleep in tonight? Or was there actually some connection between me and this rock, something I didn't recognize? Something the child we were traveling with did?

This bizarre state was nothing like opium. Opium was a comfort, a soothing blanket of protection. But this, this was pure intensity; the world was unraveling to expose the beautiful and frightening perception beneath. This was anything but safe. Fear and awe flowed through me in equal measure.

As I wandered, or rather floated, through the chamber, I could barely sense my legs working and found everything else in the underground chamber had taken on a living, buzzing energy. Distinct boundaries, those that separate one object from another soon lost meaning. From this angle, I found it increasingly difficult to define what I was seeing. Those are rocks, I thought to myself. And that over there is water. Try as I might, distinctions seemed utterly useless and contrived.

Overwhelmed, I sat down and allowed my world to dissolve. Suddenly, something deep inside shook me as if abruptly awoken from a dream of falling. Not knowing where this panic originated, my first impulse was to stare at my wristwatch for some reason. I gazed longingly at the numbers on the display, searching for some logic, something solid to grab hold of. The numbers read 10:27 p.m. My mind told me that those digits used to mean something; they once held the promise of keeping my world in order. Now, they were nothing more than empty, electronic bars that symbolized whatever I wished them to be. The infinite number of subtle ways this truth changed my reality was deeply unsettling. And I quickly devolved toward panic. Out of utter frustration, I ripped the watch from my wrist and threw it into the dark recesses of the chamber.

I wasn't just throwing away a watch! No, this action held immense significance! I was relinquishing all the compulsive dividing, organizing, and boxing of time itself! And then! I found a gentle hand on my shoulder.

"Good for you, Michael," Eden said. "Time is a stupid human construct. Watches are dumb." She hadn't simply witnessed my little outburst, she had genuinely understood it. What I imagined was a terribly unique moment of realization about the untameable force we refer to as "time" was already well-tread, familiar ground for her. I knew my handle on scientific fact and research was superior to hers, but this was a brand new world; one where I was a mere child and she a fully educated adult. Kaylah's psychoactive alkaloids had only been in my system for an hour, yet I felt I had already absorbed insights that might have taken years to uncover.

Only now could I fully appreciate the possible psychological benefits these drugs had to offer. Medicine indeed. It was secret knowledge like this that had always kept me at a slight disadvantage in Eden's presence, regardless of my intellect. Only now could I truly consider the full impact of her assertion that these chemicals would indeed have had extraordinary consequences on the minds of primitive humans.

"I'm going to crawl up to the waterfall." Eden decided with a slow, euphoric grin as she lifted her face to the ceiling. In the diffused glow of the chamber, her pupils had transformed into gaping, black holes that once again devoured her irises with a force that even light could not escape. This alone made me uneasy and exposed beneath her gaze. She rose to her feet and moved off toward the opening in the wall from which we had emerged and disappeared up, into the dark tunnel. A birth canal.

Then, for the second or third time this evening, the symbolic relevance of the task that brought us here gained more power under the light of my newfound consciousness. Running into uncharted territory to chase down monsters, my life had become a lame metaphor. And I was fairly sure this represented an even larger metaphor for something else, but decided not to dwell on it much longer; for sanity's sake.

I got up again and moved about the camp to see how everyone else was faring. As I wove my way around the luminescent stream, I noticed the water level had risen a few centimeters since we first entered the cave. If we stayed here too long, we theoretically could drown down here. I found Sabol sitting crosslegged just beneath his orange geode staring at the electrical components of the smashed sat-phone. In slow motion, he delicately poked and prodded at the exposed wiring with a pair of tweezers.

Further off, Gomez lay flat on his back near the mouth of the stream. With his arm overhead, his hand waved gently back and forth in the current. For a moment, I thought he may be sick or distressed, but as I stepped closer I detected a barely audible, Spanish melody rising from his lips. I stood in awe, stunned by the smooth purity of the man's voice. My God, he could have been a professional vocalist. I didn't know why, but I was certain he was singing something his mother used to sing to him when he was a child. "No querido estas sentir, quien es mi amor . . . "

Pavlik was propped against one of the earthen walls staring intently into his pocket Bible. He didn't appear to be reading, just gazing over the pages with a subtle smile on his face. "Eden is right," he muttered. "It's all making sense now."

Still fidgeting with the radio on the floor, Sabol suddenly broke the trance. "All these tiny circuits are like the nervous system of some primitive, little animal," he said slowly, turning the circuit board toward me. "See how they all branch off into these tiny transistors along the board? It's like veins leading to major organs. Or some basic, neural network. They're so . . . small and fragile." He looked up with a sadness in his eyes. "I don't know if I can fix it, professor," he whispered.

"I believe you can rebuild him, doctor," I said, trying to be reassuring and cheerful. As soon as the words left my mouth, I wasn't sure if my positive tone was for his benefit or mine. At the mercy of such boundary dissolving drugs, it seemed far too easy to slip into a never-ending pit of dread, and I couldn't let him pull me in. To my dismay, my statement weighed heavily on him.

"My dad wanted me to be a doctor, just like him," he said quietly, moving his attention back to the radio. "He shouted when I joined the military. God, he was pissed. He said, 'smart move, Billy. Now you'll be an instrument of death instead of the healer you were supposed to be.' But, I wanted to help too, you know? Go over there and stop those terrorists."

He quietly laughed at his youthful ignorance, and my mind's eye began focusing on the abyss below once more. No, goddammit! I'm not going to start thinking about my own parents. Leaving was their choice, not mine. I was just a fucking kid for Christ's sake. "I thought he'd be impressed," Sabol continued. "I thought he'd see how brave I was for going to the desert to

. . . help. All I found was death and hatred. I come home and everyone treats me with fuckin' sympathy. They felt sorry for me. I spent years out there in the sand and the heat thinking I was saving the world from Jihadists. I come home and my dad just shakes his head."

I had no idea what to say, but his depression was infectious. There was a visceral motion to the medicine's effect, a sense of riding waves. I kept finding myself caught in a current of horror followed by joyous wonder, only to be pulled under by another wave of fear. But now, Sabol's mood was adding gravity to my own dark pit. How long I stood contemplating over the young soldier, I could not guess; gauging the passage of time was now impossible. Somehow, I needed to find a way to pull him from his suffering. Saving him was the only way to save myself from the growing dread.

"I don't know what happened to you in Iraq," I said gently. "But I do know you saved my life today more than once; mine, and everyone else's. We're all indebted to you. If that doesn't make you a healer, I don't know what does." This was possibly the first time in my life I had said something truly meaningful to another person. But I couldn't take any credit; I had no idea where it came from. My mind was too jumbled with stimuli to form coherent thought. My mouth was on autopilot.

Sabol's head fell into his knees and he began crying softly. A muffled, "Thank you, professor" rose from beneath his locked arms. I stepped away to leave him to his own catharsis and realized Tina had also disappeared from the chamber.

My gaze fell to the hole leading up to the waterfall; there was nowhere else she could have gone. The dark orifice beckoned and terrified me. Under great apprehension, I shimmied my way up the damp tunnel of earth. Upon reaching the surface, I tumbled ungracefully onto the ground, behind the sheet of water. With the light of a full moon flickering through the thin, translucent veil, I was able to make out a dark form showering beneath the stream, framed by heavenly blue, night sky. As the figure turned, the water glistened along the curves of a naked female form. Sometimes I wondered what inspired Eden to ever wear clothing.

"Oh my God!" Tina's voice cooed in ecstasy. "You have to try this! The water feels like silk."

"Shit, I'm sorry!" I stammered at the realization that I had been staring at Agent Flores. I hid my eyes and lowered my head. "I didn't know you were naked, sorry."

"Stop it!" she laughed. "Get in here!"

"Oh . . . oh, no, I can't," I stammered. Oh, God, what is she doing? "I, uh, I didn't pack my swimsuit." I began shuffling back into the cave, hoping my joke would be enough to divert her line of thought. No such luck.

"No!" she demanded. "Any clothing would ruin it."

I tried not to stare, but the soft, liquid glow of moonlight dancing over her breasts, along the smooth curves of her hips was pure bliss to my cranked-up perception. I struggled with a form of anxiety I hadn't felt in years. She must have confused me with one of the soldiers. "Um, you do know this is Mike, right?" I announced. "Professor Michael Huxley? Sorry, I'm just not sure how well you can see in the dark."

"I know who I'm inviting into my shower, Professor Michael Huxley!" she sang playfully. "Are you joining me or not?"

"Um, is it safe?" I asked. "I mean, the water. It's clean, right?"

She laughed at my neurosis, spinning and slinking in and out of the veil of water. I found myself sheepishly unbuttoning my shirt when I spotted Eden on the ground off to my right sitting crosslegged at the edge of the banks. I stepped closer and realized she was meditating. "Mike," she said quietly behind closed eyes. "I say this as your friend: If you don't get your ass in that waterfall with her, I'm going to beat the living shit out of you as soon as the drugs wear off."

Her empty threats didn't ease my anxiety, but they did pull me from hesitation. I undressed and stacked my clothes neatly inside the tunnel's opening with my glasses laid carefully atop the pile. A vigorous stream of shame and awkwardness washed over me like an electric shock, but it didn't stop me from moving forward. Anxiety is temporary. Feel it, truly feel it and it'll pass, Sadhu said once. Was this memory, or premonition?

I stepped into the falling water and found the bizarre sensations to be so entirely new I thought I had merged with a foreign liquid, one I had never encountered. I closed my eyes, turned my head to the sky, and let the cool stream flow over my face and drench my scalp. When I came out for air, I found Tina had moved in closer with her back arched toward me, caressing her fingers through her hair as it mixed with the glistening cascade. She was an ethereal vision of raw, feminine beauty. With fearless innocence, she yanked me by the hand back under the falls next to her. As the waters flowed down my spine, it seemed my inhibitions were washed down with them. Not since I was a child playing carelessly in the moment was I imbibed by such a deep sense of liberation. Beyond the cages of the rigid past or the ever changing future, I was free in the moment.

"The bridge is set and it's harder than diamonds," I whispered to myself, but Tina heard me clearly. She smiled as if she totally understood what I meant. How could she?

"Damn right it is," she whispered back.

We spent the remainder of the evening alone, playing and dancing in the water like children. Short of uncontrollable outbursts of laughter, our communication throughout the night was almost entirely nonverbal. At times, my mind would remind me I was involved in the quintessential precursor to lovemaking, yet our interaction didn't feel sexual. The bliss of pure enjoyment was so completely satisfying it seemed neither of us felt the need to bring intercourse into the mix. We were simply male and female forms at play, free of worry. Our individual stories of who we were became little more than background noise. We danced like gods in the Now.

Before this night I had never felt a seamless bond with another soul. And just like that, without further pretense or doubt, Tina Flores and I were in love. Beyond all rationale, beyond all logic, I instantly knew that I would, if necessary, move mountains to be with this woman. Perhaps we would both come to our senses tomorrow when we decided this was nothing but a much-needed diversion, a necessary breakdown from all the stress and trauma. But, magically enough, I didn't care; the night was ours. The only contact we shared that evening which could be considered "sexually intimate" was a gentle kiss she placed on my lips as we frolicked in the shores at the edge of the waterfall. I felt we both knew sex might come into play in the future, but tonight we shared no desire to be any more complete than we already were. After she kissed me, her eyes lit up with a sly playfulness beneath the moonlight.

"You can't catch me!" she squealed before darting to the edge of the falls into the jungle. Soaking wet and naked, I ran after her in the dark. My body felt weightless as I dodged trees, sprinted over rock, and slipped beneath vines to keep her elegant, racing form in view. My entire being became flooded by the pure, animalistic "thrill of the hunt" and all divisions between thinking and muscle response dissolved into the earth beneath my feet.

Suddenly, Tina let out a powerful wail and leapt high into the air. She kept rising higher and higher, her feet sailing far above the ground. With an abrupt shudder, her body came to a dead stop and her arms fell lifelessly to their sides. What was I witnessing? This was impossible!

I drew closer and discovered two blackened spikes jutting from her upper shoulder and mid torso. Terror rushed in and I stopped beneath her suspended body, shouting her name over and over when something dripped onto my cheek. I wiped it off and studied my fingers. It was blood. From behind her dangling body, a towering shape slowly moved out of the shadows, hovering above me with a multitude of snaking, moving parts. My spine became ice as I understood what I was witnessing. Tina had been impaled onto the claws of an animal at least three times the size of a horse. Its head bore the features of a goat and its mouth was a grotesque chasm of teeth that drew far into the recesses of a massive jawline. Every visible feature of its body left the impression of some horrible genetic mutation. Black, infected skin stretched haphazardly over a deformed skeletal structure. The curved horns wrapping either side of its massive skull along with the thick nails that held Tina's body appeared to be carved from decaying bone matter. At the center of all these monstrosities were three, intermittently blinking eyes sunk into moldy, darkened sockets in a triangular pattern. To my horror, something inexplicably human peered back from behind those pupils.

A powerful, low growl rumbled from its core as it crouched back on hind legs, prepared to strike. With an explosion of unfiltered rage, I shouted. I shouted into its terrible face until my vocal cords wanted to collapse. Briefly startled by the amount of noise this tiny animal emitted, the animal recoiled for an instant, long enough to allow Tina's body to slip from its giant daggers, into a thudding, lifeless heap at my feet.

Without thinking I grabbed the closest projectile within reach: a sharp, moss covered rock, and whipped it toward the trio of eyes with all the power my arm could expel. The edge of the stone snagged the thin, ocular membrane, temporarily blinding it with a stream of black fluid. The beast let out an agonized roar and madly thrashed at its face. I threw Tina's body over my shoulder and ran. I didn't gain more than a short head start before pure rage overwhelmed the animal's need to recover. Branches and vines crushed and twisted behind me under its enormous mass as I blindly zigzagged through the dark forest, back toward the sound of the falls.

I burst through the jungle's edge onto the shoreline and deftly spun into a forty-five degree turn to avoid plummeting into the river. The massive predator at my back wasn't quite as agile. It carried too much force to counteract its momentum. Just before it tumbled into a splashing rage, it lashed out as it passed, tearing a sideways cut along my backside from neck to waist. Within moments, the thrashing and turmoil in the rushing water suddenly subsided. I glanced back to learn that the goddamned thing could swim better than it could run. Under powerful eel-like movements, the creature snaked its way upstream to overtake me.

As the falls came into focus ahead, the impossible animal emerged in my right peripheral. With another explosion of furious energy, it burst from the water and launched high into the air, jaws open, claws outstretched. All I could do was something entirely unexpected; something prey in the wild would never attempt. I spun to my right and leapt directly in front of its snout, aiming toward the falls with all the force my legs offered. I flew passed the beast's gaping mouth, directly through the sheet of the water, onto the wet earth on the other side of the falls. Upon landing, I immediately wedged Tina's body behind me as the silhouette of a massive head atop an elongated neck swayed viciously back and forth behind the veil of water, trying to comprehend its prey's vanishing act. The shadow grew larger as the creature slowly pushed its head into the waterfall.

"Stay down," Eden whispered above me. I hadn't noticed her. She quietly stepped toward the falls while raising the barrel of Sabol's M-4 to the top of the beast's head. For a moment, she slowly waved the barrel back and forth, finding her aim.

"Where are its eyes?" she whispered-shouted.

"Top center, above the snout!" I replied. "There's three of them."

"Not for long"

Black, pulsating nostrils emerged through the sheet of liquid, sniffing madly, scanning for any trace of us. Eden stepped backward and repositioned her aim just above the nose. With a deafening blast of light she unloaded a barrage of bullets into the waterfall. Roars of agony bellowed from behind the veil as oily, black liquids splattered against the screen of water. The silhouette thrashed about as its claws slashed blindly through the falls before its shadow fell out of view. But Eden didn't let up. She continued blasting through the water until her weapon clicked dead. Without hesitation, she yanked the cartridge onto the ground, pulled another from the back pocket of her jean shorts, and with one powerful leap, dashed through the veil of water and disappeared. Moments later, more gunfire echoed further down the river. I could hear Eden shouting off in the distance between reloads. "Oh? You want more of this, asshole? This one's for my grandfather's Hudson you motherfuckers!"

I barely noticed Gomez crawling out of the cave above my head as my attention was immediately back on Tina. Under his flashlight I was able to study the full damage. She was barely conscious with two large holes punched into her: One between the collarbone and pectoralis major and the other through her external oblique. The blood appeared a normal color and consistency, so I hoped this meant it didn't puncture any major organs. But the incisions were too large to wrap. She needed stitches and God only knew what kind of antibiotics.

"Get me the med kit and more light!" I shouted. Gomez flew into action, barking orders at Pavlik and Sabol through the tunnel. I grew ill watching how much blood she was losing while I fumbled with the meager amount of clotting powder we had on hand, butterfly bandages that wouldn't stick, and gauze that needed to be wrapped around her torso, which forced us to lift her unconscious body over and over again. Gomez continued injecting her with incremental shots of morphine while Sabol kept careful count of her pulse after each dose. After some thirty minutes of work we had merely slowed the bleeding.

When Kaylah emerged from the tunnel she began speaking excitedly to us with intense gestures. Even though we couldn't understand specifically what she was saying, her message became clear: That we stick to the plan; that we should return Tina's body to the chamber below and lower her into the green geode. I didn't believe she would live through the night, but given current circumstances and my terrible confusion, I had no better plan.

Using the makeshift stretcher we had created for Eden, we slowly dragged her down into the cavern. Just as we lowered her into the hollow of the jade stone Eden emerged from the tunnel soaking wet with globs of black ooze running down her shirt and legs. She angrily threw the M-4 to the ground and shouted at Gomez, "I told you we needed to kill that fucker!" Gomez just threw his hands in the air with an exasperated, How was I to know?

Kaylah immediately clung to Eden's side and barraged her with, what appeared to be, questions about the creature.

She appeared desperate to know where the creature was and whether it was alive or dead. Disturbingly enough, Eden didn't seem to be entirely sure of those answers. After we positioned Tina as comfortably as possible, Pavlik turned to me with a confused look. "I've been meaning to ask," he said thoughtfully. "Can I get you some pants or maybe a large poncho?"

I had totally forgotten I was naked. The thought of clothing had completely avoided my detection. Although I quickly pulled a clean pair of pants and T-shirt from my backpack, I couldn't help but notice how much I simply didn't care that I had been working along with everyone to save Tina's life entirely nude. So, this is what full-blown insanity looks like, I considered, but was too exhausted to give the notion any more energy.

By the time I crawled into my purple geode, the rest of the team was fast asleep from exhaustion and stress. I had done everything I could for Tina and I knew it was far from enough, but Kaylah insisted I try to rest. I had assumed the hundreds of crystals poking into my backside would be impossibly uncomfortable, but I discovered the concave shape cradled and supported my weight, even my head, perfectly. I closed my eyes and soon became engulfed by an inner visionary state of morphing color and form. No longer certain of anything, the dream-like patterns danced and wove themselves into cohesive tapestries and fantastic symmetries. It never occurred to me that I hadn't taken any opiates that night.

Moments before I became completely swallowed by the subconscious, a tortured moan echoed through the tunnel from the jungle above; some distant, angry wail far beyond the waterfall, beyond the clearing, past the steep, muddy cliffs. All I could be sure of was that the wounded animal out there was both organic and unnatural, but I didn't know what that added up to.

I couldn't have slept for more than a few hours. Moments before I awoke, a most disturbing impression swirled up from the roots of my mind that my geode was spontaneously made whole again. The massive boulder had reverted back to an unsplit sphere—with me still trapped in its belly. Just as my air ran out gravity violently reversed itself and I was slammed into the other half of the crystalline core. The shock jolted me straight up, half awake. Consciousness and memory coalesced back into its familiar patterns as I searched the cave. I found the rest of the team pulling themselves from sleep and a seemingly random detail caught my attention. Something wasn't right about the flat surface of my geode, where the original sphere had been split in two. I had spent a good deal of time studying its unique swirls and geometric patterns the night before, so I couldn't fathom how I managed to misremember a major feature. I recalled running my hand along a thin indentation that ran from the outer edge of the stone to the center; the slightest indication of an imperfect cut when the geode was sliced. But now, this crease ran the opposite direction, a feature one would only expect to find on the other half of the geode.

Tina and her injuries exploded back to memory and I scrambled onto the surface of the stone. But before I could leap to the ground to run to her side, an intense jolt of fear rattled my spine. Something else was terribly, impossibly wrong! So wrong, in fact, my mind was straining to process it.

I was lightheaded and out of breath when it dawned on me: The dripping stalactites overhead had vanished from the ceiling! Panicked, I stood atop my boulder and my anxiety only worsened. The floor below was now completely filled with stalagmites; tall spikes of mineral deposits that spiraled from the ground, up. The damn things had changed places! I felt only minimal relief upon witnessing everyone else's shock and horror upon discovering the same anomaly.

"Wait," Pavlik grunted, rubbing the sleep from his eyes. "Weren't those hanging . . . from the ceiling?"

"Yes!" I shouted and jumped onto the ground. As I ran toward Tina's green stone, I couldn't help but drag my hand along the stalagmites as I passed. To my dismay, they were damp, rough, and incredibly dense. I quickly pressed the entirely of my weight into one of the taller cones, but it wouldn't budge. It was as real as real could be.

The only one who didn't appear surprised was Kaylah. Upon surveying the chamber, she yawned. I pulled myself up onto Tina's geode and leapt inside. She was in the exact same position I had left her in, but her bandages were soaked with blood. I pressed my fingers into the side of her neck and waited. Her skin was cold to the touch. I couldn't find a pulse. Panicked, I jabbed deeper and waited.

I waited for an eternity. Then the weakest "thump" pressed against my fingertips. I began to weep. "Michael?" Eden spoke. I looked up to find everyone's eyes on me, huddled around the rim of the geode.

"She's alive," I said, "barely."

Everyone sighed with relief until Gomez hollered, "Listen!" with his head cocked to the side. The deep rumblings of rushing water echoed from the hole in the wall with a force several times that of the waterfall we had camped below. My pulse quickened as my mind flooded with discordant data. The dimensions of the chamber are different, the air is drier, and at least twenty degrees cooler, all of our supplies, our backpacks, weapons, everything we had laid on the floor has vanished. The morphine, my OxyContin, has vanished! At some point during the night, we had all been physically moved to a different location. This is absolutely not the same chamber we fell asleep in.

"Where's my M-4?" Sabol demanded, scanning the ground. He stopped abruptly and threw his hand on his chest as he inhaled carefully. "Does anyone else feel like the air is thinner?"

We gave up asking questions, questions Kaylah either would not or could not answer, and we instead made a beeline for the tunnel. After covering Tina with another layer of jackets and emergency blankets, I clawed my way back up the dark, rocky shoot behind the soldiers. The roar of the waterfall above grew ever more engulfing the further we moved.

Once again, I tumbled headfirst from the cave's mouth, onto damp earth. I wrestled myself to my feet to join the crowd of shocked faces at the sight stretching before us. We now stood on a narrow ledge behind an enormous, deafening waterfall of sparkling whites and electric blues. This waterfall was twenty times larger than the one we had slept below. Sabol immediately removed the GPS device from his utility belt. After he stared at the readout for far too long, my patience reached its end. "Is it broken?" I shouted with all my strength, though he stood right next to me. My words emerged as a whisper beneath the sound and fury of rushing water. At first, I assumed I misheard his response.

"Oh, it's working," he shouted, "and it says we're in the southern bank of China."

Eden snatched the GPS from his hands and stared at the screen. "We're in the Tsangpo Gorge between India and Tibet," she hollered. "The last unexplored stretch of land on Earth. No one walks out of here. We're as good as dead."

# PART FOUR

## The Beyul

*"A form of consciousness beyond the veils of discursive thought, a space forever present for those who seek it, not in some far-off wilderness, but in our inner most hearts. When that realization dawns in the depths of one's being, the world effortlessly transforms into that which was sought."*

Ian Baker, *The Heart of the World*

Kaylah jumped about, waving her hands in a comically weak attempt to pull us from the barrage of asinine questions we all shouted at one another over the roar of the waterfall crashing an arm's length from our faces. With a blank mind, I peered down over our ledge to watch the fantastic deluge explode into blinding, white mist far, far below. When the child finally snagged our attention, she immediately spun to face the falls, dropped to one knee, and bowed her head to the ground. After a brief pause, she turned and flashed an intense glare that demanded we follow suit. Tina is at the bottom of that cave dangling at the edge of death, and we're stopping to pray? Anger was beginning to outweigh confusion.

The muscles in the roof of my mouth were pulled so tightly, all the soft tissues felt like stone. My entire throat was in agony. This began somewhere back in my midteens when I began to notice that whenever I was overwhelmed with problems I couldn't readily solve, the roof of my mouth would seize. Why, I did not know, but it was never quite this painful.

Just as Pavlik began to vocalize his complaints with our senseless act of prostration, an enormous shadow arose from behind the screen of rushing water. My heart clenched. When the full breadth of the towering silhouette unfolded behind the veil, its motion and form matched those of a King Cobra, one several stories high, preparing to strike. Kaylah hushed the many groans of abject fear and anxiety arising from the team.

Well, that's it. The beast from last night has returned to finish us off. And this time we're completely defenseless. Just as it had before, the creature lowered its massive head and slowly pushed its snout through the waterfall. It didn't so much as flinch a muscle under the unimaginable hydraulic force raining onto it. After the tip of the creature's nose pierced the blanket, it was immediately clear this was most certainly not the same chimera of animals that had attacked us the night before. What now emerged from the falls was a dazzling weave of pearlescent scales glistening with subtle rainbows. This was pure serpent, or, more specifically, a highly polished opal that had magically sprung to life in the form of a giant serpent. Its snout twitched and flared mere inches above Kaylah's tiny kneeling form, inhaling her every detail. As the beast studied her, the falls pounded from its scales into a splashing mist that filled the air with stinging ice. No one dared move.

Suddenly Kaylah's hair and clothing fluttered and flapped upward toward the serpent's immense nostrils as it inhaled with enough force to vacuum out the air around us. Then, without another sound, it jerked its neck backward and disappeared behind the veil once more. We lifted our heads in stunned silence while the dark shadow slipped back into the mists below, out of sight. Without further explanation Kaylah sprang to her feet and motioned us to follow.

"I have questions about that," Sabol muttered to himself. It took us all a few moments to shake off whatever the hell had just happened—these were becoming just "the next insane event in a series"—but we soon fell to a hurried pace behind our spritely guide, jogging single-file down the narrow passage between the falls and the cliff wall. When we rounded the massive arch of water into piercing morning sun, everyone paused breathlessly at our newfound surroundings, except for Kaylah.

We emerged from behind the waters to discover we were now perched atop an endless cliff nestled deep within the largest canyon I had ever laid eyes on. Slender pine trees and low-lying ferns dotted the face of a gorge extending to the horizon in either direction, reaching up into dark, gray foothills at our backs. Only by cranking my neck completely backwards could I trace the layer-upon-layer of foothills that soared into jagged, snow-covered peaks cutting the crisp, blue skies overhead. Far below our rocky ledge the yawning waterfall crashed into swirls of white mists that gave way to an enormous, raging river snaking into a shadowy canyon.

I anxiously studied the cloud cover dissipating into the depths of the watery chasm, but saw no sign of the animal we had just encountered. This offered little relief. There was no escaping the inevitable: We were still in the middle of no-man's land, but this was no landscape found in Peru, or any other country in South America for that matter. And we were most certainly at a much higher elevation. That's two more attacks waged on all rationality. First, the GPS says we're in Tibet. Second—and, this factoid packed the strongest punch—this place fucking looks like Tibet.

I had never visited the Himalayas, but I had watched enough footage on the adventure channels to make a reasonably confident identification. Before anyone had a chance to catch their bearings, Kaylah was calling us to follow her up the cliff wall she was scaling. I could only hope she was leading us to someone with a background in emergency medicine. All the other insane details took a backseat to the priority of saving Tina.

The sudden change in elevation meant less oxygen and less energy for everyone, but I was clearly suffering the most. Not only was I out of shape, withdrawal was steadily rearing its head. This was far more than the side effects of thin, chilly air and anxiety. Cold sweats and aching knees warned that my mounting discomfort had little to do with muscle or emotional fatigue. As we scrambled the slippery boulders crowning the canyon walls just south of the falls, everyone inundated Eden with questions about what she knew about our newfound environment.

"The Tsangpo Gorge is the deepest canyon on the face of the Earth," Eden panted behind me. "And the deadliest. Explorers have been trying, and failing, for years to get into the heart of the Tsangpo. This place has a way of swallowing up anyone stupid enough to walk into it."

"What can be so dangerous about this place, professor?" Gomez asked pointedly, "assuming, of course, we really are in Tibet."

"Which makes no sense, whatsoever," I mumbled more to myself than anyone else.

"No, shit," Pavlik wheezed. "It's fucking impossible."

Eden ignored our complaints and focused on the landscape at hand. "Some say the danger is due to the insane changes in elevation, others say it has more to do with unstable seismic activity. Mudslides, landslides. They say the ground here has a way of opening up and devouring anything on the surface from time to time. About a hundred years ago, a team of some fifty, rugged British explorers were wiped out after less than a week of hiking into this gorge. Only a handful made it out alive. The survivors said some of their men were killed by avalanches of snow and rocks that crushed and buried them instantly. Several more were bled dry by giant leeches that fell from the trees."

"Bullshit," I said. "You'd notice something that big landing on you."

"You'd think that, wouldn't you?" Eden laughed. "Supposedly, when they land, they inject you with a numbing toxin so you can't feel them. Anyway, the few survivors claimed that the rest of their team were sacrificed by a tribe of savages who'd been living back here for thousands of years, completely cut off from the outside world. They said that just before they escaped, the tribe had begun to toss their companions to their death into a giant pit filled with human remains."

"Well, this just keeps getting better and better," Sabol added.

"I actually met a guy once who tried to explore this area," Eden continued. "Back in the 90's this dude, Ian Baker and a small *National Geographic* team managed their way further into this gorge than any other documented trek in history. After battling extreme weather, rockslides, mysterious illnesses, and leeches, they were forced to turn around after losing one of their team members to the river. Officially, they were trying to find a series of waterfalls that are said to be hidden back here."

"Well, I think we got that one covered, at least," Sabol remarked. Eden stopped and stared down at the walkway that led behind the falls.

"Ian Baker didn't care about finding lost waterfalls as much as he was in finding lost worlds," Eden added as her mind wandered. "I believe he was looking for what the Tibetans refer to as a Beyul."

"The driver, Alto, who attacked us used that same word when he was questioning Kaylah," I said. Eden paused to catch her breath.

"Buddhists and Tibetan shaman believe that there are a few, rare places scattered around the globe where the spiritual and physical planes overlap," she said. "They say that these areas are generally found either near waterfalls or large bodies of water for some reason. A Beyul is like a portal to another realm, a realm that's impossible to get to by 'ordinary' means."

"So, which is it, doc?" Pavlik touted from the rear of the line. "Are we walking into heaven or hell?"

"Most definitely," Eden replied.

Upon summiting the ridge to a sparsely forested plateau, Kaylah motioned us to stop and quiet ourselves. A harsh wind rushed down from the mountain range ahead. Uneasily, I forced myself to stare up at the rugged, snow-swept peaks rising defiantly around us. I was on the verge of reaching a conclusion about everything I had witnessed over the days, but it was just out of reach, buried in the pit of my mind. I could sense its presence, some elegant symmetry of understanding that coalesced all of these frayed ends into one, perfect circle of truth. All the data that had dammed up in memory, frequencies that twist physical objects into random patterns at the atomic level, impossible feats of strength, real-live monsters and, apparently, teleportation to the other side of the globe, all of it boiled down to some elemental theory that I envisioned as a ring of light. I had yet to make out the details, but it was there. It had to be. I suppose, ultimately, I needed to believe there was a logical explanation behind everything we were experiencing.

I looked down at my shirt and realized something about it had been quietly pulling at my attention. Somehow, the color or the fabric was different. Furthermore, everyone else's appearance seemed slightly off. It occurred to me that the light spectrum at this elevation must be altering the colors.

As we continued walking, I drifted to a memory of Damian and Kyle arguing about how the teleporters on *Star Trek* would hypothetically work. Damian insisted that in the future a quantum principle called "entanglement" would be responsible for making instantaneous transport from one location to another an everyday reality. He argued that once two particles interact in a certain way, they will forever behave as one, single entity no matter how far the two of them were separated from one another. Kyle said this "entanglement" principle would eventually power a new species of computers with something called "quantum processing." I couldn't understand what any of it had to do with teleportation, but I was once again left feeling slightly less anxious knowing there may be some kind of scientific hypothesis behind instantaneous relocation.

Balanced on tiptoes, Kaylah scanned the ridgeline across the plateau toward the mountain range. With fingers skillfully cupped around her mouth, she released a perfect impression of a hawk's cry. Sabol and Pavlik actually looked to the skies for a moment to locate the nonexistent beast. After several minutes, a figure darted up, over the ridge in the distance, sprinting over the plains in our direction. As the mysterious figure closed in, it took the shape of a Native-African woman wrapped in a multillayered robe of beige and green. She ran with outstretched arms; her thick, braided hair held in a long, fiery orange scarf that waved behind her like a dragon kite. Kaylah shrieked with excitement and darted ahead to greet her. When the woman scooped the child into her arms, tears rolling down her cheek, it was clear we were witnessing a mother and daughter reunited.

"Well, at least she doesn't look dangerous," Pavlik remarked. Although the scene was genuinely touching, my next thought was: This woman had better be a doctor. The two were still locked in deep embrace when we reached them at the edge of a plateau sloping into thick, green valley below. Behind tears of joy, the woman nodded as we approached.

"Bless you all," she wept with a heavy, Sudanese accent. "You brought my little monkey home! My name is Eyh-boh-gayne. You may call me Iboga."

Before the woman could utter another word, two young men sprinted directly at us from the valley below, the same direction from which Iboga had emerged. Both were tall, muscular and also appeared to be of Central African descent. Neither wore shoes, but their cargo shorts and worn T-shirts were quintessentially Western. They ran with a force and determination that startled everyone; everyone except Kaylah and her mother. The soldiers readied themselves for attack, but the sprinters split off and bolted around our huddle, directly passed us toward the waterfall.

"I woulda figured . . . " Pavlik began with a confused stutter as he watched the two young men disappear over the ridgeline, "that Tibet would have more . . . Tibetans." After scanning each of us head to toe, a subtle look of suspicion crossed Iboga's face.

"Do you know me?" Iboga asked. We all exchanged glances, wondering to whom the question was directed.

Looking back and forth between Iboga and the rest of us, Gomez hazarded a reply,

"Uh, no, ma'am," he said. "Do you know us?"

Gomez's reply inspired great mirth within the woman. She let out a joyous "Ha!" to the sky before lowering her head to hug Kaylah tighter. The child bounced, screeched and hooted, mimicking a baby chimp in her mother's arms.

"I know there is no time to waste," Iboga said to me as if responding to an unspoken question. She gestured to the waterfall behind us. "Tasha and Lemm will retrieve your love and bring her to our village. Ms. Flores' life force is weak. You must come. Many forces are working against you."

"I didn't describe my relationship with 'Ms. Flores.' And just what the hell do you know about her life force'?" I demanded. Iboga lowered a small, quilted satchel from around her shoulder and opened it to reveal its contents. Along with everyone else, I bent over to peek inside the pouch to find it empty.

"Please," Iboga began. "I must ask each of you for all the money you are carrying. My daughter, my husband, my village, we are very poor. Please. We are starving and water is scarce."

I looked around the team and found I was the most baffled and disturbed by the woman's request. Without hesitation, Eden pulled her ironically bedazzled, bright pink purse from the shoulder pack she had used as a pillow within the geode. She ripped out all the bills and tossed them carelessly into the woman's satchel.

"Are you kidding me?" I nearly shouted. "This doesn't make any goddamned sense! Water is not scarce here!"

"Please," Iboga pleaded with needful eyes, "we are very poor."

Obedient to Eden's lead, the soldiers removed money clips and wallets from hidden pockets and military vests and tossed whatever they had into the pile. And, yes, yes, of course I had my wallet on me. It was zipped into my left pocket inside my jacket. Along with two credit cards, I brought just over nine hundred dollars in cash. It wasn't enough to destroy me if it was lost or stolen, but it would be enough to get me out a jam if I found myself somewhere a card was useless. Beneath a growing number of eyes, I begrudgingly removed my wallet and, with the billfold turned in my direction, I pantomimed pulling out all the cash while pressing my thumb on three of the fifty dollar bills to keep them safely behind. I slammed my wallet shut and stuffed the money into her satchel. She smiled knowingly at me and pulled the drawstring shut. Did she know what I did? How could she?

"Thank you, professor," she said, bowing her head. But, something else was distracting me now; something else out of place that I had just laid eyes on: the corner of some document stuffed into my wallet. Had I read it correctly during my little 'sleight of hand' trick? Did it really read, "The Ministry of

Foreign Affairs of . . . something, something . . . The People's Republic of China"? I had no memory of any such piece of paper in my possession. In light of current events, it seemed of little importance.

I snapped from my trance upon realizing the team had moved on, deeper into the valley on the heels of the strange woman and her child. They had left me behind on the wind-swept plateau. I watched them vanish beneath the blanket of pines, and tears began to well. I was losing my mind and my body was in agony. Without better options, I broke into a steady jog down the ridge to catch up.

The sunlight faded as the forest grew increasingly dense. For a moment, I panicked that I had become lost. As soon as I stopped to listen for signs of movement through the trees, Tasha and Lemm burst through the foliage behind me with twice the intensity as before, but this time they sprinted single file. As they darted around me, I caught a glimpse of a person on a bamboo stretcher swaying between them. It was Tina. I broke into a heart-pounding chase to keep them in sight. I caught up with the team just as they emerged from the forest into a massive clearing of tall, yellow grasses.

While I tried to digest the sight ahead, the blood-curdling aches of detox rose to frightening new levels. Lying before us in the sunny clearing within a natural, bowl-shaped indentation in the earth were twelve dwellings spread out in honeycomb formation. Though they were approximately of equal size, each hut was of a unique construction and source material. Some appeared to be made of dried mud and tightly wound branches, others were constructed of layers of animal skins pulled around wooden posts. One of the more angular homes was pieced together with gray bricks made of clay. A wooden plank hung just outside the entrance of this particular dwelling with the numbers "137" carved into it.

We followed Tasha and Lemm through the center of the village and my head spun to make sense of our surroundings. Eden gasped in wonder as she took in the sights. Only a small handful of inhabitants could be spotted throughout the camp. Two women knelt over a cast iron pot strung over a fire between the huts. One of them appeared to be from India. A delicate, gold chain draped her forehead above a reddish spot on her third-eye center. She was dressed in a dark, ochre robe and sandals. Her companion appeared older and was also clearly not from this part of the world. Her smooth olive skin, bright almond eyes and rounded cheekbones were clear indications of Asian Pacfic ancestry. They both raised their heads, smiled widely, and waved as if greeting old friends. An elderly Chinese woman stood motionless on the front stoop of a "V" shaped home constructed of bamboo overlaid with massive, dried palms. With eyes lightly shut and knees slightly bent, she held her hands in front of her stomach as if cradling an enormous, invisible pot belly. "Where the hell are we?" Sabol muttered.

Upon crossing a massive fire pit at the center of the small village, a pair of Native American Indians, a man and woman, from which tribe, I could not guess, emerged from the forest hauling a deer carcass over their shoulders. They nodded respectfully just before I followed the team through the arched doorway of a larger, dome-shaped dwelling. When my eyes adjusted to the dark setting, I found we had entered a hut constructed of a swirling latticework of white Aspen branches. I was pleasantly shocked to find the temperature at least fifteen degrees warmer on the inside. Delicate aromas of lavender and mint filled the air.

The two men transferred Tina's body to an oblong, wooden table at the center of the floor, just beneath a rounded light beam. We huddled in tight formation around her until Iboga demanded we give her room to work. The light they worked under passed through an opening at the ceiling's apex where the Aspens spun counterclockwise to form a skylight, and then down to form the walls. My mind drifted briefly while I tried to imagine how such a feat of architecture was performed. Beneath me, Tasha and Lemm carefully washed Tina's wounds. As I cringed at the physical damage, detox overwhelmed my focus. Waves of nausea and aches marched through me with greater intensity. I began to wonder how much longer I would be able to stand upright.

In quiet desperation, I studied the rows upon rows of wooden shelving that lined the hut. Each held perhaps a hundred or more glass jars, stone bowls, and handmade baskets filled with plant extracts, flower petals, and dried roots. Though I couldn't begin to identify anything in the collection, there didn't appear to be any opium pods.

"It's like some ancient pharmacy," Sabol exclaimed, examining a small bundle of dried, red roots.

"Maybe these people really are healers," Eden said hopefully, squeezing my arm. Suddenly, a man spoke from the darkened periphery of the hut, beyond the reach of the skylight.

"Perhaps, young Miss," he said with a polished, Southern accent, "but a true healer is also capable of bringing about unspoken agony."

Before I could pick out the man's form amongst the shadows, it was too late. He had unsheathed a hunting knife, leapt around to my back and pressed the cold blade against the side of my neck. With a precise flick of the wrist, he quickly sliced down and back before expertly returning the knife to its sheath. I could only assume he had just cut my throat and the pain had yet to set in. My greatest misery was that I would die with so many unanswered questions.

Then something fell to the stone flooring at my feet with a wet splatter. I looked down to find the writhing mass of a dark brown leech; the absolute longest, fattest I thought possible. The man then stepped into the light at my side and patted my shoulder as if we were old friends.

"You need to watch out for those things. They fall from the trees and if you're not careful, they'll eat you alive," he smiled. "Good to see you again, Professor Huxley."

# Harsh Reality

*"If you believe that you are NOT omnipresent, omniscient, and ultimately omnipotent—you are delusional. If you believe that you are separate from that which you call God, then you are living a lie."*

Kevin Michel, *Moving Through Parallel Worlds to Achieve Your Dreams*

Not only had I never met the man standing before me in the medicine hut, everything about him seemed out of place. Caucasian, midfifties, unshaven with shoulder length, jet-black hair with gray streaks. His glasses were slightly scratched, but the frames were modern. His black, snap-buttoned shirt and jeans were well worn, but definitely store-bought.

"You're . . . " Eden stuttered, trying to wrap her head around the man, "you're white."

"That's what they tell me around here, yes," he smiled, leaning over to study Tina's wounds. His accent sounded Texan.

"Sorry," Eden said, trying to add it up, "it's just . . . I thought we were being taken to a tribe of shaman."

"Maybe your idea of what a shaman looks like is out of date," he replied kindly. "Some men come into knowledge through religious practice, others arrive through science. They call me Sadhu."

Eden shook her head with further disbelief.

"It's true, it's not my birth name," he admitted. "Everyone who lives here must drop their history. Relinquishing the arbitrary word you are identified with is as good a start as any, I s'pose."

I didn't like the sound of this, but I pushed aside the possibility that we were at the mercy of another brainwashed cult and focused on the men working on Tina. Tasha and Lemm gently peeled the soaked bandages from her shoulder and abdomen to reveal damage worse than I remembered.

"Her wounds have not improved," Iboga commented. The hole punched through her upper waist was so enormous, it didn't seem possible she could still be alive. Iboga handed

220

Tasha a wooden bowl filled with a thick, gray mixture of what appeared to be wet clay and crushed leaves, while Lemm filled a long, wooden pipe with a dried, green herb. Kaylah helped light the pipe with a burning twig she had pulled from beneath an iron kettle.

"Is that . . . marijuana?" I asked.

"Oh, no, that's a concentration of oregano," Sadhu whispered, resting his hand on my shoulder again. I couldn't tell if he was joking with me, but he continued as if he were entirely serious. "Plant extracts are more efficient at fighting infection and repairing damage than antibiotics or pharmaceuticals; the body or other bacteria doesn't build a resistance to herbal remedies. Some of the healing methods we keep alive here date back more than fifty thousand years. If the patient is receptive, there is nothing they can't accomplish. I've witnessed them cure cancer and bring people back from the dead."

"I sincerely doubt everything you just said," I whispered back, only partially involved in the discussion. "No offense," I added, trying to maintain composure. He chuckled easily.

"I bear no interest in your trust, son." Son? You're ten years my senior at the most. After a moment of consideration, Sadhu chuckled again. "Ya know, partner," he said, leaning closer, "it's the people who want your faith you really need to watch out for. But I don't need to tell you that, do I? You're a man of science. You doubt everything."

"Yeah, what's wrong with that?" I growled.

"Nothing at all. I doubt those who don't."

With my attention on Tina, I couldn't help notice 'Sadhu' studying me from the corner of my eye. I couldn't get a lock on this guy. He looked and sounded like a man who just walked out of a 1960s cigarette commercial, yet he spoke like a monk. Sadhu leaned in again with a hushed tone. "I bet you think the frequency you're chasing after flew outta some electronic gadget, don'tcha?"

After basking in my blank stare, he slapped my back with a laugh as if we had just shared a private joke. "Well, I suppose technically you wouldn't be wrong. Technically."

I glared at him momentarily before Tasha and Lemm began scooping up dripping handfuls of the chunky, gray-green mush to slather over Tina's bloody incisions. She moaned weakly as they worked. I hated to see her suffer, but was relieved to see her respond to stimuli. After Tasha would spread a layer of the clay, Lemm would inhale a chest full of smoke from his pipe, lean in and blow over the soaked area with considerable force. It was mesmerizing to watch the surface of the mixture lighten and dry under his powerful exhalations. When I knelt to help them turn her body, I realized that Tasha was wearing a faded Run-D.M.C. T-shirt, and my anxiety crept a little higher. These don't look like medicine men. Cold sweats were now tearing angrily up and down my spine.

"Is this going to heal her?" I asked Sadhu. He shook his head while watching the men work. When he realized I had directed the question at him, he coughed with surprise.

"Oh, hell, I don't know," he gasped, studying me again. "They're the healers, not me."

"This will absorb the toxins in her system," Iboga answered with mild irritation, as if I should have known to direct the question to her. "It will stop the bleeding for now, but it won't repair the internal damage fast enough. She will be dead by the end of the day."

"Okay," I said impatiently, straining under mounting agony. "Then, what do we do?"

Noticing my struggle to stand upright, Iboga moved her attention to me. She removed a rag from a copper bowl of water on the shelf and placed it on my forehead. Whatever was infused into her water left a cool, tingling sensation on my skin, a brief, but welcomed relief from the discomfort that was quickly rising to unbearable levels. My nerves had now declared mutiny and were actively working to either escape the boundaries of my skin, or reach up and strangle me.

"We cannot heal her," Iboga said gently, dabbing my forehead again. "If we intervene, it will be a waste of time, precious time that you do not have. By tomorrow evening, you all must return to Peru, those of you who are still with us. It's the rainy season and the waters are rising." She pressed her index finger into the center of my chest, directly on the incision from my surgery several years ago. "And on this side of the Dreaming Tree, doctor, you must return through the green flower for the Beyul to accept you."

"What the hell does any of this mean?" I hollered, swiping the woman's hand from my forehead. My stomach twisted into knots and my legs crumbled. All the warmth and energy steadily drained from my muscles to be replaced by freezing acid. I caught myself just before collapsing to the floor. "You're just going to let her die?" I wheezed, bent over with hands on my knees. Tasha and Lemm leapt up to help me, but I pushed them back.

"Professor Huxley," Sadhu exclaimed, jumping down to face me, "you don't understand. We don't have time to heal her . . . but you do. The only way any of you are going to survive is if we kill two birds with one stone, so to speak."

"More like six birds with one stone," Iboga added before turning to her daughter. "Your father should have finished preparing my roots by now. Bring them quickly." Oddly enough, Kaylah seemed to understand her instructions in English and quickly vanished through the doorway.

"As for the rest of you, your guides will be here shortly to take you on your respective journeys," Iboga said, addressing Eden and the soldiers. "Each of you, including Professor Huxley, must find your own way through your unique pattern of darkness. I promise you will find the answers you are ready for. Or death. The result is the same."

"Excuse me?" Pavlik asked angrily.

"This has gotta be a joke," Sabol agreed, turning to Gomez. "What the hell is going on?"

"You're not dividing us up," Gomez said firmly, crossing his arms. "We're here to protect them."

"That is most certainly not why you are here, soldier," Iboga smiled.

"I'm not leaving his side," Eden added as she helped my shivering body into sitting position. "If you're giving him what

I think you're about to give him, he's in for one hell of a ride. He's not prepared for this. He needs me."

"Does he, child?" Iboga laughed. Lemm handed me a leather canteen of water gesturing that I consume all of it. Once I did, Tasha wrapped a warm blanket that smelled of tobacco and lilacs around my shoulders, another welcomed, but temporary pause from my agony.

"We know why you're here and what you need to know, but I'm afraid there's no other way to proceed," Sadhu explained. He pulled a hand-rolled cigarette from his shirt pocket and lit it with a snap of a black, Zippo lighter. "We can't reach all of you with the same technique. Each of you needs to approach this from a different angle in order to see what's really happening and just what's at stake."

"Oh, Jesus Christ!" Eden hollered, leaping to her feet. "Enough of the coy bullshit already! Save the Zen koans for the tourists. We need answers."

"Why does everyone here seem to know us?" Gomez demanded. Sadhu took in the tired, frustrated faces around him and conceded with a subtle nod of the head. After a heavy sigh, he broke into explanation.

"Ya know, I was working at a particle accelerator facility in a little town called Waxahachie in Texas before I came here," he began before reconsidering his words with a half-smile. "Moments before I came here, to be precise. My job was to . . . "

"I'm sorry, you're a particle physicist?" I interrupted in utter disbelief. Nothing about this man fit into any of my stereotypes for "scientist" or "shaman."

Sadhu smiled and continued, "You could say my job was to peer back to the first moments of creation. After many years of research, I've witnessed enough incomprehensible phenomena to bring most men to the brink of insanity. Some of the truths I've come to understand concerning just how matter and energy take shape in this universe took years for me to accept. And there's a good deal more I know to be true which my noodle simply isn't designed to grasp. Our brains aren't evolved enough to handle what physicists are uncovering. Given that,

I'm never sure of the best way to break news to folks which completely conflicts with their heavily entrenched schemas."

"Sir, our 'schemas' have had their asses kicked over the last couple days," Sabol replied. "The thing that punched a pair of holes into my client here wasn't human, that I can say for sure."

"There's nothing you can tell us that is going to shock us at this point," Eden added. Iboga let out another boisterous "Ha!" from the other side of the medicine lodge where she tended a kettle over a small fire.

"Accepting that monsters exist is easy," Sadhu explained. "That's something happening out there. It's actually fairly easy to accept that sort of shit." He gestured toward the center of his forehead. "But, when we're forced to question just what it is that's really looking out through our eyes, well, that's when the real horror sets in for a lot of folks. That can bring the strongest man to his knees." Sadhu began to clean his glasses with a handkerchief when he found himself surrounded by several, impatient faces. He folded his arms tightly and lowered his head.

"Fine, but I bear no responsibility if one of you freaks out; you came huntin' for us," he announced, staring at the floor. "So, let's start with the easy stuff. Everyone in this village knows you because from where we're standin' you all showed up several days ago. Your most recent visit, that is. An Agent Downey of the FBI, I believe his name was, arranged the diplomatic negotiations necessary for you all to pass through China into the Tsangpo Gorge with three chaperones from the Chinese government, two of whom died along the way. The third now lives with us as an intern, if you will. Your team was searching for an uncontacted tribe hidden deep in the canyon, a village of shaman from every walk of life. Sound familiar?"

Sadhu took a brief bow while Iboga did a halfhearted curtsy. My heart rate rose higher.

"You were following the trail of a religious cult from a small mountain town back in the States," he continued. "It took your team nineteen days to pass through the gorge this time around. Almost all of your gear and belongings have been either lost or destroyed along the way. When you arrived on our plateau, most of you were at the edge of death."

"You said 'this time around,'" Sabol reminded him. A jolt of electricity shot up my back as I recalled the document stuffed in my wallet. Eden clutched at my arm and leaned into me, taken by the man's ridiculous tale. Her fingernails cut like daggers in my bicep.

"Utter bullshit, Señor" Gomez sighed and lowered his head dismissively.

"Dude, I don't know who you're talking about, but that ain't us," Pavlik said, his voice growing louder. "Last night, we were sleeping in a cave in the middle of a rainforest in Peru! All of us know that, right?" He performed a quick check to be sure we all agreed with him. "Ask that woman's daughter for God's sake!" Pavlik barked, pointing at Iboga. "She's the one who led us there!" Sadhu waved his hands in surrender.

"I understand that, son," he said quietly. "What I'm saying is, you weren't teleported here. From our point of view, you were all already here. Now, that's a golden detail, perhaps the most important. When you really understand what that Beyul actually did do to you, you'll know everything you need to know to save your lives, as well as Agent Flores'. Only then will you understand what's hunting you."

"Only then will you see why Reverend Kane is a dangerous man," Iboga said with remorse.

"So you do know the reverend?" Eden demanded. "Okay, that's a start. He did spend time here with you?"

"What do you mean by, 'this time around?'" Sabol repeated louder.

"Are you the ones who made Kane a dangerous man?" Gomez asked. At that, the wry smile fell from Sadhu's face and he lowered his head. Before he could speak, Kaylah burst into the hut with a hulking, middle aged man in tow.

"We should have let them die," the man said, framed in the doorway like a brick wall, bearing features of a full blooded, Mexican Indian: Piercing, dark eyes, chiseled features, and sharp cheekbones. His heavily tattooed arms held a wide, stone bowl filled with a dark, green powder. Beaded necklaces and hammered, metal cuff links adorned his neck and arms. Shimmering, black hair draped his back covered by a sleeveless, yellow tunic falling just below his knees. With a nod of his head, the man stepped under the skylight on obscenely muscular legs.

"So, why didn't you let him die?" Gomez asked, turning his attention to our new arrival. The man ignored him as he moved around Tina's bed. "What happened to those Christians when I tried to heal them was whispered in tales long ago by my ancestors," he explained in a voice rumbling with an ancient accent I couldn't begin to decipher. He laid the heavy mortar on a narrow, wooden table between the two beds. My attention was divided among my quickly depleting physical state, the Indian and the contents of my wallet.

"When the Spanish invaded our shores, they came bearing the cross," he continued, staring into the skylight, losing himself in memory. "Our medicine men offered their priests to participate in our ceremonies, with the hopes of demonstrating that we, too, had religion, just as they did. Perhaps if we could prove our gods as powerful as their Jesus, the invaders would leave us in peace."

He shook his head and touched Tina's forehead.

"My people would tell a story about something terrible that happened to one of their priests during a healing ritual, a man who had become deathly ill during the long, ocean voyage. But in his case, the ceremony was akin to throwing water on a grease fire. They spoke of hideous transformation and acts of unimaginable savagery. Whatever happened to this priest of theirs convinced many of our people that at least part of their holy book was true, the parts about hell and what lives there. I never thought I'd see this curse come full circle."

Iboga quietly thanked the man with a gentle kiss on the cheek before he silently exited the hut. For some time, no one spoke. Eventually, everyone began to draw their attention to me with expressions that screamed, "Well, YOU'RE the scientist. "Science" us out of this shit!"

Suddenly, the terrible frequency boomed through my

memory and I found myself in the most dreadful state of mind, one I had only experienced for a few, brief moments in my life. What felt like a massive, empty pit inside my stomach was something far sinister. The sensation was that of a dark crossroads where I stood imprisoned by a thousand and one equally valid, equally insane possibilities. Each option branched out before me without solid reason, "supporting data" or even an instinct to take one step closer toward any one of them over the other.

"I imagine this is all a lot to take in," Sadhu said quietly, shaking his head. "We are indeed the Craneo Roto clan, though we go by a lot of names. We carry the torch of knowledge long forgotten and dismissed by civilization, and yes, rare loopholes in the law of physics which have brought you all here to us. Furthermore, Reverend Kane and his people have hijacked, if you will, a formula intended for spontaneous, radical healing of the physical body. They know how to follow a technique but they have no understanding of the mechanics behind it. And that, we now know, is terribly dangerous."

With shivering hands, I mustered the courage, the sheer will, to snatch my jacket from the floor. I yanked out my wallet and hastily removed the foreign document I had glimpsed earlier on the plateau. Everyone leaned over my shoulders as I studied the seemingly official travel visa I now held. It was badly beaten and frayed at the edges as if it had been thrown into a washing machine. Every last detail about me was typed into a section on this mysterious form titled "Temporary Visa Holder": my full name, address, social security number, and the airport I had apparently departed from: Denver International. It was dated several weeks ago along with my signature just below the "personal data" box.

This could be a forgery. This paper could have been easily shoved into my jacket while I was asleep. Just because I don't have a better explanation doesn't mean this guy's ridiculous story is true.

Eden shook me harder by the shoulder the longer she studied the Visa I held. "What does this mean?" she whispered with growing fear. "How? . . . How?!"

After a confused search through the many pockets on his military vest, Sabol removed a highly weathered paper identical to mine. "This has my name on it," he said. Sadhu sighed deeply before cocking his head with a wince.

"Also," Sadhu said, contemplating his next words. "If you all check your bodies, paying special attention to your palms, your feet, you'll certainly discover calluses, bruises, and scarring from your journey through the gorge, ones you've never seen. And perhaps others that have vanished. In fact, your clothing may even be slightly different. There's an infinite number of little variations from one multiverse to the next."

I turned up my palm, though I absolutely did not want to study the details. Indeed, my hands were badly scraped and weathered, far worse than the damage they had suffered in the jungle alone.

While everyone broke into their own self inspections, I pulled up my pant leg to expose the stitches on my lower calf. Assuming I'd forgotten which ankle had taken the damage outside the biker bar, I fiercely jerked the opposite pant leg up to my knee, nearly tearing the hem in the process. Though both of my legs were bruised and filthy, neither betrayed any indication of the wound I had suffered just a couple days before in Boulder. I reached around to scan my back for the scar the creature had inflicted the previous night. Again, no marks whatsoever.

Sadhu rested his palm over Tina's forehead. "Unfortunately, as is often the case with major, life-altering changes to the body," he began, "the damage to Agent Flores here represents a dramatic shift in the quantum blueprint that is read by the rest of the incarnations. All the essential physical and emotion repercussions of, for example, a major automobile accident will generally bleed through an untold number of closely knit universes, but the specific details of the event may change from thread to thread. Consequently, Agent Tina Flores here slipped and fell from a cliff last night while on a vision quest with one of our Tibetan shamans. She was impaled on the jagged branches of a dead tree just before impact. That's why her wounds appear slightly different to you on this side."

"You mean, that's what happened 'this time around?'" Sabol asked with growing frustration.

"That is absolutely not what happened to her!" I grunted.

"We appreciate that," Iboga called from the far side of the hut. "My daughter explained what happened on your end."

"Your team has been visiting our tribe here in the Tsangpo for years," Sadhu continued. "It's always a slightly different story and there's always small changes among each of you."

"Okay," I conceded for the purposes of discussion. "Then why would that be the case?"

"Now that you've entered a Beyul, your lives will forever be entangled with it," Sadhu said with hint of a smile. "It's confusing, I know, but now that your team has merged with a singularity, the boundaries between one multiverse and next will begin to weaken. Be patient. It gets stranger."

My head spun in a blurry mess as my stomach spun the opposite direction. I lunged forward and staggered to the exit. I had to get outside, away from the madness. I collapsed onto the grass just outside the doorway as all the air rushed from my body. With a frightening amount of force, my stomach clenched and I dry-heaved in one agonizing wave after another, but I couldn't throw up. Eden rushed to my side and wrapped me in her arms, frantically massaging my neck and scalp, not so much for my benefit, but for her own.

"You'll be okay," she said shakily. "Everything's going to be okay." When she could no longer pretend my health was her primary concern, she took my head in her hands. Her lips trembled and eyes watered while she held my cheeks. I had never seen her so frightened. Why now? After everything we've been through, this is what breaks you?

"You're weren't supposed to let this happen!" she sobbed. Her head fell to her chest. "You were supposed to keep it straight! I don't know what to trust." Oh? I've lost YOUR trust, have I?

She stared into my eyes as if deeply betrayed. "And now . . ."

she cried, looking to the sky, "now what?"

For a moment, I almost wished her sudden, unbendable faith would kick back in, but it was just as flimsy and unstable as I imagined it was. She dumped my head into the grass, leapt to her feet and exploded into a full sprint. I had no energy to chase after her. She darted to the edge of the village and disappeared into the thick of the forest.

"We need to go after her!" Sadhu hollered from within the hut. "The last time she did this she nearly threw herself off the cliff!"

"Lemm!" Iboga shouted, and without hesitation Lemm burst through the entrance and leapt over me in fast pursuit. With the last of my strength, I rolled onto my back. High beyond the tiny village, past the foothills rose a line of charcoal peaks that sliced a crystalline sky with jagged, white-daggered points. A blinding vortex of snow spun silently from the highest peak in slow motion, like the minute hand creeping round the clock. I lost consciousness as the swirling mist dissipated behind the mountains.

# The Fabric of the Cosmos

*"Only after disaster can we be resurrected. It's only after you've lost everything that you're free to do anything. Nothing is static, everything is evolving, everything is falling apart."*

Chuck Palahniuk, *Fight Club*

I was awoken to the sensation of red-hot, razor-scaled snakes tearing their way through my muscles, joints, and tissue. A firm hand on my chest kept my body from jolting violently from the wooden table I lay upon. Rivers of sweat leaked from every pore in wretched waves of agony.

"Calm yourself, professor." I heard Iboga whisper. I anxiously scanned my surroundings to find I had been returned to the medicine hut. Tina remained unconscious on her bed a few feet away, parallel to mine. The rays pouring through the round skylight had grown weaker and I guessed it to be mid to late afternoon. Iboga and Sadhu began to speak inaudibly near the doorway. They appeared to be having a heated debate, but I couldn't hear their words. Clearly, these people are insane. But I'm alone, at the height of opiate withdrawal and at their total mercy.

"Where is everyone?" I hollered as nonconfrontationally as possible. "Where is Eden Jessup?"

"Eden and your soldier friends are fine," Sadhu replied, stepping away from Iboga with a calm smile. He lifted my wrist to check my pulse. "You'll be okay without her for a few hours. Trust me, she's more afraid of being away from you than you from her."

I had no strength to laugh beneath the agony, but I managed a disdained grunt. "You should see what she's capable of," I groaned.

"What's that?" he asked, dabbing my forehead with a cool rag that smelled of mint. "Impossible acts of rage? You were drawn to her because she was smart enough to question faith, but she does so out of revolt. We should always beware of anyone who loves religion with a fervor. Or hates it. Their final behavior is often identical."

"Eden isn't weak," I said.

"No," Iboga broke in, "but she thinks she wants freedom when the ultimate price scares the hell out of her. She'll condemn the beliefs of others while entertaining her own delusions. We only hope you can focus her energy in a constructive manner."

I shook my head. Iboga studied my face for a moment before smiling knowingly. "You think you are weaker than her because you are passive," she said, carrying a jar of mushy, green liquid.

"Drink all of this," she instructed, "and do not puke it up." I was in no position to argue. I could only hope that whatever sludge sat in that jar would somehow ease my suffering.

"Some people are passive because they fear what a fight will do to them," Iboga continued as I forced down the bitter liquid. "And some people are passive because they fear what they would do to another. Which are you?"

"Professor Huxley," Sadhu broke in before I could consider the question, "Eden is perfectly happy with the world being bizarre. But, now she's been presented with something about herself that truly scares her and she's folded. In desperation, she's turned to her father's blind faith; an image she's carried of 'God' to avoid knowing herself."

"I can't tell if you're being vague on purpose or because you think you're actually saying something deep," I grunted. What did I really expect when I agreed to track down an entire village of wise men? "I just want to know where you've taken Eden and my friends," I demanded as sternly as possible through the pain. Iboga gently lifted my head and positioned a handwoven pillow filled with dried herbs behind my neck.

"She and the rest of your friends have each been taken by a different member of our tribe, one who we believe can unlock their precise mindset," she explained. "Each shaman here is a master of a unique method of tapping into energy. Some, as myself, have mastered a specific medicinal plant; others, a martial art, or a meditation technique, or a healing process.

Although the objective with each of you is the same, our methods must speak to your individual egos."

"Why is that?" I asked. Sadhu shrugged his shoulders as if the answer was obvious.

"So they can be deconstructed. If you're to stand a fighting chance, you must be taken off your leash. To some extent, at least. It goes against everything you've been taught, I know. You've been brainwashed by your culture to strengthen your identity, to continually build it up and defend it at all costs. But if you want to tap into real power, you need to master step one of the formula for shapeshifting: Unlock the cage of your ego."

"You want to deconstruct my personality? That's brainwashing! What the hell are you doing with us?" I hollered, struggling to lift myself. With a single finger, Iboga pressed my forehead back to the pillow. Iboga and Sadhu both laughed. Sadhu leaned down to my face.

"You really think you aren't already brainwashed, professor?" he laughed quietly. He straightened himself and folded his arms contentedly. "Do you know how brainwashing works?" I stared at him with confusion while he awaited my response.

"Brainwashing is repeating the same thing over and over again," he finally answered himself. "It's the trenches we carve from walking back and forth along the same path in our head all day. The brain is molded by repetition. And the body follows the mind."

"We must wipe your slate clean so that you may start anew," Iboga said.

"You mean born again?" I asked angrily.

"That was the original intention behind the notion of spiritual rebirth, yes," she replied.

"You need to be deprogrammed, how's that?" Sadhu offered. "Reminded that you really don't know anything." He and I both laughed, but for very different reasons. What they had just suggested was ludicrous.

"Is there even a single thing you're sure of at this point, Professor Huxley?" Sadhu suddenly barked. "Professor, are you even sure that you're you? Have you really looked at your hands since you woke up this morning in the Dreaming Tree? Are you certain they're yours?"

Once again, I lifted my palms before me. I studied the thick callouses coating the top of my palms and the dozens of tiny cuts carved into my fingers. These hands don't look familiar. These were hands that had been beaten, bruised, and healed over, again and again, for weeks. From my perspective, I left Boulder two days ago. In my weakened state, I was in no condition to protect myself from yet another onslaught of insanity.

I ignored the agony required to turn onto my side and curl into a fetal position. In a few short days my entire world had been ripped apart, piece by piece. I had lost everything. Everything I knew, everything I trusted. I didn't know where I was, I didn't know who I was with, including the woman I had known for years. My opiates were gone, along with all my belongings. I didn't know what to believe about a scientifically reliable universe or even how much I could trust my own logic or judgment. And now, I doubted the skin I wore belonged to me. For the first time since I was a child, I stopped holding back and began to weep uncontrollably. I stopped caring, I stopped trying. I. just. fucking. stopped.

With the crash of floodgates thrown open, I let myself cry as hard as my body allowed, free of all resistance. I didn't care what these people thought of a grown man acting like a baby, and I didn't care who heard me.

Against all rationale, the longer I sobbed, the less miserable I felt. Stranger still, my fear seemed to be draining right out of me, into the table. And along with it, I no longer felt sorry for myself. In my mind's eye, I could actually see the very essence of my anxiety and self-pity seeping from my veins like a heavy, black tar; a pitch-black ooze the likes of which I had witnessed earlier, dripping from the creature who struck Tina. I pictured this acrid tar draining into the tabletop, down through the wooden legs and into the floor. I let it all pass. I even stopped fighting the insane predicament I was in.

Okay, the world doesn't work the way I thought it did. Maybe

I've gone completely insane. I don't care anymore. I give up. By this point, crying was just another open valve in a complex system; an unfiltered stream of emotion, as natural as blood flow. I watched as this stream died into a trickle, and then eventually fizzle out altogether. Sadhu laid a gentle hand on my shoulder and eased me onto my back. He leaned in and spoke quietly.

"I'm still waiting, professor," he whispered. "Just what is it that you know? What are you still sure of?"

Whether the force that burned through me was born of pure frustration or passion, I did not know. It moved with such intensity, I did not stop it to ask for identification. This explosion of energy punched through my body, into every fiber of my being, launching me into the air toward Sadhu. Like a starved animal, I pounced directly onto the man, pinning him to the floor, his eyes wide with pleasant shock. Every abdominal muscle turned to stone under the strain of shouting with all the force I could muster directly into Sadhu's face: "Nothing! There isn't one, goddamned thing I'm sure of! I have no fucking idea what's going on!"

After an extended, frozen pause, a grin sneaked across his face. "Well, that's the first step," he sighed, picking himself from the floor and straightening his shirt. "That's the quickest way to unleash yourself: Be at one with your total ignorance. Of course, the secret is that they're all first steps. Only when you've lost everything can you see what they can never take from you."

"That which does not come or go," Iboga said.

"Every particle in this universe is in constant motion, continuous change," Sadhu said. "Whether you realize it or not, you've come here to understand the secret of shapeshifting. But to do that, you have to see what never moves, what doesn't shapeshift."

I leaned backward and collapsed to the floor. A strange sensation washed over my body; one I was unfamiliar with, a quiet humming that penetrated my skin down to the bone. It took several moments to realize I was no longer roiling in agony. The razor-bladed snakes tearing through my veins had transformed into gentle streams of vibration, bizarre pulsations that twirled and danced in and out of my muscles and joints.

How is this possible? My gaze fell to the floor and I realized I was also seeing these swimming streams of pulsating rhythms move in and out of me through the ground. Solid matter, including the surface of my own skin now appeared almost translucent. Ethereal, white orbs flowed within a network of invisible webbing that stretched throughout my nervous system, down my spinal column and into the ground to connect with root systems deep below the earth. I looked up and found Sadhu and Iboga patiently observing me. They both sat cross-legged on the floor with a quiet intensity.

"Am I . . . am I tripping?" I asked, trying to find my grounding. "I'm in no condition for a drug trip right now." They smiled.

"Relax, professor," Iboga explained. "Everything I do is aimed at getting you to shut up for one, complete minute."

"You want me to stop asking questions?" I groaned. "That's not going to happen. I don't give up."

"I'm referring to your incessant thinking," Iboga said, tapping at her temple. "It takes more courage to sit in absolute silence for one minute than it takes to go into war. And to answer your question, I've given you the root from the apocynaceae family. You could say that the plant and I are One. I am the embodiment of its spirit. Ibogaine has taken you out of pain by temporarily filling in all the many gaps in your system."

"Only another opiate or a close derivative can do that," I mumbled, no longer sure of what I knew.

"And yet your withdrawal symptoms have vanished," Sadhu added.

"Next, it will cleanse your system of the toxins," Iboga explained. "That's going to be a slightly rougher ride."

I was still focused on the part about me shutting up for a minute. Could anyone blame me for asking questions? "So, you've given me a drug?" I asked, "to cure me from the drugs I've been doing?" The moment the words left my mouth I had the most peculiar realization of holding no investment in my question, or the answer. I dropped my concern about it immediately. That, in and of itself, was so unnatural, so against my instincts that I no longer felt like myself. All I could do at this point was watch.

With that, something moved through my newfound consciousness: The years I had spent hiding behind opiates washed through me, unveiling a sorrow in the center of my heart; a pain both physical and emotional, one that had been allowed to remain undisturbed for decades. Under the influence of Iboga's medicine, the source of this agony was now brutally obvious in full color and sound. Had I never been introduced to such powerful plants, ones Eden was so familiar with, I may have spent the rest of my days happily ignoring the quiet misery in my chest.

My parents chose a holy man over me, their own son. A lifetime passed as I let that settle in; what it had done to me. "I feel like a coward for numbing myself for so many years," I said aloud.

"Don't be so quick to condemn your addictions," Sadhu said firmly.

"You didn't make the final decision to come here until your opiates had taken effect," Iboga added. "They brought you here, to the most important time of your incarnations. Do not curse it. It served an important purpose."

I stared at my hands again and found that my layers of skin, muscle, veins, and bone were no longer impenetrable, separate entities. My bodily tissues appeared as one, interconnected pattern that vibrated into existence as I stared at it. It was almost as if I were actively manifesting my hands from thin air, microsecond to microsecond. "But," I began. Iboga sighed loudly.

"Everyone has such a big 'But,'" she said. "What is it going to take to shut you up for one, single minute, I wonder?"

"This 'sacred plant' of yours," I insisted. "It is a hallucinogen, yes? I haven't just gone completely mad?"

"Hallucinogen?" she asked with a polite smile. "Professor, I don't know what that word means to you, so I'm not sure how to reply. Your world is your description of it. And you talk to yourself about your world constantly. You plan, you comment, you judge. You've been doing it since your parents taught you language. And, along with it, they passed down their own brainwashed ideas about the world."

"Passed along like a gene," Sadhu mused.

"Or a disease," Iboga replied.

"Either way," Sadhu said, "shapeshifting requires one to break that chain. And because it's a chain of thought, our methods are aimed at the more subtle levels of existence."

Iboga paused to stare at me with mild suspicion. "This isn't a 'spiritual lesson', by the way," she said. "We're illustrating a very real mechanism that exists in the universe. Call it what you will, but ever since you've learned to speak you've been narrating your life at every turn. And, what's more, you have built a cage for every word that fills your head. You must rid yourself of this disease first if you are to save Agent Flores' life tonight. You must awake from the dream you've built. You have to learn to stop talking to yourself and create your world intentionally."

"Even if that were possible, how am I supposed to do that?" I asked, moving my attention back to Tina. A million points of buzzing light danced to life as my eyes moved over her sleeping body. Once again, I forgot the question and became mesmerized by the whole of everything quietly vibrating into reality. This is what Kyle and Damian were photographing with their Feynman Squid.

"You're doing it now," Sadhu said.

"Doing what?" I asked mindlessly.

"Manifesting your world according to your description," Iboga replied. "You think your internal dialogue keeps you sane, but it also keeps you asleep. It narrows your experience into a constricted reality from an endless expanse of possibility. In many ways, that is exactly why Eden relies on you. She craves the controlled lines of your scientific mindset. In turn, you see her lack of boundaries as potential freedom from your own leash. Anyone who wishes to enter power in this world must first learn to control the inner dialogue, the constant commenting that goes on in the head. These cages cannot survive in a quiet mind. And, professor, you come from a culture that despises silence. Your people actively avoid quiet space."

"But, don't demonize your thinking, either," Sadhu added. "The fact that we humans have the power to shrink our world into a manageable experience is the real magic, if there is such a thing. Whenever you feel the world is too much to handle, you can always tell your story of how you came to be where you are. Pull the wave back to a particle. The stories we tell ourselves repeatedly are the ones we believe, the ones that directly shape our world like clay. The trick is to remember that it's just a story to serve the purpose of keeping your wits intact. Ultimately, we're treating your addiction to your storyline."

"The reason you're really panicking right now," Iboga continued, "as well as your friends, is because you cannot weave a solid story of how you came to be here, in this place, with us. You want to tell yourself, 'First I was in Colorado, then I flew to Peru, and then I got in a truck, and from there we hiked to a cave and . . .', and now there's a gap. Now you're in the Himalayas and your storyline has betrayed you." I waved my hands in front of me and shook my head. This was too much at once. By now I was barely processing what they were saying.

"I believe Beyuls exist on this plane to create just these sort of gaps in our storyline," Sadhu said.

"So, what you're suggesting is," I began, "the solution to all we're facing is to teach me how to meditate? Is that about right?"

"No," Iboga laughed. "We don't have time for that. We'll have to take a far, far more direct approach with you; a dangerous shortcut."

Sadhu cut in, "There are shortcuts to this knowledge, ways to temporarily trip the ego-consciousness, techniques that allow one to dip a toe into the ocean of possibility long enough to pluck out a miracle. But shortcuts come at a price. These loopholes-to-enlightenment tap into rare powers and tend to leave much of the brainwashing intact, unfortunately. Iboga's husband used one such technique with the intention of saving Reverend Kane and his people when they were poisoned by a medicine man in Peru during an ayahuasca ceremony. Evidently the medicine man had added a highly toxic dose of devil's breath to the mixture. Kane was seeking a connection to the heart of darkness. He theorized that such ceremonies were communing with the devil himself. Now Kane believes he has proven that hypothesis."

"Devil's breath?" I asked to no avail.

"Evidently, Kane and his church represent a 'perfect storm' of things that should never enter the Zero Point Field," Sadhu mused.

"We never imagined there were entire collections of people who still believed their internal dialogue was the voice of God," Iboga added with growing frustration. "We believed— we assumed—the bicameral lineage of humanity to be mostly extinct. We had no idea what effect our techniques would have on such a mindset. No one could have suspected they were catalysts for something so bizarre, so hateful. It was foolish to meddle with them."

"Wait," I weakly tried to interrupt. "Kane's entire church is bicameral? How did they find . . . "

"And your daughter brought them to us!" Sadhu nearly shouted at Iboga before calming himself.

"They were already here!" Iboga hollered back.

I had no idea what they were talking about, but one thing was clear: the "Kane" topic was a well-worn argument around here.

"Kane and his people were at the edge of death when Kaylah took pity on them and brought them to us from Peru," Sadhu explained. "She's wise beyond her years, but she still follows the whims of a child. Sometimes she does, well, whatever catches her fancy." Sadhu paced back and forth, still trying to make peace with it all.

"They all seemed eccentric, yes, but besides that, they appeared to be typical missionaries 'spreading the word of God to the poor savages,'" Iboga said. "The shaman they encountered in Peru had added the flower of borrachero to the mixture with the intention of making them terribly ill, or perhaps turning them into slaves, why, I can only speculate. We needed to act fast and the intervention had to be vigorously transformative in order to shift their physical energy signatures to a balanced state of health."

"Though our intentions were pure, we accept responsibility for . . ." he paused, searching for the right words, " . . . what Kane has become. We didn't create the monster, but we did unlock its cage. They've taken an ancient healing technique and twisted it to meet their own, unique worldview. Kane is a man who learned how to enter heaven just long enough to throw a grenade into it. We have to do what we can to bring balance to the disharmony this has created. And, that requires another, dangerous shortcut."

"And just how do you plan to fix this?" I asked, slowly realizing the full weight of what he was suggesting. "Wait, you mean through us? You mean to use me and my team to fix the mess you made?" I shouted, waving my hands in dismissal. "No, no, no, no. Eden and I are university professors! We're only here to gather information for the government. I don't know what you imagine we're going to do about Kane and his church, but we're in no position to wage some kind of battle with nutjob fundamentalists!"

"You're already at war!" Sadhu said, laughing gently. "It's too late to drop your involvement in this. You and your friends were what the cosmos offered up as a response to this disaster, and may I add, what an unusual response you all are. But I have to work with what I've been given. We won't leave the gorge to take a direct part in this conflict, but we will do what we can to counteract an unusually negative and obscenely powerful wave of energy in the quantum field with, hopefully, an equally positive and energetic one." Sadhu glared at his watch with an anxious shake of the head. "And we have less than twenty-four hours to put that response in motion."

I let out a heavy sigh of surrender. I had no idea what was going on, yet I noticed myself beginning to trust these people. First and foremost, Sadhu clearly had a strong background in science; he was a man of logic and reason. And, they obviously meant no harm. They were doing what they could to help and, from what I could gather, they had a strong sense of morality. Plus, they held an extensive knowledge of plant medicine which, if nothing else, wasn't arrived at by blind chance. Whatever knowledge they held on the secrets of the universe were clearly beyond my own. One way or another, they were able to whisk all of us from the jungles of Peru to be here with them.

The more I dwelt on the issue, the clearer it became that it would be arrogant, if not flat out ignorant, of me to be in anything short of wonder and gratitude to be in their presence. By the time I had made up my mind on the subject, I concluded that if I could find a way to stay here in Tibet a while longer and learn from these people, it would be time well spent. I recognized superior knowledge when I saw it. Or maybe it was all the drugs on my brain. Or the exhaustion or the confusion. Either way, it was time to let someone else take the wheel.

"So, what's it going to be, professor?" Sadhu finally asked with a knowing grin after a full minute of watching me stare blankly at the floor.

"Okay, I give up," I said with a weak smile, shaking my head upon hearing the words fall from my lips. "Whatever you say. Just tell me what I should do next."

"Oh, so you've decided to put your faith in us?" Sadhu asked with a raised eyebrow. "You wish to hand the leash over to me, so to speak?"

"Yes," I agreed. Oddly enough, I felt good about this decision, as if another great load had been lifted from my shoulders. "Where do we start? I'm at your mercy."

Iboga and Sadhu exchanged glances. "Well, in that case, we start at the end," Iboga said cryptically. "Your end. As long as Professor Michael Huxley is alive and well, he will be trapped within the cage he has built for himself."

"Which means what?" I asked, thrown off by her statement.

"Which means we have no other choice but to end this particular incarnation you presently inhabit," Iboga replied gravely. "I'm afraid you're indeed the weakest link in the chain, professor. You just proved that beyond a shadow of a doubt."

"What?" I replied with a chuckle.

"I told you," Sadhu said severely, "We have no interest in your faith,"

I tried to lift myself, but I found Iboga's medicine had brought on intense dizziness, a seasick kind of motion sickness. Every turn of my head sent the walls of the hut spinning into a blurry mess of nausea and color. My arms gave out and I fell to my back under the growing suspicion that I had been poisoned. Sadhu moved in and stood over me while checking his watch.

"You have twenty or thirty minutes left before your kidneys fail, professor. How will you spend your final moments?"

"He can still walk," Iboga said as she washed her hands. "I don't need two dead bodies fouling up my medicine hut."

"Oh, of course," Sadhu agreed. "We'll throw him in the Jain's Pit with the others." My heart pounded my rib cage as each and every movement in the room turned my vision into a churning swirl of motion and light. I shut my eyes and gasped for air. I felt Sadhu bend down to speak into my ear. "You call yourself a man of science and, just like that, you fold and put all your faith in us," he said. "You'll go to any length to fill in those gaps, won't you, professor?"

"We are the Broken Skulls," Iboga said pointedly, stepping in closer. "We sacrifice all the weak links to the Jain's Pit."

"How do you think we managed to remain a myth for so long?" Sadhu asked quietly. "You don't become the stuff of legends by allowing every idiot stupid enough to hunt you down to just walk back to civilization and start running at the mouth."

"Maybe he trusted your white face," Iboga chuckled. Sadhu wheezed out a maniacal chuckle of a man who had been painfully restraining his true personality for too long. He shook his head so vigorously back and forth, for a moment I thought he was entering a seizure. When his head snapped to an abrupt halt, I knew he was shaking off the pretense of the 'amiable wise man.'

"Or maybe it was the psychospiritual bullshit mixed with the half-baked science we've been feeding him!" he laughed out loud with a far less measured, Southern accent. "Jesus Christ, partner, you're just as dumb as your parents!"

# The Ring of Fire: Crossroads, Part One

*"The central idea of string theory is quite straightforward. If you examine any piece of matter ever more finely, at first you'll find molecules, atoms, sub-atomic particles. Probe the smaller particles, you'll find something else, a tiny vibrating filament of energy, a little tiny vibrating string."*

Brian Greene

**B**lindfolded, with hands tied, I stumbled and crashed over branches and rocks. Lemm and Tasha shoved at me until I would collapse, at which point they would violently snatch me to my feet and begin pushing harder. Nausea had never been so intense. Every part of my solid form seemed to melt down to a liquidy mess. Soft tissues, organs, and bone gradually surrendered all sense of rigidity. I could only guess that my muscles were now powered by pure adrenaline alone. Off in the blind distance ahead, several drums pounded out a rolling, angry rhythm that grew louder with each agonized step. The roar of the waterfall became ever quieter behind us, so I guessed they were driving me deeper into the gorge.

"So, you're just killing us all off?" I coughed.

"You shouldn't speak," I heard Iboga say off to my right.

"Oh, no, son," Sadhu exclaimed with the easy drawl of a cowboy about to string a bandit from a tree. "For now, just you. I s'pose you could call it ritual sacrifice if you want to be dramatic about it."

"It is an honor to die by our hand," Iboga called out.

"If you ever manage to break free of your leash, don't hand it to another man," Sadhu exclaimed before shouting into the heavens. "Ye shall make you no idols nor graven image, neither rear you up a standing image, neither shall ye set up any image of stone in your land, to bow down unto it!" his voice boomed as if preaching to the masses. "For I am the LORD, your GOD!"

These people are raving lunatics. This can't be happening. Maybe this is some trick they play on outsiders. 'Let's fuck with the white man; make him look like a fool'. Or perhaps it's some tactic, some psychological manipulation to teach me about the 'true nature' of 'self' or some such bullshittery.

"If this is some kind of radical strategy to enlighten me, I assure you I'm a reasonable man!" I called out. "I'm willing to cooperate, I swear! We can talk this out!"

They laughed but said nothing. Either way, I was at their mercy. There was no way to fight them. In my condition, a child could overpower me. Behind my blindfold, the world spun and sloshed in darkness. It was obvious I was in the final throes of a losing battle with a highly toxic substance. Can I talk my way out of this? Doubtful. I can barely speak.

The high altitude forced me to save all lung capacity for heavy breathing. The rhythmic drumming ahead grew louder and echoed from the canyon walls. Ever since they forced me to my feet and out of the hut, I was expecting the ground to slip out from beneath me, and my entire world would become falling, until . . . until I died, I guessed.

I tried to imagine death. What will that really be like? How will that experience play out, blow by blow, the one I will be enduring any moment now? My body will be gone, my mind will be gone, everything I know will end. I can't picture that. It's not possible to picture that.

At the end of my little story about falling there remained nothing but dark, blank space. My death stood before me as a massive, gaping hole. So many possible ways it could play out. At what point will I forever lose consciousness? I couldn't bear it. "Please don't kill me," I finally wailed. Sadhu laughed behind Lemm and Tasha who were now equally pushing me forward and holding me upright.

"Oh, you're going to kill yourself, professor," Iboga added. It seemed I was now leading a single file line along a narrow ledge. The rising drum beats now lay directly ahead, echoing from the far side of some enormous chasm. A cold wind rose in a slow spiral from below with a low, empty howl. Suddenly, Lemm and Tasha yanked me to an abrupt halt.

With a swipe across the back of my head, Sadhu ripped the blindfold from my face and I found myself in near total darkness. The sun had long set and dazzling starlight stretched overhead. I didn't realize I had been in the medicine hut for so long. I searched the cobalt sky for the moon, but it was nowhere to be found. A few moments passed before my eyes adjusted to my dim surroundings to a most heart-stopping sight.

Without my glasses, all I could make out was a tiny ring of brilliant yellow-orange light spinning in the distance at the edge of the clearing beyond the forest. A ring of fire? The longer I stared at the fiery circle, the more details of the surrounding landscape below emerged in its glow. The tips of my boots lay inches away from what I could only imagine was the result of an ancient meteor strike. I stood at the furthest edge of a dead-man's plank over the mouth of a massive hole carved deep into the earth.

Upon taking in the entirety of the dark space yawning around me, I dropped to my knees and immediately threw up a burning stream of bile into its depths. I wanted to puke again, but something in my gut held back. Sadhu lowered himself to one knee to speak behind my shoulder as I tried desperately to make out any features inside the giant, black hole.

"Let me guess," Sadhu laughed. "Now you're wondering if this is all just one, big 'teachable' moment; some grand lesson of self discovery? And maybe you won't die here tonight?" Sheer confusion and lack of oxygen kept my lips from making words. "I promise you this," he began quietly. "When your body crashes into the rocks at the bottom of that pit, your head is going to split open like a gourde." He spoke gently as if his words were soothing. "Your skull will literally crack apart and everything you are is going to seep out."

I weakly raised my head to study the sole light source ahead at the opposite edge of the crater—the spinning, orange glow of fire—and found a trio of tribespeople facing us, a woman and two men. Though they were a good distance away, I believe I had spotted the woman earlier when we first entered camp. She spun a fiery torch on a rope in wide circles while the men beside her pounded out a steady rhythm from wide drums of wood and hide. Although I couldn't be sure from my vantage point, their features appeared Asian Pacific and their outfits of leather and palm leaf barely covered their rich, glowing skin. A garland of white flowers flashed intermittently around the woman's neck in the firelight. Her muscled companions were bare-chested and adorned with necklaces made of polished, white bone. A soft whirling sound rose and fell in the night air with the varying speed of the woman's torch. My stomach muscles clenched inward with painful contractions, but I couldn't, or rather, I wouldn't throw up again.

"Their song is just for you," Iboga said. "It beckons you to step forward." I coughed, barely able to hold my head off the floor of the ledge. My body was shutting down and I was fading fast.

"And, look, professor!" Sadhu exclaimed. "Here comes the frequency you've been chasing after!" He pointed across the crater to the trio of natives who had entered some type of trance. The whirling song wafting from the woman's torch and the drum rhythms all blended together to create a low, thrumming noise. Before long, the frequency began seeping into the atmosphere from their direction. The tribespeople were creating it!

My God, the frequency is manmade! But how? "Their instruments make the sound?" I muttered. The discovery was so shocking, I nearly forget I was about to be thrown to my death. "How are they doing it?"

"Oh, it isn't their instruments," Sadhu exclaimed. "But, yes, dancing and drumming can assist in generating the frequency."

"What are they generating it with?" I demanded. I had to know!

"The only instrument on earth at the moment that can channel the Zero Point Field," Sadhu began. "The right temporal lobe." He waved his hands for me to be patient with his explanation. "Specifically, if you must know, it does this in response to the vibration of the pineal gland, which is located just above the roof of your mouth. If there's a part of the human body most responsible for the frequency of your consciousness, it is the pineal gland. If you ask me, it's the crowning achievement of evolution on this planet. So few humans have scratched the surface of its power. Those who master their consciousness are essentially masters at controlling the pineal gland." My jaw was locked open by his explanation. I was in no condition to judge the man's words as either brilliant or utterly insane.

"Humans coevolved with centuries of hallucinogen use and practice to tap into the Zero Point Field as incarnate flesh and blood," he continued rather matter of factually. "But all I can offer is the perspective of a physicist," he admitted, taking a seat behind me. "When all of the endless, complex possibilities that can take place in this universe are broken down to the simplest of options, I'm talking from the large stuff here, like whether a star has enough mass to fizzle out quietly at the end of its life or if it will become a black hole, down to whether we'll have rain tomorrow in the gorge or not, if you choose to go left or right when you're lost in the woods, all the way down to if a raindrop will land on the wing of a dragonfly, or just miss it and hit a leaf instead. The most rudimentary movement of reality we can study is this: What will happen when a single particle is given a fifty-fifty option of passing through one hole or another."

"The double slip experiment," I whispered. "Kyle and Damian used to talk about it."

"In many ways, that experiment was the boundary for what we humans call reason, where pure logic and math leads us straight off the edge, as you're about to experience," he explained. "We now know that the particle passes through both holes when its options are narrowed down to only two. You have to appreciate all that implies, professor." He slapped my shoulder again as if we were old friends having a friendly discussion on scientific research.

"My point is, when the universe is given only two options, it chooses both. At the most basic level of existence, a particle does everything that it can do simultaneously within what your physicists refer to as a 'probability wave.' There, all options coexist simultaneously."

"You mean, until we look at it," I replied. "Damian and Kyle said that once it's observed or measured in some way; once we look at it, the wave collapses and the universe chooses. What does this have to do with what's been going on?"

"You're still stuck in your Isaac Newton-style mindset with the rest of the planet, a definition of reality that's outdated by several hundred years," he scoffed. "I spent my life working tirelessly with quite literally the largest, most complex machines ever built on this planet to try to show people the proof that reality is far, far more than we observe it to be! Religion failed to wake the world to this truth, so I figured if I showed the world the actual math proving we live in a world of endless possibility they would have to open their eyes!" A tinge of anger rose in his voice the longer he spoke.

"But all I found was that my efforts were useless! It seems the world wants to stay chained by the necks to Plato's Cave. They insist we live in a world of division, black or white, up or down. That's their trench, their leash . . . and yours as well! And it must be wiped out, once and for all. You haven't evolved, Professor Huxley, so we have no real use for you. You see the world as stable, reliable chunks of matter that follow predictable patterns and you call it 'reason' even when your own science does not. You've been living a lie inside a dream world and you've been suffering from it. The whole planet has been suffering from that point of view. Well, now I say to hell with it: I'll prove to you how wrong you are about black and white."

The conversation was turning back to sacrifice and my mind spun to do whatever was needed to keep Sadhu talking. Just a little more time . . . someone or something has to intervene. "So, what the hell does particle physics have to do with any of this?" I asked.

"Your physicist friends failed to tell you one, very relevant detail, professor," Sadhu continued. "And, when I tell you what it is, you're going into the pit. Our fire dancer and drummers are growing weary, so you're either smart enough to understand the relevance of what I tell you or you aren't. No more discussion. You'll have to find a way to process it all very, very quickly, partner."

Yes, anything for even a few more minutes of life. As long as I'm alive, I have options. I may get out of this. Maybe Eden will come save me. Or maybe Pavlik, or . . .

"Forget what you know and allow what I'm telling you to really sink in, partner," he said before a measured pause. "There is no such thing as wave collapse. Probability waves don't collapse down to the single possibility of 'left' or 'right' from the quantum field. This is the truth: The particle still goes through both holes even after it is observed, so . . . deal with that. Your physicists invented the idea of 'wave collapse' to try to explain how we ever see reality go only left or right, up or down, but they have no actual proof of it, they have absolutely zero evidence that wave collapse happens, there's no math for it." He paused to let his words digest. "Now, from your limited perspective, this is only goin' one of two ways: Either I'm throwin' you into this pit, in which case you're at the mercy of death. Or, you're throwin' yourself in, in which case, you have an option. Only with intention do you get an option."

My mind went blank. Nothing of what the man said fit into my experience. No wave collapse? I live in a world where things go one way or the other. But there must be wave collapse. When I come to a fork in the road in life, I go left or right. Not BOTH. The moon is always in the sky WHETHER I LOOK AT IT OR NOT! I was about to die with yet another loose thread hanging in my mind.

"You're all fucking insane," I wheezed. The waves of nausea were building to a fantastic crescendo and I began to wonder what would fall into the crater first, the remaining contents of my gut, or the rest of me. "That's not how the world works!"

"But, what if he's right," Iboga whispered. "Then that means . . ."

Then that means . . . Once again, I stopped panicking. Or, rather, I decided to give up on the option of panic for a moment. Maybe it was the psychoactives flooding my nervous system or perhaps it was the fear of death. Perhaps it was simply my kidneys shutting down, but in a brilliant flash of light, all normal, rational structure in my brain exploded in a chain reaction.

Within my mind's eye, I watched a million numbers, data, conclusions, equations, and geometric configurations burst into fire, one after another. Every piece of my logic went into flame, everything I thought I knew and trusted about chemical processes, cellular division, the transfer of DNA, gravity, the stars, the earth, and everything in between exploded into fiery ash. I stared blankly from the center of my awareness with a mix of abject terror and relief as everything I held dear burned into nothingness.

Then, all my relationships followed. Who I thought Eden was burst into tiny, glowing fragments, and then Tina exploded, along with all my thoughts about her, followed by everyone I had ever met. It all rose into flames. Everything I imagined that everyone I had ever met had expected of me, or even simply thought about me, I let it burn. All gone. Deconstructed down to the particle and beyond. Then, finally my parents caught fire.

For a moment, I held back. I didn't want them to burn. I had carried an idea about them for far too long to just let it go now. "Everything is going into that pit," Iboga said quietly behind me. "Might as well let it go now. It will make your death easier."

"You need to take full responsibility for everything in your world before you die down there," Sadhu said. "Let it all burn, son."

My stomach relaxed and I stopped clenching. Soon, the internal flames consumed my mother and father. Everything that I thought I knew about their intentions, their motivations, burst into a raging blaze. As it all burned into a glorious smoke, it exposed a curious, soft greenish glow of energy in the center of my chest. All the many, many preconceptions I had been carrying on my shoulders, all the notions and judgments I had balanced atop my head all turned to ash and began to fall, like iron girders melted by jet fuel. I could physically feel a massive weight plummeting from the terrifying, glorified heights of my tower of intellect, crashing through my chest, into my stomach.

My entire being went into a gut-wrenching freefall of weightlessness, a waterfall crashing to a river and opening doors in the process with an explosion of energy. This was the floor pulled from beneath my feet. This was my ever-growing fear of falling come to pass; an anxiety which had grown more powerful with age, or rather, the stronger my intellect had grown. My storyline had reached its end.

With the force of stampeding horses, my stomach muscles pulled inward and I puked the most foul smelling—and tasting—stream of toxic waste. Wave after wave of burning acids poured from well-worn trenches and down, into the mouth of the dark pit below. Everything that I ever thought I knew to be 'true' spewed into the darkness. I couldn't imagine how my body was able to withstand such a noxious substance.

As my stomach unclogged itself and the dust settled within my mind, I found only a few, small concepts remained; those ideas that couldn't be toppled over or deconstructed. These intrinsically harmonized, geometric patterns held some special property; an elegant simplicity of exquisite symmetry like the crystalline structures at the core of the geodes we had encountered.

These were the concepts I had encountered in my lifetime that had no need for outside structure or authority. Some of these ideas I had retained from my scientific education and simple observations of the world, and some had been handed down from my parents, others from teachers, many more from books, and a great many truths from Eden. There were even a few indivisible concepts I had obtained from the media, books, and movies.

As I gazed at these few ideas, they slowly transformed into vibrating circles of pure energy, crystallized truth. I knew without doubt, without the slightest tinge of hesitation, that I was directly observing the most elemental structures of the physical world; the absolute smallest, most basic energy at the deepest core of matter. I was seeing beyond the veil of solid structure, beyond the 'atom,' beyond protons and neutrons. I searched the unadulterated emptiness of consciousness and saw that at the heart of everything I had ever laid eyes on, all I had ever touched, tasted, heard, smelled and, especially, thought, there had been an infinite ocean of these indivisible rings of light created by pure vibration; energy that existed at the most fundamental step above absolute nothingness.

At this level of unclouded awareness, opinions could not exist, doubt could not take root, confusion had no independent existence. And, most importantly, assumption could not take form here. The longer I held these tiny vibrations, the more details about them became apparent. Even though these miniscule apparitions had all emerged from a point of zero movement, zero heat, and light, zero energy; each of these circles could pulsate with a vast spectrum of different vibrations.

And, miraculously enough, I watched as the rate of vibration of each of these unimaginably small points of energy—the frequency they created, the song they sang—was what dictated which rings vibrated in unison with others to create ever larger, more complex patterns of solid matter. This didn't come to me as a theory, or a diagram, or even a mathematical formula: Varying degrees of resonance was ultimately behind all the seemingly complex variations of matter we experience. The very shape and position of all that is in our world, from the position of an electron around the nucleus of the atom to the black holes that devour whole galaxies, is dictated by vibration.

And, as impossible as it seemed, I not only understood this, I was somehow directly seeing this to be true as pure knowing. From this vantage point, I witnessed these tiny circles of ultimate simplicity and found the truth Sadhu was pointing to reflected within these dynamics: The universe never chooses left or right, up or down, it always remains in a state of full potential.

Everywhere energy can be, it is. Every form it can take, it does. Not in some distant past, not in a dream or an imagined future; right this very moment. Forever. "But, that's not what we experience!" some lost part of my intellect screamed, "Why?!"

"So, professor," Sadhu said patiently, "if the particle goes both left and right, if Schrödinger's cat is both alive and dead, then how is it that we only experience a world where things are only one way or the other? Tell me, son, how is the magic performed? What appears to divide this world up?"

Beneath the mere consideration of his words, my brain buckled under the weight. I could hear the sound patterns emerge from his mouth, but my world was now transformed entirely into these tiny, buzzing strings of light. I stood outside all logical context. I had no memory of who I was or where I was. Sadhu, Iboga, Lemm, Tasha, even "me" was now nothing more than nameless, meaningless vibration humming away in an endless expanse of silence, for no particular reason what-soever. I stood at the core of chaos; a place that I had always oh, so carefully kept just out of reach, just beyond the veil of words I had shrouded myself within.

So, this is what it means to lose one's mind. I gazed at waves of vibration running through a majestic ocean of light rings. It was, beyond a doubt, the most exquisite sight of unspeak-able beauty I ever beheld. The patterns rolled out in every way; some flowing in tandem to exchange patterns with one another while some collided and burst into new arrangements of energy.

And once again I directly knew what I was witnessing within this play of vibration: I was directly seeing every possible energetic reaction take place simultaneously! I'm looking at the world from the perspective of the probability wave; the point that lives a microsecond before we experience a world that goes left or right.

At this level of reality, the idea of a single point, a specific, individual particle, had no meaning. Here, there were only waves. This was the world as it truly was: Every possible posi-tion the electron could take, every possible direction an atom could move, every molecule chain that could form, every chemical reaction that could ever be. All of it happening at once.

And beyond this surface of light and form at play I found a hollow abyss so massive, so expansive, I couldn't help but

shrivel in its presence. It stood motionless, changeless just behind these infinite surges and swells of force as a dead stillness;
a silence without boundary or form, a knowing darkness filled
with attention. And I knew that this emptiness had always sat
quietly in the background, quietly unaffected by the dance of
light appearing on its surface. This infinite spaciousness would
always remain perfect in its own right, silently giving rise to
vibration. The absolute essence of all physical form. This was
consciousness itself: undivided, unfiltered awareness without
aim or desire, fear or motivation, before the storyline, before
the ego claimed it as its own.

Consciousness is the ground state of all energetic fields in
the universe; the core of reality that never shapeshifts. Indeed,
the only power that does not ever change.

In the face of this massive nothingness, I realized that, when
it came right down to it, I could choose one of two reactions
to the immensity of it all. I can pass through one hole or the
other. On the one hand, I could explode into a world of terror and expend the rest of my energy, perhaps the remainder
of my life running and hiding from the truth of this massive
silence. I could rebuild all the structures in my head, all the
cloaks, the divisions, the opinions, all of my assumptions, and
I could make them stronger than ever! Behind my fortress, I
could deny ever witnessing this expanse, I could wrap a story
around it like a cage and I would contain it until it collected me
at the end of my life. I could wage war on this silence until my
heart stopped beating . . . which, should be any moment now.

Or . . . or, perhaps instead I could muster an impossible
amount of courage and embrace it. I could surrender to this
and accept it. But, I knew to do that would mean total oblitera-
tion; the tiniest drop of water meeting the widest ocean.

Well, I was about to die anyway, so what did I have to lose? I
let anxiety go and allowed all extraneous details to be dumped
into the void. Gradually, I allowed myself to slip into this dark
quiet. And the entirety of the world's momentum began to play
around me while I sat centered within myself; pure consciousness that had always remained motionless. Never reaching,

never grasping, never wanting for anything.

I am . . . the void. No. Even that was too much. I Am.

I stood at the center of this bizarre crossroads as a god looking over his territory; a god with a million arms and a thousand eyes. I stood and gazed through an endless number of rings, like a vast honeycomb of windows, each vibrating with an ever-so-slightly different song, each holding the potential for a different combination of matter and energy. I bore witness to a billion possible universes.

My consciousness passed over a vast mosaic of possibility and I witnessed all the ways this could all go from here; every possible "branch" reaching out from a point called NOW.

Through a million and one vibrations I could see my body dying right here in the Tsangpo Gorge in a million different ways. Through countless patterns of mass and energy, I saw Sadhu throw me to my death. Through others, I threw myself in. Schrödinger's cat is indeed both alive and dead. In thousands of other configurations of matter, I witnessed Eden (and, in others, Sabol or Pavlik or Gomez) bursting in and saving me with varying degrees of techniques and skill.

In some versions, their rescue attempts were successful. In others, they failed miserably and were thrown into the pit along with me. Countless other versions held realities where Sadhu changed his mind, or Iboga changed hers. All the millions upon millions of likely ways that matter would configure and take shape flashed before my eyes at the speed of light, through the vast ocean of tiny bands of vibration. And it was directly made clear to me: the key to unlocking each and every possibility lay in my ability to match its unique "vibration."

The longer I gazed, the more I noticed that there were also highly bizarre possibilities; ways in which molecules could suddenly arrange themselves in rare, unlikely, yet, physically possible  patterns. These paths represented a mere fraction of the far more likely conclusions of my scenario, standing at the precipice of this giant crater. These were the few combinations lying on the fringe; events that would take place perhaps once out of a trillion and one replays of the same dynamics.

258

Within these rare rings of light and vibration, I watched as sudden gusts of wind roared down from the Himalayas in upwards of 200 miles an hour to dash Sadhu, Iboga, Lemm, and Tasha from the ledge and launch my body into the air, over the mouth of the crater and deposit me safely on the ledge on the far side. Insanely unlikely? Absolutely. Physically possible? Yes.

In others, lightning spontaneously exploded from the heavens and ignited everyone around me into burning ash. Within one of these vibrational patterns I witnessed all the atoms in the vicinity suddenly vaporize into swirling gases; in others, all atomic movement nearly stopped altogether to create drastic drops (or rises) in temperatures where everything; the trees, the grass, our bodies, suddenly froze into blocks of ice, or sizzled into glowing, orange ash.

There were even a few vibrational patterns so "unnatural," so very alien, that they were difficult to witness under the vantage point of "Professor Michael Huxley," like abstract scenes viewed through the wrong end of a prism. These passageways were encircled—perhaps guarded—by frequencies entirely foreign not only to myself, but to the rest of humanity I would imagine.

In this small handful of "honeycombs," the nearly impossible atomic configurations lived; realities where, for example, my cells spontaneously turned on locked, dormant gene patterns for ancient DNA. In some cases, I watched chromosomes take over that haven't been coded in a hundred generations of my ancestors, where my physical form underwent radical transformation. Here, enzymes burst into spontaneous activity to devour and replace collagens, where bone and marrow was deconstructed in a matter of moments.

In some of these rings, I watched my shoulder blades sprout wings moments before I flew into the night air. In others, all my genetic information shut down completely except for that of a wild cat, or a dinosaur, or a horse, or combinations of several lifeforms, and on, and on. After some of these incredibly grotesque shifts, I would turn around and devour Sadhu right where he sat. Or I would mindlessly gallop off the ledge and plummet to my death.

I stood at the apex of this crossroads, locked in time. I stared, unable to move, unable to act. Unable to choose. Frozen, I could not enter into any one of the trillion paths laid before me. How do I merge with any of these realities? Panic began to rise again from a trench carved over a lifetime of anxiety. Am I dead? Perhaps this is what death is: Stuck forever in the last place you stood, like a player in a frozen video game.

"Only awareness can choose," I heard Iboga's voice speak from just behind me. "That's the key behind it all. Only awareness can vibrate with one of these patterns. Unclench the roof of your mouth."

"What's that?" I heard myself reply.

"Your unique, incessant thinking patterns," Sadhu said gently. "It tightens the soft spot at the roof of the mouth, behind the tongue. Above that is the pineal gland which produces DMT, the hallucinogen your body naturally produces. DMT quiets the centers of your brain that processes language and metaphor. Now, unclench your mouth, breathe normally, and control which vibrations pass through the emptiness of your consciousness. Harmonize with patterns that vibrate with the path you want. Only identity divides a path within the infinite probability wave. Identity is the magic that divides the wave."

"What does that mean?" I heard myself ask. "Identity divides the wave?"

"It means that only Professor Michael Huxley can choose," Iboga replied. She repeated my name loudly as if it were an incantation.

"Professor Michael Huxley," she whispered again with force. Arrrgh! That pattern! Those words!

Upon hearing my name spoke aloud, my world of infinite probability began crushing in around me! The sea of vibration suddenly took rigid shape, smashing reality into sharp lines and compressed surfaces. Wrapping the apex of my consciousness were complex layers of energy that vibrated in unison from the totality of my memories, notions, and beliefs of Professor Michael Huxley. It was an absolute lie, a tale that I had allowed to take shape and form, a story I had made manifest from all the incredible wonders of possibility. An idol cast before God. And its name was "Professor Michael Huxley."

A vibrational pattern, a habit, an addiction born of continuous use and repetition. All the waves of light began to vibrate in harmony with my ego pattern, isolating "me" from that infinite sea of waves. And it hurt. It was painful to be a separate, individual "object" set apart from an infinite sea of energy formation. There was pain in existence, terror in being ripped from the womb! I found myself encased in a small, separate bubble of light, a sphere created entirely of my own habitual patterns of energy. In perfect response to the unique frequency that "Professor Michael Huxley" emitted, the waves of energy that passed into my bubble were starkly, violently, cut down from the infinite combinations of possible form and movement into a very finite series of paths.

I loosened the roof of my mouth and allowed myself to breathe normally. The rocky ledge I was prostrated on now took form and shape beneath me once more. Below that, the dark pit opened up and at the edge of the massive crater, pine trees emerged from the vapors of the probability field. In the distance, snow-capped peaks rose into a charcoal sky. The fire dancer, the drummers, Sadhu, Iboga, the hands in front of my face; everything took shape by harmonizing with all the many complex frequencies that had entrenched themselves within my mind. All my thinking patterns, my fears, my anxieties, my beliefs, all fell back into place like a web of tiny rivers finding their paths through well-worn canals in the dirt.

And, like magic, I felt like myself again! The simple processing of my name brought my world back into order. But, now I could see that the frequency my consciousness emitted was one that I had been building and maintaining, organizing and sorting for decades; a mantra of internal dialogue that I had repeated to myself over and over again to bring order from chaos. The identity of this "Professor Michael Huxley" created for one purpose and one purpose only: To cut the world down from the many to the few, from all possibility down to the one, single path. To make the world match the vibration of MY ego, MY pattern, MY identity!

"Yes, ego-based awareness has less options to choose from," Iboga said as if seeing into my soul. "You come from a culture that considers awareness to be an abstract concept when we know it to be an actual field of energy that affects the world. But every consciousness represents a different vibration; some tempered by love, others by fear, some by belief, others by meditation, or drugs, or laughter, or . . . well, the point is, everyone carves up their world a little differently. But when several people harmonize on the same wavelength, the power to shape their world increases exponentially with each matching frequency."

"For where two or three gather in my name, I am there among them," Sadhu added. Peru . . . my God. With these new synaptic connections I could now directly see how it all began. I saw how the original recording of the frequency was made. Ramirez's cameraman, Torres, had simply recorded several members of Kane's church when they all become transmitters for the Zero Point Field simultaneously.

But when Kane and his people entered the probability wave, something went deeply wrong. What exactly happened and why, those patterns still had yet to take shape in my mind's eye, but I saw with unbending certainty that the members of Kane's church represented a perfect storm of things that should NOT enter the Zero Point Field. Yet, unlike a computer, Kane's men had awareness, twisted as it was; but awareness that could choose, nonetheless. They held a dark consciousness tempered by images of jealous gods and damnation, hellfire and demonic rage. They entered a quantum field of possibility where their own conglomeration of identity patterns directly shaped their immediate environment at the particle level.

It was crystal clear: That which I imagined I had come looking for. I followed this thread of insight and saw what the laptop did back in the physics lab. Whatever emitted the frequency of the Zero Point Field entered a field of full potential for particle configuration. But only consciousness chooses. A laptop computer does not possess consciousness, so it couldn't choose "order from chaos." The computer emitted an amplified frequency of the Zero Point Field, which pulled everything in the near vicinity into a probability wave. Every possible combination its atoms could take! But once the laptop ceased to "be a laptop," the frequency was instantly cut off, and we were simply left staring at one of the billions upon billions of combination patterns possible.

But that was only from our limited perspective. In the physics lab Friday afternoon, in yet another "branch" of possibility, we were left staring at a completely different organization of matter. In some patterns, its atoms had arranged themselves into a pile of ash, or different shapes, or liquids, or gasses. I imagined that in at least one, very rare version, it simply snapped back into the shape of a laptop. And our resulting response to each of those combinations was different. In some cases, Eden and I decided to have nothing to do with this investigation whatsoever. In others, we decided to pursue this information with entirely different tactics, methods, and resources.

With the speed of light, a new set of synaptic bonds formed, an entirely new way of seeing the world built on my new perspective. Why, there would even be a possibility where Agent Tina Flores and Agent Thomas Downey had brought their anomaly to us weeks earlier, where we had learned of the connection between the mythical Roto tribe in Peru and the one in Tibet, hidden deep in the Tsangpo.

In such a case, Agent Downey could have found a diplomatic passage for us through China, into the gorge. This, of course, would have brought another version of our team, from a slightly different version of energetic configuration, to the Tsangpo days earlier.

Sadhu was right. The Dreaming Tree didn't teleport us here. What it did was even more incredible. It entangled our egos, our identity patterns, with one of the other countless pathways our physical forms were also treading. We were indeed already there, crossing paths with ourselves; working from a slightly different set of dynamics and options.

My mind was so empty it could hold only undivided clarity. With a powerful grip, Sadhu seized the back of my neck and held me over the ledge, forcing the black pit to fill the boundaries of my vision. But I had no fear or care whatsoever.

"Now what's going to be lost at the bottom of that pit?" he demanded. I felt and then heard the answer emerge from my lips.

"Nothing," I replied. "Professor Michael Huxley is just a bunch of words and stories, empty worries and assumptions, all wrapped in dead memory that emits a specific frequency."

"Excellent." he whispered.

Now I saw it. This had all been one, elaborate game to wake me up. Iboga had not poisoned me, Sadhu was not here to kill me. I was brought here to see how the universe took shape, specifically, how the frequency of Professor Michael Huxley vibrated his world into shape.

"Then, there will be nothing of value lost down there," Iboga added. "That branch must be killed off if you're ever going to save this world. And, my, there are so, SO many ignorant branches of you that we've had to remove over the years."

"Pruning you like a bonsai we are," Sadhu said.

"I see what you're trying to do," I said weakly. "I see it now."

"Do you?" Sadhu replied. Before I could respond, he spun me around to face him and shoved the tip of a long, wooden pipe into my mouth.

"Wha ith this?" I mumbled.

"This is two things," Sadhu replied. "It's the second half of the combination to reach the Jain and it's also a failsafe, I hope."

"Wha tha hell doth tha mea . . .," I began to ask but Sadhu quieted me with a raise of his hand. Iboga winked at me and produced a wooden match in her fingers which burst into flame with a snap of her fingers. Cupping her hand at the far end of the pipe, she lowered the match and illuminated a bowl of tiny, yellowish granules.

"Breathe deep," Sadhu instructed. I was in no mood for

whatever was in his pipe, but I inhaled, nonetheless. An inorganic, acrid taste filled my mouth and throat. I pulled as hard as I could, expecting to choke, but my capillaries seemed to open up and readily accept the full onslaught of the strange smoke rushing in. It was as if my lungs were made for just these sorts of vapors, whatever they were.

"Now hold it," Sadhu demanded. He turned me around to face the dark abyss, wrapped an arm around my shoulder and pulled me in.

"If there is one instruction of ours that you take to heart, let it be this one," he said fiercely. "Do not, I repeat, DO NOT accept that man's offer. Your only job now is to find a way to turn that man down. Find a way. It may take all of your resources, but you must."

My face turned red and my blood vessels bulged under the lack of oxygen. Gradually, my vision took on a shimmer, as if everything were wrapped in a soap bubble. "Exhale and leap," Sadhu demanded.

Leap? Does he mean, 'Into the pit? On purpose?' A million reasons why I shouldn't jump rushed through me. A deluge of excuses to turn and run sprayed up from the crater like a geyser.

"Now!" Sadhu shouted. "Jump into your doubt! Jump in direct defiance of reason! You're at the boundary of logic, so the only thing left to do is to jump! Become the wave!"

Somehow, something about his words clicked, or rather, his suggestion inspired some basic primal instinct of self-preservation to shatter and I found myself tipping forward, over the ledge.

And I fell. Wind rushed into my chest and blasted at my ears. Cold air tore at my eyes, my stomach twisted into a knot, and fear screamed from every pore. Moments before I crashed headfirst into the jagged rocks below everything came to a screeching stop. The world suddenly moved into ultraslow motion and I hung suspended in midair as I inched my way downward. The final medicine they had fed me leapt into full effect. My heart slowed to a crawl and my brain stopped processing linear thought.

I peered into the darkness and saw the floor of the pit blanketed by stone spikes that reached to the skies above. Draped over these dagger-like rocks were dozens upon dozens of human corpses in all manner of decomposition. In every direction, broken bodies of men and women were impaled above rivers of skulls and bones that had fallen between the many crevices.

Before I could process a reaction, a jagged boulder crashed into my spine, launching a number of vertebrae into my rib cage, smashing every organ in its path. Then my head bounced from a cold, hard surface with a deafening crack, followed by a rapid-fire succession of tiny crunches as every major bone shattered over stones and dead branches at the base of the pit. Warm blood poured down my forehead and into my eyes while my heart shuddered violently in my chest before sputtering to a crawl. All sense of hearing faded immediately afterward, and then a numbing of my extremities; fingers to arms, toes to legs, up my torso and, lastly, my head.

So, that's it? "This is death?" was the final thought my demolished brain managed to leak. This was hardly worth all the time I had spent worrying about it. A moment later, my heart gave out and my muscles went limp. I died staring at a decomposing skull that looked suspiciously like my own.

# PART FIVE

## The Jain, Crossroads: Part Two

*"Silent, conscious awareness is naturally naked of phenomena and is nakedly present in the core of all phenomena. It is only our distraction with phenomena—"clothing" made of thoughts, images, sense impressions, and memory—that keeps our core cloaked from recognition. By inquiring into your life story, you can recognize the layers of ephemeral distraction that keep your attention busy with entanglement. When you recognize them, you can reclaim your attention. You can allow the distractions to fall away, or you can see through them all the way home, to the silent core."*

Gangaji

Out of a black, empty nothingness, a familiar substance filled my consciousness and I began to feel enclosed by a smooth, constant pressure. Shortly thereafter a great discomfort arose when I recognized the substance as water. My God, I'm drowning.

Instinctively, I found my center of gravity and swam "upward." Without knowing where I was, who I was, I became the act of swimming; clawing my way up, desperate for air. When my stress reached its peak, the next stroke broke the water tension and I exploded to the surface of what, I did not know.

Air rushed into my lungs while vision and stimuli gradually took shape. I was floating in the center of a warm, tiny spring lined by tall grass. As the temperature grew considerably warmer near my feet, it must have been heated by fissures beneath the earth. An azure blue, moonlit sky stretched above a forest of Banyan trees and the longer I searched my new surroundings, the more certain I became. This was not Tibet any longer. The air was humid and heavy with the scent of earth, moss, and the most subtle hints of jasmine. Delicate water lilies of electric pinks and violets hovered silently on the surface of my small, tepid pool along with a single, white lotus in full bloom.

"That flower is in continuous full bloom," a voice spoke from within, one I did not recognize as my own, internal dialogue.

I swam to the edge of the spring and parted thick swaths of grass to discover fine, white mists dancing just above the ground, coating the forest floor with specks of dew. Everything was wet, from the low hanging palms to the flowers in the spring, to the blue fungi nestled at the base of the trees. Bathed in the full moon, the banyans reached to the heavens and corkscrewed down, into the earth in a writhing network of roots.

Slowly, I pulled myself to the grassy shore and after a clumsy struggle, up to my feet. My strength had begun to return but I had little memory of what had happened; only a subtle intuition that my mind had endured a thorough . . . cleansing. Had my brain been washed? I looked about and found no particular direction different from the next: Everywhere I searched, tall reeds and massive ferns waved lazily in a humid breeze winding through the forest. I finally decided to go with the flow and follow the vague scent of jasmine.

After weaving the network of coiled trunks and twisted branches, one particular banyan tree stood out; one holding a dark, bulbous mass near the base. I stepped closer and the bulk became a massive network of vines. At first, it appeared to be nothing more than a random bundle of foliage, but as I continued forward something else appeared: A form hidden, or more precisely, mingled within a spiderweb of branches. It was a human body.

I was staring at the corpse of an Indian man who had died sitting cross-legged in the nook of the Banyan. After further inspection, I decided he must have passed fairly recently as there remained a paper-thin layer of moist skin over his muscle and skeletal structure. The withered membrane that covered his bones and skull had turned a greenish-gray, nearly indiscernible from the plant life entwining it.

To my sudden dismay, I found that many of the vines had woven into and out of the man's epidermis. Stranger still, two larger branches passed directly through the man's chest and navel area. This made no sense. It would've taken more than a year for roots this size to make their way through solid, organic matter. This man hadn't been dead for more than a month. What is this? Where in hell am I?

"Why did you come to my Beyul?" a voice asked in a heavy, Indian accent. I didn't rightly "hear" the words, rather, this was more of a foreign vibration that moved directly through the center of my forehead to coalesce into language. My heart froze as I sensed movement from the body and my breathing shuddered to a halt as I watched the corpse's eyelids creep open. Bits of dried skin fell from his eyes in the process and soon, two brilliant, sky-blue irises were now beaming through the foliage, staring into me. Beyuls. The Tsangpo. The Roto. My memory churned and I began to form linear connections again. The pit they threw me into was another Beyul.

My attention was pulled to one of the bright green vines wrapping the tree, a different species of plant that had entwined itself with the Banyan. I traced the coiled vine from its roots to a flowering tip dangling just above the emaciated man's head: a bunch of succulent, green grapes.

And another foreign stream of information unfolded within my mind's eye: This was a Jain who survived by this random cluster of fruit hanging just above him. He would remain in meditation until the fruit ripened. Impossible.

I studied the man's torso, arms, and legs to find little more than skin and bone. I doubted the withered muscles in this body even held the energy to lift its hand and pluck a fruit from the vine. Hesitantly, I reached out and twisted off the largest and ripest grape from the cluster. I leaned forward into the network of branches and placed the fruit on the edge of the man's dry, cracked lips. When he didn't respond, I pushed the grape further into his mouth, wondering if he still had a pulse.

Suddenly his eyes lifted open to meet mine. I jumped backward and froze. With steady, progressive movement, he lowered his jaw and ever so slowly opened his mouth. Just as I thought he was about to speak, his jaw closed again. It wasn't until he lowered his jaw once more that I realized he was chewing. By the incredible amount of time it took him to crush and swallow the single piece of fruit, I had long struck a cross-legged seat before him, held in complete, utter awe by the biological miracle before me. His electric gaze never broke from mine.

Then, another wave of information entered directly through the center of my forehead, yet this time the flow of awareness was far more intense, concentrated like a laser. I could actually see the flow of attention; a subtle bending of space that poured from the top of the Jain's head like a water fountain, into a perfect semicircle, down into the top of my own cranium. His consciousness passed directly through my brain, down my back, and exited at the base of my spine into the earth beneath my body. I looked down and saw this circle of energy pass below the earth and arch back up to enter the base of the Jain's spine, thus creating a full circle, a closed circuit of conscious energy between the two of us. The longer he allowed this circuit to exist, the faster the vibration pulsed around the ring of light we shared. As the frequency gained momentum, more and more conscious thought poured into my spine, allowing me to access the Jain's memories directly.

This was the first human to ever enter this region of the Tsangpo. He traveled here from India thousands of years ago in search of Nirvana. An echo of his meditative practice in this gorge can still be tapped into today.

The forest around us remained silent while the ancient man and I sat face to face, held in an ever-intensifying, organic circuit until I felt my awareness steadily harmonizing with his: A highly refined frequency of consciousness few had ever attained on this planet, one that could readily tap into probability waves. My vision became flooded by a soft, white light allowing me to hear the Jain's only inner dialogue: A sort of chant he repeated quietly to himself:

*Om asato ma sadgamaya,*
*tamaso ma jyotirgamaya,*

*mrityorma amritamgamaya*
*Om shantih shantih shantih*

The words were gibberish to my untrained mind, but the
longer he chanted, the deeper my perception became flooded
by a now-familiar sound: the deep, resonant hum of the Zero
Point Field, a frequency powerful enough to rip me from the
safety and comfort of my home, out to the farthest reaches of
the globe. A vibration that spoke to the highest truth of the
physical universe: The song of everything happening at once.

My vision of light gradually consolidated into shapes and
movement. Once again, a vast ocean of tiny vibrating rings
enfolded me and I found myself at the center of the probability wave once again. Before Schrödinger opens the box, before
the particle goes left or right, where reality exists in a wave
of potential. From here, a billion and one possible directions
stretched before me, awaiting me to harmonize with whatever
path I wished.

But this time something was exceptionally different. My
consciousness was now linked with the greater focus of the
Jain. And his attention was far more pliable than what my own,
limited ego could harmonize with. His was a consciousness
tempered by years, lifetimes, of training and meditative practice. It possessed a potential spectrum of vibration far wider
than I would have thought possible for a human to tap into.
His was an awareness unleashed, unhindered by ego; an awareness that could pull any vibrational pattern into existence. With
my attention bound to his, I could harmonize with literally any
possible combination of matter and energy.

Why, by piggybacking on this man's attention, I could whisk
myself back home with Tina in my arm and a diamond the
size of a baseball in my pocket. All the riches I could imagine
could be mine, right now! Any desire, no matter how unlikely.
Power, fame, sex, all the poppies on the face of the globe! Or,
I could get really creative: I could leap into a configuration of
matter and energy where I am a king! A living prophet! I could
emerge from the clouds and alight upon the earth like a god of

my choosing.

And . . . and what a strange time to learn that when every possibility is laid before me, it's hard to move. Just as with imprisonment. I wanted all of it and I wanted none of it. I was frozen once again. After an indeterminate amount of time—ten minutes, a day, a lifetime—something entirely unexpected arose. I found that I was rather enjoying the simplicity of residing in this not-choosing. There was a hidden pleasure to be found in resting in the potential of choice. And a subtle question arose from the periphery of my awareness which quietly asked, "What do you want?"

What did I want? Within all the chaos, I had forgotten what I really, really wanted. I remained in this state for so long I began to sense the vines of the Banyan trees creeping around me. What do I really want? Slowly, I began to picture it. Images of what I truly desired arose in my consciousness and settled into my heart. I didn't want extremes of power or fame. I didn't want riches or drama. Now that the offer was made real and accessible, I didn't want to shape the world, or even save it for that matter.

When I thought of my true ideal, I pictured a quieter life. I wanted the world I had been building for myself, maybe with the addition of the woman I loved, and perhaps with a bit more confidence, humility, and wisdom for the wear. I wanted to better appreciate what I had already been given. Was it too much to ask? From my current vantage point, with all the insane scenarios at my fingertips, it shouldn't have seemed so, yet somehow it did. Was going home after all this really an option? Was my ability to ever return home destroyed the moment I left my front door?

I directed my attention again to the shell of the man sitting across from me, a man whose entire bundle of energy resided in the wave, short of a single toe he kept dipped in our limited world of particle and form. Our eyes met.

"No thank you," I said aloud. "It's too much. If I ever get there, I'll do it myself, on my own power."

An almost imperceptible smile appeared on his face and he

closed his eyes. Like a magnet pushing against its polar oppo-site, I was suddenly thrown backward and up, into the air. I was pulled through the forest and back toward the spring as if my consciousness were on a retractable line. With a splash, I was slammed beneath the waters of the lotus pool and down, down into the warm bowels of the earth.

And everything went black once more. No light or move-ment, no water or air. Not even the act of breathing. But something began to shimmer on the surface of this pure, empty nothingness. The sea of vibration born of an infinity of vibrating rings slowly emerged from the depths. For a brief moment, something in this vast ocean of energy glistened above the others. A sort of fiery shimmer spun through one of the tiny circles which, upon closer inspection, appeared to be more like "strings" of vibration, ever-so-delicate, elastic bands of buzzing energy. A random memory bubbled up from my ego's past. Kyle and Damian had once spoke of something called a "Unified Field Theory" in theoretical physics they had referred to as Super . . . and there it was again! A blaze of fire spinning in circles amongst the infinite ocean of rings!

I mustered all of my awareness and held my attention to this particular band of light, this one circle of energy that sang just for me! I held on for dear life with an effortless, unbend-ing intention. The longer I held my attention on it, the closer the ring became, the larger it grew. Soon the spinning energy sizzled, hummed, in wide circles that encompassed my entire range of vision! A spinning torch of fire! In the center of this glowing circle, an image appeared. A woman's face! Am I looking at Tina? Perhaps Eden? The woman smiled at me and the rest of her body emerged into view. And then I, too, was standing on solid earth right before her! She was a vision of raw beauty, held within a circle of glowing, orange light.

But I did not recognize this woman. Or perhaps I had seen her somewhere before; in another lifetime? She wore clothing made of leather and palm leaves, a wreath of small, white flow-ers graced her neck. Kneeling on either side of her were two men who pounded furiously into large, handmade drums. At the edge of my peripheral, the woman's fiery torch spun with a deep, whirling sound, a sound that had been filling my ears for what seemed an eternity.

Suddenly, the woman swung her torch into the ground. The fiery tip snuffed out in the dirt with a loud whoosh! and the men abruptly stopped drumming. There was a moment of silence before the three of them suddenly broke into cheering and howling into the night air with joyful celebration.

I stood before them, utterly confused as to what was going on: where I had been, where I was now, who I was. I could almost see the spinning computer icon that read, "Loading . . . please wait."

The woman leaped at me with unbridled enthusiasm, wrapping me with the most powerful embrace I had ever received. Hesitantly, I returned the hug, trying to understand what we were celebrating. While she adorned me with excitement, I turned my head to survey my surroundings, and it started to come back to me. I was now standing on the opposite side of the crater. Far behind me, on the "deadman's plank" Sadhu, Iboga, Lemm, and Tasha were on their feet beaming at me. The woman pulled back from the embrace and stared into my eyes.

"This is the first time you have ever made it across!" she said, struggling through tears of joy. "I thought I'd never see the day!" At that, she pulled me in hard and kissed me passionately on the lips before yanking my head to the side.

"The medicine wears off quickly!" she said fiercely. "You don't have much time!"

"What?" I managed to utter.

"GO SAVE HER!" she shouted.

And somehow, it all clicked. My God. It's all so clear. I know how to save Tina's life.

With a speed and agility I never imagined, I darted out of the clearing and into the woods, back toward the medicine hut, back to the woman I loved.

# Meaningless Miracles

*"When we look at our lives from the viewpoint that everything is every-where all the time, the implications are so vast that for many they're hard to grasp."*

Gregg Braden

**M**y body leapt over rocks and bushes, ducked branches, and dodged trees in total darkness with such flawless grace, any onlooker would think I had navigated this path a hundred times blindfolded. How I was performing these feats, I did not know. I was in a frame of consciousness that did not know error. Or, more precisely, doubt.

But time was running out. The hallucinogens were wearing off, along with my vision of the probability wave. I sensed tiny fragments of "darkness" enter my consciousness as I ran full speed toward Tina. I could feel it happening on the periphery of my mind; the old structures of my identity as a scientist, as a man of reason and respect began to settle once more in my well-worn trenches. Doubt was trying to rear its head again and divide me from everything happening at once.

I've been doped on drugs for days without proper sleep. Maybe I hallucinated my death, entering a probability wave, emerging at the far end of the crater. I probably just walked around the periphery of that goddamned ravine; I just don't remember it. Maybe this has all been one, giant mind fuck and the tribe is back there laughing their asses off.

I exploded into the medicine hut and slid to a halt at Tina's side. She was still unconscious, with a pulse weaker than ever, her breathing so subtle I could barely detect it. Okay, I know how I can fix her. It's all vibration. Vibration is the root of all structure, all atomic configuration. I just need to alter her vibration. I fumbled with placing my hands over her body like I had seen in movies where mystics psychically healed their patient. Then I tried waving them in circles, then holding them still with eyes closed in concentration.

No, that's not right. Those dramatics are just for show. It doesn't matter where I put my goddamned hands. I stared blankly at her dying body for a moment. For the life of me, I could not imagine why in hell I thought I knew how to heal her. I have absolutely no idea what I'm doing. I don't even know where I really am. Or who I am. Yes! That's it. The first step to shapeshifting.

At that, something at my core unhinged. Just as before, I could sense my identity disconnect from my perception. But, this time, it was a far smoother transition.

The once hard lines and defined edges of my ego were less rigid, lighter, more accepting. I put my hands in my lap and sat on my heels. Soon I settled back into my vision: That whatever the "I" was, that center of awareness that was perceiving the world from behind my eyes, it was immoveable, a something that has always existed in its rawest, most elemental form. That which could never shapeshift. Rather, it was the world that had always been transpiring, manifesting around it.

The longer I sat in this state, the more the rigid features around me, from the clay covering her wounds, to the wooden bed she lay upon, to the earthen floor, the entirety of it slowly moved out of focus. My world broke down once again from molecules, down to atoms, down to particles until nothing remained but an endless ocean of vibrating rings of light. All my lingering doubts, all my questions, all my discontent, even my very motivation for entering this field, all fell back into the abyss. My consciousness moved from particle back to wave. And now I saw the truth: There was ultimately never a duality among the two.

There is no particle. It's an illusion created by ego. And in response, humming softly in the background was the frequency that brought me here to begin with. I focused my attention into the billions and billions of potential vibrations and witnessed the possible combinations of matter and energy from this point of now.

From the vantage point of the probability wave, I witnessed each and every way the dominoes could fall from here. In a billion of the most likely scenarios I was forced to endure watching Tina's heart give out where she died before my eyes. In the majority of these patterns, she passed quietly; in others, she struggled under the asphyxiation and pain before going limp. All of these projections lay behind frequencies that the ego Professor Michael Huxley could readily vibrate with; patterns that easily harmonized with my education, my beliefs, my ideas, and doubts, my understanding of biological processes. If it were up to ordinary chance and my typical viewpoint, my leash, Tina would be dead within the hour.

But now I saw why healing required that I was also the one who changed. If I was to see a different outcome play out, I would first have to alter the frequency my ego was connecting with. Otherwise, the only patterns of reality I would merge with would forever remain ones where Tina died before me. I have to reach a different frequency of particle configuration.

The very moment I focused on exactly what I was looking for it appeared: A rare network of rings that vibrated with the lowest probabilities of outcome. These projections were carried by highly foreign patterns, circles of vibration my identity was entirely unfamiliar with. Within these limited, uncommon configurations, I witnessed the oddest scenarios play out: The sort of things which, out of a billion, trillion playbacks of the same dynamics would only transpire once. The very reason such phenomena rarely see the light of day in our world. The majority of these realities would perhaps never come to pass within the short lifespan of a universe that was, unless a consciousness were to come along that knew how to intend such a rare event to manifest.

In one of these projections, I gazed in terror and wonder when all the molecules of Tina's body along with the bed she laid upon spun into a vortex of swirling plasma and vanished beneath the earth, the result of some near-impossible, brief convergence of cosmic radiation that had been passing through space for a millennia. In yet another, she spontaneously burst into flames when a series of internal chemical reactions ignited the fatty acids to torch her body spontaneously from the inside out. In others, extreme blood loss shut down her higher mental functioning leaving only the lower, reptilian brain in command. Combined with a sudden burst of enzymatic decoding, she would physically transform into things other than human. In a few of these scenarios, she leapt from the table like a wild animal and killed me with her bare hands. In other cases, her claws.

In many other configurations, brilliant waves of light danced from her skin and flowers bloomed spontaneously from her hair. Each and every possible chemical reaction—no matter how unlikely, no matter how beautiful, or how terrifying—that could take place, did. All happening at once; all contained perfectly in the potential of the moment.

As I looked through the vast ocean of energy, I saw that it was even possible that, with a rare surge of chemical energy from her mitochondria, all the macrophages within her system were swept into unimaginable speeds to destroy the damaged and dead cells, where the fibroblasts and proteins ignited to rebuild soft tissues while collagens repaved her wounds right before my eyes.

But, just like the other bizarre and completely unlikely scenarios, this configuration of reality lay guarded behind a frequency so alien to anything I had ever experienced, I had no clue as to how to enter it. It sang at such a high, delicate pitch! How would I ever harmonize with such a reality to merge with it? As if she saw my dilemma, Iboga began speaking as soon as she entered the hut behind me.

"The shift need not be permanent in you or her," she said. "Just long enough to make the jump from one pattern to the other." Before my mind could process the routine of asking just what the hell she meant by that, my body burst into action. It was obvious. I leapt to my feet and frantically searched the hut. That's why they collect herbs—each medicine alters the frequency of awareness in a unique and specific way.

Like an addict searching for his syringe, my hands fumbled over bowls of powdered leaves, jars of dried fungus, and shredded roots. I tipped over ceramic pots filled with flower petals and ran my hands through dozens of berries, pods, and essential oils. As my eyes passed over each medicine, I could sense the energy it emitted. I could feel the vibration the plant gave off just by laying my eyes on it. There must be one that can instill that frequency. This wasn't a perception born strictly of touch, vision, or hearing, rather some subtle combination, one that belonged in its own sense category.

And there it was. I felt it before I saw it. The corner of a dark, wooden shelf near the floor at my feet hummed with the same vibration as the projection where Tina's cellular composition spontaneously snapped back into place and her wounds rapidly healed. I dropped to my knees and grabbed the source of the frequency: A round, white vase of hand-molded clay. I greedily snatched it up and dashed it to shards on the floor. Gradually, the entire hut smelled like shit.

"That wasn't necessary," Iboga lamented with a compassionate tone, one that appreciated the state of mind I was in. I furiously dug through shards of clay and cow manure to discover what had been calling to me: A network of spongy, orange-capped mushrooms with whitish-blue stems. Before I attempted to stuff the entire mass of fungus into my mouth, Iboga called from the far end of the hut.

"Okay, Jesus, hold on, professor," she said, scurrying to my aid. She yanked the mushrooms from my hands, doused them in a bowl of water and shook them lightly.

"You might want to wash the cow shit off first." She smiled and presented them to me anew. As I shoved a handful of bitter caps and stems down my throat, Iboga tried to calm my nerves. It was clear she knew her efforts would be useless, but she tried nonetheless.

"Chew those before swallowing, professor," she advised. "Your stomach is empty and quite fragile. It won't take long for the sacred mushrooms to work on you, so take it slow. You're ingesting the First Medicine."

"Ah, you've chosen cubensis to reach her," Sadhu said upon entering the hut behind Iboga. "Interesting choice. They are the Golden Teachers; the first psychedelic humans made contact with. It changed us forever."

I was too busy chewing to reply, so instead I glared at him angrily with a mouth full of mushrooms and pointed angrily at his face: a gesture I intended to convey, "I'm pretty sure you coaxed me into throwing myself off a cliff to my death, so I'll get back to you later. But just know . . . I've got beef."

I pushed past the two of them and knelt at Tina's side once again while Iboga and Sadhu seated themselves on the floor at the far end of the bed. They closed their eyes in unison, placed their clasped fingers into their lap, took a deep breath, and began to chant; a low, resonant hum forged deep within their diaphragms. At first, I thought their chanting would distract me, but I found I could make use of it. The sound was a nearly continuous droning much like the sound of a honeybee at ultra-low speed. I allowed my attention to ride their song back to the Zero Point Field.

Their humming helped me sneak out of the ego's leash and into the probability wave with ease. Within moments, I sat at the center of awareness within the sea of potential energy, each feasible pattern passing through my heart as well as my head. Within moments, I had pushed past all the "more likely" possibilities where Tina's death played out a trillion times over, each a bit different than the last. I peered into the realms where she survived, but only barely; suffering lifelong paralysis or loss of limbs, or a million other maladies. And again I moved steadily on, into the stranger frequencies and saw the truly bizarre; the far more unlikely organizations of matter and energy and I gazed at all the possible horrors that could come about, as well as manifestations of such subtle, elegant beauty they were difficult to witness. For most of these patterns, I wondered just what it would take, what would be required to bring a human consciousness down these roads.

"Things that Professor Michael Huxley still cannot begin to conceive of," I heard a voice reply. Though I knew I was hearing my own internal dialogue, I believed the words to be true.

And then some tiny river moved into my consciousness, a stream of energy that I didn't recognize as my own. Soon, this unusual sensation overwhelmed my perception and I noticed a shift on the deepest level of my awareness. The very instant I realized "Oh, the mushrooms are kicking in," a cluster of vibrations emerged from the ocean bearing realities where Tina was healed spontaneously.

My consciousness sang in ever-increasing harmony with the world I so desperately wanted, the tiny window of possibility that held my love healed. And slowly my personal frequency began to merge with its patterns. As the two songs integrated, I watched behind closed eyes as Tina's wounds spontaneously healed under the coating of dried clay. I envisioned muscle tissue repairing itself, nerves building new connections, and a network of healthy cells bridging the puncture wounds. Yes, this is what I want.

And on some highly refined level, I sensed that this convergence of energy was affecting Tina's consciousness as well. Though her body was inert, her awareness was readily accepting of the unusual exchange taking place. She has some experience of this from her grandfather, was my intuition. None of this could take place without her ultimate consent.

Finally, I felt a change in myself as this "handshake" took place. While the frequency altered the patterns of biological matter within her body, I could see the physics behind every incredible dynamic, how everything taking place was indeed in no way "supernatural." All of these sudden shifts at the particle level was somehow completely within the realm of physics at the biological level. And under this unusual frequency, Professor Michael Huxley was completely okay with that, without the slightest doubt clouding his view.

When I saw the last of Tina's incisions sealed, Tina let out a soft sigh. I opened my eyes just as she turned her head. As if waking from a thick haze, she groggily looked up at me. For a moment we gazed into each other, then her lips rose to a weak smile.

"I love you," she whispered. I wept and joy poured from my being. A quiet realization fell upon me that I was now forever changed. My heart now held greater power than my head.

"I love you," I replied. With a gentle hand, I leaned down and peeled the layers of clay from her shoulder and waist. I had to see it with my own eyes. Beneath the crumbling chunks of clay I found nothing but smooth, healthy skin. Tears poured from my eyes in a combination of shock and gratitude. More than anything else, I was overwhelmed with how entirely okay I was with this, as if I had just watched a plane take off for the thousandth time, an incredible sight, for sure, but nothing out of the ordinary. We have the math to explain exactly how it happens.

I just saved her life. I reached into the vast myriad of possibilities and plucked out a specific vibration like a surgeon. I leaned into her for a gentle kiss, but stopped halfway. The larger, dark reality of it all hit me with the impact of a freight train. No, I absolutely did NOT save her life. I didn't change anything. I didn't heal anyone!

How could I ignore the larger truth here? All those many possibilities still existed in their full potential. I had only chosen to personally experience one specific band of color from the spectrum! In a trillion other scenarios, Tina still died right there. Who the hell am I to leap around from one possible combination of atoms to another?! It was more than self-serving, it was delusional. No vibration of patterns was any more or less "right" than any of the others! Every path had an equal claim to existence.

I leapt to my feet and stared down at her body. The endless variety of what could have been pounded through my memory. After witnessing one of the greatest truths of reality, my insight and knowledge were unmasked as ultimately meaningless. Confusion crossed Tina's face as I stormed out of the hut into the cold night air.

Outside, the camp was quiet. The only sounds came from a weak fire crackling in a large stone pit at the center of the village. The horizon to the east glowed with a faint sweep of pink and, above it, a dark blue expanse dotted with starlight. The sun would be up shortly and I would have spent one full day in the gorge. I felt like I had been here for years. Leave it to me to feel depressed after taking part in the most utterly profound, spontaneous acts of healing. I took part in a miracle and now I was as lost and alone as ever.

"So after all your trouble, now you're not certain if you should have saved her?" Iboga said upon exiting the hut. She wrapped a warm, woolen blanket around my shoulders and stood at my side.

"You know the truth as well as I do," I muttered. "Now that I see it all for what it is, I feel I've been scammed somehow. This isn't what I imagined. She lives, she dies. It's all there at the same time and there isn't any combination that's any more "correct" than any other. Some are just more rare than others. I don't feel like I did the right thing just now. All I know for sure is that I did some thing. I could've chosen a billion other outcomes to experience, so what's the point?"

"Who says there has to be a point?" she replied. "Points are for the ego to feel righteous in the choices it makes. But you are right. All choices are ultimately arbitrary. It's an equally great and dangerous realization. Lesser minds would use that insight to justify the hatred they would unleash upon others. The wisdom you glimpsed is something that our "shortcuts" to enlightenment often skip. I'm happy you see the futility in miracles."

"Oh?" I grunted. "You're saying it's a good thing to know my efforts are useless a moment after I unlock one of the biggest secrets of the universe?"

"Absolutely," she replied confidently. "It's one of the ways the universe balances personal power with insight. The people we should be concerned about are the ones who stumble into heaven for a moment and believe for the rest of their days that the choices they make are uniquely right. They forget to continue to act from love, to choose from the highest compassion. You've been drained from this experience, professor. When your energy returns you won't feel so depressed about this, I promise."

"Yeah?" I shot back. "Like the love it takes to persuade a sick, drugged up man off a cliff to his death?"

Iboga smiled wide, nearly to the point of laughter, "You look pretty healthy for a dead man. Look at you, dead in a ditch one minute, up and rescuing his princess the next. The mind will find any reason to complain."

"You two turned on me back there," I said, not sure if I was really angry about their supposed betrayal.

"We had to make you believe we turned on you, professor," Sadhu lamented when he stepped outside. "To make all those leaps, you had to act from your own power; yours and yours alone. It was absolutely necessary to make you safe."

"What the hell does that mean?" I said, shaking my head, unsure if I really wanted an answer. He pulled another cigarette from his pocket and lit it behind cupped hands.

"We are deeply concerned about anyone who knows the shortcuts to tap into the probability wave," he said. "A damaged ego with a means to replicate god-consciousness makes for a deadly combination."

Iboga grunted in agreement. "Hopefully our plan to fight fire with fire will work," she said and returned to the medicine hut.

# Sloth Monkey

*"You get there by realizing you are already there."*

Eckhart Tolle

Just before sunrise, Sadhu escorted Tina and I west out of the village through the forest toward the mountains. The valley floor took a sudden turn into steep terrain and we soon broke treeline into scree and shale. Rising just ahead from the base of the Himalayas rose a silent barrier of foothills that seemed to emit a steady, frigid wind. Sadhu forbid us from asking any questions on the way up, saying only that we should "clear our minds and allow the sediment to settle." When the two of us followed him from the village, he would only say that he was guiding us to a spring to heal. We lodged no complaint on that note. My body and mind were equally exhausted; my joints ached, my feet hurt, my back was an absolute mess, and my brain was barely processing. I didn't even trust my own thinking.

I found myself fantasizing about a point down the road when I had managed to put all of this into some kind of perspective. But I couldn't begin to imagine what that might look like. One thing I was sure of, I wasn't detoxing. Every muscle and joint was sore, but I was far from withdrawal, neither was I high. Whatever Iboga fed me had performed a feat I assumed impossible. I guessed I just had to get used to such things.

"This gets pretty steep, but it's not much farther up the ridge," Sadhu called from ahead. The man was now in "stoic field guide" mode. I was coming to accept that the man changed personas faster than I could change my shirt and decided to give up trying to get a lock on him for the time being. Tina and I walked hand in hand in silence, but after some time I allowed some distance to fall between us and our guide. We were both desperate for privacy. From what I could gather, she had no memory of anything since she and I were running naked through the jungles of the Chambira Basin.

"I want to thank you for what you did," she whispered once

we were alone. "I had several visions while I was unconscious. Most of them were just crazy, hallucinatory dream states, but many of them were based on things that were actually taking place around me, I could feel it. On some level, I saw how you healed me."

Ah. That. I was also quite certain that I had no idea what to think about that detail, either. Did I like the notion that I faced death to emerge, reborn with some cosmic insight that allowed me to spontaneously heal the woman I loved? Joseph Campbell would have been so proud. Of course, I liked the sound of that. Not a bad trade, to be elevated to "spiritual healer" after having my carefully sculpted identity of "atheist" knocked from the mantle and shattered to a thousand pieces. I could still picture a version where she lay dead in the medicine hut. The layers between those realities now seemed frighteningly thin. Tina patted my hand when she saw me struggling with her compliment.

"I know you didn't just magically cure me," she said. "It was more like you bridged the gap between here and there. You helped light a passage for me to reach a place of health."

I nodded my head in reluctant acceptance and we both chuckled weakly at the absurdity of it all. Neither of us were really sure of where we were, what was happening, or where we were going, but we were grateful for more time together. Other than dealing with having been unconscious under extreme agony, she was functioning surprisingly well. And she was coping with all the unanswered questions with a hell of a lot more grace than I was.

After scrambling along a near-ninety degree incline, Tina and I trailed Sadhu around a narrow ledge. For some ten meters, we treaded gingerly around a curved cliff with our backs scraping the wall and the sheer ledge just beyond our toes.

Yes, this is just the kind of rest and relaxation I needed, I thought as I gazed down at the yawning expanse below. From here, we enjoyed a bird's eye view of the forest and the Roto village in the clearing. Oddly enough, I found the dizzying views no longer bothered me. Instead, I found myself soaking in the majestic sights of the canyon and the green plateau beyond as the sun peaked over the horizon. We rounded the corner to find an enormous, east-facing wedge in the cliff where the ledge beneath our feet opened into wider, more forgiving opened space. Nestled in the corner where two walls of rock met was a bubbling pool of steaming water, just as Sadhu promised.

He opened his leather satchel and removed a wrapped handkerchief filled with dried venison, coconut, and papaya. From around his shoulder, he unstrapped a bladder of water which he handed to me. I was clearly the one most in need of hydration after the climb.

"You have until the sun reaches the top of that tree," he instructed, pointing to a lone, jagged pine jutting from the cliff. "About two hours. You can find your way back down." Before he began his return journey around the ledge, I grabbed his sleeve.

"How did I make it over that crater last night?" I asked, or rather, pleaded. "How did I get to the other side?" He smiled and shook his head.

"What does it matter what I tell you?" he replied. "All you'll ever have is your experience of what happened. Whatever I tell you, you'll doubt."

"But, I believe you'll tell me the truth," I said.

He raised his eyebrow and nodded. "Okay," he said. "From my perspective, you fell forward and disappeared into the crater. A moment later, an enormous whirlwind rose from the pit, powerful enough to lift you into the air. It carried your body to the other side just before it dispersed. Obviously, the chances of that happening must be astronomical." I studied him, trying to decide if he was making a joke. When he didn't flinch, I lowered my head in thought.

"I remember dying in that pit," I whispered.

"Yep," Sadhu said. "That too. The particle goes through both slits. But you choose to continue the story of Professor Michael Huxley." I rolled my eyes at his suggestion of how this was all connected to physics.

"Told ya," he replied, slapped my shoulder and disappeared around the rocky wall.

Although the sun had barely broke the horizon, we could feel the heat on our skin as we peeled the filthy clothes from our bodies. The cold, mountain air was still unforgiving at this hour so we wasted little time submerging ourselves into the rolling spring. Well, at least, Tina didn't hesitate; she lowered herself right in with a prolonged, "ahhhh," and rested her head against the rim. I poked a cautious toe below the surface and found the temperature was searing. I couldn't imagine how she dropped into water that hot.

"Get in, you pussy," she cooed, but with her accent it sounded more like pooo-sey. I laughed and shook my head when she asked what was so funny. Several dramatic moments later filled with me screeching "Ow!" and "Shit!" with every inch gained, I finally eased the full girth of my body into the pool and found the water didn't seem nearly as hot once I was in.

I didn't realize how hungry I was until I began devouring the fruit and deer jerky. In a weird way, I had begun to enjoy the empty feeling in my stomach. Soon after gorging ourselves, we fell asleep in each other's arms with warm spring water bubbling up to our necks and the sun on our faces. At this point, I found I didn't really care what was real. I was content to take the moment as-is.

After a short period of dreamless sleep, my eyes began to open. I was confused to find my surroundings dark. Had we slept through the day? No, I was no longer in the spring. And Tina wasn't next to me. I felt the urge to panic, tried to focus and, slowly, the dim surroundings came into view. Above me, white cones of mineral deposits stretched down from the ceiling. I knew this view. Kaylah suddenly appeared overhead. She studied me with a concerned eye before leaning in and crawling on top of my chest. Before I could ask just what the hell she was doing, the girl bent down and locked her lips with mine. I froze with awkward fear and a stream of smoke passed from her lungs and into mine. I lost consciousness beneath her vapors while I heard her speak in clear English, "Not yet, professor."

I awoke with a jolt to the sound of scurrying over rock. The moment I opened my eyes, something darted around the far corner of the cliff wall. A segment of coconut on the edge of our pool spun in circles on its back. I looked down to find Tina still snoozing happily in the nook of my arm. Slowly, I eased my head back and pretended to fall asleep. After a couple minutes of studying the edge of the cliff through peeled eyelids, I nearly passed out again. Then a subtle movement shook me back to the present, but I kept my eyes mostly closed.

Through blurred vision I saw what appeared to be a tuft of white fur steadily peek around the corner. And then a tiny arm reached out for a finger hold on our side of the wall. With creeping, continuous movement, its small hand studied the crevices of the rock until it found its grip. In successive, gentle degrees of progress, a small white and gray monkey, no larger than a house cat, crept its way around the bend. Its round, tan face never broke eye contact with me throughout its entire journey from cliff wall to ledge, less than a meter distance. Moving at a snail's pace, it took nearly twenty minutes for the creature to cover the stretch. When I opened my eyes a little wider, he would come to a full stop and stare at me without blinking.

After another few moments of keeping perfectly still, he would continue his sloth-like crawl along the far rim of the spring. With no sudden movements, I nonchalantly turned my head down to see if Tina was witnessing the same event. She was sound asleep. Waking her would surely send the overly-cautious animal scurrying out of sight.

With the same, smooth pace, the monkey perched itself on hind legs and began reaching for our scraps of papaya. One by one, it would raise the peel to its mouth and slowly scrape off a chunk of flesh, all the while staring into me with undivided intensity. This display went on for maybe a half an hour. The longer the little beast ate, the more mesmerized I grew by its gradual, conscious movements. Each motion was deliberate and soaked with attention.

After finishing every last morsel of fruit on the pool's edge, the tiny creature made its way into the hot spring across from us. First, it stretched its foot out and dipped its toes into the bath. I spied a slight wince as he adapted to the water's extreme heat, but it never broke eye contact. Ever so slowly, it lowered its weight into the spring up to its chest. After coming to rest, he carefully cupped his hands below the surface and scooped a teaspoon of water over his head. For the briefest of moments, he closed his eyes when he rubbed the water over his forehead and back through his scalp. He repeated this same movement again and again, washing his face and hair in slow motion. With each successive pass, he allowed his eyes to close just a little longer when the water washed over them.

By the time his bath was done, he allowed his eyes to close while he nestled his head between two small rocks where the water rose neck-high. All I could see now was a small, furry face poking out of the spring. A short time later, his jaw fell open and I could hear the creature snoring softly over the rolling bubbles. I stared at our little friend until my own eyes went blurry and I slipped back into sleep.

The next thing I knew, Kaylah was poking and prodding us from the edge of the hot spring. She chattered in her native tongue, but it was clear she meant for us to get dressed and make our way back to the village. Dazed and confused, Tina and I both lazily dried ourselves and pulled our clothes back on. As we followed the child back around the corner of the cliff wall, I took one, last gaze at the pool. There was no sign of the creature; only the peels of papaya and coconut scraped clean by tiny teeth.

# Sastuns

*"Thoughts don't become things; thoughts ARE things."*

Eric Micha'el Leventhal

Kaylah led Tina and me to the fire pit at the center of the village where we found Iboga smoking from her long, wooden pipe, staring intently into the flames. We took a seat on one of the large, flat stones on the rim of the fire. Tina had regained her energy and was now bubbling with questions, but Iboga redirected her with a wave of her hand before she could speak.

"The human ego; the totality of your internal thinking, your very identity," Iboga began as she expelled a cloud of smoke into the fire, "represents a unique frequency that harmonizes with the sleeping potential of a billion and one forms that your world can take. I call that potential 'spirit.' You may call it what you wish, a quantum field, or whatever word you've decided to assign to it this generation. To me, it is choiceless awareness. And, therein lies the ultimate trick. The awareness that is attached to your identity pattern will experience only those energetic patterns that it can attune to. Our song, our story, our beliefs, all our mental constructs are forever reaching into an ocean of infinite energy and building bridges between our consciousness and a select series of vibrational patterns within that ocean. We create frequencies that literally shape our world. Most of us do this unconsciously from habit, from brainwashing."

"You do know that's a lot to digest, right?" Tina asked with a look of shock. "I mean, if that was true, wouldn't every human being experience a completely different world? If my ego is shaping what I see at the same time yours is, then why would any of us even agree on what this village or this fire pit in front of us looks like?"

"That question is based on the assumption that there are, in fact, other people," Sadhu chuckled, appearing behind us.

"She isn't ready for that," Iboga scolded him. "Ignore him for now."

Sadhu waved his hands in surrender. "Okay, fair enough," he said with a smile. "Here's one way to satisfy your question: The vast majority of human perception lives in a very narrow bandwidth. We've been weaving stories across the globe about what this world looks like, what is possible, what isn't. In doing so, everyone is continuously fine-tuning the dial on their internal radios in order to connect with other minds in a meaningful way. Brainwashing spreads much like a virus and you see the world your parents handed you. That's why we separate ourselves from the masses. Why do you think people treat religion and philosophy as if it's a life and death battle for the world itself? Because for them, it is! It threatens us when others don't subscribe to their bandwidth! It makes them wonder just how reliable their own tuner is."

"Tuner?" Tina asked, "as in a radio?"

"Of course," he replied. "The ego is just another station on the radio and it always confuses the description of the world for the world itself. You aren't the body any more than the radio is the source of the music. You're a wavelength, one that can be moved or altered."

"And there absolutely are differences in how people from different walks of life experience their reality," Iboga added. "If an uncontacted aborigine suddenly walked into your home, Ms. Flores, they would see a very different view than you do. Just as you would if you walked into their terrain. Since the beginning of humanity there have been those who sense very different phenomena than the herd."

"Yeah, so do insane people," I added.

"Absolutely!" Sadhu agreed. "What a schizophrenic sees is a different, perfectly valid wavelength of reality that you don't have access to."

"So then, just what is the difference between your tribe and a bunch of insane people?" I demanded. With that, Sadhu and Iboga broke into hysterical laughter. Tina and I just stared at each other anxiously. It was a question we both desired an answer to, and one that would be ultimately ignored; however, Sadhu nodded in appreciation of my discomfort.

"Okay, okay," Tina said. "How does this connect to the Dreaming Tree you claim brought us here? How did I wake up in Tibet?"

"You're everywhere," Sadhu shrugged.

"Because we are not, I repeat, NOT the song our ego sings," Iboga replied as if it answered Tina's question. "We are not that narrow bandwidth we live in. It is that confusion, and that confusion alone, that has ultimately led to every act of rage and ignorance that has ever transpired on this planet. We are that which animates the identity."

"I generally just call it 'attention,'" Sadhu said. "But I prefer to demystify this whole process."

"As you wish, but my point is that you must realize that the real power, the real mystery lies in your own attention!" Iboga said. "You must be very careful how you use it, where you direct it, and who you hand it to, especially when that someone still grooms their own identity, one who would see their desires fulfilled, whatever they may be! Attention is a force that people crave after in ways that can defy comprehension. Babies require it to live, you can feel it when it's directed at you even when your back is turned, and if you're suddenly denied it after steady access for long periods of time, you will go into withdrawal just like a drug addict. Most people who have acquired large amounts of it have access to incredible amounts of power to connect with even greater combinations of possibilities."

"How's that?" I asked.

"Constructive interference," Sadhu mentioned quietly. He looked around and found everyone waiting for him to elaborate. He sighed. "When two waves of equal amplitude interfere constructively, the resulting amplitude is twice as large as the amplitude of an individual wave," he said matter-of-factly. "If one hundred waves of the same amplitude interfere, the resulting amplitude is one hundred times larger than the amplitude of the individual wave. Don't kid yourself into thinking Kane doesn't know that. That's why he preaches. He wants to absorb the power of his faithful converts."

"That's one way of describing it, yes," Iboga continued. "Consciousness that is freely given to another can be used to tap into possibilities that few have access to; that is, provided the receiver remembers the truth about who they really are, what they are made of. But most channel that energy back into their own ego and they go insane from it. Or worse. That's one of the reasons so many of your rich and famous fall apart. They can't handle the influx of attention in a balanced way."

"And, that's how we arrived in Tibet!" I cheered as if their words had explained anything about how we were pulled hundreds of miles across the globe instantaneously. Without missing a beat, Iboga stood and shouted, "Rosita!" into the early morning air. For several minutes, no one moved, no one spoke.

I was about to ask another question when a tall, slim woman with curled, black hair stepped from a grass hut on the periphery of the village. The tone of her skin and facial features appeared to be of Spanish or Mediterranean descent. After Iboga spoke with our new guest in hushed tones, the woman approached us and gestured that we stand.

"This is Rosita, Professor Huxley," Iboga said with a reverent tone. With a smile, Rosita fanned out her fingers like a magician proving there was nothing in her hands before cupping them together. She then closed her eyes, inhaled forcefully and held her breath . . . And she held it. And she held it longer. The woman held her breath so long I feared she would soon lose consciousness. This Rosita was clearly in good physical shape, but I feared just how long she could keep this up. When she finally exhaled, she lifted her hand slowly before my eyes. Resting in the center of her palm was a translucent, dark green sphere about the circumference of a dime. Tina and I leaned in for inspection. Judging by its tint and surface features, I guessed it to be a naturally occurring garnet.

"What is that?" Tina asked.

"It's a Sastun," Rosita replied with a Spanish accent upon opening her eyes. "Consciousness takes both the form of wave and raindrop. This is one of those raindrops, born of pure consciousness. This particular Sastun was created through the intention of a powerful emerald torrent."

"Like a stream?" Tina asked.

"I envisioned a green river, to be specific," she said and placed the tiny gem in my hands. "This is for you, professor. May you use it to fill one of those gaps of yours someday."

I held the stone up to the firelight and asked, "You're telling me that I'm holding an idea? Of beautiful, emerald liquid." After a delightful smile and a bow of her head, Rosita disappeared back into her hut, leaving us to stare at the artifact in a stupor.

"I know you think that woman just pulled a sleight of hand trick on you," Iboga said. "But the point is that focused intention can become a physical manifestation. That Sastun will remain in this state until it is unlocked."

"Unlocked?" I asked incredulously.

"Yes, by vibrating with the awareness that manifested it. Just as you had to do to enter the Dreaming Tree properly. Just as you had to do in order to heal this woman. It'll all come together one day, I promise."

"Hold on," I said with outstretched palms. "You just took a giant leap over a gap there."

"You're the expert in that field, professor," Iboga laughed gently and paused to consider another way of explaining it. "With enough time and intention, Rosita could have focused on another idea, an idea broken down to its simplest, most elemental structure. She could have held that idea under the pressure of her focus until she had a diamond; pure, crystallized thought. Or . . . " Iboga stepped in closer to look me in the eye. "She could have focused on being in a specific spot in Peru," she said. "Rosita could have ingested a medicine that would help her vibrate with what you call the Zero Point Field. And from there, she could have focused on the truth that, within all the many possible realities, she was already in Peru. And it would be the truth. Just as you are both in Peru and Tibet."

I felt my brain clenching the longer she spoke. I feared these people's worldview was beginning to actually make some kind of twisted sense, but Iboga didn't let up. "Furthermore, professor, Rosita could have vibrated with one of the billion and one possibilities where that truth crystallized into physical form. And a manifestation of that intention would be left in her wake; a stone with a crystalline structure containing the potential of bridging the illusion of space and distance between here and there, waiting to be unlocked by whoever vibrated with the same frequency as she had when she created the manifestation. Its sole potential would actualize you to the single truth that, in this specific case, you are equally in the Chambira Basin and the Tsangpo Gorge. The Dreaming Tree doesn't move people. Or even consciousness, for that matter, since it cannot come or go."

"It removes the illusion of separation," Tina said with awe. She held her fingers to her mouth at the realization that she was beginning to understand. "I'm beginning to see what you're doing to us. You're trying to change our bandwidth."

"You're suggesting that the geodes behind your waterfall are crystallized awareness of an intention." I repeated to be sure I had it right. "Specifically, that a person is both in Peru and Tibet. You're saying that crystals are thoughts manifested into physical matter."

Iboga laughed, "All of matter is."

After a lengthy pause of digesting the woman's suggestion, I finally had to ask the obvious.

"So, did Rosita create the Dreaming Tree?"

"She is one member of a long lineage that has been building that bridge for generations," she replied. "And my family has been entrusted as its stewards, but I don't possess the intention, desire, or will to manifest such abstract ideas into physical entities. I've helped pave the way for many other Beyuls in this world, but not that particular one."

"What about the crater past the forest?" I asked. "Did you help build that one? The one you led me off of?"

"That wasn't my hand, either," she smiled. "But, a shaman much, much older and more focused than myself does appear to be the only soul responsible for that particular bridge, a man who barely exists on the plane of physical existence."

"I believe you met him briefly," Sadhu added. My mind spun, trying to comprehend who he was referring to.

"Oh, you remember," Sadhu said, poking me in the spine. Suddenly my vision of the skeleton man wrapped in foliage sprang to memory. I had begun to imagine I had hallucinated him.

"So, the Dreaming Tree isn't the only Beyul?" Tina asked.

"There's hundreds of spots scattered around the globe that vibrate with the Zero Point Field," Sadhu replied. "Some appear to be naturally occurring. Others were created with transmissions of the field through the frontal lobes, spots where holy men have meditated again and again, or places that once held great, shamanic ceremonies. When the frequency of the Zero Point Field is transmitted into this realm, it tends to leave an imprint behind. Some objects, like the crystals in those massive geodes, are just better at retaining that imprint than others."

"Also waterfalls," Iboga added.

"Yeah, that one is still a conundrum," Sadhu admitted thoughtfully. "Something about the negative ions retaining quantum field information . . . ," he mumbled, trailing off before he snapped back to his original line of thought. "Regardless, most Beyuls I've discovered over the years were created over incredible lengths of time from entire lineages of holy people entering the ZPF in the same location for generations over. But, a few like the Jain's Pit were created in the blink of an eye."

"By whom?" I asked.

"The Jain himself," Iboga replied. "He was the first holy man to enter this part of the gorge. He was meditating, smoking Reed canary grass when an earthquake opened a hole right below his feet."

"Instead of being swallowed by rubble, he entered the field and returned to his banyan forest in India," Sadhu explained. "That's one of the reasons I gave you canary grass before you leapt: It helped you match the frequency he emitted when the

Beyul was formed."

"And if I hadn't smoked your canary grass?" I demanded, "then what?"

"You would not have merged with the frequency of the Beyul," Sadhu said with a shrug.

"You would have plummeted into just another hole in the earth," Iboga replied.

# 137

*"Feynman, I know why all electrons have the same charge and the same mass. Because, they are all the same electron!"*

John Wheeler

Kaylah led Tina and I to one of the huts to rejoin the others; a brick structure I had noticed earlier demarked by a wooden plaque with the numbers 137 etched into it. When we entered the angular dwelling we were greeted by the rest of the team; that is, the team was there, in the hut. I can't say we received much of a "greeting".

Gomez and Pavlik were fast asleep in a pair of hammocks strung up side by side. A Tibetan monk stood between them waving a golden incense burner back and forth. Pavlik finally found his Tibetan in Tibet, I thought.

Sabol, however, was in a completely different state. He paced the floor, brimming with energy and talking to himself. Eden was seated quietly near a clay stove with a small fire in its hearth. She slowly sipped tea from a wide, plaster bowl, betraying no sign of awareness that we had entered the hut. Sabol tackled us with a powerful bear hug and raucous laughter the moment he saw us. As if reunited with long lost family, he nearly burst into tears when he squeezed us hard enough to make it difficult to breathe. We both accepted the rare display of affection after sharing a quick glance under raised eyebrows.

"Oh, Thank God you guys are here!" he cried. "I didn't know if I'd see you two again, ya know?! I mean, I thought … this is IT. Everything changes from here on out, you know?" He pulled us in and landed a hard kiss on each of our foreheads. We had never seen this version of Sabol. He leapt back and spun excitedly in a circle.

"These holy people, man," he hollered. "I mean, who the hell woulda guessed, right? That these guys talk to Jesus? I mean, I can't believe it all. My mind is just . . . blown!"

He pantomimed his head exploding. I took him by the

shoulders and forced him to focus for a moment. Clearly, the shamans had also exposed him to "some shit" last night and he was struggling to process it all. I couldn't blame him, but I needed him sober. That, and he was starting to freak me out a bit. I pointed firmly at Eden, who still hadn't torn her gaze from the fire.

"Is she okay?" I demanded. He turned his back and pushed his hands forcefully over his scalp before spinning back around to face us. Wide eyed, he threw his hands out with a Fuck, I forgot about THAT situation! This is WAY too much for me to handle right now!

"Ohh, her!" he hollered, rolling his head in circles with an Ok, how do I explain THIS? He crouched next to Eden and madly waved his palms over her head. "She came in and saved me last night! The shaman who took me, she threw me into a burning ring of fire! But Eden came in and . . . you see . . . she's like this radio, right? And, like, Christ . . . man, Christ is like this radio station! Well, fuck, it turns out that Eden Jessup can, like, tune-in the station of Christ. You get it? I saw the whole thing last night! She is an honest-to-God prophet!"

He shook his head and closed his eyes. "Arrggh!" he moaned, massaging his temples. Exasperated, he finally collapsed to the floor. "I'm not explaining it right," he said angrily. "I know it sounds crazy, but now I know that I'm here for a reason. I've been entrusted by God Himself to carry out a mission for one of His prophets! I thought I was about to die last night and I kept thinking there's got to be some version of this where someone saves me. And she did!" He clutched at his chest, his eyes watering. "I've never been so blessed!"

A few days ago, I would have had absolutely no doubt in my mind that this man was in dire need of professional, psychiatric help, but now I could see his basic point of view. If he was exposed to any of the same, essential insights that I had been, I could understand how his Christian background might interpret all of it.

"Actually, Sabol," Tina spoke for both of us. "We've been through quite a bit ourselves, so that doesn't really sound all that crazy." She crouched next to him and rubbed the top of his head. That either means he's making sense or we've all gone mad. The soldier immediately raised his head and beamed behind tears of joy.

"Oh, thank God!" he said. "Thank God we're all on the same page! It makes it so much better if we all know what we have to do! We're so much stronger if we all have faith!"

Umm, hold on. I raised my finger. "Sabol," I began gently. "I think perhaps the details of your religious beliefs may have imprinted over some of the truths that you've been exposed to ..." Before I could finish my sentence, Sadhu burst into the hut behind us.

"Professor Huxley!" he called as he passed us. "I've been meaning to tell you that I think perhaps the details of your scientific education may have become imprinted over some of the truths that you've been exposed to here."

"That's not the same thing and you know it!" I hollered. Sadhu moved around a tiny, wooden desk on the far end of the hut. It was only then that I noticed the entire perimeter of the dwelling held row after row of books in all manner of condition. The majority of them appeared to be dedicated to experimental or theoretical physics, but the rest were devoted to either other fields of science, philosophy, religion, or a combination. There must have been five hundred books stuffed into the tiny dwelling. The shelves seemed to be loadbearing walls essential to holding the place together

I scanned the author's names on the shelf closest to me: Feynman, Hawking, Planck, Faraday, Greene, Higgs, Schrödinger, Sagan, Krauss, Dawkins, Hitchens, Randi, Harris, Castaneda, Gangaji, Maharshi, Tolle, the list went on and on. When Sadhu took a seat behind the desk it dawned on me that we were standing in his home. It also dawned on me that I had been standing there completely quiet with my finger still wagging in his direction.

" . . . that isn't the same thing," I repeated slowly, trying to catch my line of thought. "I didn't come here with a head full of religious luggage. What I experienced last night was the unfiltered truth! I saw the world from a genuine, spiritual perspective!"

Sadhu laughed and shook his head. No! You're not taking this one from me! Not after what I've been through! You can't take away both my atheism and my spiritual insights at the same time!

I angrily marched over to Tina and yanked the sleeve on her shoulder to expose the area where her puncture wounds had been just the night before.

"There's the evidence, right there!" I hollered. Sabol leapt up and studied the surface of Tina's skin.

"My God!" Sabol cried. "Christ healed you too! I've been walking among angels this whole time and now, oh Lord! Now my eyes are open!"

"Isaac Newton was a genius," Sadhu announced as he stuffed a pinch of tobacco into a rolling paper. "Possibly the most intelligent man yet to walk the Earth. You're a lot like him."

When it seemed he wasn't going to elaborate, I threw my hands into the air.

"What?" I sighed angrily.

"You know, f=ma?" he replied with a wry smile. "Newton discovered all the essential laws of force, motion and acceleration hundreds of years ago; equations we still use to put rockets into space today. He could prove his hypothesis about how gravity acted on mass with repeated experiments, but he absolutely did not see the entire picture. Einstein's theory of relativity was hundreds of years away, as was quantum physics, which would throw his neat and tidy system of 'every action has a one hundred percent predictable reaction' straight into the garbage heap. Just as what I know today would throw a lot of modern quantum theory on its ear. But again, his equations are just as relevant now as they were back then. Why? Because they work."

"Are you actually suggesting that there is some deeper truth to Sabol's dogma that I have yet to discover?" I asked pointedly.

"I'm saying his model works," he replied, lighting his cigarette. The Tibetan monk hovering over Gomez and Pavlik briefly twisted up his face when Sadhu exhaled a ring of smoke in his direction. "His model has been working for his advantage, as well as for yours, and it will continue to do so, so don't knock it. They're all just models!"

"Well, it all seemed pretty clear last night when I apparently magically floated through the air over your crater," I groaned. "Or, are you taking that back, too?"

"Okay, relax." Sadhu sighed throwing his feet onto his desk. "Christians have their healers and miracle workers too and they can work just as effectively. I'm not taking anything of value away from you, but your ego is already trying to snap right back into its old trenches, only now with the label of "miracle worker" slapped over your ego, or whatever your personality is cooking up now. But, okay, go ahead: tell me about your newfound perspective. What great, unfiltered, spiritual truth did you encounter last night?"

I bit my lower lip and struggled for a clear beginning, a firm starting point. This is absurd! We just discussed this and I basically agreed with them! Why is he fucking with me? I spent several moments piecing together the flow of other-worldly experiences from last night into a clearer perspective; one I could verbally explain and describe. "I saw the world behind the veil of illusion," I said hesitantly.

"Perhaps you're a Buddhist now," the monk uttered in a Tibetan accent. I waved my hands back and forth.

"I'm not a Buddhist now." I insisted. Slowly, I began to explain what I had witnessed. I told them how I directly witnessed the essential building blocks of reality; how all atomic structure boils down to vibrating strings of pure energy.

"... and when bundles of them vibrate together, they form the particles that makes up our protons, neutrons, atoms, everything! I saw an infinity of possible branches of the universe through this vision!"

"String theory," Sadhu interrupted. "You just essentially described what theoretical physicists refer to as 'String Theory.'

You know, 'All fundamental particles in the universe are really just manifestations of one, ultimate thing: A ring of pure energy.' Depending on how that string oscillates depends on whether it forms an electron or a photon or a quark. String Theory. You probably heard your colleagues discuss it over the years."

"I'm not talking about some hallucination of a scientific theory!" I hollered only to be treated with a round of kind, blank stares.

"What the hell is he talking about?" Sabol asked Tina. Tina shook her head and studied me.

"I'm not sure," she replied.

"Okay, stop fucking with me!" I shouted at Sadhu. "Don't act like you don't know what I'm saying! This is basically the same shit you and Iboga have been talking about since I got here!" Sadhu shook his head and tapped the ash from his cigarette into a plaster cup.

"I'm not saying I disagree with you on any specific point," he said. "Obviously you tapped into something indescribable that you haven't begun to comprehend. But you imagine you tapped into some unique, spiritual insight about the world. You're trying to package last night as a spiritual experience. You may not have come here with religious baggage, but don't think you came here free of scientific dogma about the world; insights that you yourself don't fully understand. I mean, you must realize you're a man who's been subjected to all sorts of scientific hypotheses over the years, both consciously and subconsciously. And you've accepted a lot of models of the universe from trusted, fellow scientists. You must realize that what you've just described isn't a spiritual insight about the mechanics of the world at all, nor is it original.

"The brain's only job is to sort through millions upon millions of pieces of data. Maybe your mind used your memories of scientific theories to try to make sense of the random synapses firing off from all the hallucinogens your system has been processing over the last few days. If I were you, I'd drop it. Just forget what you think you learned."

My anger grew steadily. Once again, I felt like this man's only purpose was to try to make me feel insane, or worse: Completely worthless and ignorant. I was beginning to hate him. "You think the world is made out of little rings of energy?" Tina said. "Sweetheart, that's cute. I like it."

"Hate to break it to you, Doc," Sadhu said. "But, your insights were anything but religious."

My face turned red and I clenched my fists.

"This is bullshit!" I hollered. "I saw my own death last night! I was reborn with important, divine insight!"

Sadhu smiled and shook his head. Sabol approached me with a gentle hand on my shoulder.

"Professor, relax," he said. "It takes time to accept the power of Christ."

At that, my blood boiled. I darted from the hut and instinctively ran back into the forest. I knew what I had seen. That pit was filled with dead bodies, at least one of which appeared to be my own. I had peered into another layer of reality, faced incredible truths, cheated death and I had performed miracles, only to be called a fraud by the people who were right there with me. I jogged through the pines until the forest turned abruptly sparse. I had to know. I had to see for myself in the light of day. As I broke the clearing, I was once again standing at the edge of the crater; the Jain's Pit.

Without hesitation, I ran to the outcropping of rock I had been taken to last night. I jogged along the narrow stretch toward the center of the crater and dropped to my knees. Leaning as far over the ledge as balance would allow, I stared into the depths below. The walls of the pit tapered so tightly, the morning sun hadn't yet reached the base. I couldn't detect any features of what may lay at the bottom.

It could've been filled with water, stones, or a hundred corpses.

# Back to the Pit

*"It is surely harmful to souls to make it a heresy to believe what is proved."*

Galileo

After several minutes of searching for any hint of form at the bottom of the crater, there was a rustle in the trees behind me. Sadhu emerged from the forest blazing a path for Tina, Sabol, and Eden. Tina shot a half-wave with a head-tilt at me that asked, "Are you okay?"

I held my palm into the air to reply, "Yeah," but I certainly wasn't sure if that were true. I turned my back, saddled the furthest tip of the ledge with feet dangling over the abyss and continued to stare into the emptiness. I was in no mood for company. Sadhu walked the plank to join me while the rest of the group stayed behind. He took a seat just behind my back at the edge while he finished his cigarette, tapping the ash into the crater from time to time. He now carried a long, coiled rope around his shoulder. Before I could ask what it was for, he broke into another diatribe.

"Did you know that up until some four hundred years ago people used to think that light wasn't a real thing?" he asked casually. I sighed. I didn't care where this was going. The sweet tobacco vapors reached my nose and imbibed me with the strangest sensation that I wanted a cigarette. I had never smoked in my life.

"Back then, people thought of light as this abstract, holy essence that God created," he continued between slow drags. "It wasn't an actual, physical 'thing' like water or sand. You couldn't hold it. You couldn't move it from place to place. Il-lumination was just another God-given quality of the ether."

He stared at me while I gazed into the pit. As if sensing my unusual desire, he pulled another cigarette from his pocket and handed it to me. Without hesitation, I accepted and allowed him to light it. I inhaled deeply and found an odd sense of relief wash over me. Goddamned it, I needed one of these.

"The Michael Huxley who arrived here through the gorge

was a smoker," Sadhu whispered as if it were a secret. "Habits and intense events have a way of carving themselves into the quantum field. Just another one of those trenches. We pick up a lot of garbage from our other incarnations. A lot of good luck, too, I would add." I hoped he wouldn't elaborate on the subject. Fortunately, he didn't.

"Anyway," he continued. "Then Galileo burst onto the scene and said 'bullshit' to all that. 'Light is Outside the Realm of Man' was total nonsense to him. 'Light is just another thing and I can prove it,' he said. Well, that was heresy at the time. I mean, that was like saying you could bottle up the sweet grace of Jesus Christ himself and put it in your pocket. I tell ya, scientists have been pissing off the church for generations. I wonder if Galileo was the world's first atheist!"

The longer he spoke, the higher the sun rose and, ever so steadily, the morning rays reached deeper and deeper into the base of the crater, allowing me to see a little further into the crevice.

"So Galileo goes to the university and pulls these rocks from his pocket and he shows them to his Aristotelian colleagues," he explained. "He tells them, 'With these rocks, I can capture sunlight itself!' and of course everyone scoffs. He's out of his mind! But Galileo was a smart man; he knew how to put on a show and prove his point at the same time. He asked the students to close all the blinds and gather around. Once the room was dark he asked everyone to take a closer look at these magic stones of his. There was nothing to see! They were just ordinary, gray rocks that vanished into the darkness with everything else. Everyone was about to walk out and ignore the old lunatic when he shouts, 'But, wait! Watch what happens now!'

"So Galileo marches outside under the morning sun and everyone's following him, still laughing at the old fool. He walks into the middle of the courtyard and lifts these magic stones of his to the sun. What the hell is he doing? He's mad! 'I'm capturing sunlight!,' he announces. After a short while he marches back into the dark lecture hall and he opens his hands for everyone to see. And the rocks glowed! Right in the palm of his hand sat the same rocks everyone had just witnessed a few minutes ago and now the sun itself was pouring out of them! Light was a real part of our world; an object that could be moved from here to there! It changed the way the world thought about light forever," Sadhu giggled to himself and tapped his ash into the pit.

"Yep, with a little barium sulfide Galileo single-handedly proved that light was a thing, something we can quantify," he sighed. "He surmised that the rays we see must be made of tiny 'corpuscles', he called them; individual pockets of light, every bit as real as raindrops. Centuries would pass before anyone had the equipment to prove that light waves were made of photons."

I took another drag from my cigarette and smirked. "I'm guessing there's a larger point here," I said quietly. He smiled and patted my back.

"See?" he said. "You are getting to know me! I say the same thing is true about our awareness. It's just another thing in our world, every bit as mysterious and amazing as everything else, yet we secretly believe it's outside of our realm, something un-approachable. It can behave as a wave or as a particle or both. It can be an individual thought or background noise.

"Now, you and I have both witnessed what some would refer to as the 'supernatural', but I say there is no such thing. The mysteries the cosmos provides are more than enough for our brains to handle. Absolutely nothing is beyond the bounds of nature; some things our monkey brains just don't compre-hend, or at the very least we can't accept at this point in our evolution. I would argue that some combinations of particles are simply more rare than others. I suppose that's why I still consider myself an atheist. Of course, that too can be a leash, another word that will mean whatever the listener chooses."

I couldn't believe what I was hearing. After all the 'guru-like' wisdom, all of his work with impossible phenomena, living here amongst medicine men and shaman: this man was an atheist! Sadhu slouched forward, sighed heavily and scratched the back of his head. Again, he seemed to be deciding on the right words.

"I was raised in a strict Christian household," he admitted hesitantly. "My parents taught me everything, provided whatever I needed to live. They fed me, taught me how to walk and take care of myself. We owe so much to our caregivers. Why wouldn't I totally trust them when they told me there's one, supreme being who controls all of it? And He sent His only begotten Son to offer us eternal redemption? Why on earth would I not take their word on that? They're the ones who kept me safe by telling me the stove was hot and they were right.

"And that's how models are passed down, from generation to generation. They literally shape our collective world so that there is unified 'agreement' on what this world of ours looks like. I like Jung's term for our mutual agreement: The Collective Unconscious. Yet as powerful as those models are, they're all just maps. Some of those maps are better at describing the actual territory than others. But, the truth of the universe will never be affected by any of those frameworks, I don't care how accurate they are."

"So what inspired you to break from the model you were handed?" I asked.

"I suppose I needed an upgrade," he replied. "I had this need to know at a young age: How does God do it? I would spend hours alone in my backyard which opened into North Fork of the Appalachians. I would get lost studying the trees, the leaves, the rocks, the bugs, the animals, everything! I wanted to know, I needed to know, what God built everything from. The church taught me  that in the beginning, there was only God. He just was. He was never born and he would never die. So, by that logic, everything MUST be made of the very essence of God. Even though the world was filled with all these apparently different things that looked and felt different, things that are rough to things that are soft to the very large or fantastically small, hot and cold: I decided at a young age there must be some basic essence at the root of it all; an energy that cannot be divided further."

"You were looking for . . . the fabric of God?" I asked.

"I suppose," he replied thoughtfully. "And then I took my first physics course. It was the first class I ever had that I found useful! I actually paid attention to the teacher. She told us how matter is made up of these tiny packets of energy we call atoms. Okay, I thought, now we're onto something. So, what do we really know about atoms? Is it anything more than just a label we slapped onto something we can't possibly understand? We do that in science: we give a name to some incredible combination of matter and energy and it dupes us into thinking we understand it.

"And I learned there's over a hundred different kinds of these atoms and they absolutely can be divided into smaller pieces. Well, that's not what I was looking for! I wanted the most basic element; something that resided in its simplest form that would explain everything, connect everything! I would barrage my teacher with questions after class. I wouldn't wait for the next chapter or the next semester to know the answers! What are atoms made of then? So, she taught me about electrons, protons, and neutrons. Do those exist in their most fundamental form? She eventually had to direct me to theoretical physics because, it turned out, no one really knew for sure. Our tools to study the very, very small are limited."

"So, what did you do?" I asked. "Was your question ever satisfied?"

"Indeed it was," he said with a smile. "But not in the way I imagined. I also realized that I wanted far more than a logical answer to that question. Seeing the solution to String Theory at the end of an equation wasn't satisfying. I wanted to directly experience the answer. But I also had no idea what that meant. Later in life, I found myself working with enormous machines to answer just those types of questions; a particle collider in Waxahachie, Texas over fifty miles long."

Now, if Damian and Kyle imparted anything to my gorilla brain concerning physics, it was this: Texas never got its particle collider. The largest super collider in the world was supposed to be constructed in Waxahachie, but the Republicans pulled the funding for it when they couldn't see the use of knowing the deepest secrets of the universe. What's the point when everything we needed could be found right in the New Testament?

Instead, it was built in Switzerland. Even years after the Large Hadron Collider was up and running successfully, Damian and Kyle continued to bitch and moan, often quite loudly after a few drinks about the injustice of it all. In their opinion, it should have been built in the USA as a monument to our dedication to Science. When I shared this information with Sadhu, he didn't seem surprised.

"Oh, you remember that particular timeline now," he replied with a chuckle. "Funny, you didn't when you arrived here. Regardless, I ultimately found the same thing that you described, professor: Tiny rings of vibration; the most fundamental structure of all matter and energy. An ocean of them, singing and harmonizing together in a spectrum of wavelengths to form leptons and quarks, all the way up to atoms; everything!"

"So you do agree with me," I grumbled. "Perhaps I directly witnessed the fundamental essence of reality last night after all."

"It's still just a model. There's still another perspective where there are no waves or particles; where there is only one electron in the entire multi-verse; the one appearing to be many. And that, too, is a perfectly valid perspective. Deeper still, I could rightly say that there are no particles at all in this world, not a-one; that the very nature of emptiness carries the illusion of matter and energy.

Professor, use your model to your advantage until it no longer serves you, up until it's become a comfortable cage you've grown accustomed to. That alone may just be enough to get you out of this jam."

At that, he flicked the butt of his cigarette into the pit and slapped his thighs. I was still staring into the depths below. The sun was moments from revealing the features at the bottom.

"Okay!" he hollered and turned to me. "You ready?"

"Ready for what?" I asked nervously as the shadows moved aside to reveal some confusing shimmer of form and color.

For a moment it appeared I was looking down at clear, blue sky, but quickly realized I was seeing the sky overhead reflected on a pool of perfectly still water at the base of the crater. Surrounding this tiny pool were jagged rocks that splintered haphazardly upward toward the heavens. My eyes had just began to perceive unusual shapes dotted throughout the daggers of stone when Sadhu abruptly answered my question. Those aren't just rocks down there.

"To watch the rest of your companions leap into the abyss," he replied. "It's been decided that Eden Jessup, Tina Flores, and Bill Sabol must also meet the Jain before we'll allow any of you to leave. We must know that the rest of you will turn down the Jain's offer just as you did."

"What?" I shouted. The spell was broken; he now had my full attention. At the time, his answer confused me. It no longer does.

"The Craneo Roto can't have egos walking out of here with the full potential of the Probability Wave at their disposal. Egos get jealous, they find reasons to be angry, to feel separate. It would serve you to remember this: Even the holiest of holy on this planet can channel pure beauty or pure rage. It's just a more efficient use of energy to be at peace; however, an ego can distort that truth. And, son, trust me: you do not want a god pissed off at you."

"Would that be a big G or a little g?" I asked.

"If it calls itself a god, it's always a little g," he replied.

# Offer Accepted

*"God has no religion."*

Mahatma Gandhi

**"**You want to run that by me one more time?" Tina hollered after I detailed the final trial they would each have to endure. Eden simply smiled to herself with feet dangling over the ledge, eyes closed. Sabol was bouncing nervously in the background, brimming with panic.

"I'm supposed to send Sabol down next," I explained. Before he complied, he asked what the hell was going on. I had no answers for any of them, only that we had no other choice. "They won't let the four of us leave until we pass this test of theirs." I said, not really understanding what I was saying.

"What test?" Tina asked. "Jumping off a cliff?"

"What about Gomez and Pavlik?" Sabol asked. "Why don't they have to throw themselves into a crater?" I had no answers. I couldn't guess why Gomez and Pavlik were exempt from this final trial of theirs, but the fact alone left me uneasy. Sabol peered ahead where Sadhu patiently awaited his presence at the tip of the rocky plank.

"You'll be fine," Eden called out from her meditation. "Have faith." That was all Sabol needed to hear. He straightened up, nodded firmly as if heading out on an official military excursion and marched his way towards Sadhu. Tina and I took a seat arm-in-arm to watch the insane show from the sidelines.

Sadhu pulled the same, basic maneuvers with Sabol as he had with me. After a brief discussion, he stuffed the pipe into the soldier's mouth and spoke his final words of warning: "Whatever you do, do not accept that man's offer. Find a way to turn it down."

A moment later, Sabol leapt over the edge followed by a loud splash. Then the world went quiet. Even the air stopped moving. At the point of noticing my mind had come to a dead halt, another splash echoed from the depths of the abyss. Sadhu tossed the rope over the cliff and fished out a soaking wet, rather wide-eyed Sabol. Upon reaching the ledge, Sadhu seized him by the collar with a ferocity we had never witnessed. "Who are you?" Sadhu shouted. Sabol straightened his back and came to attention.

"Corporal William Sabol of the US Marine Corp," Sabol replied firmly. Sadhu smiled and returned the salute.

"Good to have you back, soldier," Sadhu replied. "You are dismissed."

"Thank you, sir," Sabol replied before marching his way back to us. Upon his return, he spun on a dime and remained standing at ease against the cliff wall with hands clasped behind his back. "Agent Flores," he abruptly shouted. "Your presence is requested on the ledge."

"You okay, buddy?" I asked delicately. He continued to stare straight ahead and his eyes began to water.

"I believe I passed the test, professor," Sabol responded quietly. "I did not give into . . . unearthly temptation."

Tina and I shared a long gaze followed by a longer embrace. "You'll be fine," I comforted her, hoping I was right. "I'll keep an eye on these two. We'll be right here when you get back."

After a long kiss, Tina slowly made her way along the ledge. I stood next to Eden and watched nervously as Sadhu repeated the same maneuvers. My heart lodged into my throat as she leapt over the cliff. An eternity passed while I listened for her to break the surface of the pool again and, just as before, everything seemed to temporarily 'pause'.

"She's going to be fine," Eden suddenly spoke from behind closed eyes. "Have faith". Sure enough, another splash echoed through the ravine and Sadhu tossed the rope to her. Feeling slightly more at ease, I took a seat next to Eden to try to get a lock on her. I felt like I was the only one worried about her current state of mental health.

"Are you okay?" I whispered. She smiled at the question, but didn't open her eyes. Instead, she reached down and took me by the hand.

"Everything is exactly how it should be," she said, opening her eyes to stare into the pit. She looked up and squeezed my palm.

"I'm sorry I ran off earlier," she admitted quietly. Shit, that was genuine. I couldn't remember her ever sincerely apologizing for her behavior. "I've just been processing a lot of new information. I've been confused. Last night, the tribe sent me on a vision quest with a Christian mystic. She opened my eyes to what I've been dealing with."

"And what is that, exactly?" I asked. She returned her gaze to the darkness.

"That I've been in a chrysalis state," she replied, putting her arm around me. "I know it's been confusing, but I need you to have faith in me. Everything that has happened to me, you, the entire team, has been for one, very specific purpose. The visions I've been having, the energy I've been tapping into are just ripple effects from a radical turning event in my life. Like shockwaves rolling out from a point of impact."

"Oh?" I asked. "And what event was that?" She smiled at the question.

"It hasn't happened yet," she said quietly before leaning in to whisper the rest in my ear. "Ripples in the quantum field move forward and backward in time from our perspective. I need you to trust me; trust me and not these shaman. They don't give a shit about our world. Can you do that for me?" I simply nodded in agreement, not understanding what she meant.

"Sabol thinks you're Jesus Christ now or something, by the way," I mentioned, trying to add some levity to a dire and confusing situation. Eden smiled.

"After my 'spirit journey,' I was walking back to the village and I found him writhing in the dirt in a circle of stones." She explained, "One of their shaman must've given him something that packed a serious punch cause he was flailing around, hollering about being burned alive. I took his hand and tried to comfort him. I mean, that's it: I helped him to his feet. Well, that must've meant something pretty damn relevant to him at the time."

I looked back to the ledge just as Sadhu barked the same question at Tina. "Who are you?" he demanded fiercely.

"I'm agent Tina Flores of the National Police," I heard her

reply. Sadhu gave her a hug and sent her along the walkway.

"He wants you next," Tina said to Eden as she approached.

"Oh, I know what they want," Eden replied softly. "And they're not going to get it." At that, she stood and walked defiantly along the ledge toward Sadhu.

"What did that mean?" Tina asked. I shook my head. A steady wave of nervousness rose along my spine once again as I watched Eden inhale the smoke from Sadhu's pipe.

"How long was I under?" Tina asked, staring at the sky. She was clearly in a mild state of shock, but appeared lucid. Ahead, Eden leapt into the Beyul out of sight, followed by a loud splash.

"What do you mean?" I asked. "You dove down and came right back up," Tina shook her head, trying to comprehend my answer.

"It felt like I was in that banyan forest with that man for hours," she whispered. "But the sunlight never changed there. It's like he lives in a perpetual state of dawn."

"Strange," I mentioned. "It was night time when I met with him."

"Yes," Sabol said quietly, still standing at full attention. "It was forever dawn."

As worried as I was over their collective states of mind, I couldn't listen to their personal interpretations of the Jain. Something wasn't right. Eden hadn't surfaced. Too much time had passed and she was still under. I leapt to my feet and followed the narrow ledge to Sadhu who laid a gentle hand on my back.

"Relax," he assured me. "We know what we're doing. This isn't the first time we've been through this routine, obviously." Several more moments passed and Eden still hadn't come up. I peered at Sadhu and felt a subtle wince of dismay cross his face. Without hesitation, I immediately moved into position to dive in after her when he restrained me with a hand over my chest.

"Just wait," he said firmly. "This can take time."

"Yeah?" I argued. "And what if she's had another seizure?"

"What do you mean?"

"She's been prone to seizures lately," I replied angrily. "How do you not know that? You all act like you know everything!" I stared into the pool below and saw only ripples. My heart raced.

"What kind of seizures?" he demanded. "When did they start? Does she dream?" I was barely aware of him. My vision went blurry and my breathing quickened. The surface of the tiny spring became still as a highly polished mirror. "Does she dream?!" he shouted again.

"Yes! So?" I hollered back. "She's been having visions where she wakes up inside them. She calls them 'lucid dreams.' How do you not know this about her?! You said you've met all of us a dozen times over!"

"That woman has never come to us as a lucid dreamer!" Sadhu hollered.

"Why does that matter?" I cried. He looked to the sky and shook his head as if he couldn't put into words how relevant that detail was.

He whispered to himself, "Why didn't Kaylah tell us that? Kaylah is a dreamer. She must have known."

Another long minute passed and a loud splash echoed through the pit below. We leaned over the edge to find Eden pulling herself to the gravel shore of the pool. Sadhu paced and stared anxiously at the ground. It was disturbing to see him this worried. When I realized he wasn't going to help her, I yanked the coiled rope from his shoulder and threw it over the ledge. Eden appeared perfectly at ease as she clamored up, soaked and emotionless.

Sadhu backed away cautiously when she finally summited. After a moment of mustering his courage, he slowly approached Eden who remained wide-eyed and silent on the tip of the rocky plank. "Who are you?" he asked. Eden didn't answer. She raised her palms and stared into them.

"Ohh," she whispered. "I'm dreaming."

"No," I said firmly. "No, you're not." For the briefest instant, a series of static pops and electrical discharges buzzed just above her cupped hands. I assumed, or rather I hoped, I was still coping with the aftereffects of the hallucinogens.

"Who are you?" Sadhu demanded louder. The electrical snapping abruptly stopped when Eden raised her head.

"I am…," she responded hesitantly and stared into her palms again. Sadhu leaned in, awaiting her to finish her answer. Once more, a static field appeared to hover just above her palms. "I am… Eden Jessup," she added before bringing her attention back to Sadhu who lowered his shoulders with a sigh. "and . . . I . . . am . . . awake," Eden concluded.

Sadhu's eyes grew wide beneath his lowered head, but he stepped aside to let her pass. Ever so gracefully Eden made her way along the walkway, staring intently at her hands. The very moment her back was turned, Sadhu gripped his heavy, wooden pipe like a club. He arched back and, before I could protest, swung down with all his might. The end of his pipe landed directly between her neck and shoulder. With a small crash, Eden collapsed face-first onto the ledge in a cloud of dust.

"What the fuck are you doing?!" I shouted, dropping to my knees next to her.

"Saving our lives," he lamented.

# Split Decisions

*"When we look with the 'I', we dream. When we look for the 'I', we awaken."*

Mooji

After Sabol and I carried Eden's unconscious body from the ledge of the Jain's Pit, we reconvened at Sadhu's lodge. Just before we entered, I spied Kaylah kneeling before a wide, flat stone between two of the huts crushing down yet another pile of green leaves into a powder with a wooden mallet. She winked as I passed.

Sadhu positively forbid we attempt to revive Eden, swearing profusely of its dangers. Pavlik and Gomez were both awake and sipping tea in their hammocks when we returned. They barraged us with anxious questions so quickly we had no time to reply.

"I'll explain everything in time, brothers," Sabol replied cryptically. "We have been tasked with a great burden."

I rolled my eyes and laid Eden's limp body on the floor near the stove, placed a pillow behind her head and checked her vitals. Her pulse was strong and breathing was steady, which made me feel only slightly more at ease. Tina huddled next to her near the fire to dry off while Iboga and Sadhu spoke in animated, hushed tones just outside the door. Suddenly, Iboga stormed away and left Sadhu with a pained uncertainty on his face. When he finally decided to enter the hut, he locked the door behind him and took a seat at the edge of his tiny, wooden desk.

"I'm not sure how best to explain this to all of you so that it makes sense," he grumbled, massaging the bridge of his nose. "Our worst fears have come to pass. As a man of reason, I suppose I would say that the specifics of Eden Jessup's characteristics, her rather unique electromagnetic field, allowed her to accept the Jain's offer."

Sabol, Tina, and I sighed, "ohh," in chorus, as if we understood the full implications of it. Pavlik and Gomez stared blankly.

"What the hell does that mean?" Pavlik demanded.

"Basically," Sadhu began, "she has total access to the Zero Point Field whenever she closes that circuit with the Jain. A convergence like that is something that requires decades, lifetimes to acquire, and it is generally only accessible to those who can disconnect from the frequency of their own identity.

"As I've been saying, ultimate power is supposed to be readily accessible to those who have no desire to gain from it; who have purified their obsession in bolstering their own individual power. And, therein lies our problem. Professor Jessup allowed the Jain to forge a connection between her energy pattern and his own, to be unlocked with the blink of an eye. And she does indeed still groom an ego. Unbeknownst to us, Eden has experience with lucid dreaming; the ability to become fully conscious while in a visionary state. Subconsciously, she's been forging a bridge between our world and the infinite long before she came to us."

"So what?" Pavlik asked weakly from his hammock.

"Yeah, what does Professor Jessup's dreaming practice have to do with anything?" Gomez added.

"Lucidity in the dream state is the last step of conscious evolution before a human reaches what the masters refer to as 'enlightenment'; a Buddha, a Christ, one who is fully awakened to their potential. It is the utter realization that you and your waking environment are connected in ways the ego alone could never imagine. However, her connection with the Jain will allow her to skip the fail-safe of dropping the ego and deposit her into total access to the Probability Wave. From there, every combination matter can take could theoretically be pulled into our world. If she can imagine it, it could manifest."

"Even if what you're suggesting is possible, what's the problem?" I barked at him from the floor. "I thought enlightenment was what your tribe has been after, so why the hell did you beat her unconscious?"

"Because that woman may now have access to more possibilities than even Kane and his people do!" he replied firmly.

"Kane's people enter the quantum probability field with techniques they dimly comprehend, so they do so from a limited perspective. We believe they've continued to add a deadly combination of nightshade to their mixture of ayahuasca. It temporarily shuts down higher mental functioning and leaves the reptilian brain intact; the base of the brain that handles our predatory survival instincts to kill and consume, all of humanity's darkest fears, all of our base, primal desires. They enter the Field just long enough to trip it!

"Eden, on the other hand, would continue to have access to the full capacity of the Field from her higher brain functioning. But, like Kane, she would still view that myriad of possibilities through the filter of her ego, a limited concept of who she is!"

"She's an agent of Christ!" Sabol said angrily. "You're standing in the way of a real messiah!" Sadhu shook his head and folded his arms.

"Son, that's only a story she's dreamed up to shield her from the full onslaught of the Field," Sadhu replied cautiously, knowing he needed to tread carefully with Sabol's religious views. "It's how her ego shrinks all that power into a neat, tidy package. But the moment she allows the Jain to grant her total access to power, the larger truths open up along with it."

"And what truth is that?" Sabol asked. Sadhu shot out his hands as if the answer was obvious.

"That she's far more than just an agent of God," he said. "When she's pulled into the wave, she'll remember the truth that, essentially, she is god. Anyone who has total access to the Zero Point Field can rightly be called a supreme being. But her consciousness isn't ready for this. It'll put a face on the Supreme; a mask, an idol cast before God. Her ego will continue to harbor a need to personify infinity. Typical, human consciousness runs from total chaos, so she'll put it in some kind of box again. She'll wrap an impossible amount of power in her own version of what godliness looks like. And I fear that she'll be far more dangerous than a few missionaries shapeshifting into abominations of nature."

"What are you suggesting exactly?" Tina asked, more curious

and less frustrated than I. "That if she enters this quantum field of yours then she'll drag her own, unique ideas about god in along with it?"

"Exactly!" he replied. "Just like Kane's people do, except they're convinced they're communing with the Satan from their old religious beliefs. They imagine they've forged some kind of deal with the Devil! They're completely insane. But who knows what Eden would do? She's a free spirit with a mish-mash of New Age, Hindu, and Eastern mythologies rolling around her head. There's no telling what she would unleash on this earth! There's no telling what she would become." He rubbed his eyes and scratched his head. This was clearly giving him a headache.

"Listen," he finally said. "We wanted your team to walk away with a little more insight into what was going on out there before you confronted Kane and his church again. We hoped you'd be able to overcome your fears and act from a place of deeper power and insight, but this is far more than the world can handle. We have an obligation to do as little harm as possible."

"So, what are you going to do?" Pavlik asked. "What's your plan now?"

Sadhu stood up, moved to the door and studied the floor. "Iboga is calling for a meeting of the entire tribe," he said. "We're going to decide the best way to handle this. All of you need to stay right here. Do not leave this hut for any reason. Keep Eden Jessup quiet and safe."

"What if she wakes up?" Pavlik asked. "Are we in danger?"

I quietly harbored the same question. Sabol laughed at the absurdity of the suggestion. "We're not in danger from her, brother," he announced. "She's at the Right Hand of God."

Sadhu crossed his arms and cocked his head to the side. "If she wakes up," he said, firmly pointing his finger at us all. "Do not, I repeat, do not give that woman any psychoactives! None of any kind. I don't care what she says to convince you. It may be the only thing holding that dam in place."

"What?" Tina asked in disbelief.

"Her consciousness hangs in a balance between the safe

structure of her ego as a mere 'messiah' and the direct power of a god," he said fiercely. "The dimethyltryptamine in the canary grass you each smoked from my pipe was only meant to last a few, short minutes and it will have worn off by now, so Eden's normal ego pattern should have fallen back into its trenches at this point. But we can't have anything, and I mean anything, nudging her consciousness back toward that connection with the Jain. Once that circuit is made whole, it's over."

"You said the medicine in your pipe was also a fail-safe," I reminded him. "What did that mean?"

"Yes," he admitted. "I gave you all a powerful dose of DMT before you entered the Jain's Pit. That helped your conscious energy match that of the Beyul's, but it also gave your awareness a specific vibration when you each met with the Jain. The connection he forged with Eden was made under the specific energy signature of the extract of canary grass. Theoretically, she shouldn't be able to fully realize that connection again until she consumes dimethyltryptamine. I always hoped that will afford us some measure of control over the ensuing chaos if anyone ever accepted that man's offer, but I don't really know. The pineal gland manufactures DMT when it chooses too, so it's possible that any psychoactive alteration in her chemistry could reforge that circuit to some extent."

"What do you mean you 'don't really know'?" I hollered at him.

"I've never seen this before," Sadhu lamented. "Everyone who's come to us runs in the other direction from the Jain's offer. Real power like this scares the living hell out of most humans. Limitation defines our existence." As Sadhu opened the door to take his leave I spied a bustling of activity in the village behind him. Dozens of people from every walk of life made their way between the tiny dwellings toward the fire pit.

"Just keep her quiet," he said in a soothing tone. "The tribe will decide the best way to deal with this. Stay here, keep her calm." He pulled the door closed and an eerie silence filled the room. Suddenly, Sabol leapt down between me and Tina by the fire.

"That guy is insane," he whispered. "We can't trust him. His idea of what's really going on here is fuckin' nuts! We need to get out of here!" He put his hand over Eden's forehead. "We need to get her out of here!" he added.

"The man said to stay here," Gomez said quietly. "After what I've seen last night, I am convinced that these people are a hell of a lot wiser than we are. We should do as he asked."

"I have to agree with Gomez," I said firmly. "You heard what he said. We don't know what we're dealing with here."

It was only then that I remembered the promise I made to Eden mere minutes ago at the Jain's Pit. Pavlik quietly watched the conversation take place with a look of anxiety and lack of any comprehension. I looked down at Eden, and at the dark purple bruise on her neck from Sadhu's blow. I've known this woman for twenty years and I have no idea what she's capable of. Tina took my hand and stared into my eyes in search of answers. Something in my heart softened under her gaze, and I searched the room, exasperated.

"Look, even if we did leave, where are we going to go?" I asked Sabol. "We're literally in the middle of nowhere."

"We're strong together!" Sabol said, wide-eyed. "We're right and they're wrong! The Lord will find a way! We need to have faith in Eden as a prophet and not in these assholes."

That's when Kaylah breathlessly burst into the hut, spun around the door and peered through the opening while closing it smoothly behind her. When she was convinced no one had witnessed her stealthy entrance, she swooshed her hands up and down to get us to our feet before yanking a leather canteen from around her shoulder.

"Get up!" she whispered loudly in a native, South American accent. "Grab all your stuff! We must go. Now!"

"Since when does the kid speak English?" Pavlik asked in a fit of surrender. Kaylah turned to him with fire in her eyes as she tossed the canteen into his lap.

"I speak better English than your stunted schoolgirls who stare at their phones all day!" she hissed, pointing to the leather bladder. "That is datura. Take the biggest mouthful you can and pass it around! Be fast! They will be back soon!"

"What the hell are you doing?" I demanded. "Where are you taking us?"

"I'm getting you all out of here!" she shouted, pointing at Eden. "They decided it's safer to kill her, and I did not come this far to let that happen."

With no time to argue or to think rationally, I moved once again into pure action. Lingering doubts that we were making an awful mistake, an earth-shattering, terrifying mistake, circled my brain as we pulled ourselves together, downed every last drop of Kaylah's bitter concoction, and threw Eden over Pavlik's shoulder. After a quick peek through the doorway, we tiptoed single-file to the rear of Sadhu's lodge and into the forest just as the sun began to set. Within minutes, we were back on the trail leading to the waterfalls. Back to the Dreaming Tree.

# PART SIX

## The Great Escape

*"Shapeshifting requires the ability to transcend your attachments, in particular your ego attachments to identity and who you are. If you can get over your attachment to labeling yourself and your cherishing of your identity, you can be virtually anybody. You can slip in and out of different shells, even different animal forms or deity forms."*

Zeena Schreck

We fought to keep up with Kaylah as she blazed a trail through the forest, up and over the plateau toward the roaring falls that grew louder with each panicked step. Except for her, none of us were in any condition to flee. Even Pavlik struggled with Eden's unconscious weight draped over his shoulder. To the west, the sun sank low in an orange blaze while starlight shimmered in a dark violet sky to the east.

Just before Kaylah began to make her way down the steep crevice at the waterfall's edge, a siren echoed from the forests behind us. Everyone froze in wonder at the low moan booming through the canyon: the bellow of some enormous horn. Kaylah turned, eyes wide with fear as she stared into the black masses of pines at our backs. We had never seen her this frightened.

"They know what I've done," she cried. "They will do anything to stop us. We have to stay ahead of them."

"This is fucking insane!" I shouted. "How are we that much of a threat?"

Kaylah shook her head at my asinine question. After a second blast of the horn, Eden slowly lifted her head as she dangled over Pavlik's shoulder. After a brief struggle, she lazily rolled herself down, onto her feet, at which point, everyone including Kaylah took a measured step back.

While massaging her bruised neck, she noticed everyone's

apprehension. I took a quick study of her eyes and found nothing out of the ordinary, just my friend; sore, groggy, and confused. I extended a cautious hand toward her face. Without hesitation, she pressed my palm to her cheek.

"I'm okay," she said, looking into my eyes. "Where are we?"

"Do you know who I am?" I demanded. "Do you know who you are?"

She twisted her face with an arched eyebrow that asked, "Are you fucking kidding me?" For now, it would have to suffice.

"They will burn this entire canyon to keep us from pulling her across the rift!" Kaylah shouted, pointing to Eden. "For the first time, they're afraid! There is no telling what they'll send after us! We have to keep moving!"

At that, Kaylah turned and scrambled down the crevice, glaring fiercely in our direction until she disappeared below the ledge. After sharing a brief round of blank stares and shrugged shoulders, we followed suit and clamored down after her.

"So she speaks English," Eden said.

"I'll fill you in later," I explained.

"As much respect as I have for these people," Gomez mumbled, swinging his girth over the cliff, "I have no doubt they would do us grievous bodily harm if they believed it necessary."

"You're also facing trouble on the far end of the Dreaming Tree in Peru," Kaylah's voice echoed from the rocky cliff wall below.

"What does that mean?" Gomez shouted back.

"The waters rose faster in the Basin than I guessed. You're all about to drown on the far side in the cave." And as an after-thought she added, "Also Kane's missionaries are closing in on you. They've got a small army to hunt you down where you sleep. You'll want to be awake before they find you."

"Yeah, I wouldn't want to sleep through something like that," Eden added with a sigh. In the dimming light, it was nearly impossible to find hand and foot holds along the slippery rock face under a continuous siege of icy spray from the waterfall at our backs. Twice I lost my footing and twice Pavlik caught my heel and repositioned it in a solid crevice for me. As I inched my way along the wall, a familiar pain began to take hold at the back of my shin; the same area that had sustained damage when Eden and I were attacked in her car back in Colorado. But I had no time to theorize about why it suddenly hurt again.

Upon reaching the ledge that snaked behind the enormous arch of water, I felt another shift of awareness. I simultaneously felt high and cold, but not the sort of cold from the brisk, mountain air. This was an otherworldly chill that pooled around my spine and seeped into my bones, as if my soul had been thrown into an ice bath.

As we jogged single file between the cliff and the roaring falls I grew dizzy, nearly drunk. My gaze fell to the plummeting sheets of water to my right and terribly strange images began to form in the currents. Faces appeared within the rushing falls. Scowling, piercing eyes opened everywhere I looked, witnessing and judging our escape.

I fought to ignore these visions. They gradually possessed me with deadly intent; one that beckoned me to take a final, small step to my right, into the raging falls to sudden death. Reason and logic swiped back at the hallucinations with hard science; precious biological knowledge: Humans evolved with a strong instinct to find eyes and faces within their environment. Hundreds of thousands of years of searching for hidden predators among the foliage tends to do that to an animal. My confused brain had simply moved into survival mode to make sense of the chaotic, hallucinatory stimuli. Yeah, that's all this is.

"Does anyone else feel weird?" Gomez shouted over the roaring currents. I was both relieved to hear I wasn't the only one feeling drugged, as well as deeply concerned for our collective sobriety.

"That's the datura, sergeant," Kaylah hollered from the front of the line. Just outside the cave's entrance, she abruptly turned to the falls, dropped to one knee and lowered her head just as she had when we first 'arrived' here.

"I ask you: Hold them back. Give us time," she chanted several times before repeating the request in another language

I did not recognize. She then leapt into the tunnel's entrance carved into the cliff wall on hands and knees. No one dared ask about her incantations, but Sabol snagged her by the ankle before she disappeared down the rocky shoot that led to the Dreaming Tree. His pupils were dilated, his movements shaky and uneasy.

"What did you do to us?" he demanded. Kaylah sighed with a "we don't have time for this," but explained as quickly as possible, nonetheless.

"To get back to Peru you need two plant medicines," Kaylah shouted at us impatiently from her perch. "Both of them need to work together to unlock the rift. We didn't have time to wait for the first one to work, so I had to give it to you earlier. The second part will kick in fast though. Follow me!"

"What about her?" Tina asked, gesturing to Eden. "She didn't drink the datura! I thought you said all of our 'frequencies' had to match." Kaylah turned, took a quick study of Eden and shook her head.

"It's too dangerous," she replied. "I'll give her the second medicine only. That should be enough for her. She'll be able to fill in the rest of the pattern herself to complete the circuit back into your sleeping bodies in the Basin. I hope."

Eden turned her palms up; just as confused by Kaylah's explanation as the rest of us. One by one, we crawled on bellies and knees back down the narrow passage that bore into the heart of the cliff. As I moved through the crevice, the rounded walls of rock seemed to lose their rigidity. Gradually, the tunnel leading to the Dreaming Tree transformed into moist flesh that undulated with its own rhythmic breathing; a sort of birth canal of the earth. I tried desperately to ignore the stimuli and remain focused on my sole task of pushing my weight forward.

Just as I became certain this 'organic passageway' was about to constrict entirely and suffocate the life from me, the world opened and I dropped face-first onto the floor of the massive cavern of stalagmites. Gomez helped me to my feet and the seven of us stood before the row of half-shelled geodes once again. Kaylah bolted to the center of the underground chamber to shout directions.

"Everyone must sleep in the same flower as before!" she hollered, ushering us into our respective crystalline pods. "Except for Professor Huxley and Agent Flores. You two must trade stones! Quickly! Move! The waters are rising! I have to send you back now! I can't pull any of you from the Tree myself!"

"Why?" Pavlik asked without really understanding what she was suggesting. Kaylah shrugged her shoulders and cocked her head to the side.

"I dunno," she mumbled. "Cuz you're all full-grown adults and you're kinda heavy. And, I'm only ten years old."

Without further debate we crawled into the geodes; however, I did level a silent, "Why?" concerning the switch between Tina and me as I scrambled ungracefully into my jade bowl of crystal points. I peered over the edge to find Kaylah leap atop her white/violet geode at the far end of the line, remove a slender, wooden straw from her leather satchel and begin packing a dark charcoal powder into the tip.

"Your energy patterns have changed while you were here," Kaylah said as she worked. "I don't have time to explain. Maybe you'll figure it out for yourself."

"Our energy patterns have changed?" Tina asked. "What about Professor Jessup's? It sounds like her 'energy patterns' have been massively altered, but she's in the same, golden geode as before." Kaylah briefly rose her head to study Eden sitting on the edge of her pod.

"I believe Professor Jessup is still just where she needs to be for this to work," Kaylah said apprehensively. "Her energy patterns are higher, but not changed. She's still our solar plexus. I only hope her power doesn't throw us off during the trip. Who knows where we would find ourselves. You could all wake up in another world, or the moon, or you could wake up not knowing each other. You could find yourselves in some close copy of the world you once knew where the changes are so tiny you don't even notice them."

"Okay, enough," I said, regretting I asked. Eden shrugged her shoulders.

"What's this about my 'boosted energy pattern'?" she asked. Kaylah ignored her.

"Do you remember meeting with the Jain?" I asked. "Or climbing out of the pit? Anything before Sadhu knocked you out?"

Eden's face twisted. "Sadhu did what, now?". Before I could answer, Kaylah leapt to the top of Tina's stone.

"Lay back," the child instructed. Tina curled into the concave bowl of purple crystal while the rest of us leaned over to observe Kaylah's work. The small girl jumped into the bowl and straddled Tina's stomach with the slim, wooden pipe in hand.

"Stick this up your nose until it hurts," Reluctantly, Tina did as requested and stuffed the wooden straw deep into her nostril.

"Now, tilt your head back," she demanded. "This is going to feel odd, but this will not kill you."

Fear consumed Tina's eyes while Kaylah inhaled deeply. With fierce exhalation, the girl blew into the far end of the pipe with a loud wooot!, blasting her medicine into Tina's sinus cavity. After a violent muscle contraction, Tina's head jerked backward and her body instantly went limp. Her eyes shut and she appeared completely unconscious. Without a moment's hesitation Kaylah leapt from Tina's geode over to Gomez's to repeat the same maneuver.

"Why didn't you tell us you spoke English?" Gomez asked after her straw was stuffed into his nostril. She leaned in with a whisper.

"Because before now, your stupid questions would have been a waste of my time and energy," she replied with a wink. After another powerful blast into her pipe, Gomez immediately dropped out of consciousness just as Tina had. Moments before the child leapt into my geode, the back of my shin screamed in pain once again. I pulled up my pant leg and searched my ankle. Running from ankle to mid-calf was a thin, reddish scar with a series of small hatch-marks crossing through every quarter inch or so. It was as if I were looking at the wound the doctors had just stitched up back in Boulder, after several weeks of recovery. My mind spun until Kaylah jumped onto my stomach and smiled wryly, reloading her pipe.

"Old scars coming back, professor?" she asked while packing a fresh bowl of the dark gray substance.

"Yeah." I said, trying to make sense of it. "They vanished when I awoke here, but now they're coming back. How is that?"

"Your mind remembers the scar," she replied under a raised brow. "Didn't my mother teach you anything? Your story carries the song of that injury. With enough time, your story would sing everything you remember about your world back into your body. All the cuts and scrapes on your hands have been slowly sinking away from this body's journey through the Tsangpo Gorge. But you don't remember it that way; that isn't your song, so those scars are disappearing. To heal, or shape-shift, or pull a rabbit from your hat, you have to change your story."

I was already lost in studying my palms before she had finished talking. Indeed, the callouses and scars I discovered upon first waking here in Tibet were almost completely healed. "I can feel all your questions bubbling up from your bones." Kaylah said, patting my belly in amusement. "Hopefully you'll piece it all together into one, clear vision; one you can really make use of." She finished loading her powder and lifted the pipe to my face.

"Now when it comes to bringing about change to others, you have to change their mind. Or at least get it to shut up for a few moments. Just as I am about to do for you. Just as you did for Agent Flores."

"Yeah, I don't suppose you're going to tell me what you've loaded that pipe with?" I asked nervously.

"Would it really matter if I tell you it's anadenanthera pereg-rina?" she asked rhetorically, shoving the tip of her wand into my nostril. Kaylah inhaled deeply while overhead, a terrible rumble echoed through the tunnel leading to the waterfall. A new level of fear crossed the child's face as she twisted her head around to study the commotion. Behind the roaring falls, some violent eruption grew ever louder. To my ears, it was nothing short of a ferocious battle amongst several, wild animals.

"Just a little more time," Kaylah whispered to herself. "Hold them back, Nagis."

Roaring, pounding and splashing all blended into one, tumultuous rage. "They're here." She announced, turning to me, "Safe travels, professor. I hope you're a strong swimmer. We enter dark waters now."

The child inhaled deeply and blasted a chest full of air into her pipe with all her might. A bullet fired into my brain and my world transformed into piercing white, agonizing pain. Gradually, the torturous sting subsided and leveled into a highly intense vibration. And under this vibration, all solid matter was undone; Kaylah's skin, her muscles, bones, my green geode, the cavern, the terrible sounds above. Everything fell back into the ocean of pure, silent awareness.

# Bilocation

*"Just becoming more aware of the stories we live, along with their infinite plotlines and subplots, begins to wake us up. In lucid dreaming we become aware of ourselves as both in dream story and outside it. In lucid living, as in lucid dreaming, we are no longer tyrannized by the story circulating around and inside us. The demon in the nightmare can be faced directly; the flying dream can be enjoyed in its ecstatic moment. As we face ourselves in our stories, we have space for perspective. We can stand back and see our personal story as part of a bigger whole."*

Gangaji

Out from the abyss, a tingling sensation arose; a subtle tickle at the back of the throat. I heard a voice call my name and I felt I was waking from a dream, yet I knew I hadn't been asleep. Not exactly. The next sensation was of a haunting aftertaste; one of being drained from one container into another as though I were a liquid. The tickle in my throat grew ever more intense and a wave intruded into the center of my awareness, obstructing some essential pathway. And the voice grew louder.

"PROFESSOR HUXLEY!" it screamed. The tickle had now grown to a full-blown cough and the intrusion became more severe. Panic set in and I found myself back inside the confines of my brain, my nerves, my limbs, followed by a terrible assessment: I'm drowning.

"PROFESSOR HUXLEY!" A hard slap across my face and my eyes burst open to find Kaylah straddling my chest, pulling frantically at my collar. Small rivers of glowing, phosphorescent water fell around her. It blurred my vision and flooded my mouth. I jerked up and choked water from my lungs as Kaylah leapt to the surface of my geode.

Where am I? What am I?

"Help me! They're heavy!" Kaylah screamed before leaping out of view, leaving me to stare dumbly at a ceiling of stalactites. Stalactites. Peru. And some part of me was perfectly fine with that. Repetition does that, no matter how insane it is. A long moment passed as I sat in a quickly-rising pool of water within my violet, crystalline bowl while comprehending the current situation: Our cave is flooding.

In a flash, I shoved doubt and hesitation aside and launched myself to the surface of my pod. Water was filling the entire chamber and had just begun to breach the tops of everyone's geodes, sending glowing rivers over the sides, down into the hollow cores. Tina was draped over the edge of her geode, coughing and scrambling for traction. Behind me, Kaylah was trying to fish out Eden. The soldiers were nowhere in sight. I automatically began making my way to Tina's aid when she stopped me with a raised hand.

"I'm okay!" she coughed, pulling herself to the surface. "Get Gomez! I'll get Sabol!"

I looked down to find Gomez passed out cold at the bottom of his blue, crystalline cradle,  his mouth ajar, slowly filling with water. Without thinking, I leapt on top of him, shoving my palms into his chest as I landed. A small geyser launched from his mouth upon impact. He snapped to full attention and I ordered him to his feet while studying his eyes. When I was certain he understood our dire situation, I leapt out to help the others.

Within a few, short moments, we were all standing atop the geodes' slick surfaces, coughing and soaking wet, searching for an exit, all of us now waist-deep in water. The available space between the water's surface and the spiked ceiling was rapidly deteriorating. I was forced to move between two stalactites for a slightly larger pocket of air above my head when I noticed Kaylah swimming frantically passed us, dodging the mineral spikes along the way. Everyone leapt into the water and followed after her. We swam in a tight group to the far wall of the cavern and huddled in a circle, treading water up to our chins. The thin pocket of air space above our heads had nearly vanished.

"The exit is directly below!" Kaylah shouted while she still could. "Take the deepest breath you've ever taken and follow me!"

She inhaled and vanished below the surface. We had to crank our necks to take a full breath of air, our gaping mouths inches from the rocky ceiling. After Tina dove below the surface in my peripheral, I did the same and went after her.

Vision was little more than a series of dark blurs beneath the glowing, murky depths. I managed to isolate the blurs that were in motion and swam after them. Swimming and lung capacity were never my strong suit; I let too much air escape far too quickly with each stroke. In the fuzzy expanse, panic threatened to overwhelm me when the burn of oxidation tingled in my chest. I fought to keep my hands paddling in pursuit of the undulating orbs ahead and not give in to the ever-growing instinct to break off and swim upward where, rationally, I knew there was no air to be found.

I had to make the impossible decision that if I was going to die, I would die swimming forward. My world became engulfed by the pain of suffocation as the moving blurs disappeared into an even darker spot that suddenly encompassed my entire range of vision. Though I had no idea where I was going, I pushed toward the point where the swimming shapes had vanished and soon, dark walls closed in from all sides. It dimly occurred that we had entered the tunnel leading up to the waterfalls. The burning agony in my chest reached its breaking point and I felt consciousness slipping. In the confusion I gave into the natural instinct to inhale. I opened my mouth and warm water poured down my throat, while any lingering hope of survival swam out. Then a pocket of air followed just behind the water as something yanked my body upward into glorious open space. I coughed in a blaze of pain, expelling the water from my lungs and straight into Tina's face.

"Good to see you, too," she chirped and kissed me on the cheek. I was still coughing when she shimmied herself up ahead of me, further along the narrow, rocky tunnel. The water level was at my waist when I felt something slam into my feet from below. I reached down and something squeezed my wrist. I pulled with all my might and Pavlik's head splashed up from the surface, coughing and gasping for air.

After a short scramble to the mouth of the cave, I fell into an exhausted heap on a mushy layer of mud. Before I could catch my bearings, Pavlik landed with a hard thud on my back and rolled into the earth beside me. I found the rest of the team crouched against the wall facing the thin waterfall, a mere fraction of the size of the one in Tibet. Brilliant moonlight shimmered quietly through the liquid veil. I broke into uncontrollable coughing as my mind processed the reality that we were back in the Chambira Basin. Kaylah slammed her palm over my mouth.

"Shhhh!" she whispered, wide-eyed with intensity. "They know where we are. They tracked us!"

"Who?" I asked, bumbling to my feet. "The Rotos?"

"I wish," she replied, studying the ghostly images through the waterfall. "Kane's missionaries and a small army of brainwashed locals."

After a stealthy escape up the slick, muddy ridge into the cover of giant ferns, everyone collapsed - except for Kaylah who literally ran circles around us, peeking through the giant leaves from every direction. As I lay in a stupor, I assumed everyone else was also coping with the effects of the instantaneous, transcontinental, multidimensional astral travel. When she finally decided we were safe for the time-being, Kaylah dropped to her knees to catch her breath.

"Maybe I stayed ahead of them," she mumbled confusedly before she drew in everyone's attention. "Listen! Up to now, you've only brushed shoulders with the Dark. From now on it won't be hiding, it won't hold back. It will leap out, grab you by the throat and possess you. We're a threat to Kane and his people and they know it now. Their anger wants you off balance."

"Can you be a little more specific on what the hell you're talking about?" Gomez asked.

"I certainly don't believe in possession," I said flatly.

"Words, words, words," Kaylah sighed.

"What do you know about what's hunting us?" Gomez demanded. Kaylah gestured for everyone to be silent, peeking through the bushes once more for several long moments before she continued.

"While you were all awake in the Tsangpo Gorge, I followed Kane's missionaries through the forests here," she explained quietly. "I've been spying on them: Giddeon, Bowen, and Braun. They've gathered up a team of shapeshifters to kill us. Whatever happens, don't let Giddeon or any of her followers look you in the eye."

"What?" Gomez whispered angrily.

"Kane's missionaries can touch the deepest part of your mind," she explained. "We go to those places to heal, but I think Giddeon is using that bridge to find the vibrations of your darkest fears. She can shapeshift or make her brainwashed slaves shift according to what she finds inside you. I'm talking about shifting made just for its target. So, don't let her in."

"That actually makes sense," Tina whispered to me. "The thing that Alto turned into, it was meant for me."

"Giddeon is more dangerous than all of them," Kaylah said. "That bitch's stare is a black-hole, worse than Medusa's."

Sabol laid his head back in agony. "Anything but that. Uggh. I hate snakes," he muttered, wringing his hands. "The way they writhe, the way they slither makes me…nauseous."

"Better than insects," Gomez added, flicking a shiny, black beetle off his jacket. "Cold, robotic creatures." Everyone stared briefly, assuming he was aware of the irony. If Gomez was capable of emotion, he kept it well hidden. When he found us all staring, he hollered mindlessly, "What?"

"Fuck that, I ain't afraid of anything," Pavlik concluded.

"You're not afraid of dying?" Tina chuckled incredulously, "Really? I doubt that."

While the team gave in to pondering their worst fears, I could barely process the insanity that poured from the child's mouth. Obviously, I had connected with some truths about the nature of spontaneous healing through the manipulation of vibration, but I had serious trouble accepting the darker, more sinister potential behind the same dynamics. Without thinking, I reached up and lightly rubbed the surface of the one of the giant tear-shaped leaves dangling above my head. It was smooth, damp and slightly rubbery to the touch, but more specifically, it was absolutely real. This was not a dream. This was South America. I still couldn't accept that either. Somehow, we really were back in the rainforest, over ten thousand miles from Tibet.

I pulled my pant leg up to find the bandage around my lower calf was right where I had left it, filthy and blood-stained. Tina stared in mild confusion when I rolled next to her and shoved my hands under her shirt, studying the surface of her skin. "I like where your head is at," she whispered. "But this really isn't the time."

"Are you hurt?" I demanded a little too loudly, causing Kaylah to hush me beneath a fiery stare. Tina suddenly broke into her own, fevered self-examination upon realizing what I was doing. She, too, found no sign of injury. Clearly the thought hadn't immediately occurred to her that, if we were somehow zipped back into our 'Peruvian bodies', then she should still have two, massive holes punched through her shoulder and hip. And I should be detoxing. I quieted my nerves to take full inventory; joints, muscles, nerves. No aches, no shivers, no abnormal sweating.

As my brain tried to piece it all together, my eyes drifted to a dark mound of objects at the center of our huddle. All the supplies we had left behind in the cavern were in a pile: the soldiers' weapons and gear, our backpacks. My backpack, the one carrying the bottle of OxyContin. Normally, I would have risked giving away our position to noisily scramble over each and every person there to return that bottle to my greedy hands. But now I hesitated. Yes, every muscle burned from exhaustion, but I had to admit that I simply didn't need it. I wasn't certain if this also meant I didn't want it.

Tina took me by the hand after seeing the turmoil in my face. When her fingers interlaced with mine and I felt her warmth, I instantly surrendered to all the frayed ends and dark gaps. For now, at least. As soon as the soldiers noticed that Kaylah had pulled our supplies from the cave, they immediately began strapping on backpacks and utility belts, checking the status of their rifles, handguns, and knives.

"My M4 isn't even wet," Gomez whispered to Sabol as he inspected his ammunition clip.

"Neither is my pack," Sabol replied, turning to Kaylah. "Wait, when did you pull our gear out?"

"Yesterday," she replied casually. "Before the river started flooding the chamber." Everyone exchanged a round of confused glances.

"Wait. So, you were…awake here, too?" Gomez asked, searching for the right words. "On…on this side?" Kaylah stared as if we were being deliberately stupid.

"I just told you I was spying on Giddeon while you were out," she repeated. "We're awake everywhere at once, all the time. The trick is to remember that it's impossible not to be awake to everything. Anyway, I can be awake in three places at once now. Well, four, if what I'm doing in one of those stories doesn't take much of my noodle," she added, tapping her head. "If I'm just monkeying around, being in two places at once is easy."

After searching the team of bewildered faces around her, she sighed heavily. "We learn to do it first in dreaming," she explained. "Anyone who knows how to lucid dream can practice being in a bunch of places at once. It's the ultimate smack in the face to the ego."

"Why is that?" Eden asked.

"Because your identity has to believe it's . . . special," she said, searching for the words. "It likes to think of itself as a solid object with hard edges that lives in one place at a time. One that doesn't move or shapeshift."

"It has to believe it's a particle," I said to myself, once again worried that their worldview was beginning to seep into my core. Kaylah nodded.

"That's why we practice shapeshifting," she whispered. "It keeps the ego at bay." It was then that she said something even more confounding. "It's also why average people forget most of their dreams."

"What?" Tina asked. Kaylah rolled her eyes. Stupid adults.

"The ego needs to pack away those other worlds into a little, tiny box that it pretends it has control over," she said as if it were obvious. "Your identity deals with impossible stuff in one of three ways: It either wraps a new storyline around it that lets the impossible thing happen, or it calls it a dream or a vision. Or, it just simply forgets it happened. Because none of you were ready for being in two places at once, I had to mix in a powerful sleeping medicine with the cactus I gave you before you entered the Dreaming Tree on this side. That helped you believe that you were in one place at a time. My plan was to make your ego a little weaker . . . " Kaylah, paused as she eyed Eden, "not break it into a thousand pieces." Kaylah then nudged at my arm with a smile. "Of course, my drug wore off on you for a moment there, didn't it professor? Probably because your body is used to such medicines. But I kept my eye on you in both places." At that, she giggled with a hand over her mouth. "Whoot! Whoot! Whoot!" she howled quietly like a small monkey.

My mind spun to catch up to her suggestion and, for a brief moment, I recalled a half-forgotten dream when I was in Tina's arms in the Tibetan hot spring Sadhu had led us to; a dream where Kaylah blew smoke into my lungs. Bilocation. Details of my time in Tibet steadily faded in the same way a dream does in the morning, regardless of how vivid it was when it took place. Was this my ego's way of sweeping the impossible under the rug? Under this new sensation, I couldn't help but entertain the new round of questions that bubbled up from the abyss; questions aimed at snapping my world back into some kind of familiar stability. Were we simply asleep in that cavern for the last couple of days? Were the Roto just a dream? If so, was it only my dream? I squeezed Tina's hand with a panic.

"Hey," I whispered. "You do remember being with the Roto clan in Tibet, right?"

"I think that's what I remember, yes," she replied. "But the details are starting to fade. I'm starting to doubt what really took place the last couple of days. But, then again, my body is healed. I can't argue with that." Kaylah giggled with delight.

"If you're trying to figure out what's real and what's fantasy, why would you trust what another character in your own dream has to say about it?" she asked. Everyone else was clearly suffering from the same dilemma. Pavlik poked at Kaylah as she lay next to him.

"So… was it all just a dream?" he asked.

"Were you aware that you were dreaming at the time, soldier?" she whispered.

"Well . . . no," he answered after some consideration. He began detailing what he remembered about the Roto, but the child firmly interrupted him.

"Then it was a dream," she replied. "It's always a dream until you're awake. The same is true right now! As you hear the words I'm speaking right now, wake up!"

Deflated and troubled by her answer, Pavlik turned and dropped his forehead toward the ground. Kaylah patted his shoulder, realizing he wasn't ready for her explanation. "For now, just focus on your job," she said. "Have faith that keeping Eden Jessup safe is most important."

"Yes!" Sabol said elatedly at hearing his God-given priority spoken aloud. He scooted next to Pavlik and grabbed him by his vest. "She's right," Sabol said fiercely. "We'll be right with God as long we accept his infinite power so we can protect His prophet!". Something about Sabol's words clicked hard for Pavlik. His eyes opened wide with realization and his hands shook wildly.

"Yes!" he shouted excitedly. "I remember it now! I see it! I understand what that Tibetan dude was trying to show me last night!"

"Shhh!" Kaylah warned him. "Keep your voice down!" But Pavlik was rolling with religious fervor.

"He was teaching me how to merge with the explosive, raw power of God!" he hollered. "He was showing me a path where I give myself over to something greater! He was trying to teach me how the Lord is like this continuous Big Bang and I need to stop resisting it!" Kaylah put her hands on his shoulders and tried to quiet him.

"The Roto did the same for each of you in way," she explained. "You need to calm down." But Pavlik didn't hear her. He jumped to his feet and rose his palms to the air. "Yes!" he hollered. "I am awake, I am ready to fulfill my holy purpose!"

Four, five, then six bright green laser points suddenly shown through the leaves around us. Three of them landed directly on Pavlik's chest. The moment he noticed them he shouted a final order at us: "Run!"

Before any of us could react, rapid gunfire echoed through the jungle. Under a series of deafening blasts, Pavlik was slammed onto his back while bullets ripped into leaves and severed branches. We dropped to the earth and pressed ourselves low to the ground. Gomez and Sabol crawled next to Pavlik with tree bark and foliage exploding and showering around them. Following Kaylah's lead, Tina and Eden scrambled to lower ground, away from the gunfire, while I lagged behind to scramble closer to the soldiers, not to help, but to snatch my backpack.

As soon as Tina and Eden reached the bottom of the ravine, I turned just in time to see Pavlik pull two large canisters from his military vest and hold them to his chest while Gomez and Sabol shouted protests into his face over the gunfire.

"What the hell are you doing?" I barely heard Gomez holler. "Your wounds aren't fatal, soldier! We're carrying you out!"

"No!" Pavlik wheezed. "I see it now! I wasn't afraid of dying. I was afraid of dying for nothing. Run!"

The onslaught of gunfire moved in closer, forcing Gomez and Sabol to give up on changing Pavlik's mind. They both tucked their tails and charged toward me. Gomez waved his hand that I should keep running as bullets zipped around them.

"Move your ass, professor!" Gomez shouted. "Those are anti-structure grenades!"

"What the hell is he doing?" Sabol shouted at Gomez, pointing angrily back at Pavlik! "He could have made it!"

The moment we reunited with the women on lower ground

everyone broke into full sprint, deeper into the jungle. We ran for our lives, dodging vines, ducking tree limbs. Soon the gunfire was replaced by a multitude of boots pounding the earth at our backs. Behind us, branches snapped and mud splashed under the weight of dozens of people chasing us through the dark foliage. Only a rare beam of moonlight breaking the canopy illuminated our path; all I could do was keep Tina and Eden in view. When Sabol's lean, muscular form caught up to my lumbering, shameful pace he slapped a handgun into my chest. "It's loaded," was the only instruction he offered as he passed. "Safety's off!"

I could hear our assailants begin to overtake us from either side and I knew we were beaten. We weren't agile or fast enough and I guessed the locals on our tail knew this territory well. But I kept running forward when suddenly a terrible explosion shook the forest at our backs. Agonized screams and shrapnel rode an ensuing shockwave that sent us all flying head-first into the air.

Now, this was something I had witnessed a thousand times in action movies. They always made it seem like a 'fun ride' to be launched from one's feet via dramatic explosion. I never imagined just how frighteningly painful it was to be lifted, torn, from the ground by a highly compressed wall of air. It slammed into my spine like a massive baseball bat whacking a fruit fly, while the air displacement created a vacuum in its wake. Inhalation became temporarily impossible, my lungs collapsed as all the oxygen was sucked violently from my chest. Without air for sound-waves to travel upon, everything went eerily quiet, far worse than suddenly going deaf. I could only watch in horror as Gomez and Sabol soundlessly gasped for air beside me. My head turned to ether and everything went black.

# Prey

*"Now, clear your minds. It knows what scares you. It has from the very beginning. Don't give it any help, it knows too much already."*

Tangina Barrons

I awoke to a most peculiar view: The underside of trees slowly sailing beneath a starlit sky. A glorious burst of oxygen filled my lungs and I knew I was being dragged by my heels through the mud. Eden's face appeared overhead as she pulled me in by the collar, slapping her palm over my mouth. She had double-backed and somehow managed to pull my fat ass to safety behind a ring of dense foliage. We peeked through the leaves to study a commotion just ahead of us where we spied a bloodied man wearing Peruvian military fatigues furiously kicking Gomez and Sabol back into consciousness at gunpoint.

"You killed our brothers!" he shouted into Gomez's face with a lazy, Southern drawl as he landed the tip of his boot into his ribs. "Hablas Englis, asshole? You think a few grenades are gunna win this fight? Boys, you have no idea."

Just as the man pulled both soldiers to their knees, a woman emerged in the glow of one of the larger moonbeams splitting the canopy. With a quick snap, she downed the final swig from a canteen before angrily dashing it into the mud. She was slim and muscular with short, mud-coated hair that hung over her eyes in twisted knots. Both of her hands were covered in blood. With a repressed grunt she dug into a sizeable gash in her upper shoulder and fished out a chunk of shrapnel which she threw at Gomez.

Although she brandished Sabol's military knife with precision, her expression was far more intimidating. The hard creases cutting her cheeks and forehead were forged by decades of repressed rage. This fierce women circled our soldiers, quietly sizing them up. Just as her male cohort, she wore camouflaged pants two sizes too big, black military boots and a tight, black T-shirt far too small. A badly tarnished, silver cross hung from her neck on a thick, metal chain.

These weren't soldiers and their uniforms didn't belong to them. I recognized their faces from the FBI recording. These were two of the three missionaries left unaccounted for and presumed dead: Giddeon, the woman, and Bowen, who busied himself smacking Sabol around.

"How is our brother?" Bowen asked quietly. She shook her head. Bowen exploded into another fit of rage, kicking and beating Gomez and Sabol. "You murdered Braun you motherfuckers!" he spat.

I searched myself and realized I had dropped the handgun Sabol handed me. Christ, I'm fucking worthless in this world.

"Did . . . did Pavlik sacrifice himself for us?" Eden whispered in a daze.

"For you," I snapped. "Religious fanatics tend to do insane shit like that for their prophets." Her eyes watered and I felt guilty for my outburst, not enough to apologize, however.

"Oh, God," she whispered.

A pair of screams sliced the air from the far right of our small hiding spot. We both immediately recognized the voices. Two native Indian men with straight, jet-black bangs wearing little more than leather loincloths and beaded cuff links emerged from the foliage dragging Tina and Kaylah by the hair. They both struggled to cling to their captor's wrists while being hauled roughly through the mud. Overwhelmed by rage, I nearly leapt from the bushes at the sight of it, but Eden held a firm hand to my chest.

Tina and Kaylah were thrown to the ground next to the soldiers as another dreadful sight stepped from the shadows in the background: A small army of native men and women. They gathered around their victims to join Giddeon and Bowen. Judging from the vast array of clothing, hairstyles and jewelry, most of the natives appeared to hail from different tribes. I only spied two children among the crowd: A pair of twin sisters who couldn't have been much older than Kaylah. Eden quietly identified each clan as more Indians emerged, or limped, into view depending on how close they had been to the blast. "Maca . . . Culino . . . Yagua . . . Zaparo . . ." Eden whispered fearfully. "Jesus Christ, they've been recruiting from miles around."

I counted two dozen Indians before my heart sank. Every one of them appeared to be brainwashed with an irrational amount of rage toward their captives. They leaned over our team huddled in the dirt, growling and seething in a variety of tongues. Sabol and Gomez silently held their ground while Tina shriveled to shield Kaylah beneath her. Giddeon let out a high-pitched whistle into the night air and everyone instantly fell silent.

"Spread out!" she hollered. "She's here somewhere. Find her!" Her instructions were immediately translated into multiple languages by several members of their clan and a dozen natives dashed into action. With coordinated precision they began scouring the grounds, searching bushes, kicking and swatting at branches. It wouldn't be long before we were discovered. Giddeon slapped Sabol's knife against her palm as she approached Gomez, whereupon she dropped to one knee and lowered her head in frustration.

"I am so close to being done here in this godforsaken place," she growled in a low, harsh drawl. This was a woman at the brink of insanity, struggling not to weep as she spoke. "I have just one, final task and I will be allowed to return home. Why you people insist on being on the wrong side of this is beyond me. We have been ordained with holy purpose! How can you not see that? Your blindness: Is it willful?"

She lifted her eyes to meet Gomez's. Once his attention belonged to her she reached off to her side and placed the knife to Sabol's chest. Her arm shook with rage as she continued speaking.

"When you see what waits for you in hell, ya'll are going to spend the rest of eternity wondering how you could have been so arrogant as to toil against the hand of God. But I clearly cannot open your eyes, soldier, and so you are forcin' my hand. You're forcin' me to deal with you in a manner you would likely judge as . . . less than Christian. I'll only ask you this once."

She whimpered uncontrollably, tapping the knife harder into

Sabol's skin with each word.

"Where . . . is . . . Professor Eden Jessup?" A terrible pain crossed her face that forced her head down once more. "And, son, if anything, and I do mean anything, spills outtta your mouth that falls short of a direct answer, I am going to tear this man's heart from his chest and make you watch me devour it right here and now, I swear to God."

Giddeon closed her eyes and waited. We had mere moments to intervene. I leapt into action without thought, without doubt. I spun Eden around and dug into her backpack, pushed past her extra clothing, canteen and Power Bars, and pulled out her cigarette lighter, glass pipe, and zip-lock of marijuana.

"What the hell?" she whispered as I stuffed a sticky ball of herb into the bowl. "One, last toke before dying?"

"Do you trust me?"

"Of course."

"Take one hit," I demanded, firing up her lighter. She inhaled deeply while I kept the bowl burning. I snuffed out the fire as soon as she pulled a chest full of smoke. I peered through the foliage to find Gomez at his wit's end. He shook his head slowly at the ground, knowing that any response he offered would mean Sabol's death. Giddeon tapped the knife harder into Sabol's chest, leaving a bloody gash in his skin as Eden exhaled behind me.

"Ahhh, there it is. I can feel the medicine working," Giddeon said, cranking her neck back. "Your time is running short to cooperate. The bridge will soon be opened. I'm already beginning to smell what all of you are hiding." Giddeon turned to Gomez as her pupils widened, "I can see those insects of yours, soldier."

I turned to find Eden staring into her surroundings with amusement. Her gaze caught mine as she considered something. "Was that . . . " she began. "Was that . . . my weed?"

"Are you dreaming?" I asked. "Or are you awake?"

She was about to reply but instead she paused, raised her palms and gazed into them. Just as before, upon crawling out from the Jain's Pit, a static field of electric pops and snaps appeared around her hands. Her eyes widened with astonishment. I fought the inclination to freeze up at the impossible sight.

"Oh, I am dreaming," she whispered. "And . . . it seems . . . it seems that I can . . . " While she pondered her next words, Gomez had decided on a response.

"I don't know where Jessup is," he replied mournfully. Giddeon didn't move. She continued to stare into the mud until she called to her troops waiting patiently behind her.

"Atau!" she cried. A young, native man rushed to the front of the line and lowered his head. "You are fortunate today," she said to the boy. "Kneel." Atau did as requested, keeping his eyes lowered in holy reverence.

"It seems like you can what?" I prodded Eden while studying the scene through our wall of ferns. Giddeon's search party was closing in on either side of us. We would be discovered at any moment. Eden had begun to chant quietly to herself; an ancient Hindu chant, one I had heard somewhere before in a half-forgotten dream. Though strangely familiar, the incantations were gibberish to my ears:

*Om asato ma sadgamaya,*
*tamaso ma jyotirgamaya,*
*mrityorma amritamgamaya*
*Om shantih shantih shantih*

"It seems like I can create an electromagnetic field," Eden said when she completed her chant, bewildered by her own statement. "Or . . . it's more like I can merge with some version of . . . here . . . where an electric field forms around my hands. I can't decide which."

I turned away from the terrible scene playing out with our team and grabbed her by the shoulders. "Yes, that's right!" I whispered firmly. "The human nervous system can behave like . . . like a particle accelerator!" Her face twisted up.

"How is that possible?" she asked, moving her attention to me, her eyes glazed by another realm of existence. "I mean . . . that doesn't make scientific sense, does it?" Your opponent is allowed up to three clarifying questions in the game of bullshit-tery.

The static pops fizzled as the field around her hands went dead. My mind spun aimlessly for an answer. She trusts me. She needs a "scientific" explanation. I have to bridge that gap for her. But there wasn't an explanation; at least not one I had time to explain. I had no choice but to lie. I grabbed her wrists, held her palms a few inches apart and began making circles, rotating one above the other. I made it up as I spoke.

"Because . . . uhh . . . the nervous system, well, it's electrical, right?" I stuttered, struggling to sound sincere. "You see … your left and right hand can carry opposing, magnetic charges that can hold a field of valence electrons."

She stared blankly, taking in the utter nonsense I had just suggested. But as she did, the snaps and pops in the empty space around her hands appeared once more, steadily growing in intensity. Just above her head, a vibrating ring of white en-ergy took form that gradually picked up momentum, burning a perfect circle into mid-air. One hemisphere of my brain said, "super-string" while the other whispered, "halo." As her hands spun faster, a single point of white, hot energy materialized between her palms that seemed to draw its power from the "halo" above her head.

Ghostly wisps of electrical discharge siphoned from this "halo," down through the top of her head, along her arms and into her hands. The point of pure light at her command gradually expanded into a vibrating circle of energy; a buzz-ing ring that amassed size and strength the longer she worked her palms around it. I was watching a human being manifest a particle accelerator in empty space. But the real magic, the most amazing trick, was my ability to temporarily set aside my framework of reason. It was so unlike the Michael Huxley I knew, I wasn't sure I recognized him.

What had become of the old me? He's dead in a pit on the other end of the globe, of course.

"Good riddance," I said, trying desperately to ignore the 99.99 percent impossibility taking place between Eden's hands.

"Uhhh . . . yeah . . . just keep doing that," I said reassuringly. Her face was aglow with awe and delight. I peeked back to the team to find Giddeon raising her furious head.

"You've made your choice," Giddeon announced to Gomez. With a sudden snap of her arms, she clamped her fingers around Sabol's throat. "Atau!" she cried. "Surrender!"

The young native lowered his head in prayer and laid his outstretched palms face up in the mud. What took place next pulled at my chest and twisted my stomach. A nearly imperceptible sound of a vacuum filled the air while Giddeon's eyes became empty, black holes. The moonlight on her face faded from a soft white into a sickly gray; indeed, the very space around her body became an inky black.

Sabol clenched his eyes shut, refusing the madness taking place before him while Giddeon's skin crackled like dried clay and the soft flesh around her eye sockets shriveled into the cavities of her skull. Everyone, including the natives, gasped in terror when the woman's entire body aged twenty, thirty, forty years in a manner of seconds. And with it, the frequency began to seep into the atmosphere from deep within her.

"What the hell are you?" Gomez gasped.

"I am no one," Giddeon hissed.

Witnessing this terror unfold firsthand allowed me to peer behind their technique, providing valuable insight into the cult's mentality and the many ways they had twisted the Roto's wisdom. If Iboga had taught me anything, it was that shapeshifting demands the price of the ego, the conglomeration of everything we believe to be true about ourselves in order to purchase entrance into the Field. But much like myself at first, Kane and his people imagine the ego to be the very essence of who they are.

"They can't make a distinction between dropping their identity and physical death," I heard myself say aloud. In their eyes, transcendence of ego was a dynamic wrought with terror, death, and decay. I was watching nothing more than this woman's unique vision of death play out; the necessary surrender of limited self to merge with the probability wave.

In her mind, dropping the ego was fatal. And this cult feared death above all else. Beyond their purported faith in an afterlife in heaven, their fear of dying was unmatched.

A raspy, shrill sound exploded from Giddeon's throat; a noise that was only partially human. "Look at me!" it cried. Sabol cringed and shrunk back in agony as she pressed her peeling, skeletal hands into his cheeks. But he wouldn't open his eyes. Tiny whirlpools emerged in the space just beyond the woman's pupils: the essence of attention draining into the void. The frequency she emitted grew ever louder, and though I had imagined I had developed some kind of peace with this particular wave pattern, seeing it misused in the most vile way imaginable was steadily dragging me into a state of shock.

"Keep your eyes shut, Sabol!" Kaylah shouted next to him. "Don't surrender to her!" When the soldier could no longer handle the pressure, his eyes burst open and immediately his attention was drawn into the recesses of Giddeon's void. My God, this is an actual transference of energy! Awareness can be moved from here to there. Sabol let out a scream as some deeply held secret was ripped from his subconscious. Only then did Giddeon release him from her skeletal grip.

"Thank you for letting me taste your darkness," she whispered to Sabol after the "transfer." The soldier fell to his back in exhaustion. "Your terror was delicious," she added just before the bones of her face began to collapse inward. Her words became a garbled hiss as her throat and larynx contorted.

"I saw what you hide, soldier. That dark nest of seething, writhing serpents. It's a good fear; there is no shame in it. I too am terrified of snakes. Perhaps it's the Christian instinct in us to shrink from evil?"

Suddenly, Atau's body collapsed into a dead heap next to Giddeon. Upon seeing the young boy's lifeless form, I instinctively knew: Had Sabol freely surrendered his attention over to this woman as the young native had, he would be in the dirt lying next him without any physical signs of trauma.

The sound of tissues sucked dry of all fluid filled the air as Giddeon's form continued to deteriorate. In one, swift motion she reached her bony, petrified hand into her gaping mouth, curled her fingers around her teeth and yanked them to the side with a Snap! When she removed her hand, her jaw hung loosely inside her mouth.

A new level of terror coursed my spine upon realizing that she had unhinged her jaw. A deafening, high-pitched shriek poured from her throat while the hair on her head fell from their roots, strand by strand, exposing a quickly graying skull. I tried to pull my eyes from the horrific transformation before me, but I couldn't turn away.

Through the bushes, I saw Giddeon's eyes rolled back into their sockets, her teeth became black and crumbled from her mouth like ash. And then, with a series of cracks beneath her scalp, a dozen slippery coils oozed through the puncture holes, twisting and slithering amongst each other until they took the form of eye-less snakes. Each serpent emerging from her skull hissed and writhed as if their very existence was torturous.

The color drained from Sabol's face before he screamed so hard he collapsed under his worst fears of snakes made manifest before his eyes. Giddeon's body stretched into an elongated cable of pulsating, scaly flesh while her torso lurched backward, preparing to strike. From the black spaces in her gums sprouted curved, razor-sharp spikes when she stretched her mouth to full, horrible capacity.

Suddenly, the strobe-lights and whirring sound pouring from Eden's electrical discharge pulled everyone's attention, including Giddeon's. Her serpentine form suddenly twisted and shrieked in our direction. Behind me, Eden knelt at the center of a spinning disk of blinding white light that steadily expanded with intensity. Her fiery ring burned the back of my shirt, forcing me to fall to the ground, out from the bush. I stared up at Eden's "super-string" as it crackled and rippled into the surrounding air with tiny arcs of electricity, sizzling the foliage all while leaving her own body and clothing completely untouched. Judging by the crescendo, I sensed an ensuing breaking point where Eden would no longer be able to contain the energy. I scrambled to my feet and ran toward the team shouting, "Duck! Drop to the floor!"

With arms stretched wide, I took a running leap and tackled everyone to the ground,  followed directly by an abrupt, low-frequency boom as Eden's palms exploded apart. Detonating out from the center of her hands was a circular shock-wave of scorching heat; a white-hot disc of fire that burst through the jungle, boiling the moisture from the air in its path with the sounds of sizzling timber, branches and foliage racing behind it. The discharge soared mere inches over our heads, singeing our hair as it passed. With a fading roar, the string's circumference expanded off into the distant jungle as it lost momentum. In every direction just above the ground, the world had been sliced through.

A silent, breathless moment passed before enormous palms began tipping beneath crackling trunks, crashing into each other, pounding the forest floor. The earth shook angrily from repetitive impact as we huddled together and shielded our heads. I managed to throw myself over Tina while trees stretching thirty meters collided with rocks and each other in a series of rolling, heart-pounding thuds.

I stole a glance to see Giddeon and Bowen recoil before they screamed in agony upon being pinned by several, massive trunks right next to us. Before the ring of fire sputtered out altogether in the distance, Gomez was on his feet with Kaylah over his shoulder, pulling at Sabol's arm.

Disoriented and nearly deaf, I fumbled to my feet and grabbed Tina's hand. Except for the largest boulders, the foothills and the muddy cliffs, nothing stood above our waist. The canopy had vanished, leaving nothing but the expanse of moonlight and stars overhead. As far as we could see along the dimly lit landscape, every tree trunk, every root, bush and fern crackled with glowing orange and gray ash at a perfectly straight line. And the world fell quiet.

As soon as we pulled Sabol around, we made a mad dash, leaping over smoking stumps and downed branches to collect a very stunned Eden Jessup. While the team ran mindlessly toward the mud-drenched cliffs, I stayed behind to steal a quick survey of the carnage we'd left behind. The sight was bloodcurdling. Mixed within the chaos of crumpled wood and sizzling foliage were the bodies of perhaps a dozen people, sliced just below the midsections. My eyes grazed over the incomprehensible amounts of blood and torched flesh and my stomach twisted inward until I was drawn down to hands and knees. Tina yanked at my shoulder just as I puked a stream of burning acid into the mud. Was I also responsible for this? Did I talk Eden into doing this? Did my bald-face lie about the laws of physics play a role here?

Tina managed to get me to my feet when I noticed Giddeon struggling beneath a mound of dead branches. She had nearly returned to human form. Behind her, her partner Bowen, along with a half dozen Indians, began struggling for freedom. Those who witnessed the ensuing lightning burst soon enough dropped to the ground. With her legs crushed beneath a massive trunk, Giddeon screamed as we fled.

"Do you see this?!" she shouted with unbridled rage. "Do you see what she is now? How much proof do you need?" Pale as snow, Eden stared dead-eyed at the wave of mutilation encompassing us. When it was clear she wasn't processing outside stimuli any longer, Sabol forced her to run alongside him.

The world became a blur that we pushed through following the river downstream. We ran single-file over trunks and dodged piles of insurmountable burning foliage toward the cliffs we navigated just days before. The further we ran, the scope of the wreckage became increasingly evident. Terror overwhelmed Eden's eyes as we treaded entire football fields of cut trees and smoking ferns, severed birds, decapitated monkeys and butchered wild cats. When we rounded the cliff wall to an area shielded from the electron burst, Eden could barely keep up. She was consumed by the sight.

"I bulldozed a rainforest," she muttered.

A solid thirty minutes had passed in silence when we finally reached the outer edge of the blast radius. I guessed the damage we left behind to be at least three square kilometers. Soon after the jungle opened once again into untouched, thick terrain, Sabol's attention was abruptly drawn to a tree wrapped by thick, gray-brown vines. The longer he stared at the network of twisting branches, the more he shuddered and whimpered. Kaylah patted his back and snagged Gomez's blade from his belt sheath.

"Good eyes, soldier. Relax, they aren't snakes," she whispered and ran off trail, scampering over rocks and grasses to the base of the tree. When she began chopping small chunks from one of the lower hanging vines I questioned her on the detour.

"Banisteriopsis caapi; half of the ingredients," she replied. "I need two medicines working together to make ayahuasca. Now we need to find psychotria viridis leaves. You're a smart man, professor: With a billion plants in the rainforest, how did people ever find the right match to brew together? What are the odds, do you suppose, that the right combination would ever be found?" I hoped her question was rhetorical. I treated it as such.

"And why would we want to make ayahuasca?" I hollered, baffled and frustrated. Kaylah ignored me and continued cutting. She didn't reply until she had rejoined the group and had stuffed the vine segments into the pack slung over Eden's shoulders. Eden didn't appear to notice the commotion at her back.

"Ayahuasca is liquid DMT," Kaylah explained once we were leading the pack in relative privacy once again. "It is the same basic medicine Sadhu gave you all at the mouth of the Jain's Pit. But this will last much longer than his little smoke. The bond between Eden and the Jain won't be made whole again until she vibrates with the same patterns she did when she accepted his gift."

I almost exploded at the child. For everyone's sake, specifically Eden's, I contained myself and shouted in whispers at her. "Are you seeing what she just did?" I quietly hollered. "That was after a little THC! And you think it's a good idea to feed her DMT?"

Kaylah shook her head at my stupidity. "You still want to think Kane is just a sick, confused old man. That storyline is easier, I know. It also scares you that Eden Jessup's gift may be our only hope. And still it may not be enough to save our world."

For the first time, I began to seriously wonder if we were merely pawns in this child's game of gods and monsters. What if she was completely out of her mind? This was a nine-year-old who's brain had been subjected to powerful hallucinogens for God knows how long. At the back of the line, Eden's body shivered and went limp with a soft thud into the ground. She rolled into fetal position, forcing the soldiers to carry her once again.

By the time Kaylah decided we were no longer being chased, the eastern sky burned with electric pinks and warm reds. We took refuge in the shadows of towering boulders at the base of the slope; one we were all too familiar with. Several sections of our claw marks were still visible trailing down the muddy wall high above. Now that I could survey the full, clear geography of the slope without the fog blinding my view I decided once again that the feat we had collectively performed seemed even more impossible. Sadhu's voice whispered in my ear, "Collective interference," but I had a burning need to bury those memories for now.

The moment my ass hit the dirt I broke into my pack and ripped into my OxyContin. At this point, I simply didn't care if I needed it or not. Had there been tequila available, I would have downed half a bottle with the same gusto. I savagely chewed two tablets like a starved animal before I fell to my side in exhaustion.

# Closing the Circuit

*"Chaos is what we've lost touch with. This is why it is given a bad name. It is feared by the dominant archetype of our world, which is Ego, which clenches because its existence is defined in terms of control."*

Terence McKenna

After a half hour of rest and refueling in relative silence, Gomez broke the spell. He had been at the brink of losing his temper but had instead busied himself with the dry oatmeal squares Sabol had passed around from his supply pack. While he ate, Gomez leveled an angered focus at Kaylah, who stared mindlessly at the cereal bar in her hands. She looked defeated, and that made everyone nervous.

Eden sat outside the circle facing the raging river. I wanted to see if she was all right, both mentally and physically, but I found myself apprehensive of being near her. Everyone else was coping with the shock in their own way, but Sabol seemed to bear the worst of it. He wouldn't eat or drink. He laid on his side, clutching at his stomach with tears in his eyes. It was far more than just losing Pavlik. Whatever Giddeon had done had broken him.

"So, this was all part of your grand plan?" Gomez finally growled at Kaylah. "Waking up in a flood and walking into an ambush? Was Pavlik a necessary sacrifice in this scheme of yours?" Kaylah looked up with mild surprise.

"She didn't know what was going to happen," Tina said behind closed eyes as she rested against the slope. "It's not her fault."

"Isn't it?" he shouted, spitting a mouthful of oatmeal into the mud. "It sure seems like this kid knows all sorts of shit that she only doles out in bite-sized fragments. And then, only when circumstance demands it."

I certainly couldn't argue with the sentiment, but I was in no frame of mind for another fight. Before Tina could retort, Kaylah placed a gentle hand over Tina's. "I pulled you out as soon as I could," Kaylah replied quietly. "I cannot see the future and I cannot see who among you will survive. I can only move toward balance."

"You call this 'balance'?" Gomez shouted.

"We have to know how far the balancing pole extends on either side before we walk the tightrope," she replied quietly.

"Fuck that," he grunted, shoving a finger at her. "That's the shit I'm talking about, right there."

"I made the mistake of bringing Kane and his people to my tribe in the first place," Kaylah admitted. "That's my fault. I didn't see who he was this time around, what he had become. But all of you have to make peace with the part you have to play in this. I didn't ask you into my forest and Kane left three missionaries behind for a reason. He knew someone might follow his tracks and he knew that could make them dangerous to him. What his plan is exactly, I still don't know, but I do know he has one. And now you've seen for yourself the sort of things they can call up. Whatever this adds up to, you all have a duty here to help."

Kaylah turned to Eden who's back was still turned, facing the river, meditating, praying or God only knew what. "I believe we need Professor Jessup to really screw up Kane's plan," Kaylah said. At the very mention of Eden everyone fell silent again. Even I temporarily stuffed what I had witnessed into a dark corner of my brain marked, Do Not Disturb.

"Okay, so what's the next step in balancing this mess out?" Tina asked Kaylah. "What are we up against?"

"When I tracked down Giddeon and her merry band, they were holed up in a Yora village in the highlands to the west," Kaylah explained. "They had been using it as a sort of base of operations while they searched for you and planned their attacks. At the time, Giddeon, Braun, and Bowen had gathered fifty soldiers, only a select one or two from every tribe in the region."

"How are they choosing which people they take?" I asked, but I suspected I knew the answer. Kaylah took a moment to consider before she answered.

"They seem to take only the most confused members of

the village," she said, "those who don't appear to know the difference between the little voice in their heads and the voice of God. Anyway, Giddeon's tricks are powerful. Anyone who doesn't join them are either eaten alive or they go insane from seeing the angry hand of God firsthand."

"Oh?" Tina asked.

"Sure! Giddeon simply picked up where Kane left off. I'm guessing it didn't take long for Kane to realize that what he was able to do with his power out here in the jungle would work just as well in the States. Maybe even better. Americans are really stupid creatures."

"So what has Giddeon been doing with these tribes exactly?" Gomez asked.

Kaylah sighed at the thought of it. "First, she preaches hellfire and brimstone; her vision of God from the old Bible, enough to get the tribe's attention. Giddeon has been fed a story that the good lord above has blessed their church, and theirs alone, to make a deal with evil to wipe us sinners off the planet. I think the way they see it, sending people like us to hell is good for both God and Satan. Hell gets what it wants, and Earth can be cleansed for the Second Coming. And I don't just mean Jesus Christ. They claim that God Himself is coming back, whatever that means. Some of these tribes out here have never seen a white person before in their life, or any outsider. They don't know what to make of it.

"Giddeon preaches about a world where hellhounds run around gobbling up all the nonbelievers, dragging their souls back to where they belong, "Cleansing the Soil" as they call it. But then, just like any good salesman, she offers hope! She promises heavenly peace for those who cooperate. And for those who don't, well, I would guess after you've seen a family member gobbled up by the demons this crazy woman just warned you about you'd be on your knees, too. They claim they will be the last church. Ever. And if we don't stop them, she may be right." She leveled her gaze onto Gomez.

"And the moment I learned of their plan to bring an army of shifters to you at the Dreaming Tree, I did everything I could to stay one step ahead of them," she said firmly. "Pavlik's grenades killed one of Kane's missionaries and took out almost half of Giddeon's army. We would all have been shot dead back there if it wasn't for him."

Gomez began to grumble at the insinuation that Pavliks' death carried some larger relevance, but Kaylah interrupted him. "Giddeon knows you may be the only ones on the planet now who understand the power they stole from my clan and that makes her very nervous. She knows now that you plan to fly back to the States through Panza's base and they will do anything to stop you. They'll do anything to stop *her*," she said gesturing to Eden. "Giddeon will throw everything she has at us now to keep you from bringing Professor Jessup and your knowledge back to Kane's doorstep."

"It's a two day journey back to Panza's airstrip," Gomez said.

"Not if you talk Panza into sending a truck of soldiers after us," Kaylah said, staring at Sabol.

Gomez growled and shook his head. Picking up on her suggestion, Sabol lifted his head, pulled the broken satellite phone from his backpack and shook it at the girl with frustration. "This is completely busted," he said. "We can't contact anyone. I tried everything to repair it before we . . . went to Tibet."

Kaylah smiled. "But you haven't tried to fix it since then, soldier. You see things in a new way now. My clan showed you how paper thin your identity is, but the ego heals itself. It will come back in a thousand ways. It hooks you with a worry, a little voice in the back of your head that whispers that something is still left unfinished. It always pushes heaven off to some distant future. For now, the only way to peel your mask off again is by ripping it off by force. It'll fall back into place, but we only need to pluck out a miracle."

Kaylah reached into her leather satchel and removed a tiny, bright green tree frog. The creature was so still, so serene, I wondered if it was real. When she cupped it in her hands, I saw its vocal sac beneath its chin flutter ever so gently. It was alive and, my God she's been carrying a live animal this entire time. "Say hello, Francis," Kaylah announced. "Hello, Francis!"

she replied to herself in a high-pitched voice, shaking the tiny creature gently. Sabol's head fell against the wall behind him.

"Oh, God," he muttered. "No more hallucinogens. Plee-aase."

Kaylah shook her head. "Sorry," she said, petting Francis' head with her finger. "You can't do it on your own yet. Think of this as a helping hand from God to pull you closer to His knowledge."

"Are you saying he can't remember what your shamans taught him?" I asked. "In the same way Eden can't reconnect with the Jain until her consciousness is . . . nudged, or whatever?"

Kaylah seemed somewhat surprised by my question. "You're all kind of dealing with the same problem. What you learned from my clan cannot be held by the average mind. I'm guessing that you can only remember a little of what you learned in the Tsangpo, so be careful! Memory has a way of filling in gaps so that your story seems to go in a straight line. It's always running from chaos and death."

I didn't know what to think about her suggestion. At this point, I couldn't decide if I even believed I had actually experienced being in Tibet at all. Kaylah snagged the tiny amphibian by its hind legs and dangled him upside down. The creature began to struggle as she lifted it to her face.

"Sorry about this, buddy," she whispered. Everyone including Eden jumped in shock when the child screamed with all her strength, the most ear-piercing yell I'd ever heard, directly into the frog's face. The animal shook with violent contractions to break free, but the child held tight. Her screaming came to an abrupt halt and she once again lovingly cupped the creature into her hands. With a stroke of the frog's spine, she gathered a clear, jelly-like substance onto her finger.

"I'm going to spread this onto your gums," Kaylah warned Sabol. "Francis here is a Sapo frog and it's the last of the medicine I've got, so it's going to have to do. Clear your mind and hold your attention on the satellite radio during the entire journey."

"Yeah, how do I clear my mind, exactly?" Sabol asked confusedly. Kaylah considered how to reply to him in a meaningful way.

"Just stop asking questions for a minute," she said and pointed to his forehead. "For the next two minutes, stop all your planning. Allow a space of zero movement, zero doubt."

"You mean faith?" he asked.

"Yes!" she said. "Enter a state of pure faith!"

Sabol pulled a small, all-utility blade and driver set from his pack and quickly unscrewed the back of the radio. A twisted mess of wires and green electrical panels burst from the casing when he pulled it apart. How anyone could make sense of such a tangled chaos was beyond me. Kaylah reached into Sabol's mouth and massaged his lower gum with her index finger.

No more than two minutes passed before his pupils dilated into shark eyes. He let the radio fall to his lap as he gazed in wonder at the sights around him. Kaylah gave him a moment to adjust before she gently lifted the radio before his face.

"How do you heal him?" she asked quietly. "He needs a good doctor." Sabol steadily turned the device in his hand and cocked his head. He gazed into the network of twisting wires and recoiled in horror.

"Snakes!" he whimpered and threw the component to the ground. "It's a nest of snakes!" Kaylah retrieved the radio, but this time held it at a safe distance from Sabol's view. Terrified, the soldier hid his face, cradling himself.

"Come on, he's in no condition for this!" Gomez hollered. Kaylah angrily hushed him, pulled open Sabol's arm and sat in his lap like a child holding a toy.

"Breathe slowly and look at what I have here," she said gently. "They aren't snakes . . . they're blood vessels."

"Blood vessels?" he asked curiously, lowering his palms.

"Yes," she replied. "And they're injured. They need your help." Slowly, he returned his focus to the exposed wiring and soon the fear withered from his eyes. After a few moments of staring mindlessly into the network, he picked up his tweezers and poked delicately into its innards. With a gentle flick of his hand, he disconnected a tiny, black processing socket with a half dozen metal pins protruding from the base.

"The blood won't pass through this organ," Sabol whispered, rolling the processor around his palm.

"What does it need?" Kaylah asked. Sabol stared into his hand and went completely still for several, eerie moments. Just as I began to fear that his mind had shut down for good, a wave of energy flashed over his face.

"I need fire," he whispered. Kaylah immediately pulled several wooden matches from her satchel and awaited further instruction. With sudden precision and focus, Sabol snatched the front casing of the radio from the rocks beside him and shook it upside down. Three strips of metal the size of finger-nail clippings tinkered quietly to the ground. He plucked them up one at a time and inserted them into the base of the socket before snapping it back into the panel. His speed steadily increased the longer he worked. After removing a file wrapped with soft, metal cable from his pack, he nodded to Kaylah, who flicked the match head aflame. Sabol heated the wire over the fire until it melted to a near liquid. With a blur of furious movements, he began soldering wire after wire into various ports.

Before he understood what was taking place in his own hands, he had reconnected the two halves of the radio, twisted the tuning dial and unleashed a noisy stream of static from the receiver. I couldn't believe what I was hearing. For a full min-ute, he stared into the radio controls with utter shock. "How the hell did that work?" he asked.

"You don't remember yet, but you spent much of your time with the Roto learning how to fix breaks in paths of energy," Kaylah responded. "You could become the very best electrician on the planet when you get home. Or a surgeon."

Tears filled Sabol's eyes as he took her words to heart. "If you survive, that is," Kaylah added gravely.

# Collecting the Pieces

*". . . DMT can allow our brains to perceive dark matter or parallel universes, realms of existence inhabited by conscious entities."*

Rick Strassman, *DMT: The Spirit Molecule*

After a rather awkward call via our newly repaired satellite phone to Agent Downey and to a very pissed off Colonel Panza, we continued east along the river toward a canyon where we could make our way to an extraction point on drier highlands without traversing the mudslide cliffs. From there, we would rendezvous with a team of Panza's men on a rarely traveled logging route and return to base where our cargo plane would be waiting to carry us back to the States. It all seemed so simple.

Deciding how best to "debrief" the powers-that-be on our current situation forced me to realize there was no "normal life" back home waiting for me or for the rest of us, assuming we survived. I could never relate my story without them suspecting I had gone mad, present company excluded. As if I wasn't disconnected from my fellow man enough already. Common ground with others was now a thing of the past.

It was late afternoon by the time we reached the rendezvous point at high ground where the air was cooler and less humid. Downey ordered us to stay put near the logging path as we waited for Panza's men, but to remain out of sight. No one could argue with that advice. Gomez led us to a ditch lined with tall grasses, close enough to the road to hear approaching vehicles without advertising our presence. The moment everyone was well hidden and settled, Kaylah darted back into the jungle for reasons unknown. No one had the motivation any longer to question a child who seemed older and wiser than us all.

Luckily for me, the OxyContin was working its magic and I mildly cursed myself at how wonderful it felt. The effects were stronger than ever. The edge it cut from my anxiety and confusion seemed necessary at this point even if I wasn't experiencing withdrawal. Living outside the safe, gentle haze of opiates proved far too prickly and harsh for what we were facing. The volume on all incoming stimuli was cranked to eleven.

Surprisingly, I did manage to offer the rest of the team access to my stash. Gomez and Tina both readily accepted and that made me feel a little better for some reason. Two days ago, I would never have offered my precious, limited supply of opiates to anyone unless they were in extreme agony. I decided that that alone counted as an improvement. Or maybe I was just rationalizing.  Regardless, I believed that if it weren't for my fuzzy, ecstasy cocoon, I probably wouldn't have been so cavalier about joining Eden where she rested alone outside the group. It was Tina's suggestion that I check on her, but I knew it was the right thing to do. Eden had been isolating herself ever since the "clear-cutting" incident. I found her reclining against the grassy slope with eyes closed, but I knew she wasn't sleeping. I stretched out next to her and tried to seem at ease. For a long while, neither of us spoke.

"Well, aren't you the brave one?" she finally said, eyes still closed.

"I ain't afraid'a you, bitch," I lied, trying to make a joke of it, quietly cringing at my poor attempt at levity. I pulled back to find genuine ground with her. "Sorry, it's hard to put into words," I started anew with genuine sincerity, "but I think I kind of understand how you were able to do what you did back there. At least, I understand it in a way that makes sense to me. I believe there's a solid, scientific explanation from a quantum physics perspective. If the human nervous system really can harmonize with this Zero Point Field, then . . . "

Eden scoffed. "It's strangely comforting to know you're still an atheist after all this insanity," she muttered, "but, you're hung up about the 'hows.' I'm hung up on the 'whys.' Good to know there's something left over of the people we used to be."

"You saved our lives," I reminded her. Of that much I was certain.

"I cut down two dozen people," she replied weakly before she began to ramble anxiously. "I clear-cut a fucking rainforest.

A couple days ago I was preaching Christianity to you. I don't know who I am anymore. When I'm awake, I feel trapped in an insane dream I can't wake from. Mike, I'm trying to stay functional, but every hidden aspect of my personality is exploding out of proportion one at a time until I'm forced to stare it in the face."

She opened her eyes and faced me. "I used to think these supernatural ideas were fun. But I had no idea how scary it could get. All the crazy shit I've ever seen happened either while I was high or asleep so I could always secretly rationalize it away. My head was full of chemicals or I was dreaming. Now I'm awake and sober and the world is impossible. When I enter these ecstatic, fully charged states of consciousness, these realms of utter perfection, there's always something tugging at me, something that still seems . . . unfinished." Tears filled her eyes as she hugged her body.

"You know what I'm really afraid of?" she asked, clasping my arm. "Fuck, it's all so goddamned ironic it's insulting; the universe must be laughing at me. In the end, I'm afraid that I'm what's unfinished, that I don't deserve to wield that power. Hilarious, right?"

"False idols before God," I said, suspecting I understood it now on another level. Great, now I'm referencing the Bible.

"Yeah," she agreed, shaking her head. "And I take responsibility for that. I've done everything I know to find an honest path to Nirvana. My attitude was, if there's a way an ordinary human like me can touch grace, I'll do anything to find it. Anything! I'll stay that course until I'm dead. There is nothing else worthy of my time."

"Well, your dedication was always obvious," I said, turning her wrists to expose the religious icons inked along her forearms; the many hieroglyphs and symbols hailing from ancient Egypt to Mesoamerica and everywhere in between. "But, I guess I always kinda figured all the tattoos were to make you look more interesting," I smiled to let her know I was kidding, even though I wasn't, not entirely. My attempt at levity again only fueled her frustration.

"You're right, though!" she said, angry with herself. "I've fantasized about being closer to God—whatever that means—all my life. Of being some wise, powerful woman, a force to be reckoned with. But when I really had to face the truth that the price of admission was my precious ego, my answer was, Hell No! Anything but that! I mean, fuck, if I can't look cool doing it, what's the point? I'm fucking ashamed to see that in me," she laughed ironically. The longer she laughed, the more she teared up.

"Shit, Mike, Kane doesn't even scare me that much. Maybe you should have left me back in the gorge with those shaman. Mixing God with human emotions shouldn't be allowed to happen."

At least she was calling me "Mike" again. That made me feel a little less anxious. "I had a hand in that destruction back there, too," I reminded her. "I helped point you down that road."

"You didn't know what was going to happen when you made up that pile of bullshit about manifesting an electrical field," she laughed gently, wiping her eyes. "I did. And you know what? It felt good to wield that kind of power. Too good. And I want more. I could see exactly what kind of improbable version of reality I was tapping into. What I couldn't see was that it would leave me feeling afraid of myself. Christ, I'm afraid to go to sleep because of what I'll do in my own dreams."

Her last remark left us both silent. We jumped in fright when Kaylah burst from the bushes at the top of the ridge and slid into the ditch next to us. She reached into her satchel, removed several handfuls of long, narrow leaves and stuffed them into Eden's pack.

"You have to crush those vines I gave you into a pulp and chop up these leaves. Grind them down if you can," Kaylah explained. "You'll need to simmer them together in water over low heat as long as you can, at least five or six hours. Toss in some . . ."

"I know how to make ayahuasca," Eden muttered. "I've just never taken it. It's not the 'how,' it's the 'why.'"

"When the time comes, you'll know why," Kaylah replied, removing the satchel containing her hallucinogenic pet frog, Francis. Now she handed the creature over to Eden. "In the meantime, this is in case you need something with a little more punch than your marijuana."

"With more punch?" we both asked in unison. Kaylah smiled and nodded.

"Sure, the test was a success. Now we know for sure: Any shift in your consciousness allows you to tap into the Jain's spirit to some, small degree," Kaylah explained. "Again, that circuit won't be completely closed until you ingest Sadhu's failsafe, DMT. What you'll be capable of in that state will be fantastic; you'll reach the highest level of godliness possible within a mortal, physical form."

"I'll swim in Little Big Crooked," Eden said quietly.

"You'll shift into the highest vision of god your identity will allow," Kaylah replied. "But, remember, you're not enlightened. None of you are. You haven't dropped your leashes, not completely. My mother would say that your personalities are still going through their death throes. Then again, perhaps by the time you have to take the full plunge, you'll all be ready to give up the 'doings' racing in your head; let the 'unfinished' be unfinished, get it?"

"Sadhu said true enlightenment can take years," I said. "Even lifetimes."

"The Rotos are old," she replied, rolling her eyes. "They think enlightenment takes lifetimes of meditation, but then they'll turn around and tell you that time is a manmade idea. I say enlightenment is easy, so easy a child can do it. It's the simplest thing in the universe because it's already ours. Right now, not when we sit down to pray or even after we die. And that doesn't make any sense to a mind that only understands problems. We like to pretend there's work to be done, a puzzle to solve first. So silly humans walk around with the big idea that something must be done first, gaps need to be filled. My mother says we have to stop pretending and start intending. It drives us mad because we can't accept what we already own.

"So maybe by tomorrow you'll drop all of your ideas about unfinished work, everything you believe is *you* and you'll give in to even greater possibility. Or even sooner. Maybe it'll happen within the hour. Or, by the time I'm done with this very sentence."

She paused and smiled at us both with a raised eyebrow. Eden and I shared a blank stare, wondering what she was waiting for. She only smiled and stared into the jungle.

"But, until you remember that the best version of you has and always will be only available right now," she continued, "you'll put it off and make excuses. You'll hold back, and that blinds you from the big picture. No matter how much power you collect, as long as you believe in a small idea of you, death will keep hunting you."

"Are you saying Eden could still be killed in that state of higher consciousness?" I asked, trying to wrap my head around it all and see it from her perspective.

"Absolutely," Kaylah replied, shrugging her shoulders. "As long as there is ego, there is always the option for death. And birth. So, yes, she could be killed in that state. Or she could collapse every single version of our reality, just as my people fear. Or, she could do something we can't imagine. Or maybe she'll chose to do nothing at all and let Kane devour the Earth. I don't know, anything can happen." After a long gaze into Eden's eyes, the child wrapped her arms around her and squeezed warmly.

"I have to go," Kaylah said quietly, sending anxious chills through us both.

"You're leaving?" Eden nearly coughed in disbelief. Kaylah nodded with subtle sadness.

"I've done all I can to put you on the right track,." she explained. "Every time, I'm only in the way after this point. Maybe I just have to take my own advice: Let go and trust. It's a hypothesis, at least. Right, professor?"

"You're talking like you've seen this play out before" I said. "Like you've seen all of this fail already." Even though I spoke the words, I didn't really want an answer. What this child had been doing with the power of the Dreaming Tree at her fingertips, I couldn't fathom. As she considered my comment, Kaylah gazed at the ground and exhaustion swept her face.

"The choices you make from here will be from necessity," she replied. "I am sorry for my part in all of this."

"Where are you going to go?" Eden asked.

"I have to find what is left of the Quechua. On this side, they're my family."

"What about the Craneo Rotos?" I asked. "Can you ever go back there?"

Kaylah giggled and patted my cheek. "I'm already there," she reminded me. "I never left. You still only have faith in the particle, professor. The particle, and not the wave." That left me with another set of questions I knew may never be answered.

"And, yes, the Craneo Roto were totally pissed I brought you back in your condition," she explained. "But, they won't leave the gorge to do anything about it. They did everything they could to stop me from pulling you across, Eden Jessup, but once they saw I got my way, they dropped it. That's how they are. Our world isn't their worry. They don't have roots anymore here like I do."

At that, she stared with heavy intensity at Eden. "Believe me," she said pointedly, "if you ever step foot onto their soil again, they'll kill you without blinking. They believe your energy is safer spread out over a distance like a wave. They fear you like a walking, talking bolt of lightning; a super-concentrated burst of energy that shouldn't rightly exist—just a stupid human holding the power of a god in her pocket. But I know the truth. I know it's beautiful."

"Trust me," Eden sighed, resting her head. "If I ever make it back home, I may not leave my bedroom ever again. In fact, a couple years in a padded cell is starting to sound pretty good right about now."

"No shit," I agreed.

After a few, short goodbyes to the rest of the team, Kaylah disappeared into the bush once again. Her departure left everyone uneasy, as if yet another piece of our armor had been pulled off.

It was early evening by the time Gomez detected the first sounds of tires rolling through mud and gravel off in the distance. We could hear Panza's soldiers talking loudly amongst each other as their covered, flatbed truck came to full stop. The driver whistled loudly out the window to get our attention.

"Well, that's just great," Sabol grumbled. "They only sent three guys."

Gomez stepped in front of the slowing truck, waving his hand with a "cut throat'" gesture for the men to lower their voices. They laughed and ignored him. The driver impatiently motioned toward the back of the truck, grunting, "Vamanos!" Sabol and Gomez both attempted to quiet the man as we passed.

"Vamanos!" he shouted louder. As Tina ducked through the canvas entry to the flatbed, the Zero Point frequency echoed from the distant jungle. Everyone froze in place upon recognizing the now-familiar sound, except for Panza's men. It was impossible to determine which direction it originated. It seemed to emanate from several positions around the forest.

"Que es eso?" one of Panza's soldiers yelled, hanging out the window. The driver peered into the wilderness and shook his head.

"No se," he replied.

"Fuck," Gomez said, signaling us to move faster. "We need to go. Now!"

"What's the hurry, señor?" the soldier barked. "Relax, the real soldiers are here to protect you gringos from the scary sounds of the forest."

# Racing Hell

*"A warrior considers himself already dead, so there is nothing to lose. The worst has already happened to him, therefore he's clear and calm; judging him by his acts or by his words, one would never suspect that he has witnessed everything."*

Carlos Castaneda

Only one of Panza's three soldiers, Segundo Miguel, rode at the back of the covered flatbed along with the rest of us. He laughed when Gomez and Sabol readied their weapons and struck positions at the opened rear. Through the sliding window on the cab we could clearly hear his other two men up front as they cursed the job they'd been stuck with.

"Deberías prepararte," Gomez warned Miguel. You should prepare yourself. The soldier turned his head down in disgust. It was clear the general attitude was now that we were all insane. Tina busied herself loading two handguns next to me. She snapped them into her thigh holsters before inspecting the bulky, automatic weapon Gomez had collected from Pavlik. "Laser sight, night scope, duel fire controls," Tina mumbled, twisting the rifle in her hands to show me a second, enormous barrel beneath the primary cylinder. "He's got a goddamned grenade launcher on this," she laughed quietly. "There's only one in the chamber, but I'll take it. Fan boys of war. Christ, I'm surprised he didn't add gold spinning rims."

"Okay, so, now do I get a gun?" I asked anxiously.

"What happened to the one I gave you?" Sabol asked. I only barely recalled him slapping a handgun into my chest when we were fleeing earlier.

"I, uhh. I dropped it," I admitted. "Sorry. It was my first encounter with antistructure grenades." Sabol quickly smirked with a "I'm just fuckin' with you" expression. It was good to see him coming back around to a state that resembled normal functioning. He removed a flat, black pistol from inside his vest, checked the cartridge and indicated the tip of the barrel.

"Point that end at the bad guys and squeeze the trigger," he said with a grin.

"Now for the million-dollar question," Tina grunted, "do bullets stop these shapeshifters, or whatever we're calling them?" Silence fell over the team until Eden finally spoke. She had been in lotus posture near the rear, leaning against the cab in silent meditation.

"I unloaded a fifty caliber into one of their faces back in Colorado," she explained to Tina while removing her grandfather's handgun from inside her pack. "I'm guessing that was Christopher Aldon, Kane's right hand at the compound. Fucker didn't even flinch. Then Mike and I trapped him inside my Hudson and blew the tank, twenty gallons of gas. But Downey said there was no sign of a body at the scene, so I'm guessing he survived that, too. Then I shot Alto outside the falls with Sabol's M4 at close range. I reloaded twice before it escaped."

"I guess I have my answer," Tina huffed. "Bullets slow them down. Eden is the only real firepower we have." I cringed as Eden lowered her head.

"I'm not a weapon," she mumbled. Before Tina could apologize, the truck slammed to a skidding halt, throwing everyone toward the cab. We scrambled up from the metal flooring and listened quietly. Even Miguel seemed mildly concerned. Beyond the thin tarp, the jungle was perfectly still. Everyone's heart jumped when the driver blasted the horn, and held it. Soon we heard him yelling through his window, "Mueve tu culo!"

Gomez leapt from the trailer to investigate and ordered us to stay put. After a long, dead silence we heard the cab doors opening and slamming shut, followed by footsteps and cursing. Tina jumped to the ground to investigate. When I began to follow her, she held her hand for me to wait behind.

"I'm not any safer back here!" I reminded her. She nodded in agreement.

We crept along the side of the truck in total darkness while Sabol stayed with Eden. Miguel simply pounded once on the cab door with irritation at the holdup. I wrestled with the ethical vs. survival question: Do I tell Eden to ready her pipe, or perhaps even the psychoactive frog Kaylah gave her? After witnessing what she was capable of with a bit of THC in her system, what effect the secretions of Kaylah's Amazonian Tree Frog might have on her, we were all afraid to guess.

With arms extended, I pointed my gun at the ground as I stealthily stepped sideways toward the front of the truck and immediately realized I was only mimicking what I had seen in the movies. I considered how, thus far, the information I had picked up from film and television had been terribly inaccurate. No amount of posturing would make me feel safer. I was a total fraud.

We stepped into the empty road and joined Gomez and the driver, bathed in the headlights, gawking at the sight ahead. Some twenty meters down the path, standing side by side were two native girls, eyes wide open, staring mindlessly into our high beams. They weren't much older than seven or eight years old, unnaturally thin, frozen in place. And I recognized them. Eden and I had seen these girls the night before amongst Giddeon's army.

The driver sighed in disgust. "Niños espeluznantes," he groaned. "I hate creepy little kids." He gathered his courage and shouted down the road, "Sal de la carretera!" They didn't budge. Except for the fact they were standing upright, they exhibited no signs of life whatsoever.

"Gomez, we're in trouble," I said severely. "They're with Giddeon."

"Shit," Gomez said, turning to the driver. "We need to keep moving. Mow them down if you have to."

"Are you mad?" the driver barked. "I'm not going to run down children. I don't care how awful they are! What the hell happened to you people out here?"

His two partners leapt from the truck with weapons readied, not from any sense of emergency; they were impatient. With a nod of the head, the driver ordered his two men to go deal with the bizarre road block. With Miguel leading the way, they strolled down the path and holstered their weapons. As they approached the twins, some vague commotion in the distant forest caught Gomez's attention. He readied his weapon and tapped the driver on the shoulder.

"We have movement from both directions, lieutenant," Gomez whispered, "I'm telling you, we're in danger. We need to move."

"Danger, señor?" the driver asked sarcastically, though his anxiety was beginning to show. In the headlights his soldiers stopped midstride when the odd pair blocking our path stretched their mouths wide open and released a nearly imperceptible hiss into the night air. The hiss steadily grew to an ambient, white noise, and dropped to a low roar, a sort of rumbling no human vocal cords could possibly muster.

The soldiers scanned the area around them before looking back to their commanding officer in utter confusion. Snapping branches and crunching leaves continued to echo from the dark expanse on either side of the road. Slashes of moonlight illuminated a multitude of heavy forms zigzagging through the brush, dense masses that moved low to the ground.

On the road just ahead, the soldiers confronted the twin girls who continued to scream into the night, never once pausing for air. Miguel turned back for new instructions when suddenly, both children appeared to rapidly grow taller. Their spines and necks began to elongate with a series of fleshy snaps until they towered over the soldiers while their heads drew together until they stood cheek to cheek, all while releasing the never-ending, terrible wail from their lungs. I became ill as their heads spun counterclockwise in tandem, their necks stretching together into one, twisted knot of muscle and flesh. The rifles fell from both soldiers' hands in shock as, tendon by tendon, the girl's bodies fused together into a single aberration of the human body—a two-headed nightmare riding atop four legs.

Overcome by fear and insanity, the caravan driver raised his weapon and fired aimlessly at the road ahead, shooting his own man in the back in the process, who fell to the ground and rolled into the ditch. On thin, bony legs and gangly joints the beast approached Miguel, who managed to raise his weapon. Before he could fire, the "twins" opened both mouths and swiftly sunk two sets of jagged teeth into either side of his throat.

"We should get back in the truck," Gomez decided, over-taken by current events.

"Really?" Tina responded absentmindedly, backing away. "You sure you don't want to see more?"

Gomez snapped from his trance and fell into action, pulling furiously at the driver's shirt while motioning us to get our asses back in the truck bed. But Gomez's efforts were useless; the soldier's mind was gone. He yanked free of Gomez's grip with a swift yank, stumbled toward the entity as it continued to munch on Miguel and mindlessly unloaded his weapon at the bloody scene. Tina and I bolted to the rear of the truck. I fought the instinct to gawk at the flock of dark forms converging on us from either side of the road.

Gomez leapt into the driver's seat and stomped the gas the moment Tina and I dove through the canvas flaps onto the flatbed. We barreled down the road toward a head-on collision with the creature whose shrieking soon blotted out all other sounds. When our engine revved into high gear we rolled over something massive, tossing us around the flatbed. Sabol struggled to recover his stance while crackling screams of agony and snapping bone could be heard directly underneath. I spied the receding road through the canvas flaps, but found no monstrous carcass in our wake. Where did it go?

My eyes fell to the ground just as three, elongated, skel-etal arms slashed through the canvas from either side. Sabol shouted at us all to drop back to the floorboards. With finger-nails the size of steak knives, the beast ripped straight through the metal framing while clinging to the truck's underbelly—until a second, more explosive jolt of the rear tires shook it loose, sending it flailing into the mud behind us, along with the shredded frame of our canopy.

With the cargo area exposed, our vehicle had now been re-duced to an oversized pickup. Gomez skidded around a sharp turn and the jungle broke into open space where the moonlight exposed rolling, grassy plains. We were allowed but a brief in-stant to catch our breaths before Giddeon's forces poured into the road at our backs; a hunting pack comprised of a dozen four-legged creatures. They burst onto the plains and skidded to a collective halt in a cloud of dust, as if awaiting further instruction. I scrambled to the front of the flatbed and pushed open the sliding door on the cab.

"I see them!" Gomez shouted before I could warn him.

Although the finer details were shrouded by shadows, their overall dimensions and grotesque shapes were undeniable: Bulky heads laden with spikes, torsos armored by heavy bone plating, powerful hind legs. It would have taken an impossibly harsh and highly unusual environment for such a breed to evolve naturally, where the most adapted animal survived by smashing down enormous barriers standing in the way of its prey. The hunting party submissively lowered their heads the moment Giddeon emerged behind them. And what a sight she was.

Giddeon had now completed her transformation into Sabol's darkest nightmare of all things that slither. Intelligent design at its finest. Her naked, emaciated torso was the only hint of humanity left intact. The lower half of her body merged with the form of an enormous, black eel which propelled her to the front of the line with rhythmic undulations through the grass. Thin sheets of withered, decayed skin wrapped an impossible skeletal structure holding an ashen skull sprouting an angry nest of serpents. Her visage betrayed a soul in the deepest throes of torture; a Gorgon brought back to life after weeks of decay. The mere act of laying eyes on such a brutally shifted form inspired something at my core to want to give up and die right then and there. Then I noticed Sabol draped over the sidewall next to me. His eyes were pointed at Giddeon, but there was no sign of life or comprehension behind them.

Giddeon pointed at us as we receded into the fields and released an ear-piercing shriek, sending her hunting party of shifted natives into sudden action. Beneath pained growls and heavy grunts, the pack broke into two groups and charged over the plains in fast pursuit of our truck. Beyond the air rushing at my face, I could hear Gomez curse at the new sight in his rearview mirror. He dropped into low gear and pushed the engine harder. With a small thud, Sabol collapsed to the front corner of the flatbed and dropped his weapon.

"We're dead," he whimpered. "We can't fight this. We're done." Tina tried to pull him back to his senses while I grabbed for Eden's backpack. There would be no lighting a pipe in this wind, so I had no choice but to reach for Kaylah's frog.

"No," Eden said miserably, pushing it away. I removed Kaylah's pouch, untied the string and set it beside her as the savage groans of the animals closing in became overwhelming.

"They're going to kill us!" I hollered. She wrapped her arms around her knees and hid her face.

"What if I kill everyone else along with them?" she replied. "What if I kill you?"

I tried to form a good counterargument and failed when machine gun fire exploded into the air behind me. Tina knelt at the tailgate, blasting away at the horde as they charged our rear. My heart sank when her direct hits, even to their faces had little to no effect. The stampeding creatures would merely twist their massive heads back and wince at the bullets with irritation.

"Get ready for this!" Gomez shouted through the window. I looked up and found we were advancing on a steep, muddied hill, one that would soon drain our speed. With nerves rattling my bones, I slid down the truck bed next to Tina, snagging Sabol's rifle along the way. Sabol had succumbed to full-blown shock; expressionless and curled into a shivering ball near the wheel well. I wondered why I wasn't lying next to him in the same condition. My answer appeared from some deep corner of my brain: Because there's nothing to lose. I'm already dead. Maybe not here, not yet. But, at every moment, a version of me dies. I'm alive, I'm dead. It's all happening at once.

The moment I swung the barrel over the gate, I mindlessly squeezed the trigger out of panic upon seeing our horrendous predators up close. They had nearly reached our bumper.

"No!" Tina hollered, leaning over and flicking some lever on my weapon. "Together! Three-shot bursts!" She indicated the closest target: A particularly fleet-footed creature in the lead on a direct collision course with our side panel. I did what I hoped was "taking aim" at its snarling face when Tina rested her hand on top of my weapon. "We have to wait until they're right on top of us!" she shouted. "Otherwise we're just wasting ammo!"

Under the unpleasant advantage of closer range, these creatures resembled the animated skeletons of rhinos wrapped in moldy skin. An oozing, black tar dripped from their tiny, dead eyes, eyes that were still horrifically human. Gliding over the grassy plains just behind the horde was Giddeon, snapping and shrieking, coercing her attack dogs to charge faster.

"Now!" Tina shouted, and we unleashed a barrage of bullets into the pack lead. Its front legs collapsed, sending it into an uncontrolled tumble. A moment later, the creature righted itself in the distance before it resumed the chase with ever more fury. Not terribly effective, but it was all we could do to keep them at bay. We continued beating them back in this fashion for what seemed like an hour, although it was probably less than a few minutes. Just as we feared, when the truck neared the top of the hill, our speed plummeted and the entire pack closed in fast. For the fourth time, Tina's trigger clicked dead. "I'm out!" she hollered. Two rounds later, my own trigger clicked without report.

"Where's the rest of the ammo?" I screamed.

She pulled her handgun from her thigh holster. "This is it."

Her face changed upon remembering something. She reached under the barrel of Pavlik's M4 and pumped the lower slide once. "Scratch that. I've got the one grenade," she said with a weak smirk. We both knew it would ultimately prove to be little more than a distraction.

While our tires spun up the muddy incline, I crawled to the front of the bed next to Eden while Tina opened fire with her pistol. I carefully pulled "Francis" from his hiding place and discovered a film of clear jelly had already formed on his back; the result of an unpleasant truck ride I imagined.

"They're almost on top of us!" I screamed at Eden. "We'll be dead within minutes!" She lifted her head and peered fearfully over my shoulder, just in time to see the raging swarm of monstrosities reach our bumper. With a succession of violent shudders, our attackers rammed their horned skulls into our panels, forcing Gomez to pull the wheel back into alignment after each blast. As she took in the scene, Eden gradually surrendered and gestured for me to feed her Francis' magic secretions. With a firm, gentle movement I cupped the tiny animal into my hands and . . . he slipped through my fingers and hopped toward the tailgate.

"Nooo!" we shouted in horror. We both dove forward with hands opened wide. I landed with my palms cupped for a trap, but he wiggled through the tiniest opening between my thumb and index finger and then straight into Eden's open palm. The instant she closed her hand, Francis leapt away a split second faster. He zigzagged around the flatbed, hopping in one direction and another, any direction we weren't.

Tina spent the last of her pistol ammo while Eden and I continued flailing around the shuddering, slippery truck bed. After another failed attempt to snag Francis, I came to a tumbling crash just beneath Tina who lifted Pavlik's M4 into position. She shook her head and leveled the barrel of the grenade launcher to the center of the writhing masses currently gnashing at our bumper. I ducked behind the metal gate and covered my ears. At the front of the flatbed, our tiny, green friend leapt merrily onto Eden's chest. Wide-eyed with surprise, Eden loving cupped her hands around Francis and smiled.

"Good boy!" she chirped before dragging her tongue along his back as a reward.

"Here goes nothing," Tina hollered. She pulled the trigger on the grenade launcher and dropped next to me.

# Premature Enlightenment

*"What a caterpillar calls the end of the world we call a butterfly."*

Eckhart Tolle

With a brilliant, deafening boom, the hunting pack soared into the air in a fiery blaze. Our truck rounded the peak and the shower of beasts fell out of sight behind the ridgeline. Of course, we all hoped Pavlik's final gift to us had put an end to the attack, but I couldn't believe in hope at this point. It wasn't that I had become jaded, rather, it seemed the only appropriate attitude left. What good was wishing?

"There's no way that stopped them," Tina said flatly, throwing the now useless M4 aside. Her words proved true directly following her remark. The entire pack emerged over the hillside roaring louder than ever. Some were on fire, a few were smoking, all had sustained some level of damage. They pounded into the earth with a revitalized sense of revenge. The grenade had bought us a few more meters of distance. Suddenly, the flickering of firelight pulled my attention to the front of the truck. Great, now what's burning?

It was Eden. She was on her feet near the cab, her balance seemingly unaffected by the violent jittering. But something else was terribly wrong. Smoldering holes aglow with orange flame were expanding everywhere throughout her jacket, her T-shirt, jeans, even her shoes. Her clothing was literally incinerating off her body. My first thought was that she'd been splashed by some volatile chemical, or that somehow the grenade launcher had released some kind of backfire onto her.

Eden stared into her palms in utter amazement, chanting quietly beneath her breath while the frequency sailed through her essence like silk. I jumped up to extinguish the flames, but Tina seized me by the arm, forcing me to watch the phenomena before us. Eden wasn't on fire, she hadn't been doused with flammables. Beneath the circles of fire devouring the last of her socks and underwear, her flesh was completely unharmed. A spinning sphere of energy began to pulsate deep within her upper abdomen. This tiny, yellow ball bathed her nervous system with a golden glow allowing every vein, blood vessel, and nerve visible through her skin.

When the last of her garments fell to ash into the wind, Eden stepped forward to reveal yet another extraordinary sight—every tattoo on her body had sprung to life, transforming her flesh into an animated display of religious symbolism. The intricate lines depicting the Hindu god Shiva was now a living, breathing icon at the center of her chest. Shiva's third eye opened while his four arms reached out to present a never-ending manifestation of artifacts at his fingertips; blooming lotus flowers, celestial symbols, tridents and skulls. Dancing in the flames of the sun on her shoulders were Aztec and Egyptian gods, while the solar system spun slowly behind them. Catholic saints and Buddhist monks inked with precision-detail into her forearms knelt in meditation while a trio of whirling dervishes spun in ecstasy on her upper thigh.

Matching the direction and speed of the animated dervishes, Eden twirled in slow motion, illuminating another series of fantastic tattoos along her spine, complex illustrations of chakra systems rotated with interweaving geometrical patterns. Every religious icon from neck to ankle collapsed and reconstituted over and over in repeating cycles of death and rebirth.

Francis, the tree frog, suddenly appeared from behind the curve of Eden's hip, or more precisely, he "swam" in and out of her flesh. Initially, he appeared to be a living, three-dimensional creature crawling along her skin, but he immediately leapt below the surface and transformed into an animated tattoo. This inked version of Francis would then swim in and out Eden's skin as if she were a fish tank.

This fantastical version of a woman I once knew approached with a dull purplish glow appearing from deep within her skull to illuminate the center of her forehead. Sabol broke from his trance only to enter a new state of shock at the sight moving above, while I fought the instinct to drop to my knees in total surrender.

"Christ have mercy!" Sabol cried, clasping his hands together.

"I shall indeed," Eden replied as she knelt beside him. "You are my soldier, yes?"

Sabol scrambled to his knees, weeping. "Yes!" he cried. "My life is yours!"

Tina and I crouched low in the rear corner, cowering in prostration and fear while Eden spoke to Sabol in hushed tones. We could only look on and listen to the savage sounds of Giddeon's hellhounds ripping apart the tailgate. My eyes struggled to maintain focus on the entity before me, this other-worldly vision broadcasting itself into our waking state. Eden's presence hung somewhere between the worldly realm of flesh and blood and the furthest depths of the subconscious. The longer I stared, the more I felt I was both awake and dreaming loudly. In hopes of maintaining some semblance of sanity from moment to moment, I began repeating to myself over and over, "This is my friend, Professor Eden Jessup. I was warned this could happen. This isn't God. There is no God. This is my friend, Professor Eden Jessup . . . "

When she was finished with Sabol, Eden stood and looked upon Tina and I with hands gently extended. Eternally hesitant, I followed Tina's lead and accepted her hand. Her palms rippled with a warm electricity nearly painful to the touch.

As the multitude of growls and snapping jaws overwhelmed all other sound, Eden gazed at the closing pack of savage beasts and smiled. Her pupils flickered with tiny ultraviolet halos as she spoke.

"Ohhhhh . . . They're beeauuutiful," she sang slowly. Each syllable floated from her lips atop a soothing chorus of vibration. Overwhelmed by reverence, Tina broke into uncontrollable weeping. I barely managed over the numerous gaps of scientific impossibilities to form a coherent statement. I knew what had to be done, but I was hardly up to the task. I had to find a way to steer this chaos, to reign it into something constructive.

"They're abominations of nature," I said to Eden carefully. "You have to stop them."

Eden laughed quietly, knowingly. Her laughter instilled a

bubbling euphoria in my heart. If I heard no other sound for all eternity, it would be enough. Every aspect of her being exuded pure ecstasy.

"If it occurs, nature allows it," she replied through a choir of voices. "Look at them and forgive. They are manifestations of unbalanced energy, striving for peace in the only way they know. They reside within a void of awareness knowing not what they do. We should find compassion for such suffering. Such forms will not vanish from existence until they are witnessed for what they are."

Giddeon's pack animals reared up and snapped the bumper clean off the truck. I pulled Tina down lower with me behind the gate as I formulated a plan. I would have to reach in deep to grasp Eden's point of view if I were to redirect her into taking action on our behalf. She needed a why. With a trillion ways she could collapse the possibilities at her fingertips, there was no telling what she would choose in this state.

"Do you want to see us all killed?" I shouted at her.

"There is no need to fear death," the heavenly voices replied through her vocal cords.

"Okay, okay . . . but," I stuttered as the horde began slashing at our rear tires. Think fast or she'll probably smile while these beasts eat us alive! But then I remembered, it wasn't about thinking fast. It was about not thinking at all. Somehow I managed to quiet the internal dialogue and let the words come by their own volition. "You said these creatures are trying to find balance!" I shouted. "They think they're going to find some kind of peace in devouring us! You know that isn't true!"

Eden arched her brow. "No, it is not," she decided. "Consuming our physical bodies would be futile." With a sudden jolt, one of the larger beasts launched forward and dashed its skull into our sidewall, punching a dent into the tailgate that sent Tina flying forward. Delighted at the view, Eden knelt over the side to get a closer look. She extended her hand over the barrier like a child at a petting zoo.

"Such rare anomalies!" she observed. "A million lifetimes will pass without witnessing such fantastic combinations of energy again! We are blessed this evening." With furious intent, the lead hellhound lunged again and snapped at Eden's arm before collapsing into the racing ground below. Eden giggled and studied her hand with intense curiosity while blood poured from a deep slice along her palm. While holding her wondrous gaze to the wound, the blood danced away from her hand and formed tiny droplets in midair before transforming into brilliant, crystalline spheres. The tiny, blood-red globes fell into an orbit about her wrist and solidified into a bracelet of rubies.

While Eden admired her "work," a fizzle of energy washed over her hand that transformed the surface of her skin into a sort of liquid. The wound itself appeared to sink beneath the surface before her skin returned to its normal texture. She was instantly healed. "You do realize that the rest of us can't do that?" I reminded her loudly.

"You'll do that and more," she replied before furling her brow. Our little debate was becoming a mild nuisance to her, and I shrunk with the realization that this entity, this enlightened version of Eden, could become irritated. I shuddered at all the insanities that could transpire if I were to anger her. Somehow, these possibilities terrified me more than being devoured by the horde.

"All right, Michael," Eden decided, lowering her burning eyes into me. "Are you so anxious for a task? Remove the cab doors, we're too heavy. Tell Gomez to bring the vehicle up to eighty eight miles an hour and to hold it. Tell him to take the bridge ahead. Yes, that bridge. Tell him to have faith and watch for the sharp turn." It took considerable willpower to rip myself from her stare.

"What?" Gomez shouted in disbelief when I relayed her message. I looked ahead to where our road led and immediately understood his response. We were racing downhill toward a massive canyon with 90-degree ledges lining either side. Our path deposited us onto a wooden bridge completely collapsed in the middle, a gap at least 20 meters or more. Such a jump with a truck this size was impossible. Gomez cranked the wheel toward the ramp, looked back hopelessly and smirked.

"Stop thinking," Eden said, "I did the math."

"Fuck it," Gomez yelled, stomping on the gas. "Hold tight." Sabol moved back into action and crawled into the cab to help Gomez remove the doors from their hinges. As soon as the second door hit the ground, our tires hit the wooden planks of the dilapidated bridge. Behind us, the creatures pounced into a high arc that would land them in the middle of the flatbed. And the rumbling of wooden slats beneath our tires went quiet. The truck was airborne.

Our vehicle sailed across the gap as the entire pack of beasts, including Giddeon, disappeared off the edge of the bridge, into the depths of the ravine. Breathing and heartbeats shuddered to a halt as we flew. For several moments, the only sound was our vehicle whistling through atmosphere.

Crashing metal and glass broke the spell as we landed hard on the far side. Astonished that our vehicle was still moving forward, Gomez looked back to make sure I had just witnessed the same event. I turned to find Eden standing at the edge of the flatbed staring back at us. "I said, 'watch for the sharp turn,'" she repeated casually.

With a violent shock, the truck slammed to a halt into the base of a massive tree. I was thrown hard into the cab, directly joined by Tina who smashed into me after a quick slide across the flatbed. Eden was launched clear from the cargo bed, over the cab, far into the jungle ahead.

Several panicked breaths passed before I realized I wasn't dead, bruised and sore, but very much alive. I leapt out and found Sabol lifting Gomez's forehead from the steering wheel wet with blood. Just as I began to assume the worst, his neck jerked backward and he moaned loudly in pain. I listened intently for any signs of life from the ravine behind us but detected none. I ran ahead to find Eden, past the hairpin turn, into the dark jungle. Upon finding her, I gasped.

Eden was spread out in a bed of tall grass and wild flowers, naked and unconscious, but breathing steadily. She was pure, visionary art. Michelangelo's depiction of the essence of heavenly femininity. The glow from beneath her skin had faded, her tattoos had resumed their normal, earthly appearance and the wound on her hand hadn't resurfaced. I took note that her bracelet of rubies remained intact. When I knelt to check her pulse she opened her eyes.

"Miiike," she yawned as if waking from an afternoon nap, "I was just swimming in my lake. Oh, you should have seen it!"

"I've seen quite enough," I said, wrapping her in my jacket.

# Awake and Dreaming Loudly

*"The Edge . . . there is no honest way to explain it because the only people who really know where it is are the ones who have gone over."*

Hunter S. Thompson

It didn't take long for Gomez to determine the truck was useless. The radiator was nearly torn in half and the front axle collapsed. However, Tina estimated we were only a few miles from Panza's base. Soon, the five of us were jogging down the dark path, striving to stay ahead of Giddeon and her hunting pack before they pulled themselves from the canyon. For me, "jogging" merely meant speed walking as quickly as my aching sides would allow.

Though Eden carried spare clothing in her pack, keeping her covered in them proved nearly impossible. Her mind was lost in ecstasy. She danced circles around us while we hiked, skipping off in all directions, stopping to smell wildflowers or to literally laugh at the moon, which was somewhat unsettling. When she would reunite with the group we would discover she had lost her shoes or her shirt along the way, forcing me to retrace her steps. At one point, she spied a dazzling white and yellow anaconda coiled high on a branch, glistening with evening dew. Gomez had to lift her over his shoulder and place her back on the trail after she insisted on worshipping the dis-interested creature by dancing beneath it.

Unlike the rest of us, Gomez was the only one brave enough to firmly pull her under control. Both Sabol and Tina simply refused to approach her, yet for very different reasons. Sabol kept his distance out of reverence. For Tina, it was fear. I, on the other hand, continued to perform my own recently discov-ered magic trick and gave up being at odds with it altogether. It seemed reasonable to assume this attitude was due to some irreparable damage to my psyche, but I suspected I was rather at peace with the notion that Eden could perform those feats in the same way I had "healed" Tina. Scientifically speaking, I was okay with that. Or perhaps I was so exhausted that the remainder of my integrity was focused on getting our asses back on that cargo plane.

After two hours of sweaty treading through brush and mud, our sad, filthy, and very sore little team reached Panza's security gate. It must have been 3 or 4 in the morning and the place looked abandoned. Gomez shook angrily at the razor wire fence and hollered at the darkened compound, "Hello?!"

Nothing stirred. Only a few, low-level lights inside the windows promised any signs of life. I peered through the gate to the far end of the facility and spied our cargo plane awaiting our departure on the runway. The lights on the wings were illuminated and the loading platform was down. Even though there was no sign of our pilots, escape suddenly seemed like a real possibility. *It's right there. We just have to board it and get the hell out of here.* Everyone stiffened when the subtle stampede of feet suddenly became audible through the distant jungles behind us, and the hoots and hollers of war cries grew disturbingly louder. Giddeon and her companions were closing in faster than we had imagined.

"Open the gate!" Sabol shouted at the compound. Several moments later, a dreary soldier pushed open a creaking, metal door at the top of a flight of concrete steps and lit a cigarette before studying us with confusion.

"We sent a truck after you putas!" he called, searching the perimeter. Gomez slammed his fist into the latch on the fence.

"Open the goddamned gate!" he hollered. "We're being followed!" Reluctantly, the soldier strolled down the stairs, grunting and sorting through his keychain.

"It's okaay! We don't neeed a keey!" Eden sang, twirling from the rear of the group like a ballerina. The guard stopped mid-stride and slack jawed to digest the bizarre scene. Eden leapt into the air, performed a lovely pirouette, and alighted gracefully upon bent knee before the padlock. With dramatic flair she grabbed the lock and blew into the keyhole. Then, prancing atop tiptoes, she disappeared behind the group, fluttering her fingers as if presenting some fantastic feat.

The guard now scanned us one at a time with heavy suspicion. He snatched up the padlock, which, by the way, Eden had absolutely not magically unlocked and opened it with his key. I quietly apologized as we passed through. "It's been a long trip," I explained sheepishly. He shook his head and locked the gate behind us.

Upon entering, we were shuttled directly to the center of the control room where a handful of soldiers glared at us from behind screens. Clearly our situation forced more of the staff to be awake at this hour than usual. Panza burst onto the operations floor red faced and shouting.

"Where the hell is my truck?" he demanded. "Where's my men?" Try as Gomez did, Panza refused to listen to our warnings about the forces that would soon be at his door. When he threatened to toss us all into his holding cell in the basement for the rest of our lives until he had his answers, I wholeheartedly believed him.

"You need to listen! Your soldiers were killed by natives that Reverend Kane's missionaries recruited," Gomez explained angrily. "The same people who murdered Ramirez's team. The same forces behind all the other reports! They'll stop at nothing to keep us from boarding that plane."

"You've got maybe fifteen minutes, tops, before they're outside your fence," Tina added. "Go see for yourself." Panza exploded with disbelief and ordered another team to locate his men. He refused to hear logic when we insisted that they, too, would be murdered.

"Tell me," Panza laughed angrily, massaging his eyes. "How big is this 'army of locals' you've managed to piss off?" We all shared an awkward hesitation.

"Eleven, twelve?" Sabol replied.

"Maybe more," Tina added.

"So, it could be as many as thirteen people out there?" Panza asked pointedly, stepping closer. "How are a handful of Indians going to overrun my base? You do realize they give us actual, military grade weapons out here in the jungle? I have a dozen men on duty tonight armed with . . ."

"Your weapons will be useless," Eden interrupted delightfully, shimmying to the front of the group. All of us averted our eyes to the floor. We wanted to slap a hand over her mouth, but none of us dared. I tried shushing her, but Panza was far too amused.

"Oh no, by all means, let her speak!" he snorted. "I want to hear this." As if preparing for a theater audition, Eden fanned her hands and struck a pose in the center of the control room.

"Our team has traveled far and wide, in both body and spirit!" she began emphatically. "We have tracked Reverend Kane's journey through your land to a series of sacred, interdimensional rifts which pulled our souls into the deepest gorges of Tibet, and into mystical forests in India!" She paced the room, demanding everyone's attention as her momentum grew. Every soldier immediately dropped what they were doing to watch the show.

"We have battled the forces of darkness, and been blessed by the heavens!" she roared. "We have trained under the most powerful shaman on Earth, our minds have been expanded, broken apart, and made whole again by the sacred San Pedro cactus! And the Datura leaves! Yopo snuff! And the holy secretions of the Sapo frog!" She alighted atop a desk and began leaping from one station to the next, leaning down to make eye contact with each soldier as she passed.

"We have learned the ancient secrets behind the all-pervading fields of unified consciousness; techniques that Reverend Kane and his missionaries are now misusing for their own, nefarious purposes! Indeed, gentlemen, the army that charges to your doorstep this very moment is equipped with the lost art of shapeshifting! They will exploit that power in the most dreadful ways imaginable and they will tear your walls down brick by brick and devour anyone who stands in the way of their mission of striking us down." She leapt from the last desk in the row, returned to center stage at the middle of the control room and slowly drifted a pointing finger back and forth across her audience.

"The only chance any of you have of living through the night is to step out of our way and let us pass. The choice is yours." Unsure of what was taking place exactly, one of Panza's men slowly rose to his feet and began to clap until he realized that this was not, in fact, a performance.

The jail cell door slammed shut with a loud Ka-chink as Panza glared at us through the bars. "I don't give a damn what your government tells me to do with you. No one's going anywhere until I have my answers," he spat. Eden pounced onto the bars and hissed maniacally into his face.

"By the time you realize that I already gave you a straight answer, you'll be disemboweled!" she hollered. "When they get here, you're gunna beg to be locked inside this cage with us!"

Panza pushed his hand between the bars and shoved her face backward with enough force to throw her butt to the floor. By the time I helped her up he had disappeared down the long, narrow hall and back up the stairs. As Eden straightened her shirt, something caught her eye on her upper, right hip. She spun around and pulled the back of her pants down to get a clearer view. "When the hell did I get a new tattoo?" she hollered.

There, just behind her hip bone was an exquisitely detailed, full color tattoo of Kaylah's tree frog, Francis. Some newly-formed section of my brain exhaled with relief and said: Oh, good! I wondered what had happened to the little guy. He's right there tattooed onto Eden's rear end, so he's okay. And, somehow, that seemed like sound logic.

# Natural Tendencies

*"What is it about nature that is so terrifying to the modern mind? Why is it so intolerable? Because nature is fundamentally indifferent. It's unforgiving, uninterested. If you live or die, succeed or fail, feel pleasure or pain, it doesn't care. That's intolerable to us."*

Michael Crichton

At the farthest end of the dingy, concrete hall that extended the full length of the compound, two soldiers rummaged through our belongings per Panza's orders. Everything we had carried with us was now spread over a large folding table. Eden studied them intently, taking in every move they made. When they reached her backpack, they pulled out the leaves and vines Kaylah had given her along with her ziplock bag of marijuana. The soldiers were delighted with their find.

"That isn't yours!" Eden shouted at them, pointing through the bars. "Put that back!" And that's when the frequency sailed through the tiny, barred window overhead. The next level of panic set in for us all, except for Eden, still focused on her confiscated weed. No one said it aloud, no one had to. We were now feeder mice dumped into a Cobra cage. The soldiers tearing through our belongings ignored the muffled sounds from outside. One of them began stuffing a fat, green nugget into Eden's pipe while the other shoved the remainder into his pocket. "I saw that, pendejo!" Eden shouted.

"Shut up, puta!" he bellowed. His partner made kissing noises in her direction. Eden smiled playfully, pressing her breasts into the bars and cocking her hip to the side.

"Well I do declare, it would be my pleasure to give you a kiss, soldier," she sang with a sassy, Southern belle accent. She now had their full attention.

"What the hell are you doing?" I sighed. Eden put her hand behind her back and wagged a finger for me to shut up. A fevered commotion could be heard through the window slit above: branches snapping, leaves crunching, earth trampled, all followed by the faint sound of inhuman groans and snarls.

Standing on tiptoes, Sabol grabbed the bars on the narrow window and muscled himself up to take a peek. It took him only a brief glance to confirm what we already knew. Giddeon's army had shifted once again, and they were just outside the perimeter fence.

"It's hard to tell in the dark, but it looks like they've shifted into a brand new variety of awful, nightmarish shit," he lamented. From the far end of the hall the soldiers couldn't hear the trampling going on outdoors. They joked loudly and crept toward our cell as Eden twisted the bottom of her T-shirt into knots, exposing ever more midriff. They knew it was a game and they didn't care. They probably hadn't seen this kind of entertainment in a long while. I almost felt sorry for them. They had no idea what they were playing with.

"Well, now, aren't you gentlemen going to bring a lady a gift?" Eden cooed.

"I don't see any lady here!" one soldier laughed.

"What kind of gift you want, you crazy bitch?"

"Mmmm . . . weed makes me wet," she said, running her hands down her thighs. The guard lit up her pipe, took a long toke and held it out as he approached.

"You mean this weed here?" he smiled. "This is pretty good shit! But we grow better."

"Umm-hmmm," Eden moaned before turning her head to shoot a nauseated expression back at Tina. "Seriously, how do you stomach men?" Eden whispered to her. "They are such Nasty. Fucking. Pricks."

"I'm sitting right here," I reminded her. Upon reaching the cell, the guard kept the pipe just out of reach from Eden's lips as he and his partner reached their grubby hands into the cell to caress her waist and squeeze her ass, all while Eden performed the world's fakest sighs. At this point, I actually feared what she would do with the two of them.

"Tell me how bad you want to suck on this," the guard waved the pipe back and forth in front of her mouth. "What you gunna do for a hit?"

"Ohhh, once I get some of that inside of me, I'm going to

blllow yyyyour mmmminds." The guards laughed and shook their heads; they couldn't handle any more teasing. One of them fired up his lighter and moved it toward the bowl of the pipe. As casually as possible, the rest of us scooted down the bench to get as far from Eden as possible, as far from ground zero as the confines of the tiny cell would allow. Sabol crammed into Gomez who cowered in fear against Tina, until all three pressed me into the corner so hard I couldn't breathe.

I peeked between my fingers just long enough to see the flame touch Eden's pipe. Suddenly, the wretched sounds of metal bending and twisting screeched through the window above. Only the five of us knew what was taking place. The fence was being ripped to shreds. Soon all the power shut down with a loud, electrical thud. A moment later, the pitch black was interrupted by emergency flood lights that bathed everything in a sickly, red haze.

Before Eden could steal a drag from her pipe, the guard absentmindedly lowered it from the cell to wonder at the situation. She swiped at his hand through the bars, but he pulled away and shoved the pipe into his pocket. With a deafening scream, an overhead siren went off a moment before a series of explosive booms shook the concrete walls. Dust and chunks of plaster fell from the ceiling all around us with each impact. Both guards broke into a sprint down the hall toward the staircase in response.

"Fucking assholes!" Eden shouted after them. "Bring that back!" She turned and collapsed against the bars before turning quizzically to find the rest of us huddled in a tiny ball. The crashing and crumbling sounds from the floors overhead were like dump trucks caught in a series of head-on collisions. We could only assume we were hearing Giddeon's horde systematically punch holes into the concrete walls. The sounds of giant bricks crashing to the floor shook the ceiling and a number of frantic shouts soon followed along with bursts of rapid gun fire from every direction.

Sabol leapt up and shook at the bars in desperation. All we could do is stare helplessly at the ceiling, listen to the muffled sounds of slaughter, and wonder how long it would take Giddeon's hellhounds to realize there was a lower level to the station they were tearing through.

Our answer came bursting through the door in a pulsing sweat at the top of the stairs. It was Panza, bleeding and wielding a long-barreled shotgun. Wild-eyed and panicked, he backed onto the landing firing madly through the entry before slamming the heavy, metal door shut and locking it hard. With his back against the door, he reloaded his weapon under trembling hands until a thunder from the far side of the door propelled him off his feet and sent him tumbling down the staircase. After a second, explosive pounding on the far side of the door, Panza was back on his feet and running toward us, anxiously sifting through a large ring of keys. "Move!" he screamed, "I'm coming in!"

The door at the top of the stairs exploded from its hinges and crashed to the floor. In its wake, a member of Giddeon's swarm launched through the entry onto the landing. Even Panza froze a moment too long. The beast was impossibly hideous, but shockingly enough, Gomez actually screamed out loud.

Though its overall dimensions were similar to the ones from earlier, it had taken an entirely new, deadly shape. A morbid amalgamation of deceased insect and spider. Its bristly, black legs arched into a sharp "V" above the creature's body yet its torso was flattened and completely covered with segmented armor, much like that of a beetle's. At the end of a gruesomely long, jointed neck was the head of a fly with massive, compound eyes that protruded unnaturally far from a decomposing exoskeleton. "Well, that is just awful," Eden chirped.

The only anatomical feature that didn't resemble insect or arachnid was its immense mouth filled with yellow, corroded teeth. As it moved forward, its lower jaw hung low with vicious spasms that splattered black, liquid gore from its mouth. Beneath its terrible head, spiked mandibles snapped back and forth with the force of hedging shears. Gomez stumbled back onto the bench in horror. Seeing him react with such unbridled fear was almost as frightening as the beast itself.

The moment it spied Panza, this tragic configuration gracefully floated down the stairs with a rhythmic flutter of powerful legs. When it reached the hall, it struggled to stuff its massive body into the narrow passageway. I cringed at how this monstrosity could carry itself with such elegance. Somehow it made the scene even more nightmarish, as if the laws of nature had actually intended it to exist. Its girth filled the entire width of the corridor, forcing its spidery legs to punch holes into the walls to inch forward. Outside our cell door Panza dropped his weapon to rummage for the key while panning back and forth between the lock and the oncoming creature. Eden pounced onto the bars and seethed at him.

"Oh, now you want to join the crazy gringos in the cage, huh?" she hissed, shaking at the bars. Panza ignored her and jammed a key into the lock. It wouldn't budge. Wrong key. "Which one is it, I wonder?" Eden cooed near his ear. The shapeshifter had now pushed its girth halfway up the stretch. Panza fumbled with another key. "Are you sure that's the right one?" Eden asked. "I don't think it is. Doesn't look right to me." Her tone became abruptly casual to punctuate her sarcasm as the man fumbled beneath shaking hands, talking madly to himself as he searched.

"They won't get me!" he muttered. "I won't let them. I'll die in here. I'll die in the blast, but not like that, no. No fucking way. Not like that."

"You know, I have a random key stuffed into my backpack," Eden continued, ignoring his tirade. "Been there for years. Can't figure out what it's for, but, well, you know how it is when you're too afraid to throw it away, am I right? I mean, what if one day I figure out what it goes to and then I'd be all like, 'Fuck me, I just threw that little bastard away!'"

Everyone in the cell gazed at her antics in horror, too overwhelmed to tell her to knock it off. The beast was nearly down the stretch. Klink! Wrong key again. Panza snagged another; he had moments left.

"What do you mean you'd rather die in the blast?" Tina hollered at Panza. He didn't hear her.

"You know what would be ironic?" Eden asked, resting her chin on the bars. "What if the key in my backpack, the one your men just dumped all over that desk back there, just so happened to also open this lock?" she sighed and turned back to us quizzically. "Wait. Would that technically qualify as irony? I think so," she said, turning back to him. "In fact, I think that might just be the very fucking definition of irony."

"What blast are you taking about?" Tina demanded again. The insect was at Panza's back. He inserted another key. The creature raised its front legs as it moved in to attack, releasing a tortured scream that sounded almost human. Ka-chink! The gate clicked open; he had found the key.

The beast lunged down. Panza spun around the gate and shoved it closed. Before the lock could catch, the creature pushed the entirety of its terrible mass through the door and landed directly atop the poor man in the middle of the cell.

The rest of us leapt up to the bench while just below us, razor-sharp mandibles clamped around Panza's neck like a bear trap. Even Eden cupped a hand over her mouth at the amount of blood, suddenly shocked at the reality that it all ended so poorly. Sabol dashed around the writhing mass on the floor and wedged himself through the open gate.

"Let's go!" he demanded, snapping us from our collective trance. One by one, we sidestepped the feeding-frenzy while trying desperately not to draw attention to ourselves and es-cape the cell, all while a pool of blood flooded the floor. When Eden passed the skirmish, she leaned toward Panza's ear just before he lost consciousness.

"I am sooo sorry," she whispered. Sabol was about to slam the gate shut to trap the beast inside the cell when awful real-ization dawned: Gomez was still inside. He hadn't moved from his spot on the bench. His eyes were glazed over at the sight of Panza's body being devoured by an enormous insect.

No matter how loudly we screamed or pounded at the bars, it was of no use; Gomez had been pushed beyond the point of no return. We never even saw the cracks forming. Somehow, the man had shattered all at once. Sabol couldn't risk holding the door open any longer; at any moment the creature would lose interest in Panza and realize its predicament. Out of utter frustration, Sabol grabbed Panza's shotgun from the floor and fired madly into the beast's back, only to have buckshot ricochet from the smooth, black armor. Helplessly, we stood back and watched as Gomez allowed himself to be dragged onto the floor by giant pincers. He didn't put up a fight. He didn't even respond when the insect began to consume him.

If the man had ever entertained a personal theory about what was really going on with this mess, he never shared it. Only now did I realize how much I appreciated that silence. Even if he didn't mean it to, it exerted a kind of strength I had come to rely on. And now he was being eaten alive by his own worst fears. Life was stranger than I could imagine. Maybe all I've ever known in this world was what was taking place right in front of me.

There was no time to mourn. After snagging our belongings, we snuck up the stairs and listened to the violent clatter booming through the far side of the door, the only way in or out of the basement. The screams of soldiers had long died out and the only sounds we heard now were wood, concrete, and metal being smashed to pieces in the horde's unrelenting hunt for us. Without weapons (or Eden's marijuana), our only chance was to make it to the runway without being noticed and hope our pilots were still onboard, and in one piece. Hope. That's a laugh.

Sabol quietly cracked open the door to reconnoiter the situation. Horrible creatures darted furiously in every direction, tearing apart doors, overturning desks, smashing air ducts and tiling. Each beast was now a completely different, horrific shape—some unnatural combination of predatory animal, lizard, or insect. The only common feature was their overall appearance and the piercing odor of something that had died weeks ago. And still, beneath each one of them, there was a human being looking out through those eyes.

If Giddeon was among the swarm, she had shifted out of her deceased-Medusa form and was now completely unrecognizable. Everywhere we looked, blood and carnage graced the floors, walls, and ceilings; not a single soldier had been left standing.

With our team whittled down to four, Eden, Tina, and I followed Sabol along the main corridor to the exit. We ducked windows and leapt passed entryways, praying one of the creatures didn't come directly up the hall. We passed the command room where a downed but still operational computer screen in front of a dead soldier caught Tina's eye. With a limber tuck and roll, she risked being detected by the creatures tearing the room apart to move toward the desk to inspect the flashing red warning on the display. Sabol and Eden quietly seized a couple of discarded handguns from amongst the wreckage while we waited impatiently.

"We need to be a mile away from this base in ten minutes," Tina whispered when she returned. "Panza must've lost his mind. He called in an airstrike onto his own base from Lima. This entire facility is going to be carpeted by thermobarics."

Judging by his terrified expression, Sabol knew precisely what that meant. He made a panicked gesture for us to follow as he barreled straight down the corridor toward the exit. We didn't have time to look back to see what might be chasing us.

The low morning sun blinded us when we dashed through the doors and sped through the small junkyard of military equipment and broken-down vehicles to the loading bay of our plane. As we approached there was still no sign of our pilots or movement of any kind. We stopped just beyond the platform to peek up into the darkened cargo hold where we spied three wooden crates on the top of the ramp. I was nearly certain those weren't there before.

With a finger over her lips, Eden tossed her backpack to me and kicked off her shoes. Intuiting her plan, Tina did the same and the two of them crept up the platform and into the cargo hold, all without making a single creak in the metal flooring. I thought I heard a muffled thud while Sabol and I kept watch, but I couldn't tell from which direction it originated.

My heart sang with hope when the engines suddenly fired up

and the propellers began to roll into action. Could it be possible? Could we really be getting out of here? Sabol lowered his weapon and I followed him up the plank to investigate. When my eyes adjusted to the low light, the dismal sight ahead sent acid through my veins.

At the far end of the loading bay stood Giddeon, filthy and badly bruised, but in human form nonetheless, holding a gun to Eden's head while Tina lay unconscious on the floor, bleeding from her temple. Behind them, her partner Bowen leveled a machine gun on our pilots. Eden peered up at me with apologetic eyes. Sabol immediately snapped up his weapon to take aim on Giddeon.

"You pull that trigger, my brother will end you here and now," Giddeon snarled. Behind her, Bowen smiled and winked.

"Awfully kind of ya'll to arrange a flight home for us!" Bowen hollered from the cockpit. He poked one of the pilots with the tip of the barrel and the engines picked up momentum. Slowly, the plane began to pull away. "Makes it a hell of a lot easier to haul our cargo!"

I looked down at the wooden crates on the edge of the ramp. One of the boxes was filled with segments of twisting gray vines, another was stuffed with thin, pointed leaves; the same two species inside Eden's pack I was now carrying. The third crate contained a pile of white, trumpet-shaped blossoms I didn't recognize, but I knew what they were. They were the grenades for heaven; the source of the scopolamine they used to poison their ayahuasca to near toxic levels, to leave only the reptilian brain at the helm of the probability wave. They were carrying enough raw ingredients to dose a small army.

"I'm afraid we can't take you boys along with us!" Giddeon said as the plane aligned with the runway. "You two will be more trouble than you're worth, but I promise not to let your women go to waste."

"What does that mean?" I demanded.

"The Lord has great plans for them!" she replied, gesturing to Eden with her pistol. "Especially this one. My oh my, has she gathered such an incredible reservoir of potential energy to help fuel His return. I see it now. This was the design all along. You know, He really does work in mysterious ways. I have to admit, for a while there, I nearly lost faith when I saw what your Professor Jessup here was capable of. I wasn't sure how this was all going to play out, but now I see His plan! She was here to strengthen my resolve, to weed out the weak. Professor Jessup showed us the gaps in our armor! And now here you both stand before me with so many offerings in hand! You two delivered the last pieces of the puzzle just like the Roto hoped you would!"

"What the hell are you talking about?" Sabol shouted. "They thought it was a mistake to save you! They wanted to stop you!"

"A mistake!" she laughed. "You believe they wanted to stop us? Soldier, why do you think Sadhu convinced his tribe to save us to begin with? The Craneo Roto are savages. Didn't you ever ask what made us so special?"

"Sadhu told us the story!" I shouted. "You were dying! They took pity on you!" Giddeon laughed harder and cocked her head in wonder at our ignorance.

"Pity?! Is that what you think? I suppose you never had the chance to see the reverend before the cancer, did you? You never saw his true face." At that, she broke into an hysterical laughter that nearly brought her to tears. My mind spun out of control at her suggestion. The plane picked up speed and the hydraulic platform begin to rise.

"Oh, that is pathetic!" she giggled, trying to contain herself. "You spent how many days with Sadhu in that gorge and you never asked him his real name, you never recognized his eyes! I thought you woulda figured that part out by now. Professor Huxley, we're everywhere in God's eye at the same time, until we choose a single place to be in!

"From another path of choices, the good Reverend Kane turned to science instead of God, and he ended up in the farthest corner of Tibet with a godless tribe who took away his name and gave him a new one. Sadhu! What a joke. You aren't nearly as intelligent as I thought you were, professor, but, still,

I do have to thank you for these two, wonderful offerings of sacrifice! I feel awkward, really. I didn't get you anything."

Behind us, the platform was halfway up. To my right, Sabol steadied his aim on Giddeon. In the cockpit ahead, Bowen turned his machine gun toward us. "Come to think of it, I do have a couple of gifts for the both of you!" Giddeon said with a smile. "One for the each of ya!" She fired twice.

Her blasts punched into the metal flooring we had stood on a moment prior to Sabol pulling me backwards through the open hatch. Giddeon lunged forward and continued firing, pounding bullets into the plating as we both rolled down the platform, onto the receding runway a moment before the hydraulic door clamped shut. My rag doll body spun and bounced over the black gravel in a painful blur. When we finally tumbled to a stop, I lifted my head just in time to see our stolen cargo plane take flight and disappear behind the green canopy.

My ankle and knee throbbed in pain from the fall. I crawled my way to Sabol where he lay face down in the dust. I turned him over to check for a pulse, but before I could, a military jet screamed just above the treeline and dove into a tight circle around the base. After a tight, quick pass, a small hatch opened and a cascade of dark, cylindrical objects fell gracefully from its belly.

This is what a real ending looks like, I thought as a dozen bombs fell slowly around the circumference of the compound. What was worse, I had lost the fight because I had been blind to the obvious details right in front of me. Now, the only thing my newfound sight would illuminate would be my own death, perhaps the real one this time. Whatever that meant. At least it would be quick.

# PART SEVEN

## Wings of Fire

*"Have you thought of an ending?"*
*"Yes, several, and all are dark and unpleasant."*
*"Oh, that won't do! Books ought to have good endings. How would this
do: and they all settled down and lived together happily ever after?"*
*"It will do well, if it ever came to that."*

J.R.R. Tolkien

THERMOBARIC, FUEL-AIR EXPLOSIVE (FAE):
DEFINITION. A fuel-air explosive device consists of a
container of fuel and two separate explosive charges. After the
munition is dropped or fired, the first explosive charge bursts
open the container at a predetermined height and disperses the
fuel in a cloud that mixes with atmospheric oxygen (the size
of the cloud varies with the size of the munition). The cloud
of fuel flows around objects and into structures. The second
charge then detonates the cloud, creating a massive blast wave.
The blast wave destroys reinforced buildings and equipment,
and kills anything in its path.

Somewhere around twenty meters above the ground, the
plummeting canisters burst open in succession, releasing a
grayish-yellow spray of gas into the atmosphere, a far cry from
the deadly explosions I had anticipated. Evidently, those were
still yet to come. Sabol snapped upright to gawk at the scene.
"We need to be out of here before he circles back around and
detonates that shit," he growled, scanning the perimeter.

"Can we run for it?" I shouted.

"Not from thermobarics. Blastwaves'll wipe out everything
in the area. The only way we survive is to fly out," he hollered,
studying the piles of discarded military junk behind the building. "Cover your face and follow me."

Streams of smoke rained down in every direction as we ran

to the edge of the junkyard, to the old single-prop plane we had noticed when we first landed. Of course, we had no idea what sort of condition it was in, but it was our only option. We leapt into the cockpit as volatile gases steadily filled the air, burning our eyes and tightening our throats. Sabol turned the engine over several times as the view through the window became a dingy, yellow mist.

The engine didn't start, but it didn't appear he had expected it to. With fast, precise movements, he strapped a pair of dusty flight goggles from the dash around his head and wrapped his nose and mouth with a handkerchief before jumping back onto the tarmac. I stared into the skies as he worked, listening for the jet circling somewhere above the gas cloud growing thicker by the second.

Outside, Sabol siphoned gasoline from a broken military jeep through an old radiator hose, into a plastic jug. His movements grew ever more chaotic as he poured two buckets of fuel into our tank, blinded by the fumes. I desperately wanted to help him in some way, but I had no idea what to do. The moment he leapt back into the cockpit he was stomping on a lever in the floorboard, pulling a choke on the control panel and frantically switching the ignition on and off. When the engine coughed up a black cloud of smoke, I stupidly asked, "Could our engine ignite the gas we're soaking in?"

He froze as he considered the question. "I'll let you know in a sec." With eyes clenched shut, he turned the key again and the engine clattered. And then it roared to life. Directly ahead, the propeller spun into a blur. "Not so far," he replied.

Behind us, the doors on the military base exploded from their hinges and a wave of vicious, shapeshifted creatures poured onto the tarmac. Sabol did his best to ignore the latest dilemma, aimed the aircraft down the runway and began pulling the throttle. I gawked helplessly through the window at the horde scrambling over the junkyard to reach us.

Everything went into slow motion while the plane rumbled up to liftoff speed with a half dozen jaws snapping at our wings and clawing at our side panels. Our tires rose from the runway as the Peruvian military jet screamed over the treetops to unleash its second payload of canisters from its belly. Sabol slammed the stick to one side and rolled us into a vertical turn to skirt between the falling detonators. My stomach dropped into a liquid mess and I sunk into my chair, gripping my seatbelt straps with white knuckles.

After a brief, eerie pause, the world below us transformed into an ocean of light. The base, the creatures, and all of the surrounding jungle vanished behind an expanding, white cloud that rolled through the air in wave after deafening wave. I curled into a ball and pushed my palms over my ears with all my might as our cockpit shook so violently I could only wait for it all to shatter into a thousand pieces. While I cowered from the blast, the muscles in Sabol's arms transformed into steel cables as he wrestled the yoke beneath the onslaught of the growing ball of fire licking our wings.

Gradually the rumbling died away and I could hear the whine of our engine once again. When the smoke cleared, we found every window had cracked and the exterior had been severely scorched, yet the craft was still airborne. Shaky and full of holes, but airborne. When we finally leveled into a normal flight pattern toward Bolivia, I nearly passed out. My partner, on the other hand, allowed himself only a brief moment to sink into his chair from exhaustion in the aftermath.

Although we both knew what had to be done now, I don't think it would have mattered to him if I was "in" or "out" at this point. Sabol was convinced that a living prophet had personally requested him to fulfill a divine duty, and nothing in this world or the next would stand in his way. He would find Eden and deliver ayahuasca to her. It was his only purpose. Because I didn't have a better plan to save everyone I cared about in this world, it was now my plan as well. And unless we wanted to follow a trail of dead FBI and SWAT up to Kane's church at Gold Hill back in Colorado, we would have to do it ourselves. We were both in agreement that all anyone could really do to help at this point would be to stay the hell out of our way. Whatever Kane had planned was sure to dwarf whatever we'd seen from his missionaries thus far. And Eden was certainly the only one who might be able to put a stop to it.

Before we landed in La Paz to refuel and collect supplies, I had already crushed the vines and leaves from Eden's backpack against the floorboards into a fine pulp with the butt of an old shotgun I found buried beneath the seats. My overwhelming doubt and confusion about everything in my world fueled my angry pounding. I couldn't help but think about the dynamic: Strong emotion fueling kinetic energy. Fuel for work, energy converted to matter, $E=Mc^2$. It was either a mantra or my mind had been reduced to random firings.

I tried and failed to imagine just what Kane's plan was exactly. All the pieces of information I had collected over the days added up to something big, but now the massive shit Giddeon had taken on my brain was doing an excellent job of distracting me from making any meaningful connections. Was it her intention? Or was it simply the truth?

"Do you believe her?" I asked Sabol. He knew what I meant, but pretended not to. "Are Sadhu and Kane the same person?"

He scoffed at the question. "Who gives a shit?" he scowled. "It changes nothing."

I envied his black and white perspective. No matter how many times I rearranged the patterns, I couldn't make all the pieces fall into line. The moment I felt I was closing in on a coherent vision of what may be waiting for us at Gold Hill, it would fall apart just as quickly. I knew this was because I couldn't trust myself to weed out truth from fiction any longer. I had too little to work with. I questioned everything that happened in Tibet, everything I thought I learned and, especially, everything that man who called himself Sadhu had taught me. Were Sadhu and Kane actually two different versions of one person from two vastly different life choices, brought face to face with one another by the power of the Dreaming Tree? And, if they were the same person, had Kaylah been aware of it?

My gauge for determining "normal" had been shattered, and yet I couldn't deny all the insane phenomena we had all shared.

That made every scenario as equally ridiculous and as probable as the next. I felt ill. All the possibilities were paralyzing. The dark gaps in my mind were opening all over again. Enlightenment, I was learning, was a slippery abstraction, coming and going on a whim.

After a brief excursion through La Paz airport, we were soon back in the air with a small load of supplies that would suffice for now: A high powered slow cooker that Sabol somehow managed to liberate from a food truck, a roll of duct tape, a case of bottled water, and a box of energy bars. The closest we could get to Gold Hill, Colorado by plane would be Boulder's municipal airport, the same location Giddeon would most likely land. From there we'd have to drive into the foothills to the compound, where I could only assume Eden and Tina would be delivered.

"They're gunna arrest us the moment we land, ya know," Sabol mentioned casually.

"Or maybe we're just being paranoid," I offered hopefully.

"Maybe," he admitted, "but that doesn't mean they aren't after us. Panza was convinced we lost our minds in that jungle. He would have relayed info like that to Downey. It's just you and me now, buddy. We have to save the world."

I laughed heartily at his melodrama, but abruptly stopped when I realized he was dead serious. A sort of emptiness enveloped me when recent events reminded me that maybe he was right, at least on some level. Sabol reached between the seats and snagged the double-barreled shotgun I had found behind the seats. While holding the flight controls with one knee, he cracked open the chamber with an authority I knew I'd never possess. He was now in full blown superhero mode, and I envisioned myself as his trusty sidekick. I was more than happy to accept that. Not a bad upgrade from Professor Dorkus McNobody.

"Jesus Christ!" he hollered when he studied the chamber. "Did you know this was loaded when you were pounding on those vines back there?" I absolutely had not. In my desperation for the right-shaped tool it hadn't even occurred to me.

Sabol stared at me as if I were a stupid child, but eventually gave in to a disgruntled head shake of acceptance. He knew the true identity of his sidekick: A balding, out-of-shape college professor who avoided real danger, generally shrunk away from women, and feared the outdoors; a fraud who hid behind a soft blanky of opiates.

"We're gunna die," Sabol muttered to himself. Leave it to me to find a loophole in the Hero's Journey. I travel into the depths of hell to emerge every bit as clueless and frightened. At that, I popped another OxyContin into my mouth. That's my motto: Live and don't learn.

"But, this story isn't about you, you egomaniac," I heard Iboga's voice echo from the abyss as I chewed. I soon gave up fighting the nods and surrendered to the deepest sleep I'd had in days.

# Addiction to Solidity

*"True wisdom comes to each of us when we realize how little we understand about life, ourselves, and the world around us."*

Socrates

The sky beyond the small, cracked windows was a dreary, bluish black when I awoke. With a heavy yawn, Sabol explained we were only a few hours from Boulder's airport. I cursed myself for sleeping so long and leapt into action. I tossed the crushed vines and leaves into the slow cooker with three bottles of water. Steady heat for five or six hours, Kaylah had instructed, and now I was behind. I shouldn't have taken more OxyContin. The first chance I had to be of any use and I drop the ball.

I duct-taped the lid onto the Crock-Pot and plugged it into an adapter Sabol had rigged for it. If it wasn't for him, I would've been dead long ago. Only then did I notice that Sabol was half asleep. After a pointless debate over his actual level of exhaustion ("I'm fine," he insisted), we both arrived at the same conclusion: I'd have to fly while he slept. Neither of us liked the idea of me taking the wheel, but we had no other choice.

After a crash course on roll, pitch, and yaw, I was gripping the yoke with stiff, white knuckles and terrified of moving it in any direction. I kept envisioning anxiety overtaking my nerves. In a sudden, nervous flinch I would roll the plane into an out of control, downward spiral. I decided not to share my fear with Sabol as he struggled to let himself trust me behind the controls and get some rest.

Strangely enough, I began to get a feel for it all. The revelation came more so out of boredom than anything else. After I finally understood the flight controls weren't so sensitive as to send us into a tailspin with the smallest twitch, I gradually found myself incrementally pushing the control column forward and backward, left and right, farther and farther. In response, I could feel the flaps shifting up and down, how it changed the wind flow over the wings. And suddenly, I saw the elegance behind flight. I could sense the wings stretching out to either side as if they were extensions of my body. Now I understood why we imagined angels to be winged creatures.

Sabol smiled lazily behind closed eyes as I experimented with tracing slow, gentle waves up and down through the air. "See?" he said. "You're getting a feel for it."

"I hate sounding cliché," I said. "But it's new to me, so to hell with that. Flying really is an art."

"Damn right it is," he agreed and went back to sleep.

Even after Sabol was awake and alert again, I insisted on staying at the controls. Something beautifully abstract was engaged the longer I soared. The ancient part of my psyche that craved direct experience took over, and my troubles about "which way is really up"slipped into the background. Bubbling up from the center of my newfound peace was a new insight, another vibrating string of truth. I realized that, as far as our situation was concerned, there was only one thing I was truly certain of, I had absolutely no idea what was going on.

Ah, that impenetrable force field that kept blocking my path again and again, admitting my ultimate ignorance. What was it about that notion that refused to die, I wondered? Suddenly we were hit by a rising pocket of warm air that pushed up on the left wing, tossing us to the side.

"Okay, don't fight it!" Sabol instructed. "What you do is . . . " But, I had already intuited how to handle it. I allowed the plane to gently roll off the airstream before I gracefully counteracted its momentum. "Never mind," Sabol laughed quietly. "Yeah, that's what you should do."

I wasn't a trained Marine, I wasn't a shaman, and I certainly wasn't a superhero. But if I had learned anything at all since I'd left the safety of the university, it was that maybe I didn't need to add anything to my personality. This was rather a game of subtraction. I could see that what I needed to do now defied all common rationale. I, too, would have to drink the ayahuasca brew before we landed. If there was any truth behind tapping into radical perspectives that were equally as valid as the one

I had been referring to as normal, I wouldn't fully connect
with them until I was under the influence of a hallucinogen.
I would have to return to a similar frequency under which I
had first attained this new information. And, this time, the full
burden of responsibility would fall on me. I would ingest them
intentionally and retain my ability to choose. As I considered
this, I found the OxyContin to be a distraction that dulled the
full experience of flying. For the first time in my life, I wasn't
enjoying my opiates.

Just after passing over New Mexico into Colorado, Sabol
took over pilot duty once again. Flying was addicting, but I
had no desire to attempt a landing. When we were about thirty
minutes outside of Boulder's airport, I dunked an empty water
bottle into the cooker. It had only been brewing for about
three hours, but I figured enough of the alkaloids had been
extracted at this point to make a more than adequate impact
on me. Sabol had rigged the cooker to a cigarette lighter power
inverter, so I could finish the brew for Eden on the ride up to
Gold Hill. Once we found a car, that was. The universe just
needed to provide us with one.

It took all my resources to restrain my gag reflex as I downed
the warm liquid in one gulp. Ayahausca, I learned, tasted like
the blood of some old, ancient thing. "You sure that'll help?"
Sabol asked as I succumbed to a coughing fit.

"No . . . well, yes. I don't know."

"Whatever you think you need to fuel your devotion to the
cause."

"You think I lack devotion?" I said defensively. "Eden is my
heart and soul and I'm in love with Tina, how could you question . . ."

"Is that what you think we're doing?" he gasped. "You think
we're saving your girlfriends? Jesus, man, have you been paying
attention to current events? Okay, brother, whatever you need
to think."

"Yeah and you think we're walking into some religious battle
between good and evil, so . . . whatever you need to think."
He growled quietly. Before we could inflame another pointless

debate, a small ocean of flashing red and blue lights emerged from the dark valley at the base of the foothills ahead. Boulder's airport was lit up like a Christmas tree for us. As we approached, ice crystals began to form in the corners of the windows while the details moved into focus below. The entire stretch of the main runway was lined with police vehicles of all types, SWAT, unmarked black vans, two fire trucks, and an ambulance. It was a small battalion.

At first we assumed the parade was for us, and perhaps it was at first, but it appeared they had since directed their attention on the more pressing matter at hand. All of the forces below were zeroed in on the stolen cargo plane that had landed well ahead of us. Just as Sabol guessed, they had tracked it back into United airspace, just as they had certainly been tracking us, too.

We circled once more to reconnoiter a landscape that appeared more and more to be a hostage situation in full swing. If that was the case, it would likely end badly. We were low on fuel and out of options, leaving us with little choice but to land and join the party. Perhaps if Downey was down there, and he most certainly was, he would listen to our advice on how best to handle the situation. Maybe we could somehow convince SWAT to not storm the cargo plane; perhaps we could avoid another bloodbath.

Sabol laughed out loud when I shared my optimism with him. "Hell, maybe they have hot coffee and doughnuts waiting down there after the police and the FBI hand total situational control over to us," he chuckled angrily as he brought us in for a bumpy landing.

Freezing rain beaded from the windows as our tiny craft came to a skidding stop between the stolen plane and a giant, white tanker of deicing fluid that had clearly been evacuated long before the job was finished. We were careful to make no sudden movements as we exited the cockpit into a frigid downpour. The moment our feet splashed onto the tarmac, some fifty rifles were pointed in our direction. I hugged the slow cooker to my chest, half expecting to be shot at.

"Corporal Sabol, Professor Huxley, I need you both on

your knees with palms flat on the ground!" blared Downey's voice from a megaphone somewhere behind the massive line of flickering police lights. Directly to our right, a low, savage roar began shaking the insides of the cargo plane. Raindrops streamed down my face as I carefully set the slow cooker to the runway and knelt in surrender. To my left, Sabol laid down the shotgun and spread his hands in front of him.

"Agent Downey, you need to back these men away from this cargo plane right now!" Sabol shouted. "We're all in immediate danger!"

"We'll take it from here, son," Downey hollered through the megaphone. "Just calm down and come with us. We'll sort this all out later."

"If you have any bright ideas," Sabol said to me. "Now's the time to share 'em."

As we awaited arrest, I stared into a small puddle below me. In my reflection, the red and blue lights danced over my face from all directions, and another terrible thud echoed from the cargo plane, resulting in a massive dent in the hull. Everyone, including several members of SWAT, jumped back in fear. And then another thud. And another. Each crash grew more furious.

"What the hell is that?" I heard an officer ask.

"The hell if I know," Downey replied impatiently. "Maybe they brought some wild animal back with them."

The last of his words slowed to a crawl, and every minute detail sprung to life. Ever so slowly, my gaze fell back to my reflection in the rain puddle directly below me. My face moved out of focus and the emergency lights became liquid pulses that shifted smoothly from one color to the next; each shift punctuated with a deep, penetrating Boom! as though the red and blue flashes were being pounded into existence from a large drum, a drum at the edge of a crater in the Tsangpo Gorge eight thousand miles away.

And all the lights, the commotion, and the chorus of sounds seeped directly from my skin! I stared down as the rain drizzling around my head created a dreamy display of expanding rings in the puddles; rings that inspired entirely new synaptic connections in my consciousness.

"Just stay where you are and do not make any sudden movements," a megaphone screamed slowly off in the distance. "You are being detained by the Federal Bureau of Investigation."

A half dozen wary, armed officers began their approach across the runway, handcuffs at the ready, growing ever more anxious by whatever might be trapped within the massive, metal hull next to us. When the officers reached the halfway mark, the hiss of hydraulics flooded the air as the loading platform on the cargo plane began to drop. The policemen froze in place; eyes wide, their aim wavering. The lower the platform dipped, the ferocious roars within grew louder. My pulse neared fatal speeds, yet I couldn't tear my eyes from the dance of tiny rings in the water beneath me. Well, this is a fine time for the ayahuasca to kick in. I thought.

# Collective Unconscious

*"Knowing your own darkness is the best method of dealing with the darknesses of other people."*

Carl Jung

Inundated by stimuli, I remained frozen while a number of forces closed in around us. I was aware of the battalion of police and SWAT teams with weapons fixed on our position from behind the barricade of patrol cars, as well as fully aware of the arresting officers moving in ahead and, of course, the cargo platform lowering to my right, and also the rain falling into the puddle in front of my face. Of all the growing threats, why in hell would I be focused on the rain droplets?

At one point, a dozen drops fell simultaneously from my hair and landed in a perfect, circular pattern. The tiny waves quickly merged into one, large ring at the center. I've seen this pattern before. Sadhu's voice echoed dimly in my memory: Something about wave interference; how waves can positively interact with one another to create an amplification of energy.

The crucifix hanging behind Kane's pulpit. When Eden and I broke into First Life's church, we discovered an enormous stone cross with a curious design carved into the center: A series of interlocking rings encircling an infinity sign. What if that design they worshipped had a greater meaning? What if it represented their final goal? What if it were a diagram of a plan, a ceremony designed to incarnate their notion of God in physical form, here on earth? What if Kane is the infinity symbol?

My eyes were opened. Kane and the members of his parish had been multiplying their power and mass by either entering the Zero Point Field in groups, or by accepting a victim's awareness who had surrendered it willingly through faith—the most efficient way to acquire power. Now I saw Kane's ultimate plan, and now my insight was useless.

The platform continued to lower and something angry and massive rumbled in the dark confines of the cargo bay. Fear and anger grew exponentially as I wondered if Tina and Eden were trapped inside with this beast, this shifted version of Giddeon or Bowen, or, hell, maybe both. Behind rattling pistols, the arresting officers had redirected their aim to the platform beside us. Impossible gaps everywhere; gaps too wide to cross.

And there was a pressure; something nearly forgotten pressing into my thigh, some small object against my skin. I stuffed my hand into my front pocket and removed a tiny green stone. I rolled it around my palm and a word arose in memory: Sastun. Had it been there the whole time? Did I bring this back with me from Tibet? Crystallized intention. A green river, Rosita had said.

I stopped asking questions and gazed into the translucent, emerald sphere. As I stared, I lost focus of the stone's solidity. Its structure seemed to come unlocked at some fundamental level. After a moment of disassembling in the palm of my hand, its physical essence fell away and vaporized into the cold, night air. Was it a hallucination? But then I felt a shift in my attention. In the unfocused background of my mind, behind the fear, the worry, the doubt, I visualized the probability wave. A massive wall of ever-encroaching possibilities; an ocean of interlocking rings stretching beneath my wings. And I was behind the controls in the plane once again! I soared and took flight over the million and one ways matter and energy could combine in the next few moments. The winds gently guided me to a very specific point of intention below, some unusual bundle of vibrating rings holding a rare potential. This pattern carried a shimmer of jade and bursts of golden fire. I dove head first into this odd vibration of rings and was swallowed whole. And I was merged with Rosita's intention.

"Sabol," I said automatically, without thinking. "Pick up the shotgun."

"What?" he whispered angrily.

"Aim it at the release valve on that white tanker of deicer," I demanded. I had no idea what I was saying. No plan was unfolding as far as I could see. The words came automatically as if I were acted upon by forces beyond my control. My movements were the end result of a billion and one perfectly natural, physical interactions. "Sabol, that shotgun is going to be useless against whatever is coming out of that plane. But that truck is carrying propylene glycol."

"No fucking way!" he argued. "That shit is flammable!" It is? I had no idea.

But there was no time to debate. Everything happened very quickly now. The loading platform hit the tarmac and the officers took a few measured steps away from us. From the dark recesses of the cargo bay, a colossal, upside down face emerged into the strobe of flashing emergency lights; a face stretched over a head three times the mass of a normal human's. There was no doubt in my mind: These features belonged to Bowen, spread across a massive, rotting skull with a mouth carved ear to ear, sprouting several rows of stunted, jagged teeth.

"Sabol?" I called again. He was a million miles away, stunned into submission. Riding atop a hundred undulating legs, this beast wearing Bowen's face raced along the plane's ceiling, crawled out onto the exterior in a spiral, and wrapped its elongated, segmented body around the rear fuselage. Beyond the deformed skull, nothing about this creature resembled human. Its slithering neck merged with the features of a blood-red centipede nearly the size of the plane itself. A sizzling, yellow liquid sloshed angrily within the two-dozen translucent, razor-tipped claws the beast floated atop. Each claw punched into the metal paneling as it crawled, mimicking rapid machine gun fire.

As the tail section of Bowen's body continued to pour from the cargo hold, the front half lifted its girth high into the air above the plane. With an ear-piercing cry, the beast shrieked at the tiny humans now scrambling madly below. Its hind end was still crawling from the plane when total chaos broke out on the runway.

"Sabol!" I shouted. Long before Downey and his men had a chance to scream in shock and terror, frantic gunfire broke out from behind the line of vehicles. Bullets pinged from Bowen's thick exoskeleton without leaving a mark. Overwhelmed by the nightmare that towered above them, a few of the arresting officers fell to their asses in shock; others fired their pistols aimlessly while the rest simply ran blindly in the opposite direction. For some reason, the reaction I found most distressing were those few who broke into uncontrollable laughter at the sight, as if hearing the funniest joke ever told.

The moment the full breadth of Bowen's form emerged from the plane's belly, its segmented, trident tail lashed out and snagged the nearest arresting officer clear from his feet. The beast pulled the screaming man underneath its body, drove a half-dozen spiked claws into the man's abdomen and pumped him full of frothing, yellow venom. The officer's body went into spasms while bloody foam bubbled from his mouth.

"Sabol!" I shouted louder. "Eden Jessup needs us!" This time he heard me. He snapped into action and, lacking a better plan, he followed my instruction. He raised the shotgun to the back of the deicer truck and fired twice. The valve on the tank exploded, releasing a violent geyser of fluid; a bright, green river that arched across the runway, onto the cargo plane and the beast's tail. Upon seeing the results of his actions, Sabol needed no further instruction: He was back in action-hero mode.

He leapt to his feet and confidently fired a third shot into the tarmac, igniting the deicer. When the brilliant, orange flame raced onto the creature's hind end, the soft flesh began to cook beneath the exoskeleton. Bowen's horrible eyes glared down at the two, puny creatures responsible for the assault and released a soul-shattering scream. He writhed in spiraling circles around the length of the airplane trying to escape the growing flames.

Sabol scrambled behind police lines and began pulling the agents and officers away from the destruction while I darted in the opposite direction, up the loading platform of the cargo plane in search of Eden and Tina. The first thing I noticed was that the wooden crates holding the vines and flowers had vanished. I pushed further into the dark recesses as the creature's shrieks and moans continued to echo from above. Suddenly, a barrage of gunfire slammed into the side panels and I dropped to the floor to make myself as small as possible. When the ricochets died down, I could hear Sabol hollering angrily at the agents and police units outside, begging them to stop firing toward the plane.

I shouted into the blackness for Tina and struggled to listen above the noise for a response. Nothing. Everywhere around me, the metal sides began to buckle. Outside, Bowen's centipede form was coiled around the hull's midsection and squeezing increasingly tighter under a series of pained muscle spasms. I shouted for Eden. No response. Steel beams creaked and buckled as the cargo area steadily collapsed inward. I crouched lower and ran to the front of the plane. Inside the cockpit I discovered the pilots, dead in their seats with no physical signs of damage. The sounds of bending metal behind me had nearly reached a crescendo.

The pilots had given up their attention freely. The fifteen-hour flight was more than enough time for Giddeon and Bowen to convince them to surrender themselves willingly. So, where is everyone else?

With a deafening roar, the fuselage imploded behind me sending a freight train of air through the cabin. My body was tossed into the control panel as the cockpit windows blew out. Before I could pull myself to my feet, the world shook with a thunderous blow when the landing gear snapped and the entire plane crashed to the tarmac. Deafened by the pressure blast, I slipped through the window frame, slid down the nose, and tumbled onto the runway. With gasoline vapors burning my eyes, I turned to find the craft was now hemorrhaging jet fuel. I ran toward the line of patrol cars, tried not to look back, and failed. Partially trapped beneath the flaming aircraft was a fury of squirming legs. Only when the ringing in my ears subsided enough to hear muffled sounds did I realize how the silence was helping me focus.

Ahead, Sabol ran back and forth through the line of men, desperately trying to gain a level of control over the situation, pushing the agent's weapons to the ground and ordering them to stop firing in my direction. Most of them obeyed his instructions; most of them. A few random bullets zipped past my ear as I charged toward the police barrier.

One of the itchy trigger fingers belonged to Agent Tom Downey of the FBI. When our eyes met, I darted straight at him. Like a wild cheetah, I dove over the hood of a police car and tackled him to the ground. Behind me, the cargo plane exploded in a ball of blinding light, shaking the earth beneath us.

"Where's Tina? Where is Agent Flores?" I shouted into Downey's face, partially out of hysteria, mostly because I was half deaf. "Where is Eden Jessup?!"

I gripped him hard by the collar, but I was little more than a blip on his radar. In his eyes, only the glow of the burning plane and the creature trapped beneath reflected back at me. Much to my surprise and his, I found my fist landing hard into his jaw. I had never punched anyone in my life, but if nothing else, I now had the man's attention.

"The women?" he asked slowly. I could barely hear his words. "I . . . I convinced him to release the female hostages."

"Him?" I yelled angrily, scanning the surrounding airport for any sign of Tina and Eden: nothing but police cars and SWAT vans. "Who's him? You mean Bowen? Where's Flores and Jessup?"

He shook his head. "Kane's man, Bowen, yes. He said he had hostages, men and women."

"Okay, okay, just breathe," I tried to say calmly, but I barked viciously into his face. "Start at the beginning. What happened when your team arrived?" He struggled to find the words. His brain had been turned inside out. He spoke in fits and starts.

"We . . . we thought the cargo plane was landing in Denver, but they veered off course at the last moment. When we got here, they had already landed. Kane's man, Bowen, had the pilots unloaded some wooden crates onto a white truck at gunpoint," he muttered absentmindedly. "But he ran them back inside the plane when we approached . . . that was . . . that was hours ago . . . "

"Where are those crates now?" I demanded. "Where is that white truck?" Downey didn't speak. I shook him vigorously. With a weak, shaking finger he pointed vaguely toward the parking lot just as Sabol appeared breathlessly at my side. Clearly, he had been busy. Sabol had collected the crock pot, another shotgun, and a vinyl belt of ammo draped around his shredded Hawaiian shirt.

"The wooden crates? What? . . . why?" Downey mumbled confusedly, studying the two of us. "What does that matter? There wasn't anything in them. . . just plants . . . vines, flowers. We were focused on getting Bowen to release the hostages."

His attention drifted back to the fire and his eyes grew wider. The shrill sounds of the creature bellowed within the inferno. I pulled him by the collar and swung my fist twice as hard. Rage crossed his face and my knuckles screamed in pain, but I matched his anger and doubled it, lifting his head from the ground. "What did you do with the hostages?" I shouted.

He gestured to the SWAT vans near the end of the barricade, trying to comprehend the motivation behind my questions, considering the stranger situation at hand. "Huh? The hostages . . . the women are all fine," he said, trailing off into a haze as he spoke. "They're safe inside the van, the three of them are safe."

Just as Sabol and I began a fevered sprint toward the SWAT vans to retrieve Tina and Eden, I shuddered to a halt. Three of them. Fuck. "What's going on?" Sabol hollered. "Where's Flores and Jessup?"

I didn't have time to answer. "Get his car keys," I shouted. After Sabol fished Downey's keys from his pocket he followed behind as I dashed toward the parking lot, pushing through crowds of frantic, stunned officers and agents, some of whom continued to fire their weapons into the fiery chaos on the runway.

"Don't you put a scratch on my Audi!" Downey managed to shout after us. The priorities on this guy, I swear. But not to worry. I wouldn't put a scratch on it. That is, not me personally. Sabol tossed one of the shotguns to me and we simultaneously blasted the doors open on the only two SWAT vans in the lot. Both empty. But I knew they would be. All of this, Bowen, his shapeshifting trick, had all been one, massive distraction. And it almost completely worked. Sabol stared at me with eyes pleading to be let in on the secret.

"Giddeon posed as one of Bowen's hostages," I sighed, catching my breath. "She took Tina, Eden, and the crates up to the church while everyone's attention was focused on the cargo plane. We have to get up there before they can finish the ceremony."

"What ceremony?" Sabol cried. I threw my hands into the air in disbelief at what spewed from my mouth. "The ceremony to end all ceremonies."

He nodded in strong agreement and a tumultuous roar echoed from the burning plane at our backs. We turned just in time to watch the enormous centipede break free of the fiery wreckage, scan the crowd and locate the two of us from across the runway. For this terror of genetic malfunction, the fight had suddenly become personal. After a rumbling growl, the beast pushed its burning, mangled body through the blaze and charged into the barricade of agents and government vehicles. Sabol shoved the slow cooker, Downey's car keys, and a handful of ammo into my arms.

"I'll hold it back as long as I can for you," he shouted. "Go!"

# Transitions

*"Everything turns in circles and spirals with the cosmic heart until infinity. Everything has a vibration that spirals inward or outward—and everything turns together in the same direction at the same time. This vibration keeps going: it becomes born and expands or closes and destructs—only to repeat the cycle again in opposite current. Like a lotus, it opens or closes, dies and is born again. Such is also the story of the sun and moon, of me and you. Nothing truly dies. All energy simply transforms."*

Suzy Kassem

After a couple clicks of the panic button on Downey's keys, the fog lights of a freshly polished, black Audi TT sprang to life at the end of the lot. Not the most recent model, but it was in mint condition. I strapped the cooker into the backseat, crisscrossing seatbelts and plugged it into the cigarette lighter. With the shotgun on the passenger's seat, I threw the transmission into first and hit the gas. Everything in my world still sounded as if it were underwater, so I didn't hear the approaching impact.

The car jerked to a violent halt in defiance of its all-wheel drive system. Along with a rapid-fire screech of punctured metal, a dozen dark yellow daggers punched through my roof and into both doors, just barely missing my lower left side and right shoulder. I haven't even escaped the parking lot and the car is completely disfigured. But it's not my fault.

Moving into view from the top of the windshield, the giant, fire-ravaged face of Bowen peered down at me. His giant claws sliced through my metal ceiling, dripping acidic venom onto the seats and floorboards. I spun sideways to avoid being split in half as the beast began tearing through the car like tinfoil. From a curled position on my back, I shoved the muzzle of the gun against one of the yellow daggers slicing the roof, covered my face with one hand and pulled the trigger. With a muffled bang, shards of claw and poison exploded everywhere and the centipede shivered and screamed in agony. A spray of acid sizzled into the side of my face, my clothing, and the leather interior like boiling oil. Okay, that one was sorta my fault.

Luckily, the OxyContin dulled the pain enough to keep me moving forward. Through the cracked driver's window I saw flashing red and white lights racing toward me. I had just enough time to roll into a ball before the crash. Downey's prized Audi skidded to the side as an ambulance collided with my left rear. The beast rolled from the top of the car, onto its back where it struggled angrily to right itself with a hundred legs wriggling helplessly in the air.

Sabol leapt from the driver's seat of the ambulance, gave me a thumbs up and began firing into the creature's underbelly with his shotgun. With a swift wave of his hand, he ordered me to keep moving. I hit the gas and sped from the parking lot, shocked that the small sports car was still functioning. German engineering, indeed.

As I exited the airport, I looked back just in time to see the centipede right itself and chase Sabol into the rear of the ambulance. Within moments, the beast had punched its way through the metal doors and stuffed its head into the cabin in fast pursuit. I had to turn away; I couldn't watch.

That was it. Now it was up to me and I was a complete mess. Sabol was the last form of professional defense I had in this fight. I had to admit, his unbending intent to the mission was reassuring. Even if his goal of rescuing Eden was muddied with religious ideology, his fierce dedication had most certainly served great purpose. Or maybe his tunnel vision had led to his death. Fuck, I'm losing it.

The ayahausca seemed far stronger than all the other psycho-actives thus far, but I couldn't know for sure; not in my state of jumbled nerves. My mind bounced from one possibility to the next so quickly, I had a hard time focusing on the road ahead. It probably didn't help that I kept questioning what made the road any different from the rest of the pulsating stimuli in my environment.

The longer I drove toward the foothills, the more everything would go completely silent in my mind from time to time, and that scared me even more. I preferred confused over everything going blank. But then some terrifying reminder of the storm I was closing in on would snap my world back together. A smashed-up car or a smoking truck at the edge of the road, or the fire truck I passed cut completely in half, partially dangling from a cliff. The higher I climbed, the more frequent were the signs of battle, or more precisely, an extermination. Kane and his church had been busy making sure nothing came in or out of Gold Hill.

The sun peeked over the horizon and I remembered that I was forgetting something, an essential truth that I picked up along the way that would bring me back to sanity. I had come across it before and remembered it had pulled my world into clarity, but it kept moving just out of reach. Clearly, there were puzzles I still hadn't solved, so the full picture refused to come into focus at once.

If I was going to have a chance in hell at stopping Kane, I would have to unravel every last mystery I had been exposed to and piece them together. I still wasn't sure what it might mean to save the world; that was too big to digest. But after all the many losses I had endured, I knew what it meant to save the woman I loved and the life of my best friend. I would do everything in my power to do that.

The deeper the medicine seeped into me, the more I could recall every detail from this journey—from Boulder to Peru to Tibet and back again. My time in the gorge with the Roto wasn't slipping from memory like a dream any longer. Perhaps I had imagined my memory loss. I allowed myself to entertain a piece of Sadhu's advice—which required temporarily setting aside the question of whether he had been a friend or enemy—and to consider his words on their own merit alone.

Ha. That was probably his plan all along. Sadhu struck me as a man who would indeed go through the trouble to keep his identity lingering in abstraction for just that very reason. "If worse comes to worse, retell your story," I heard Sadhu advise from deep within my mind. Great, now I'm the one hearing voices. "If you can't bear the lightness of pure being, tell the tale of you."

"Why?" I asked aloud, angered that I was considering his wisdom. "What good is that, talking to myself about myself? It's narcissistic." Yes, and you've been doing it since you acquired spoken language. Now do it consciously; bring total awareness to the story of your ego. "Okay, for what purpose?"

So that you can drop your story. You must see the ego in its stark-naked truth: That it is just a story, a description; not a solid, immoveable object. It has the power to weave your world into existence moment by moment, yet it's not the essence of what you are. It's the greatest mask ever invented. It takes everything personally, and the notion of an impersonal universe terrifies it. The idea that the cosmos is ultimately indifferent is repulsive to the ego, and yet this truth remains the most liberating to the soul.

Your story is fluid, it can be a million things at once and it can shapeshift in an instant. You can be a criminal or a saint, the most polished human being, or an animal. Instinctively, every human knows this on one level or another and they either choose to be inspired or terrified of this truth.

Okay. I can do this. I can pull myself back from the brink of insanity and drive at the same time. I just need to retell my story. They say brainwashing works by repeating something over and over until it's accepted as truth. Since I'm completely out of my goddamned mind, that's just what I intend to do—talk my way back. I'll tell my story, I'll make the chaos linear. I'll coax the wave into a particle.

# The Slippery Now

*"And along with indifference to space, there was an even more complete indifference to time. 'There seems to be plenty of it,' was all I would answer when the investigator asked me to say what I felt about time. Plenty of it, but exactly how much was entirely irrelevant. I could, of course, have looked at my watch but my watch I knew was in another universe. My actual experience had been, was still, of an indefinite duration. Or alternatively, of a perpetual present made up of one continually changing apocalypse."*

Aldous Huxley

**M**y story, my journey to the Craneo Roto and beyond has brought my awareness here, to the Now. I reside in the present. There is nowhere left to hide.

I see my entire journey, in all its beauty and terror, as one unified circuit of pure light that has blazed a path through my spinal column. A white ring, a superstring, a halo that touches a number of multivibrational bundles of human experience, from the base of my spine to the top of my skull. On one level, this is all my journey has ever been: A movement of awareness from the ground, up, from the basest of emotional reactions to the highest clarity my consciousness can attain while bound to this physical form. From my altered state of perception, I am at once the embodiment of the "kundalini" patterns inked into Eden's back and the only string, the only electron that has ever existed.

Sadhu was right, of course. I thought I was my story, and now I see my story really just adds up to another pattern, a unique configuration of information residing within an ocean of possibility; a frequency that is unique to me. My experiences, my knowledge, all my fear and love boils down to a single vibration pulling my world into existence nanosecond by nanosecond; a field of consciousness that continuously draws my world from the sea of quantum particles. And while this all sounds wonderfully fantastic and metaphorical, it is also a very real phenomena that I watch unfold. When I direct my attention to various parts of my body, I can tap into all of the energetic exchanges taking place on the physical, emotional, and quantum level; all the various organs at work behind the totality of my personal, conscious experience.

As I move my attention to the lowest tip of my spine I see all the base survival instincts—those deeply inbred, flight or fight reactions which reached a glorious crescendo on this journey. These energy patterns give off a low, thrumming vibration that I can feel in my roots and visually, they glow in my mind's eye with gentle pulsations of dark reds and brilliant pink hues.

Just above that area, I witness both the pleasures and pains of physical existence and the fiery, orange bursts of energy those sensations emit. In my solar plexus region there lay a golden orb, a tiny star continuously exploding with raw power. Here I see my battle between desire for power, and the desire to wield it properly.

The chakra above that, at the center of my chest, drums out a steady rhythm of emerald waves. Of course, chakra is probably what Eden would call these bundles of energy; however, at the present moment, they simply are whatever they are; they didn't come wrapped in labels. As I allow the lulling song of green rings in my heart wash over me, I feel these patterns are what I would call love, a force I tried desperately to tame and cage inside a box of logic and reason behind a screen of opiates. In my throat, I see the many ways I had fought with my expression; my own voice and how it was intimately bound with my trust of others, patterns that sing in waves of azure skies. And I follow this circuit of energy higher still to find a steady hue of indigos flowing from my third eye center: All the oh-so-many complex formations of my intellect.

Finally, from the top of my skull a violet light pours like a fountain into the heavens, an indescribable energy connected with the universe at large; a power beyond the boundaries of limited, human experience. I have a sense that this particular chakra is a vital part of me, and yet it stands just out of reach. This conglomeration of patterns appears simultaneously as seven, separate bundles of vibration, as well as refractions of the string of white light that connects them all.

My body, my arms stretching before me, the steering wheel, the entire car itself loses its solidity and transforms to a translucent, magnetic field in motion. I float just above the mountain road as invisible awareness. I am a ring of power, the quantum string at the base of worldly existence that reaches out to interact with a never-ending ocean of vibration and manifestation.

But, it's not over yet. I'll keep moving forward until I'm dead. If I make it to the gates of Kane's church, I'll make my way inside the compound with the ayahuasca. If I survive that, I'll find Tina and Eden. As long as I am able, I will continue toward the goal of stopping Kane and his people from completing their ceremony. Only God Himself can shake my resolve now.

The Audi skids around the last stretch of pavement to the quiet mountain town of Gold Hill. Nothing but gravel road from here on up. Above seven thousand feet, my world becomes bathed by gentle sheets of white. At this elevation, the rain turns to a light snow that sprinkles the mountainside with ghostly dust. The sky above remains a thin, gray sheet that reaches to the earth in a translucent fog, or perhaps smoke, that swirls lazily around my car as the tires rumble into the outskirts of the small town.

Gold Hill is quiet. Perhaps the inhabitants are hiding, or maybe it's been abandoned. I study the homes dotted along the steep, mountain road and decide it's the later. Doors are left wide open on cabins. Garages still have their lights on. Only frantic tire marks remain where cars and trucks should be parked. This gives me hope that at least some of them escaped.

I roll into the center of town near the top of the hill and find the locus of destruction. The few structures that once marked the downtown area, the post office, the general store, are collapsed and smoldering. A handful of pickups and SUVs are overturned, including a sheriff's truck. And then I see the signs of death. The ravaged bodies of those who didn't escape, or tried to fight off the scourge, are scattered throughout the rubble. I count at least a dozen paths cut directly through town, starting at the forested hilltop just below Kane's compound: All signs that Kane released another horde upon Gold Hill.

There is some movement to my right, just beyond the smoldering remains of a chain of wood cabins. A man waves at me frantically while helping an injured woman walk beside him. Her leg is bleeding and they're both limping, covered by ash. I study the fear on their faces, the man's grizzled beard, their worn boots, rugged clothes, and especially the woman's Buddhist mala beads. These are locals, clearly not members of First Life.

I slam on the brakes, dash from the vehicle and run to them through the cold air. They freeze at the sight of me. "I'm a doctor," I announce as calmly as I am able. "I'm not going to hurt you."

I help the man carry the woman across the wreckage and into a tool shed off the road, one of the few structures still standing. The man helps me sit her on a workbench and I inspect her wound. A bloody claw mark corkscrews her leg from thigh to ankle, but it isn't terribly deep.

"What do we do?" the man asks mindlessly.

"I'm not that kind of doctor," I admit. I pull a flannel work shirt from a door hook and begin cutting it into strips.

"You're from the university?" the woman asks.

"Yeah."

The man catches on and takes over wrapping her wound. I notice their matching wedding rings. Their eyes wide and vacant; their movements automatic. Both are in shock. "What happened here?" I ask calmly, though I'm certain of the answer. The man turns and stares through the open door to the forested peak in the direction of Kane's church. But he soon moves back into autopilot, carefully wrapping his wife's leg with an empty expression.

"A woman came down from the church up there just this morning," the wife speaks through haze. "Said her name was Giddeon. She marched right to the middle of town and she started preaching, talkin' bout the end of the world and that it's happenin' this very day, how we all needed to get on the right side of it. She even told us how it was all gunna happen. She said that first, Satan was gunna unleash his hellhounds upon the Earth. Said they would spring right outta the forest up near their church to pull all the nonbelievers back't where they belong."

At that, the woman giggles weakly, "We thought she was out of her mind; crazy fuckin' Christians." Her eyes begin to water and fear crosses her face. "I mean, who would believe something like that? But, now my eyes are open." Christ, just as I figured: Kane sent a horde of shifters to clear-cut the entire mountain. He had to be sure his precious ceremony wouldn't be disturbed. I must have slipped by the shifters on the way up. Or, perhaps, in my altered state I had actually made the car invisible?

"She said the few folks left standing were the chosen few who would see His return," the man explains monotonously. His wife points a shaking finger toward the top of the mountain and an eerie smile crosses her lips.

"She said God Himself is gunna rise up straight outta their church for the whole world to see; that He was gunna pass over the entire face of this Earth and offer all the survivors a return to paradise." The woman looks down at the Mala beads gracing her neck with anger. With a violent swipe of her hand she snaps the necklace, scattering sandalwood beads everywhere. "I can't believe we were spared, after all I done," she weeps, taking her husband's hand. "God gave us a second chance!" They close their eyes tightly in prayer, holding each other.

"You know they're insane, right?" I say quietly, finishing the last knot on the tourniquet. They turn and stare at me quizzically.

"Insane?" the woman said in disbelief.

"You don't know," her husband growls. "You haven't seen what's out there. Did you see with your own eyes what came out of that forest?"

"I've seen them, yes," I say, moving toward the door. "Listen, you both just need to stay out of sight. I have to go and . . . "

"We know what you plan to do," the wife says. "You should see your eyes, professor. Giddeon was right. You really are out of your mind. How can you still not believe?"

"How can your atheist mindset be this stubborn?" the man adds firmly. "Face it, professor, you're wrong and you've lost. The universe has shown its hand and now it's time to fold."

"Just surrender," the woman pleads. "It will make it all so much easier."

Their words stop me in my tracks. The man stands to face me. "Giddeon said that there were a few truly lost souls who might come up here, try to put a stop to His return."

"She said one of them would be a professor from the university," the woman says. "A Professor Michael Huxley. That is your name, isn't it?"

As the man turns and reaches for an axe on the wall of tools behind him I explode from the shed. I don't look back, I just run. Across the yard, the Audi is still running in the middle of the road. Scattered throughout the wreckage of the town around me, a half dozen, wide-eyed locals are slowly heading in my direction. They wield a variety of hand tools, metal pipes, and shovels. A few of them have pistols and hunting rifles. All of them appear brainwashed into committing any atrocity they deem necessary. "It's him!" the man shouts behind me, bursting from the shed. "It's the professor!"

In my peripheral, the surviving inhabitants of Gold Hill spring into action and begin charging. They close in as I leap into the driver's seat and paw at the shotgun. I point the barrel out the window and fire once into the air. The blast is so loud even I jump. The locals pause just long enough for me to throw Downey's car into gear. I slam on the gas and break through the crowd, skidding around two of them who would rather be run down than allow my escape. As I pass, metal pipes bash into my windows and shovels crash into my side panels. I duck at the sound of gun blasts but nothing hits the car. The turbo boost kicks in when I downshift, leaving them flailing in the snowy dust.

I speed to the edge of town and skid around the turn up the narrow, winding road that cuts through the forest to Kane's compound. Just before the clearing, I pull to a full stop along the side. The fencing around the property has been leveled, trampled. Before I exit the vehicle, I rip the tape from the slow cooker and dunk an empty bottle into the warm brew. The ayahuasca is now twice as dark as it was back on the plane.

With shotgun in hand and backpack slung over my shoulder, I stomp over the downed fence, up the hill. I'm rattled by the discovery that I've become a target by ordinary citizens and my internal dialogue fights for the reins once again. I close in on the front entrance of the church and hear many voices echoing from behind the structure, a crowd is gathered in the courtyard.

I creep low around the compound, trying to stay below the enormous, stained glass windows. I poke through the bushes and peer around the corner to find the exact pattern I saw in the rain puddle back on the runway, but now made flesh and blood: Twelve of Kane's disciples, all dressed in white tunics, are seated equidistant from one another in a giant circle. At the very center of this ring sits the good reverend himself looking as pale and decrepit as ever. Everyone's eyes are closed, their heads lowered in prayer as they sit cross-legged atop overstuffed, silky-white meditation cushions. They chant inaudibly, but I know their words: They are mumbling "I am no one" to prepare themselves for the death of the ego.

Trying not to draw their attention, I slowly search through the bushes to look for Giddeon among the circle of parishioners. I can't find her. Perhaps she led the horde down the mountain to begin cleansing the Earth of us heathens. I look over the architecture of this ceremony taking place and I know their plan. I see it. Essentially, they've primed themselves for constructive wave interference of the quantum field. I'm sure they don't think of it that way; the science at the heart of their practice eludes them. In fact, they would refuse to listen to the explanation if I were to offer it. That alone makes them impossibly dangerous. There will be no talking them down from chasing their goal. Reason and tact aren't options here.

In the light of day, Kane is far sicklier and skeletal than ever. His breathing is shallow and he seems to be in pain, and yet, he appears perfectly blissful seated at the center of divine attention. Everyone, including the reverend, lovingly cups a bowl of liquid in their lap. It's their customized hallucinogen to induce very customized results for bicameral minds: Part ayahuasca, part scopolamine. The first to merge them with the Zero Point Field, the second to trip it.

I look beyond the circle to the far side of the clearing where a sturdy, wooden post has been erected. Tina and Eden stand back-to-back against this makeshift column, chained to each other's wrists: A sacrifice of those less than willing to surrender to Kane's will. They, too, are dressed in the ceremonial, white robes. I cringe as I think how these people put their hands on the women I love.

From this distance, all I can tell is that both of them appear to be awake and standing under their own power. My anger is welling to the point where I find myself aiming the shotgun through the bushes at Kane. I'm being thrown off center again. Though my experience with firearms is laughably limited, I am certain that I can kill the man from this range. I have a clean shot between two of his disciples and Tina and Eden are too far down the ridge to be hit by a stray. My finger caresses the trigger and I allow myself to entertain doubt once more. One shot and I can end this. Whatever horrible thing Kane will become, I can stop this before it starts.

"And now my children, let us begin, so that we may start anew," Kane announces to his parish with his distinguished, Southern drawl. His voice booms from a small, frail body. With both hands, he lifts the sacrament to his lips and drinks. His circle of disciples, certainly comprised of those he deemed the most faithful, mimic his actions. They've certainly prepared for this moment, probably fasting for days to be sure the medicine takes effect as quickly as possible. I try to resolve my doubt by taking inventory of what I feel sure of, what my experiences have led me to understand.

In about twenty minutes or less, everyone's limited, ego-based consciousness within the circle will enter the Zero Point Field. Like raindrops on water, a chain of expanding shockwaves will converge with one another at the center as Kane's disciples surrender up the entirety of their life-giving attention. The scopolamine will shut down Kane's higher functioning and he will bond with whatever combination of matter his deeply troubled, base-consciousness vibrates with. At that point, his reptilian brain will have access to enough raw, potential energy to manifest damn near whatever nightmare he can dream up.

Of course, to be sure he has no competition for the Most Powerful Being on the Planet, Kane will devour Eden, Tina, and eventually me; anyone who has any real understanding of how he's pulled off the mother of all magic tricks, anyone who still doubts his claim to the throne of all thrones.

After that, he'll move within the wake of the hellhounds he's unleashed into the foothills. As the survivors bow at the terrible sight of him, he'll continue consuming their attention and converting it to mass and energy. His power will grow exponentially with each convert he gathers. Once the process snowballs, I can't imagine what it will take to stop him. He'll eventually devour every conscious entity on the face of the earth. I believe this is true. Everything I have come to understand over the last several days points to this ensuing reality.

And still, I can't pull the trigger. Is it because there is a part of me that wonders if I've gone completely insane and none of this is what it seems? Or, is it rather because I cannot kill a man sitting in prayer? That isn't me. No version of Michael Huxley, at least not one that I can imagine, would take this shot. If this is what it takes to save the world, I won't have any part of it. No, I'll do what I originally came here to do. Is it more ethical to hand that responsibility over to Eden, over to what she'll become after I feed her this bottle of medicine in my pack? Or does that just make me a coward? My unbending intent is wavering once again.

I don't have the luxury of time to sort this out. I slip from the bushes and make my way around the other side of the church, past the line of intricate, stained glass windows of Biblical scenes, to where Eden and Tina are held hostage. Only after I round the last corner of the compound do I realize how stupid it was to think the cult would leave their holy sacrifices unguarded.

As I pass the last window, one depicting Eve accepting the forbidden fruit from the serpent, the glass explodes. I duck and shield my eyes from a thousand shards as Giddeon lands right before me dressed in full military combat gear. The moment her boots hit the earth, she removes a blade from her utility belt, and fear slows my reflexes. She's in human form, but every bit as ugly and fierce. Before I can lift the barrel of my shotgun she shoves the muzzle into the ground. Beneath her grip, her hand begins to shift. Our eyes meet and I sense a black hole of consciousness open deep within her, awareness collapsing in on itself, as her bodily tissues shrivel and sink between the bones.

In one complete movement, her other hand swings around and lands her knife into my stomach, just below the rib cage: My final punishment for hesitating. She shoves my back into the wall of the church, pressing harder, my stomach screaming in agony as my mind processes the stark reality that this wound will soon prove fatal. My backpack falls to the ground and the bottle of ayahuasca rolls helplessly onto the lawn. Giddeon's facial tissues decompose as she seethes into my ear: "I'm so glad you survived, professor. I prayed the honor to send you down would be mine."

# Fear is Finite

*"Expose yourself to your deepest fear; after that, fear has no power, and the fear of freedom shrinks and vanishes. You are free."*

Jim Morrison

Even before the pain sets in, I've estimated from the size and location of the blade I have maybe ten minutes left. I know it's punctured my kidney, pretty sure it's pierced my lower ventricle, and God knows what else. Maybe five minutes. Now my death is inevitable. I've come so far and for what? No. I won't die afraid. I refuse to simply await internal bleeding and toxicity to take me.

The ayahuasca blazing through my system ignites a new branch of synaptic firecrackers: Another path now stretches before me, a road less traveled. I change my mind and decide rather to accept the pain. I turn my head and stare into Giddeon's eyes; her terrible eyes that turn a milky yellow, then a dingy gray, until the surface hardens and the soft tissues dissolve. I gaze into those empty, black caverns in her skull, and wave after wave of fear, pure electric jolts of searing heat, flow through my being. And I let them come. Go ahead. Do your worst.

Angered at my response, Giddeon shoves the handle with more force, lifting me from my feet, screaming her hatred at me. "I'm everything you fear!" her throat hisses. Her face transforms from one hideous vision of death and dread to the next. But I keep staring, allowing the entirety of this dreadful woman's darkness to pass through.

You'll find no solid ground with me. You have nowhere to plant your seed. You are finite.

There's nothing more she can take from me, I've seen it all and I am no longer shocked. Suddenly, all of her violent commotion is just that: meaningless noise. Under all the rage and fury, behind all the horror, I see the silent ocean of awareness waiting below. Fear is indeed finite. With the chorus a thousand monks chanting, the Zero Point Field flows through my nervous system and I witness every particle, every chain of events that can harmonize with the vibration entitled, "Professor Michael Huxley." Superimposed over my vision of Giddeon, I see a billion halos, circles of energy that hold a million and one possibilities.

And through my agony, a smile crosses my lips. Giddeon's body shivers. She has never seen such a response from a victim. She knows I'm not afraid of her and that's terribly confusing at some savage level of reaction. There is something I possess that is more powerful than her worst rage. I see into a lost, but still-lit fragment of her awareness that whispers, "What am I?" I see deeper still to a heart tempered by a life of pain and suffering; base emotions that drum out thunderous patterns of twisting, red energy and black smoke. I see that, behind all the hideous manifestations, at the core there is little more than a damaged mind riddled with confusion. I'm watching insanity materialized. And that's all we've been seeing here: insanity materialized.

Okay. Great insight. What good does that do me now? And, WAIT, What the hell is this? I look to the ground and something darts over the ridge onto the lawn. It's small. It's furry. It runs right at the bottle of ayahuasca I dropped. My God, it's the monkey from the hot spring in Tibet! His tiny, white face studies the water bottle with a twitchy curiosity before snatching it up. He tucks the bottle under his tiny arm and runs off behind the church!

Am I delirious from blood loss? Did that just happen? But my attention is immediately pulled back to my impending death. I'm growing weaker by the moment. Under the pain, the brute force, or perhaps from my system going toxic, my mind trails off and makes another series of connections, back to the beginnings of this journey; to all the tiny details. I look back through the superstrings of energy, through the many chain of events that brought me, this particular version of Michael Huxley, to this very moment. The further I drift from my body, the grander the landscape of existence appears to stretch below me. One series of events catches my awareness;

one brought to light under my realization that I am dying at the hands of insanity incarnate.

Back in the hospital in Boulder, Tina had led Eden and I into a room in the ER where a disciple of Kane's had shapeshifted and murdered a security team. But, a nurse had entered the room, a Ms. Jessica Vonfeldt, and she somehow survived the attack.

But how? I can see it all take place within the shimmering rings of light as if it were happening right before me. I am in the hospital room, standing behind the nurse as she bursts through the doors, syringe in hand. But, what's in the syringe? What would she bring to a patient who was violent and psychotic? The moment I ask, my attention focuses on the liquid held inside the syringe. My quantum superstrings dance into view and join together to form atoms, then molecules, which then bind to form a chain and a chemical formula passes before my eyes: $C_{21}H_{23}ClFNO_2$ haloperidol: antipsychotic. The nurse was saved by treating the situation as she would with any other aggressive, psychotic patient.

Again, that's all great. But, I don't have any haloperidol, and I'm nearly dead. I take one, last gaze into my ocean of vibrating light, all the millions of possible combinations and . . . but what if I did have a syringe of haloperidol on hand? What events would have had to play out for that to be a real possibility? What combination can "Professor Michael Huxley" accept as truth?

I spin through the ocean, the many formulations of possible arrangements of matter and energy. There must be some version of this situation where I have access to a syringe full of antipsychotics. And I find it. The straightest line to such a reality is through Sabol. He stands as the most direct route to put a syringe of this medicine within reach; one that, at the very least, wouldn't be any stranger than connecting to a reality where Tina was instantaneously healed.

I can see it all play out in an elegant dance of action/reaction leading to the present moment. As I watch this particular line of dominoes fall in a complex, winding trail heading straight at

me, right to where I am now, the story they weave goes something like this: Agent Downey was the one who would have
ordered that ambulance to be on hand at Boulder's airport,
and after communication with Colonel Panza, it's possible he
guessed we may have lost our minds in Peru, so it's reasonable
that the paramedics would have been prepared to contend with
people who were in a state of psychosis, and quite possibly
dangerous; hence, they would have brought along antipsychotics.

Sabol was chased into that very ambulance the last time I
saw him, and he had some degree of medical training. In his
adrenalized state, he could have figured all of this out just as I
have. He could have survived the attack by Bowen in the same
way Nurse Vonfeldt had. He could have . . .

Before I can finish watching the scene play out, Giddeon's
hideous form pulls away, releasing my body. I fall to the ground
in a heap and look up at the most glorious view above me:
Bloodied, covered in ash, and wielding a syringe, Corporal Bill
Sabol leaps from behind Giddeon and wraps his arm around
her throat as she shrieks.

"I ain't afraid of you anymore, you crazy bitch," he shouts
and yanks her off balance, shoving the syringe deep into her
neck, pumping her twisted body full of haloperidol. A weak
gurgling sound bubbles from Giddeon's chest before she collapses to the ground. Her repulsive transformations slow, then
stop completely. And now they seem to move in reverse. The
black hole within her closes, the muscles, nerves, and tissues
snap back into place, and her skin heals over. A moment later,
Sabol and I are staring at a scarred, pitiful woman curled in
fetal position, naked and crying uncontrollably.

"What am I? What am I? What am I?" she shrieks. Even
while cradling the bloody knife handle sticking from my shirt, I
actually feel sorry for her. They know not what they do.

With the largest, explosive blast of energy we've ever encountered, the frequency booms through the atmosphere from
behind the church with an earthshattering intensity, reverberat-
ing off mountain peaks for miles around. It's happening; the

final ceremony has begun. Sabol grabs my backpack.

"Stay here," he says. "I'll finish this."

I'm still processing how he came to be here. Is Sabol a hallucination? Or did I just manifest a reality where he's here, standing before me? Or perhaps I had my first moment of clairvoyance? Or a remarkably accurate insight into what was about to happen? I seize Sabol by the ankle midstride.

"No," I shout firmly. "Help me up. I can't die here without seeing the end of this." He reluctantly pulls me into an agonized, standing position. As he drags me alongside, he breaks into excited explanation on how he came to be here.

"Sorry I'm late," he begins. "I got trapped inside the ambulance when you took off in Downey's car. And, while I'm in there, I start thinking about how that nurse Vonfeldt survived the attack back in the ER."

"Sabol," I interrupt with a weak smile. "I already know what happened. That was quick thinking. You're gunna be an awesome doctor." He seems only somewhat surprised that I'm completely aware of how he survived, and nods with acceptance.

"Well, okay then," he chirps. "Let's go save the fuckin' world."

We limp to the south end of the courtyard and our hearts sink. We're too late. "Mike!" "Sabol!" Tina and Eden cry to us in unison, still held captive on a wooden post. "Thank God," Tina adds in relief, until her eyes are drawn to the knife in my stomach. They both struggle under their restraints at the poor sight of me. They're unharmed, but the ceremony has already taken place. Before us, the twelve disciples are in the process of dropping dead from complete, utter surrender of their attention. One by one, their bodies drop lifelessly from their prayer cushions.

At first glance there is no sign of Kane until my eyes draw upward. Even after everything I've seen thus far, my brain is having trouble perceiving what is actively manifesting, and rising into the air above the courtyard, floating upon free waves of electrical currents. Our jaws hang wide at the sight of it.

I had imagined Kane using the ceremony to transform into some terrible beast, even larger, perhaps more terrible than the rest of the incarnations before it. Yet, what we're witnessing now is far more terrifying.

Kane has ridden powerful wave of energy into the Zero Point Field, and is now transforming into a vision of God— my vision of God, an image I've carefully buried away since first entertaining the notion of a supreme being. Kane's body is at least ten times its original size, still seated in meditation atop a silken prayer cushion, now also several times larger. He appears as a living skeleton wrapped in ethereal layers of shimmering white skin. His entire visage is simultaneously frightful and awe-inspiring, making the scene even more unsettling. Soft, multicolored lights refract within his presence as if emanating from a massive, rotating prism. Rainbows of plasma-like energy dance and swim in and out from the crown of his skull. He is the dark essence of death bathing in the light of God.

And then the darkness within him coalesces into an isolated pattern and I know I'm witnessing the cancer that has ravaged his body. As I watch in a stupor, the cancer turns from solid masses of cells to gentle wisps of smoke, which he expels in one, great exhalation that shakes the treetops behind us. All the while, his towering form remains cross-legged with eyes closed. On the underside of the massive prayer cushion he rides upon there is a great, empty hole, a vacuum that steadily consumes the last of the living awareness from his disciples. All of their agony, their suffering and confusion, their very identity, rises into his being to be transformed into free energy to be devoured and transmuted.

The disciples' physical bodies, now empty shells, have all dropped dead to the lawn below Kane, and in the process, his physical features begin to strengthen and heal: Fresh muscle tissue, cartilage and nerves stretch into place over bone while a beautiful layer of incandescent skin splashes into place as if rained onto his form from above. His hair becomes a white river that ripples softly in the mountain air.

He is becoming every idea—conscious and subconscious,

archaic and idealized—I've ever harbored about what God looks like; everything my culture has ever shoved into my brain about "The Old Man in the Sky." A great part of me wants to immediately drop to my knees and beg for forgiveness. His image beckons me into an even more profound state of religious reverence than did Eden's last incarnation.

Now I know the truth: I have not conquered all my fears. Not yet. This is the mother of them all. Was it designed just for me? Or is this truly the great impersonal essence of the cosmos made manifest?

And the more energy this fantastic entity gathers, the less it looks like Kane, the sickly reverend—and the more it resembles Sadhu, the wise and powerful shaman: A perfected, dream-world version of him. I can't think clearly. I question my unbending intent. I don't know what I should do. Hell, I don't even know what I can do about this. I turn to find Sabol mindlessly rummaging through my backpack while holding his shocked gaze on the sight floating above. I know what he's searching for. He is still dedicated to carrying out his mission, regardless of current events.

"I almost forgot," I mutter weakly to him as God rises before us. "A monkey stole my ayahuasca."

"Huh," he replies. It's not the strangest thing he's heard all day.

# The Old Man in the Sky

*"Either God can exist or freedom, both cannot exist together."*

Osho

The godly manifestation spins slowly atop his levitating cushion, his eyes still closed in meditation. After easing me to the ground Sabol runs to the wooden post to free Tina and Eden from captivity. Ever so gradually this being's eyelids rise, and soon I'm held in the gaze of iridescent blue irises spiraling into miniature black holes that serve as pupils. Dark pools, gaps that cut right through me, imbibing me with the sense that Sadhu is still in there somewhere, penetrating my bones under his intense stare. It doesn't hurt, but I am supremely naked beneath this spotlight.

Tina and Eden leap to the ground at my side while Sabol crouches behind us to join our huddle beneath the insanity taking place above. It takes but a moment of worried inspection for Tina to realize my wound is deadly. She begins to cry, throwing her head into my chest and wrapping me in her arms. Eden nestles her forehead into my shoulder, soaking my shirt with tears, placing a gentle hand on my stomach. With a low rumble that sweeps the valley below us, this "god" begins to speak.

"There is no need for sorrow," the voice roars smoothly through a deep drum roll of reverberation. Each syllable is enunciated carefully, slowly. "I Am Here. I am the undoing of all suffering. The time of darkness for sentient beings upon this planet has passed. The furthest reaches of suffering have met their end to give birth to my physical manifestation."

The words drifting from his lips echo from the mountain peaks. Suddenly this being squints and moves his laser-beam focus onto my stomach. The heat of his concentrated attention warms my ravaged insides, the entry wound, and finally the knife. After an intense, tingling sensation, Giddeon's blade comes "undone" at some fundamental level of existence much like the Sastun. It dematerializes into a white vapor. Behind it, the pain in my abdomen is instantaneously neutralized, and my scar vanishes from sight. I gasp a sigh of profound relief as Tina breaks into tears of joy, clutching me harder. Sabol is overcome by awe while Eden runs her hand over my spontaneously healed stomach with shock and delight.

Still, none of us speak. There is no need for words; we're equally overwhelmed. But now I feel everyone's mood grow dark once more and their attention falls to me . . . me, the atheist of the group. They're desperate to know what I make of this. Even Eden seems completely taken in by this apparition, whatever its true nature might be.

"We saw them prepare for the ceremony," Tina explains.

"Kane didn't add the devil's breath, the scopolamine, to his ayahuasca," Eden says.

"So?" I reply, slow to realize her point.

"So, he didn't shut down his higher functioning before his attention entered that probability wave of yours!" Eden replies. "We may actually be dealing with an extremely elevated state of consciousness here."

She's right. This does pose an interesting dilemma. If Kane merged his consciousness with the Zero Point Field from an undiluted state of mind, it would be reasonable to assume that the manifestation hovering above us could indeed be, for all rights and purposes, considered a god. Just as Sadhu had suggested might happen. But I can't take this on faith. I must know. I must investigate.

"Who are you?" I shout with all my strength into the heavens. I don't know where I'm going with this or what I'm looking for, but I have questions, goddamn it. Quiet gasps arise from the group. Is it safe to question a god?

"What sort of a supreme being can't handle a few, direct questions?" I assure them. Damian and Kyle once spoke about a famous test that Alan Turing designed in the 1950s to identify strong, artificial intelligence in a computer program. Software that was truly self-aware, Turing argued, should elicit responses indistinguishable from those of an actual human being. I wonder if anyone ever created a test to determine if the massively improbable entity floating above one's head is the real God or not.

Before this being replies, a patient smile moves over its lips that silently says, "You may not comprehend my answer, human."

"One response is that I am the highest consciousness of a vast multitude of incarnations of the man you knew as Reverend Edward Kane and Sadhu," it replies smoothly. "Kane and Sadhu's ego-bound forms are nothing but my predecessors. I stand before you as the purest version of embodied awareness. I say this not from human ego, for I am beyond identity, but as a direct reflection of the truth. The present universe that you know will collapse a million times over before cosmic intelligence is more perfected in physical form than I. I am Christ-consciousness returned to Earth, the God-head, I am the Buddha, Krishna, the Awakened One, I am at one with Enlightenment. I Am. Yet, I represent nothing more than an open gate, a welcome invitation. You may, this very moment, drop your Earthly fears, your doubts, your individual boundaries and merge with me in eternal peace and unity. I am Heaven's Gate made flesh."

Everyone sighs at the thought, even I must admit. Total salvation, right here. Now. Sabol begins to weep quietly. "Oh, yeah?" I reply, rising to my feet. "Along with the rest of your disciples who surrendered themselves over to you, the ones lying dead beneath that flying throne of yours?"

"Are you trying to get us smote?" Sabol whisper-shouts.

"There is no true death, my son," god replies with gentle grace, and still the surrounding forests tremble beneath his words. "You know this to be true. Indeed, the physical body is surrendered when individuality merges in complete unity with consciousness. But, as you have witnessed, your body is of little consequence in the eternal nature of awareness. Reverend Kane's parishioners of whom you speak had suffered greatly in this lifetime, as well as others. Their hearts and minds dwelt in great anguish. They are now one with eternal bliss. They are not my captives; their souls are free to leave the eternity of heaven as they so choose and return to the birth/death lifecycle; a life of ego and all the wonders and tribulations that come with it. I offer you the same."

Sabol studies us in confusion. "That sounded like a pretty good fuckin' answer," he whispers. "I mean, this is God, right?"

Eden and Tina have no answer. They look to me and I realize I have the advantage of being the only one among us who is operating from a nonordinary state of consciousness. I can't imagine what impact this is having on a "sober" state of mind. But I've been tripping hard since the airport, all the while battling with insanity, the forces of evil, and contending with the heavenly reaches of my own awareness, so perhaps I'm slightly less bowled over by this being's celestial qualities.

"Why are you here?" I prod god further. "Why do you need to be in material form at all, I wonder?"

He closes his eyes, his face radiates a quiet ecstasy. "Without form, enlightenment cannot affect change for humankind directly," he says carefully, as if to a child. "I do it for you, in service to humanity. The appearance I take of form and substance is for the benefit of the human mind. Most who identify with a limited, egoconsciousness cannot bridge the gap between themselves and formless awareness. They are trapped within the illusion that such communion is abstract, impossible, or even imagined. Therefore, I stand as an offer that this gap be traversed, by appearing as a living symbol of the synthesis between man and God, to assist in the transmission from form to formless, ocean to raindrop, particle to wave."

Damn. I can't find a solid fault with any of this, and that's becoming somewhat maddening in and of itself. Everyone begins gently pleading with me to knock it off.

"Mike, I don't see a downside to any of this," Tina whispers. "What if we're actually standing before the ultimate offer? What better version of this could we hope for? How can we turn down free admission to heaven? Haven't we suffered enough?"

"If he really has transformed into some kind of open gateway to enlightenment," Eden considers. "Then we'd have to be the most stubborn idiots in the universe for shitting all over it."

"What do we have to lose?" Sabol asks excitedly. "It seems like a mistake of biblical proportions to turn our backs on this!"

The enormous, white pillow carrying Sadhu glides downward until god hovers just above the ground. With smooth, dreamlike movement, he leans slightly forward to make closer eye contact with us. "My children, there are a great many souls trapped in the illusion of separation from God-Mind," he says quietly. "Because of this, my offer can be made only once to every conscious entity upon this Earth within this present lifetime. Please decide your path so that I may proceed and present the offer to your fellow man."

We must decide quickly; it's a limited-time offer and I feel Eden's grip on my sleeve tighten. Suddenly, something presses against my back; some small form that slides around Sabol and pokes through the nook of my arm between Eden and I. I look down to find Kaylah is now sitting at my side. Neither Tina nor Eden appear surprised to see her. They had already crossed paths with her moments before Sabol and I arrived in the courtyard.

"Where the hell did she . . . ," Sabol mutters but immediately drops it.

"My suggestion," Kaylah says, "is to see if you can piss him off."

"What?" Sabol nearly shouts. "Why would we want to do that?"

"If you can piss it off, it has an ego," Eden adds.

"We can't allow this entity to leave this peak unless it is honest-to-God, pure consciousness," Kaylah says. "The more awareness people hand over to this attention vacuum of his, the longer and more powerful it will run, even well after the ayahuasca has worn off. It will be a snowball effect once he moves on."

We all know she's right. If this incarnation still identifies with even the slightest notion of an individual self, something that is limited in even the slightest way, shape or form, then it must be capable of feeling "lack" on some level. If it's capable of lack, then we would have submitted ourselves to a fraud, another cage. But the team grows anxious. At any moment, the offer will be null and void.

"Just give me five minutes," I explain to the group. "If there's no way to anger him, we'll know this really is pure awareness, just some, open gate to Nirvana or whatever." I dare a few measured steps closer to the hovering, celestial being. I must think quickly, cover every possible angle. There can be no mistakes. I inhale and take another stab at this god.

"You sure left one hell of a trail of blood to get here!" I call to him. "How many people have been brutally murdered along the way? Or the carnage that's still taking place now? What about Kane's shapeshifters who wiped out Gold Hill? Are they still tearing through the foothills, slaughtering anyone who might interrupt your precious ceremony?"

"Indeed, there is no longer use for those violent combinations of energy," he whispers, straightening his spine and placing his palms atop his knees. "I will call these agonized souls home."

From the center of his abdomen, a blinding fountain of golden light bursts into the atmosphere, pouring over our heads before arching downward along the mountain slope, into the distant canyons below. With a rumble of electrical discharge, the golden fountain moves into reverse, pulling the waves of light back to the center of his being. As if on rails, a dozen shapeshifters appear on the horizon and soar through the air toward the courtyard. Within moments we are surrounded by the beasts that Kane had unleashed, dangling and writhing in midair, each held within their own beam of magnetic light.

"God" extends his palms and speaks, "I free you from your incarnation of fear and offer you safe haven." In response to his voice, each member of the horde undergoes a sudden transformation back into human form. One by one, their bodies sail gently to earth, naked and confused. Among the crowd is Kane's henchman, Christopher Aldon, who attacked Eden and I in her car outside the bar.

Aldon rises to his feet and steps forward, taking in the vision of God before him, tears of joy streaming from his eyes. The Second Coming has finally arrived and he has the profound fortune of witnessing it. Aldon is soon joined by the others including Giddeon, who approaches sheepishly, now wrapped in a white sheet. The remaining members of the Church of First Life approach single file; the final steps of a great pilgrimage to eternal sanctuary. As the procession moves past us, Giddeon looks at us with terrible shame and sadness. She breaks into tears as our eyes meet. Even Aldon lowers his head with heavy remorse as he walks by.

"I'm sorry for what I did to ya'll," Aldon says to us. "But you see it now. I only did what I thought was right for mankind. I knew when God came back everything would be made right again."

"We couldn't turn our backs on a chance to save humanity," Giddeon says quietly. "My actions . . . they weren't personal."

"They seemed pretty fuckin' personal," Eden whispers.

Kane's disciples huddle beneath their Lord seated upon His throne, and they all fall to their knees. One by one, their bodies drop lifelessly to the ground as they surrender up their life-consciousness. Upon shedding their physical shells, I see thin, silvery contrails of bioenergy rise into the vacuum on the underside of god's meditation cushion. We bear witness to yet another incredible transfer of power as the added awareness moves directly up god's spine to add life-giving energy to his physical incarnation. In response, his visage glows with an even higher frequency of celestial light and sound.

"I am not the ego you knew as Kane, nor am I the man you knew as Sadhu," god whispers easily to us. "Do not judge the butterfly by the caterpillar. I am the phoenix, not the flame prior to rebirth. The egoconsciousness that led to my existence, Reverend Kane and Sadhu, were men who, regardless of their highest intentions, wished to control the outcome of their doings. They could not comprehend the full implications of their actions from their limited selves. I forgive them. The awareness of those who have met the end of their worldly life during the process of my rebirth are also offered eternal peace within me, divine relief from the cycle of birth and death."

That's one hell of a speech. "Well, I can't find a trace of attitude here," I admit in defeat. "Its intentions seem genuine. I don't see a desire for power or control."

"I have to admit," Kaylah says, "I don't sense fear or struggle from it. Maybe it really is a gift."

Jesus Christ, am I really going to do this? Am I going to give up my sense of individuality once and for all and enter this doorway to eternity? What will that mean? Can it be possible? Instead of a life filled with chasing after one ecstasy after another, avoiding fear and pain, always wrestling with doubt, can I finally let go and hand my faith over to this supreme being, forever?

I've exhausted the limits of my logic and rationale and I've found nothing more to question. My conscience is clear. If I am making a mistake, then it wasn't made recklessly. I suppose I need to evolve and surrender my own control. Tina holds me by the arm, tears streaming down her face. Eden laughs and hugs Sabol. We've made our decision: We will accept this god's offer. We will merge with the highest state of consciousness and live forever in bliss. I try to imagine the wonders of such an existence. Could I have ever asked for a better ending to my story?

And all of us, Kaylah, Eden, Tina, Sabol, and I take each other's hand and together we close our eyes. "You need only surrender completely," god speaks. "Let go your burden to me."

I allow my emotions, my mind, all my anxieties to relax, and soon there is a gentle sliding within my core. I can feel my very awareness begin to leave my body, like a hand slowly pulled from a glove too small, one that constricted too tight for too long. The last image my eyes perceive is the pile of bodies draped about the courtyard. I will soon add to the pile.

"You have chosen the highest path," god says, closing his

eyes to accept our life-energy. And . . . and there's a pull on my consciousness, something still left undone, some aspect I could only see now, from the perspective of my ultimate surrender. I unclasp my hands from the team, pulling everyone's attention abruptly back to Earth, back into their bodies. Everyone opens their eyes and stares at me with confusion. Even god is mystified by my sudden retreat, but he smiles, nonetheless.

"What troubles you now, my son?" his low voice booms with eternal patience and overflowing compassion.

"I just have one, last question," I say. The team sighs loudly behind me. I don't care. I won't make the same mistake my parents did.

# Beware the Double Doors

*"Life lived in the absence of the psychedelic experience that primordial shamanism is based on is life trivialized, life denied, life enslaved to the ego."*

Terence McKenna

I turn to the entity hovering before us, gesture to Eden and ask aloud, "Why were Kane and Sadhu so concerned about the connection Eden Jessup had established to the Zero Point Field while she was under the influence of Dimethyltryptamine? Where was the threat in that?"

The team shrugs their shoulders impatiently, wondering where I'm going with this. God smiles upon me. "As I have explained, my son, my predecessors believed in the illusion of division and competition," he says. "Kane and Sadhu both believed, each in his own, unique way, that once the ego-body you refer to as Eden Jessup was under the influence of the same medicine she had ingested upon merging with the holy Jain of the Tsangpo, that she, too, would become an open gateway to pure, potential energy, just as I am now.

"Both of those men, for his own reasons, feared this coming to pass. From their limited ego-identification they imagined such gateways to be individual entities; divided personalities that might engage in divisive battle with one another."

"But, you don't see it that way?" I shout. God chuckles softly.

"No, no, no. The boundless has many doors; it matters not which a soul passes through. The notion of enlightened, unidentified consciousness at odds with one another is foolish." The beaming almighty leans toward me with loving concern.

"Why let this detail trouble you, my child?" he asks. "The ceremony has come to pass. And by no fault of your own, you have failed to deliver the medicine in question to Eden Jessup; she remains bound to human ego and limited human form. I am here now, and all is well. A gateway to love and light has been opened. Do not dwell longer on who has opened it. It matters not. This is nothing more than the mind, your identity as doctor, as scientist, as atheist, stalling for time. Let it go and be at peace."

"Yeah, but the thing about that is," I add, studying Eden, who has now begun chanting in Sanskrit. "Eden Jessup did indeed ingest the ayahuasca we delivered to her."

As the frequency sails from Eden's pores, a dazzling burst of yellow light soundlessly explodes from her solar plexus. Her skin transforms into a radiance of electrical activity that begins sizzling the clothing from her body once more. For the very first time, I sense the subtlest disturbance in god's demeanor. He slightly rears back on his magic cushion at the sight of Eden as she begins merging with the wave. Her power is building far beyond her last incarnation in Peru. The circuit is being fully closed with the potential of the Jain.

"This is mystifying. I did not bear witness to this woman imbibing the medicine," god says with puzzlement. Kaylah lifts her head and smiles wryly at him.

"That's 'cause I'm a sly, little monkey!" she shouts to the heavens.

By sheer will, Eden becomes airborne, her feet dangle over the grass. She is held by an ever-growing fountain of vibrational activity; the deep hum of "Om" that steadily drums at our hearts and shakes our bones. Once more, the religious tattoos inked into Eden's skin dance to life, her spine becomes an exposed wire of glowing, hot energy and, as she raises her head, a third eye opens above the bridge of her nose. She enters a continuous state of bloom and transformation, into a mystical force of power, beauty and grace equal to the being that hovers above us on his great cushion.

"So, since it's all the same to you," I shout over the low roar of the frequency, "I ask that you shed your physical form and merge back with the ocean from which you came. Particle to wave and all that. We'd prefer to surrender ourselves to Eden Jessup instead. We'd like the job of "Gateway to Enlightenment" to be hers, and hers alone. She is our new God now."

I make a big show of dropping to my knees before Eden and extending my arms wide beneath her. The team quickly catches

456

onto the ruse and they all follow suit. Sabol is a little slower to comprehend, but he soon falls into line. One by one, we all turn our backs to "god" and dramatically prostrate ourselves at Eden's feet.

"Oh, Goddess above all beings in the whole, wide universe!" Kaylah squeals euphorically to Eden after throwing herself to the ground with hands clasped tightly in prayer. "Please be our light, our guide! I surrender myself body and spirit to your will! We will spread word of your supreme nature across the lands for all to hear! Soon, the world will bow to you. And to you alone!"

Eden merely stares blankly upon us, taking in the scene with utter passivity and total acceptance.

"You are most troubled creatures," god speaks behind us. "You are creating duality when the offer of unification has been lain at your feet!"

"Yeah, well, us humans can be real pains in the asses," Tina shouts at him before resuming her prayers. Kaylah turns an irritated eye at him and makes a flicking gesture with her hand.

"Okay, you can go now," she chirps. "We have the real God right here. You can sink back into the ether or the wave or whatever. Or you can move along and see how much of the human race will surrender themselves to you."

"Not many, I'm guessing," I add. "I have a feeling that our new religion here is going to have way more converts than yours. After people see what our religion offers, they're going to be dropping like flies at our Goddess's feet. You'll be irrelevant in a matter of weeks. I mean, just look at her! Our God is a hot, naked woman."

"Yeah, and our religion will be so much cooler than yours!" Tina hollers, squeezing my hand with a wink.

God is not amused by our antics. Not. One. Bit. The massive prayer cushion he sits upon rears back and upward to loom high above us. Mild frustration rolls over the entity's face. "You will purposefully confuse humankind?" he roars softly, growing ever more befuddled by us. The mountains shudder under his voice. "You would create another religion upon this

earth once again? A simple, direct path—a single doorway—
has been opened here to bring unity and peace to all troubled
souls! What purpose is there to make my holy offer a thing of
perplexity? It does not matter which path an ego-bound awareness follows to enter salvation! Why create division and turmoil
where there is no use for it?"

"What do you care?" I ask. "If both doors reach the same
conclusion, then don't worry about it!" An angered trembling
echoes from within his fists. Flames begin to lick between his
clenched fingers as a dark smoke rises along his translucent
spine.

"Hey, would you keep it down up there?" Sabol hollers.
"We're in the middle of prayer, so we're gunna have to ask you
to leave. You're being very disrespectful to our holy ceremony
here."

"Yeah, go fuck yourself," Kaylah snarls. With that, we have
now left god utterly speechless. His core ripples with a furious
energy, so much so that he cannot contain it.

"I will not let this stand!" he shouts with enough force to
shake the needles from every pine on the mountain. He raises
a fiery fist that now glows red hot with heat. "The honor of
saving humanity is mine! You stand as an obstacle to the path
of Enlightenment. I must extinguish your physical forms for
the greater good!"

God throws out his palm and launches a meteor of searing
heat and black smoke directly at us. We shriek and cover our
heads. Just before impact, the wing of some enormous bird
slams into the earth before us; a massive, feathery append-
age that arcs overhead like a shield. The ball of searing heat
explodes on the far side, sending flames ricocheting around us.

When we uncover our faces, we must squint to look directly
upon the shimmering, white vision that is Eden, now with the
addition of fantastic, silvery wings that extend from her shoulder blades. After the blast settles, she lifts her head and gazes
at me with all three eyes burning within her translucent skull.
Somehow, somewhere, behind her ethereal form, the same
Eden stares back at me. But she is at the crossroads; the full

expanse of the probability wave. And she needs my direction; one path over countless others.

"What shall I do, Michael?" her voice whispers. "This 'god' remains bound to ego, and I believe he means you harm. Which pattern of vibration should I sing into existence? There are oh so many paths at my fingertips. How do I proceed?"

I pull myself to my feet, brush the ash from my shirt and point to the false idol building a furious momentum of thunder and lightning behind her. "Finish him!" I holler. I always wanted a reason to shout that.

Eden nods gracefully before rotating midair to face the thing that had just attempted to smote us. In comparison, she stands a fraction of the size of this dark form, a moth facing a hawk. With an ecstatic chorus of a thousand voices, Eden speaks to the towering entity. "I cannot stand by and allow an ego to exist with access to such energy," the chorus sings. "I say: Return to the void by your own will, or be delivered there by force."

"God" is lifted high into the air, riding atop an isolated thunder storm. Angry, black clouds churn and roll beneath his floating cushion followed by furious thrashes of lightning that scorch the courtyard. We leap backward, covering our eyes from the blast. His face shrivels and transforms to a sickly gray as the prism of light within his form steadily dim. Fury and decay continue to overwhelm every feature of the giant manifestation until it resembles the visage of Kane once more, making it abundantly clear: this entity has no intention of going quietly.

Without further repose, the two forces throw themselves at one another—Eden appearing as some winged version of Kali the destroyer and "Kane" a towering visage of death cloaked by storm clouds. Much of what transpires next becomes far too abstract to explain in words, but suffice to say, the most outlandish battle ensues. Both Kane and Eden are limited only by their imagination; every strike is matched by an equally powerful, and bizarre, counterattack. Tina, Sabol, Kaylah, and I collapse to the ground in total stupefaction at the sights and sounds raging overhead.

We gawk in terror and awe as Eden encases Kane within a

sphere of solid ice which quickly plummets to the earth, only to have him burn with a red hot, internal rage to his freedom. The explosion is so magnificent that hail rains upon us for a full minute. At another point, Kane transforms into a ferocious, fire-breathing serpent the size of the mountain peak itself and is swiftly beheaded when Eden manifests a crystalline sword three times her size, which she wields with expert grace.

It seems no matter the result of each strike and counterstrike, both parties are able to reconstitute their individual awareness and continue the assault anew. We now bear witness to Eden filling the sky with a thousand duplicates of herself, surrounding Kane from all sides before each copy pummels him with concentrated blasts of high frequency sound. In response, his entire material form atomizes into a swirling black hole of particles which swallows every one of her duplicates into a crushing vortex. Just as we begin to wonder if Kane has won the battle, Eden's core energy escapes as electromagnetic radiation.

"Good girl," I whisper, leaning into Tina. "Hawking Radiation. I guess she was listening all those times I rambled about cosmology."

Each and every time, their base consciousness recovers, heals, or reconstitutes only to return fire with a brand new technique. And the war rages on, and on, and as it does the attacks come faster and increasingly nonlinear. In one moment, we are watching the two entities go at each other with brute force in the form of giant, savage animals that leap and tumble over the surrounding mountain peaks, or in the form of natural forces such as tornados or hurricanes, and in the very next moment we're witnessing counterattacks so sublime and ethereal they're impossible to comprehend.

Soon, tears in space and time are opened and resealed, superstrings are expanded and turned in on themselves, gravitational waves are multiplied and twisted into knots. There comes a point where Kane transforms into what can only be described as a complexity of interlocking, geometric patterns made of ethereal, white plasma. Eden's countermeasure to this is to morph into a highly symmetrical arrangement of ultraviolet shapes; patterns held within patterns like nesting dolls. Somehow, her response seems to "undo" Kane's move.

Tina rests her head on my chest as we watch the show continue. "Are they . . . ," she begins, trying to make sense of it all. " . . . fighting with math?"

"It looks like they're manifesting equations to temporarily change the laws of physics as some form of attack," I say, "but, I have no fuckin' clue."

And the insanity continues. This goes on in this fashion for an hour. What began as the most mind-blowing display of "energy-to-matter and back again" is nearly growing tiresome. And most certainly worrisome. It seems there may be no end to it. At the far edge of the cult's property, a few survivors from Gold Hill are beginning to emerge from the forest. They stumble forward in a stupor, their eyes drawn to the light show above. I study the cloud cover hanging just below the peak and wonder how many people can even see what's taking place in the towns below.

I'm growing ever more concerned that, given their respective connections to the Field, both Eden and Kane may indeed possess an equal capacity to pluck out realities from the probability wave. This may appear as pure chaos to us, to them it's anything but. They both essentially represent an unbroken line between thought and manifestation. They each possess total control over every punch, every deflection.

"Oh, Christ," Sabol finally sighs. "What have we done?"

Kaylah yawns. "Maybe this is what Sadhu was really afraid of. Maybe we've made a terrible mistake."

We all cringe at the notion. Perhaps this is exactly what the Roto wanted to avoid. Suddenly, Eden lands on the ground before us in ordinary, human form, weary and out of breath, but at least clothed. During her respite, several of her "duplicates" carry on in her place overhead. Eden sighs and rolls onto her back in exhaustion.

"I've tried everything to take this fucker down," she wheezes. "I'm running out of ideas, so I'm all open to suggestions here." We're dumbstruck to be asked for advice on the matter. We all search each other and my mind races for a solution. How do you fight something that's in total control of every pattern of energy it encounters? Whatever we come up with, Kane will see it for what it is, solve it, and respond in kind.

And then it happens again. All my experiences, everything I've learned coalesce and collapse in on themselves. My mind goes temporarily blank, I forget about who I think I am, and I remember the truth: I know nothing whatsoever. Maybe I'm getting the hang of this after all? And from that open field of possibility a simple notion forms; one that is truly "outside the box," I keep trying to solve it all logically, when, logically, logic isn't what will save the day.

"Chaos," I say aloud.

Everyone looks at me including Eden. "Kane can't handle true chaos."

"Mike, I've pulled every rabbit out of my hat I can think of," Eden reminds me. "Believe me, I've exhausted the bounds of human consciousness here."

"That's the problem," I explain "You're both fighting each other from the perspective of human ego; from your limited, identity-bound consciousness. You need to throw real chaos at him, something not of a biological mind."

"Yeah, how am I supposed to do that? No matter what I think of, I can't change what I am at the core," Eden shrugs, "I'm still just a fucked-up human being."

I gesture to Sabol and he immediately picks up on my intention. He rummages through his military pack, unzips a hidden pocket in the rear lining and removes a small computer tablet, the one loaded with a video of the original attack on Ramirez's men in Peru. Earlier I wondered why we were carrying a copy of the event along with us. Now I know why. With quick fingers, Sabol powers up the system, enters a password, and pulls up the video, forwarding it to the point just before the frequency is emitted in the Chambira Basin, and Kane's missionaries shapeshift.

"Whatever emits the frequency will harmonize with the Zero

Point Field," I remind her. "But a computer can't choose particle formation in the wave like we can. Everything in its radius will become truly randomized; a chaos no human mind could predict. Just like in the physics lab."

"That might work," Tina says "but, how do we get the laptop near Kane when it goes off?"

Eden snatches the tablet from Sabol's hands. The moment the computer touches her hand it becomes transparent. With a sudden burst of radiant light Eden is transformed once again into her "Goddess of War" visage. "I know what I have to do," the chorus of voices sing from her essence. "I have to give up this fight."

We gasp in terror at the thought of it. She'll enter heaven just long enough to throw a grenade into it. I leap from the grass and seize her by the ankle, her skin sizzles beneath my grip. "It'll kill you, too!" I bellow. Eden turns and places a warm, pulsating hand on my cheek.

"Yes," a chorus sings back to me, "but, only in this world. There are others." Before I can argue further, she is gone. The particles in her arm have transformed from solid matter to a gentle field of energy; ethereal enough to float into the whirlpool vacuum beneath Kane's meditation cushion, maintaining just enough pressure to grip the invisible computer tablet.

"But, I live in this one," I whisper.

All at once, the battle overhead comes to a rather abrupt stop. All of Eden's duplicates have collapsed back to One. She closes her eyes and hovers just beneath Kane who has transformed back into his sickly, human form. He leans his massive torso down with a smile.

"I won't keep doing this," Eden announces. "We'll tear this world apart. I surrender." Kane leans back to accept the addition of her abundant, potential energy.

"You have made a wise decision," he says. "As you see, nothing can come of such competition. It is fruitless. Your energy will help fuel eternal salvation on this plane."

I hold my breath as I watch Eden glide up, into the eye of the whirlpool at the base of Kane's being, but not before she presses PLAY on the computer screen. And she is gone. Kane closes his eyes as every atom that comprises his considerable form ripples with the potential of a nuclear explosion. He opens his eyes and sunlight explodes from his pupils.

"After this world," he says. "I will consume the rest until there is only One." But, before he can take over the universe, there is a shift at his core; some disturbance within his solar plexus, a contamination that has slipped his awareness. The video has reached the point where Kane's missionaries entered the Zero Point Field in Peru, and the computer is pulling every particle in its vicinity into utter chaos. A writhing, dark orb opens within Kane's abdomen, churning through a billion and one patterns of particle arrangement.

"What is this?" Kane shouts, examining the phenomena at his midsection with perplexity and fear. "I don't understand what is happening!"

"No one can," I reply quietly.

In a burst of multicolored lights and random sounds, the core of Kane's being explodes into a pulsing, primordial soup of matter and light. He flails under the impact before his entire visage becomes skull and bone, and then all solid form within him crumbles in an earthshuddering roar to dust. The dust and debris collapse into a single point of blinding light and, for a brief instant, everything goes quiet. With an overwhelming, sonic BOOM, all the combined energy that was Kane and Sadhu bursts in a white vapor that scatters across the full expanse of the sky above.

As the vapors disintegrate down to a gentle rain, the realization settles on us that it is truly over. Kaylah shrieks with joy and soon the others join in. Though I'm also immersed with relief and hope, the emptiness left in the wake of my beloved friend's passing is immediately heart wrenching. Picking up on my terrible loss, Sabol and Kaylah embrace me. Tina nestles her head into my shoulder. After a much needed, lengthy emotional pause, Sabol is the first to lift his head from the group hug.

"Did we just kill God?" he asks with a twinge of anxiety.

"For Christ's sake, I fucking hope so," Eden says upon re-materializing in the center of the huddle.

# Treasure in the Ashes

**I** awoke somewhere around eleven p.m. From what I could piece together, I had already been asleep for a full day. Though I imagined I must have gotten up a few times to use the bathroom, I had no recollection of doing so. I could hear my grandmother quietly rummaging around the kitchen, most likely making coffee. When you sleep this long, the specifics of your storyline, or "reality" as it's generally referred to, takes its own, sweet time to upload again from the Field.

A solid forty minutes must have passed before I realized I had been staring mindlessly at the play of shadows on the ceiling from my blinds. Images of gods and monsters, Peru and Tibet, shamans and missionaries swirled silently at the back of my head. Had it all been a dream? And if it wasn't, how would I continue? What does Professor Michael Huxley's story look like now?

There's a weight on my chest as I consider the possibility that Tina Flores and the deep love I felt for her had been nothing more than fantasy. How cruel dreams can be. It's supremely unfair the way they can re-create feelings of mutual love with a partner only to snatch her away upon waking. But I soon realized the weight on my chest was real, and then it all came flooding back; my story had completed its upload. I reached up, lightly squeezed the hand resting on my shoulder, and let the bliss of Tina's sigh fill my ears, her head nestled in the nook of my arm. Joy filled my heart as I caressed her back to sleep.

Eden and Sabol were both fast asleep in made-up beds on the floor on the far side of my room. After everything we had been through, none of us wanted to be alone, or with anyone else who hadn't been there to see it all go down firsthand. The four of us were now intimately linked in a way no outsider would ever comprehend. As far as my grandparents were concerned, my "little friends" could stay as long as they wished. They didn't even ask who Tina and Sabol were; they could tell we were exhausted, and I was certain my grandmother was just happy to see me with a woman again.

By the time we made it back to the safety of my grandparents' home, several news teams had begun to attempt to piece together all the discombobulated information coming out of Gold Hill. From what I could gather, the low cloud cover had indeed concealed much of the "war" that had raged on above the peak and, as far as most of the local population was concerned, there had been an unusually violent thunderstorm in the mountains. None of us, including the FBI, cared to correct that assumption. How Downey and his team would spin the multitude of stories, perhaps even cellphone footage, that would soon be emerging concerning how Gold Hill, along with many of its inhabitants, were violently wiped out would be anyone's guess, but it didn't appear that would be our problem.

After the five of us piled into Downey's Audi and fled the grounds of Kane's compound, we were passed by a fleet of fire trucks and ambulances going the opposite direction. I noticed that both ends of the line of emergency vehicles were escorted by a team of black SUVs with tinted windows. Once we reached the canyon, Kaylah said her good-byes once again and headed toward the forests of the front range on foot.

"Wait," I called to her. "Is it really over?"

She paused and considered. "Probably," she offered. "The survivors of Gold Hill saw things they shouldn't have; things they weren't ready for. That could be a problem. But we'll see. Go get some rest."

Sabol offered to arrange a flight for her to anywhere she wished, to which she responded with a boisterous, "Ha!" before prancing out of sight. We knew she could handle herself, but no one knew what to do with the confusing sense of responsibility we each held for her.

Everyone was still in a quiet stupor when we reached Boulder's airport. Another fleet of emergency vehicles had arrived to transport the wounded, put out fires, and collect the debris. We felt obligated to see if there was anything we could do to help on the scene, and of course, to return Downey's car, what was left of it. I could only imagine explaining the specifics of the damage to his insurance agent.

Amongst the commotion, we found Agent Tom Downey sitting on the rear of an ambulance, still caught in a mild state of shock, sporting a bandage around his forehead. When he took in the condition of his Audi, his eye twitched nearly imperceptibly. He looked us over and shook his head with an anxious expression that clearly said, "Oh, please, don't share any more information about whatever the hell just happened." Sensing his desire to not be "debriefed" at the moment, Tina instead laid a hand on the man's shoulder and assured him that it was "all over now." For the first time, a weak smile appeared on his face. After giving us his word to strike our names from any reports involving the case at large, Downey arranged a federal escort back into town.

So with the few people on the planet I really cared about safe and secure under my roof, I slipped back into a dreamless sleep with the woman I loved wrapped around me. I awoke again late the following morning to the sounds of pots clanking in the kitchen. Feeling, and certainly looking, as though I spontaneously aged twenty years, I painstakingly managed my robe over my shoulders and shuffled down the hall to find my grandmother making coffee for Tina and Eden at the breakfast nook. Sabol and my grandfather were in the living room sharing stories from the service. I slumped at the table just as gramma set a most welcomed mug of hot coffee in my hands.

"I like her," she whispered, gesturing to Tina, who took my hand with a coy wink. Whispering loudly in her favorite, heavy Polish accent gramma added, "She iz gud woman for you. You keep her close."

"Morning sunshine," Eden smiled wearily from behind her coffee mug with dark circles under her eyes. "How'd you sleep?"

"Like the dead."

"Poor baby," she cooed. "All tuckered from saving the world?"

"Oh, no. I'm going to leave that honor to you," Eden hissed

dismissively as she poured the cream. We all sat quietly for a moment wondering what "normal" looked like from this point forward. I found myself studying Eden, wondering just who or what was sitting at the table with me now.

"How did you . . . " I began, not sure how to pose my burning question about how she survived the computer's random frequency.

"I guess you could say I don't fear chaos any longer," she offered, staring at the cream swirling in her cup. "It's just entropy. Basically, we're all just tools the cosmos uses to spread energy out into a field. If there is such a thing as a universal commandment, it's to turn order into disorder. Kane's religion couldn't make peace with that. He believed chaos was death, so that's what he got."

"But not you, huh?" Tina added. Eden smiled and stirred her coffee.

"I think the cosmos isn't done using me yet. I still have more disorder to bring to the world."

Sabol wandered confusedly into the kitchen talking on his cell phone. "You're gunna love this," he announced. He placed the phone in the center of the table and pressed the speaker button.

Agent Tom Downey's voice roared through the device. "Hope you all slept," he grumbled, "seems now we've got a far worse and considerably stranger problem on our hands. Something tells me you're the only ones who might know how to handle it."

Eden, Tina, and Sabol sighed heavily. My forehead slammed into the countertop in disbelief. What problem could possibly be stranger?

# Just Be

*Gazing out at Spirit's sweet path*
*Am I leaving or have I just arrived?*
*There is no coming or going, only Being*
*Beholding only that for which I have ceased to search*

*Gazing deep into my heart*
*Is love leaving or has it only just arrived?*
*No, Love does not come or go, Love is*
*Embracing all with unbearable tenderness*

*Gazing into soul*
*Are you awakened, how will I know?*
*Soul answered, "I Am"*
*Time to stop questioning child—Be still, come home!*

*Barbara Prince*

# AUTHOR NOTES

I suppose an author's bio usually rattles off a laundry list of data such as where he or she is from, what sort of education he has under his belt, writing and work experience, credentials, accolades, and so forth. How dull. I'd rather try to impart a small taste of the forces at work behind this project.

I had the exceptional honor of being raised by two highly intelligent people who gave me the rarest gifts: space and unconditional love. My mother and father did not preach to or judge me. They passed along their philosophy almost solely by example, trusting I would eventually arrive at the "big" answers on my own momentum. This made much of my life terribly confusing, especially when surrounded by others who seemed so sure of what was going on, but so far I can't accuse my life of boring me. It so happens that when parents truly trust their child to arrive at his own conclusions, they unwittingly create an outcast. My brightest childhood memories involve exploring the outdoors while letting my imagination run wild, and being perfectly content with spending hours alone in my room, coloring and dreaming up stories of alien landscapes, heroes and monsters. I was and continue to be the weirdo who could never quite make sense of his fellow humans, their priorities, or what they worry about.

I began spontaneously lucid dreaming just after graduating high school, mere months after completing the first major hurdle toward adulthood, but well before I had decided on my "life's goals" and what I wanted to make of myself. By pure definition, lucid dreaming is becoming completely aware that one is dreaming while the dream is taking place. It's a point where the "dream drama," the storyline, is ultimately revealed to be illusion. To the inexperienced, the impact of even a few minutes exploring such a euphoric state of consciousness and utter freedom cannot be exaggerated. I would spend the next ten years or more working with this altered state of awareness nearly every night, with many of these visionary states lasting several hours on end.

Each and every experience seemed to impart a different "lesson" or truth about the hidden nature of consciousness. The majority of these states involved visits to fully realized realms of color, substance and complexity every bit as, if not more, real than my waking life, while others revealed locations I was quite familiar with in my daily world. While fully aware I was relating directly to hidden aspects of my own conscience, I engaged in hundreds of lengthy discussions with characters who presented equally as independent and sentient as my friends and family I'd known for years. I soon learned these would be the first of many unusual experiences I would endure which would tear at my seams and force me to question our domesticated definitions of reality.

It wasn't long before I was led to accept a natural connection between these lucid states and what is often referred to as "astral projection" and "remote viewing." Beyond all reason, I eventually began returning to my bed and body in the morning with precise information as to what friends and family had been up to while I was asleep; some of whom lived hundreds of miles away. Initially, my reaction to the discovery that my awareness was not bound to my physical body was one of terrible confusion and dread. If the "I" wasn't the body, what was it? Plus, I was suddenly forced to accept that my own dreams weren't always taking place within the safe confines of my head.

Out of pure necessity I began devouring any information I could find on the topic of lucidity while diving headfirst into any experiences that might help illuminate just what was happening to me. I consumed information and research both modern and ancient, from psychology and quantum particle theory to spiritual and shamanic traditions hailing from India, Japan, and Mexico which dated back thousands of years. I explored meditation, healing, and energy manipulation practices (or Prana, vital energy, Qi) while experimenting with altered awareness via binaural frequencies and psychoactive plants and fungi. I became convinced that my sanity and perhaps even my physical health hinged on my ability to solve the many, growing riddles I seemed to be learning about the nature of mind. Were these "lucid dreams" a natural phenomenon? Was I actively breaking my psyche on some fundamental level or was this the onset of schizophrenia? Perhaps I was having seizures or slowly suffering a brain tumor. Was I reaching enlightenment or was I about to die?

Though the questions concerning my sanity have yet to be settled to my complete satisfaction, I eventually arrived at a place of greater harmony. I still didn't have all the answers, but my health clearly wasn't failing, in fact I felt stronger and more energetic than ever. I was discovering a strange peace in not knowing all the answers, a satisfaction deeper than solid answers. The more I allowed myself to sit quietly in the center of this wonderment the dust began to settle. I gained more control of my "night life" and I found my attention being pulled to a story that had been churning and shapeshifting in my peripheral in one form or another for as long as I could remember. With the help of forces beyond my control, I realized it was time to yank this tale, kicking and screaming, out of the void and into the shared world where the rest of the world can wrestle with it on their own terms. I only hope that, through the love I've poured into this project, this story finds my fellow weirdos out there who need it most—those who still remember that our reality is stranger than we can imagine it, that our lives are always full of wonder.

# ALSO FROM GLADEYE PRESS

Available for purchase at: www.gladeyepress.com and wherever fine books are sold.

### The Time Tourists, A Novel
Sharleen Nelson

Step into time with Imogen Oliver in this first book in the Dead Relatives, Inc. series as she investigates a young girl who ran away from home with her boyfriend in 1967 and never returned, and then travels back to the turn of the 20th century to locate a set of missing stereoscopic glass plates with a mysterious connection to her own life.

### A Recipe for Dying
Patricia Brown

The old people are dying in the small coastal town of Waterton, but no one seems to notice—after all, that's what old folk do, isn't it? Eleanor and her delightful assortment of friends, most whom are getting up in age, set out to discover what is going on. Is it a series of mercy killings, or murder, and is their investigation putting them in danger?

### Dying for Diamonds
Patricia Brown

When a mean-spirited mystery writer visiting the sleepy coastal town gets murdered, Eleanor and her coffee club quickly find themselves involved. Family secrets and the bonds that we share are examined and tested as Eleanor, her retired detective friend Angus, the coffee club ladies, and Feathers, the irascible African grey parrot, work to solve the puzzles without becoming the murderer's next victims.

### *10 Takes: Pacific Northwest Writers*
### *Perspectives on Writing*
Jennifer Roland

From novelists to poets to playwrights, Jennifer Roland interviews a variety of authors who have one thing in common—they have all chosen to make the Pacific Northwest their home.

### *Washington's Festivals, Fairs & Celebrations*
Janaya Watne

Northwest native and fierce outdoorswoman, Janaya Watne has written an information-packed exploration of Washington's vibrant festival calendar. Tourists as well as the well-established who are looking to find the perfect week, weekend, or one-day trip will enjoy this handy guide.

### *Teaching in Alaska*
### *What I Learned in the Bush*
Julie Bolkan

Among the first outsiders to live and work with the Yup'ik in their small villages, this book tells Julie's story about how she survived the culture clashes, isolation, weather, and her struggles with honey buckets—a candid and often funny account of one gussock woman's 12 years in the Alaskan bush.

# AVAILABLE NOW
# from *GLADEYE PRESS FICTION*

### *Under A Dying Moon*
Patricia Brown
When a girl washes up on the sleepy coastal town's beach and two women are found murdered, Eleanor and her coffee club friends find themselves in another investigation, but are they also suspects? What is the deal with the mysterious ruby ring that seems to follow Eleanor? And who are these new people in town and what are they after?

- Visit www.gladeyepress.com for fantastic deals on these and other GladEye Press titles.
- Follow us on Facebook: https://www.facebook.com/GladEyePress/ or on Twitter at @gladeyepress
All GladEye titles can be ordered from your local book store.